Banished

AN ELEMENTAL KINGDOM NOVEL

GENAVIE CASTLE

ISBN: 978-1-962047-05-0 Paperback

ISBN: 978-1-962047-09-8 Ebook

Book Cover Design by: CRey-ative Designs

Edited by: EPONA Author Solutions

Printed in the United States of America

About This Book

Everything about this book is completely fictional. This is a why choose romance novel containing graphic sexual content, some violence and explicit language suitable for mature audiences only. Proceed with caution.

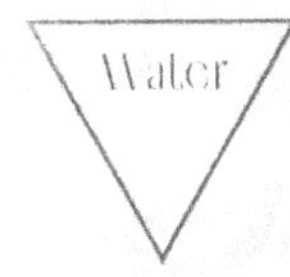

Chapter One

ZARA

The thick red liquid dribbled slowly into the glass like molasses. Its coppery scent wafted into the air and made my nose itch.

"Your boyfriend is here." Rhysa came up behind me and rested her chin on my shoulder.

"Boyfriend? I wasn't aware I had one of those," I replied.

"Back left," she said.

I turned my head and saw a tall impeccably dressed man leaning against the wall. Thaddeus Sloane smiled at whomever he spoke with. His dark hair was combed back, and he had a little stubble on his chiseled jawline. He wore a tailor-made dark blue suit which did little to conceal his lean, muscular body. Damn him, he was not supposed to be here.

Rhysa placed her hand over mine, turning the spigot off before the glass overflowed. "Go take a break. I'll cover for you."

"He's not my boyfriend." I grabbed the other glass filled with A positive and turned toward the bar to deliver the drinks.

"Boy toy? Fuck buddy? Whatever you want to call him. Take a break and go get some." She winked and went to pour drinks.

It was Saturday night, and The Convent teemed with thirsty patrons. The bar was six people deep, and we were one person short. It was not the time for a break, but I had to get Thadd out of there before the owner and my business partner noticed his presence.

"Red blend for the lovely lady and A positive for the gentlemen." I slid the glasses of blood on the counter to the vampire guests. "That'll be sixty-five even."

"Thank you, gorgeous." The male vampire slid two one hundred dollar bills on the counter towards me. "Keep the change. And what's this I hear about a "fuck buddy"?"

"Thanks." I smiled and accepted the cash. "Oh, it's nothing. Rhysa just likes to tease me."

"This is too cold," the female vampire whined.

"I'm sorry about that, sweetheart. Here, let me." Blood was usually served at room temperature, but some vamps preferred it warmed. And some were just high-maintenance bitches. I called up my fire magic and slid my fingers suggestively up and down the glass. "Try that."

The female vampire took a sip of the blood while keeping her eyes on me. "It's perfect." She licked her lips. "What are you doing later?"

"I don't play on the all-girl team. Sorry. But Rhysa, might." I winked at the couple and then turned around to ring up the drinks in the register and added the change to the tip jar.

"Break time. I won't be long," I said as I passed Rhysa.

"Take your time, babe. Oh and heads up, there's a bunch of elementals in here tonight," she said while mixing cocktails.

I went around the bar counter, sashayed my way deeper into the bar, and maneuvered through the crowd. We'd expanded a year ago and still we were over capacity. Inebriated patrons of all magical varieties swayed to the trap music thumping through the speakers. The Convent was the only bar in Silk City that exclusively catered to the magical community. Vampires, shifters, mages, Fae, witches, and now and then elementals - like me- would come in. We offered donated blood on tap, and magically brewed alcohol of every flavor.

Two scantily clad Faeries clung to Thadd. I swallowed back the bile of jealousy that snuck up on me. He was not my boyfriend and that was by choice. I had commitment issues and so did he. We got along just fine, and the physical chemistry between us was addicting. But that was as far as we wanted to take it. We understood each other and it worked.

His dark eyes met mine from across the room. His commanding presence was like a lure reeling me in. I licked my bottom lip as his gaze traveled the length of my body. His posture straightened, his body pulling me towards him like a magnet.

A few feet away from Thadd, my skin prickled as I passed the VIP section breaking my lust haze. Rhysa was right about elementals being here. It wasn't unusual for them to be in Silk City, but usually here at The Convent, they would come over to the bar and say hello. The entire elemental kingdom knew about my banishment and with my brown skin, white hair, and violet eyes, I was easy to recognize. My focus shifted away from Thaddeus as I looked over at the VIP tables. The mood lighting in the bar obscured the many faces, so I changed direction to get a closer look.

Before I made it past the second table of eight, Thadd was right behind me. He snaked his hand around my waist and guided me towards the back door of The Convent, away from the cacophony of partiers. He found a barstool usually occupied by one of the bodyguards and sat, bringing me to stand between his legs.

"Hi, baby Z," Thadd whispered in my ear. The timber of his voice made me shiver and I forgot all about the elementals in the VIP section.

"Haven't I eighty-sixed you from here, twice?" I raised my eyebrow at him.

"Three times, actually, but I have a thing for one of the owners. She's worth the risk." Thadd's lips brushed over my cheek and down my neck.

I pushed him away from me. "You smell like faeries."

He shrugged off his sports coat and threw it on a nearby table.

"Happy?" His smile told me he was pleased with my reaction.

I nodded, smiled back and then realized I had just shown him my jealousy card. Ugh, I needed professional help.

"Seriously, Thadd, what are you doing here? Magz is going to have a fit if you start anything again. And so help me, Goddess, if you've brought a date in here, I will shoot you both in the face." I ran my hands over his muscular arms. The fabric stretched taut over his skin.

He laughed. "I'm here alone, babe. I just wanted to see you before you went on your road trip. And make sure you have everything you need. And maybe steal a kiss or two."

It was my turn to laugh. "Nope, nothing's changed since the last time you asked me that, which was last night. And I am pretty sure you stole more than two kisses then as well."

He gave me a bashful smile and shrugged. "You caught me. I'm having withdrawals. You'll be gone for three weeks."

"We don't do commitment, remember? That's not our thing." I caressed his strong jaw with my long nails.

"As you wish." His breath tickled my ear. "I'll never stop wanting you, Zara. No matter how many men you date or have sex with or whatever. I will always be yours."

My heart keened. I wanted his words to be true; I wanted him to be mine because in truth I felt the same way about him.

His hands roamed over my hips. "Why aren't you wearing panties?" He cupped my ass.

The girls that worked at The Convent all wore black bodycon dresses. The style accentuated all my curves and the dark color contrasted with my hair, making it glow.

"Not that it's any of your business, but I don't like panty lines," I replied.

"Panty lines? That's the best you could come with?" His fingers toyed with the hem of my dress.

"It's the truth. And don't even think about it." I glared at him.

"Think about what?" He tried to hide his devilish grin. He was aiming to slide his sneaky fingers up my short dress.

"Don't be coy, Thaddeus Sloane. Behave yourself. I have to get back to work." Not that I wanted him to stop, but this was not the time nor place.

He kissed my neck, and his tongue circled the sensitive spot beneath my ear. I bit my lip trying to keep myself from moaning.

"Time to go, handsome," my voice husky.

"I don't think you want me to. I think you'd like it if my fingers went up a little bit higher." He slid his hand over to my inner thigh, all while peppering my cleavage with kisses.

Oh, my Goddess!

I stepped back, trying to put some distance between us, but Thadd had one arm securely around my waist keeping me close to him.

"Admit it, Zara. You want me just as much as I want you." He purred in my ear, and his thumb grazed my inner thigh just scant millimeters away from my sex.

"Yes! Yes, I do, now quit. I need to go back to work and focus." My skin felt flushed and tingly all over. I pushed him away and stepped back.

Thaddeus chuckled, placed both hands on my waist, and drew me close again.

"Good. I've made my point." A smug grin spread over his handsome face.

I rolled my eyes. "I hope you're done proving your point because I have a bar to tend."

"One more thing." He smiled at me and then pressed his forehead against mine. "Happy birthday, Zara. I wanted to do something special for you. But I know your rules, we will celebrate another day."

I hated my birthday and never wanted to celebrate it. But Thadd never forgot, and he never forgot my rules, which were no cakes, no presents, and no cards on the actual day. The day of was off limits to celebrating. And Thadd always did something to make it special.

I cupped his face and kissed his pouty lips. He tasted like cognac. Mmmm. "Thank you, Thadd."

"Can I have someone drive you home after work?" he asked when we came up for air. He always asked, and I appreciated the gesture, but it wasn't necessary.

"No. I'll be fine, it's not that far. I'll text as usual," I replied.

"Why do you always have to be so stubborn? I hate the idea of you walking home alone." He gave me a stern look.

"Stubbornness is part of my charm." I batted my eyelashes at him.

"Come here, you pain in the ass." He pulled me close for a deep sensual kiss, and the world around me faded into the background.

"I have to be somewhere, babe," he said when we broke apart.

I nodded not wanting any more info. He probably had a date, which was fine. I wasn't about to demand commitment when I wasn't ready to offer it myself.

Thadd grabbed his sports coat and held my hand as he led us back to the bar.

When we got to the counter Thadd turned and lifted me off my feet. My legs wrapped around his back, and our gazes locked. He kissed me again, his mouth stealing my breath. With his lips pressed to mine, he murmured, "I love you."

He set me down on my feet and walked away.

I felt flushed all over. Damn you, Thaddeus, and your handsome face and your l-bombs.

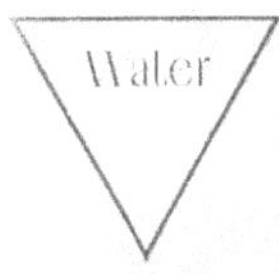

Chapter Two

ZARA

Four hours after Thaddeus left, I finished cashing out the registers and prepping the deposits that would be going straight to the bank as soon as they opened.

I changed into jeans and a T-shirt and pulled a hoodie over my head, then exited my office. Magnus Fuller was seated at the bar drinking a beer.

"Excuse me, sir, we're closed," I teased. He owned the place and could do whatever he wanted. I was a partial owner, but The Convent was his baby. Aside from Thadd, Rhysa, and mom, of course, no one else knew about my involvement on the business end, and I'd wanted to keep it that way. I handed the bank deposit bags to Magz and he nodded.

"Your boyfriend coming to drive you home?" he asked me.

"He's not my boyfriend," I replied.

"Sure he's not. Your father wouldn't approve, Zar. I don't like him much either, but as long as he treats you right and doesn't cause any fights in here." He gave me a stern stare.

Magz was my late father's best friend. He'd given me a job here while I had been in college. After obtaining my degree, I traveled a bit doing business consulting work, then returned when my father took ill. Magz was about to close up The Convent for good, but I convinced him to take me on as a partner. We renovated and revamped our business model. I still tended the bar a couple of nights per week, and I did admin work during the day. Magz and I had a great partnership, the business was lucrative, and we agreed on just about everything, except my love life.

Thadd and I agreed to keep our relationship casual. He saw other women; I was certain of it. And I dated other men, which he knew about. For the past six years it had worked, except there had been an incident where he beat the shit out of a customer in here for getting handsy with me. This may have happened more than once which was why he wasn't supposed to show up here again.

"He's not going to be a problem," I replied.

"Uh-huh. Sure he won't. Until he shows up with a date like he did the last time." Magz sipped his beer.

He was right about that. Thadd showed up with a date once, and I nearly set the whole bar on fire. "Oh no, he won't do that. If he does, I'll shoot him in the face," I assured my business partner.

"You two are so weird." Magz got up, pulled out his keys, and moved towards the door. "I wish you would drive or at least call a ride-share service rather than walking home."

"It's barely four blocks away. I can take care of myself." I had my elemental magic and my father had been a retired police officer. He had taken me to the shooting range and had me trained in martial arts since I was fifteen. I wasn't indestructible, but I could hold my own for the most part.

"Be careful. And Happy Birthday, kiddo, enjoy your time off." Magz opened the door for me. "And there's a storm headed for the coast. Don't take unnecessary risks."

"Thanks, Magz." I gave him a one-armed hug and exited.

My phone chimed with a text notification as I crossed the street. I pulled it out of my jeans pocket and checked the message even though I already knew it was Gigi, my foster mother, checking in.

Mama- Hi honey. Are you on your way?
Me – Yes. You need anything?
Mama- Donuts
Me – LOL

Gigi was an angel sent by the Goddess to save me. She and her late husband Leon became my foster parents when I was fifteen years old. They found me at the youth home where I'd ended up after my nurse-maid, Nan, passed away. Kind-hearted Gigi and Leon Parks provided a stable home and became my family after the life that I'd been born to was torn out from under me. I thanked the Goddess every day for blessing me with loving parents.

After everything Gigi had done for me, I hated to deny her anything. But her request for sugary delights was a hard no. That was the last thing she needed.

She was human and had been battling the sugar sickness she'd been born with. As she got older her symptoms got worse and her medications more costly. It made me wonder if the medications were doing more harm than good.

I was sure there were natural remedies in the Elemental Kingdom that would help her. But I had been banished by the royal family, my biological parents. For the past fourteen years, I'd had zero access to my homeland and its innate source of magic.

I stopped at the all-night coffee shop that was on my usual route home and looked longingly at the pastry case.

"Girl, one of these days you just need to give in." Bonnie, one of the waitresses said while handing me a cup of coffee.

"I wish it were that easy, but it's not for me. Gigi has a sweet tooth." I shrugged. "You know how it is."

"That woman is lucky to have you, Zara. How about one for you? On the house." Bonnie smiled and pointed at the desserts.

"No thank you. Just the coffee." I shook my head. "I'd get the worst daughter in the world award if I indulged while mom couldn't."

"Coffee's on the house then. Be careful on your way home." Bonnie waved me off.

"Thank you, Bonnie!" I waved back, pulled a five-dollar bill out of my purse, and dropped it in the tip jar near the register.

I continued walking home as the moon began to set making way for the rise of the sun. The concrete jungle I now called home was almost beautiful.

Silk City was a bustling metropolis for humans and magical folk, but at this hour it was quiet here in Zone 7, the poorest district in the city. There were lots of crime and gang-related incidents, but I had never been afraid of walking the streets alone. Although my elemental magic had waned from being away from the kingdom for so long, I was more than capable of protecting myself from an attack.

I'd assimilated to city living the best I could. It was challenging for an elemental to be so far away from nature, which was why Gigi and I were taking a road trip to the coast. As much as possible, I made a point to get out of the city. Although being away from nature came with some setbacks for someone like me,

Zone 7 was my home, and being close to Gigi was more important. Gigi and Leon had helped me deal with the traumas of being banished by my biological parents. Because of their love and support, the pain of that dreadful day became a distant memory. I hadn't forgotten or forgiven my biological parents, but I wasn't as traumatized as I had been. Sure, there were rough days over the years, but the longer I stayed away, the easier it became to move past them.

Birthdays were different. It was a day I tried to forget, even though the few people closest to me always reminded me. I knew they were just trying to help me make new birthday memories. I appreciated their efforts, truly, I did. But somehow that dreadful day wormed its way into my head and threatened to bring me down.

I shook my head. Thoughts of the past were the last things I wanted to accompany me for the next two blocks. I chugged the last bit of my coffee and tossed the empty cup in a trash can as I continued home.

Gigi and I lived in a quaint one story in the middle of Zone 7. It was modest and cozy, and it was home. I turned the corner onto my street and sighed as the familiar tiled rooftop came into view. On autopilot, I entered through chain-link gate, closed it behind me, then dug in my purse for my keys as I walked up the short pathway to the front door.

A shadowy figure appeared on the porch and blocked my way.

"Princess, your father requires your presence in the kingdom," the deep voice said to me. He wore a hood that hid his face.

I rolled my eyes. The correspondence from the kingdom had been arriving in a continuous stream as of late. I never responded to them. I hadn't even bothered to read them.

"My father passed away four years ago. And I'm not your princess. You're trespassing. Get the fuck out of my yard," I snarled but kept my voice low. Gigi was just beyond the door, and I did not want to scare her.

"You can come with me now. Or we do this the hard way," the intruder said.

He had magic, but he was too far away from me to discern what kind. I cracked my neck and thought through my options. I had access to all elements, but fire would be bad. I could burn the house down. My earth magic was the weakest of all, and even if it wasn't I wouldn't want to start an earthquake. Water magic could be useful if I expanded the water molecules in his body but that would drown him in his fluids. Gross. My air magic allowed me to fly short distances, which would allow me to run away, but I would need a running start and that would leave Gigi defenseless. Or perhaps I could steal some of the air from his lungs making it difficult for him to breathe.

Get ready to suffocate, asshole!

Before I could call on my air magic the intruder cocked his head to the side and said, "Hard way it is then."

A cloud of dust blew into my face, and then the world went dark.

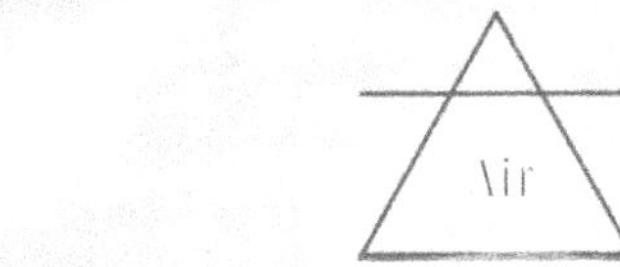

Chapter Three

PHINEAS

I threw her over my shoulder and couldn't believe how tiny she felt against my body.

"You good?" Cassian asked me.

I nodded. "Open the back door, will ya?"

"Shouldn't we put her in the trunk?" Beau asked.

"I'm sure the little size two won't be able to get away from the four of us," I answered as I shifted Zara's body to cradle her in my arms.

Cassian opened the door for me, and I slid in, keeping the princess on my lap. My nose grazed her hair. Damn it, why did she smell so good?

Patrick glanced at us from the driver's seat. He focused his gaze on the princess and smiled. He had some history with her although he never went into detail. A wave of envy rolled through me, and I had no clue why. She wasn't mine. Hell, she didn't even know me. We'd been following her from afar for the past few weeks, studying her.

Her life wasn't very exciting. For income, she worked at a bar called The Convent two nights a week. Our background check revealed that she made a good living from working just those nights. Out of curiosity, I went to The Convent to see for myself what her job entailed. I thought for sure she was swinging from a pole or spreading her legs for the amount of money she was making and was relieved to learn that wasn't true. She was quite a bartender, and men threw money at her as though she was doing so naked. Perhaps there was more to it than that, but from what I witnessed in the few weeks of watching her from afar it seemed all above board.

Aside from work, she didn't have much of a social life, and she spent most of her time with her foster mother, who was an elderly human woman. Zara seemed to deeply care for the woman and that had been both comforting and disconcerting. I was glad that she had formed a sense of family since she'd been banished, and yet this woman was all human and would not live for much longer. It was likely the princess would not want to leave her foster mother behind to help our cause, but I had a plan in place for that, just in case.

Before I knew it, Beau and Cassian hopped in the car, and we were on the road heading back to our place. Zara slept in my arms, her face in the crook of my neck. Her lips grazed my skin, and my heart rate sped up. What was this woman doing to me?

Cassian sat beside me with Zara's legs draped over his lap. He removed her shoes and began massaging her feet. He finally noticed me staring at him and shrugged. We had all fixated on the princess since we began this mission.

"She's going to be pissed when she wakes." Patrick eyed us in the rearview mirror.

"Keep your eyes on the road." Cassian's voice was low and gruff.

"He's right," Beau said. "She's going to be pissed. We probably should have restrained her."

Beau turned to face us, but his gaze was focused on the princess. He reached out to touch her hand. His finger lightly brushed her pinky. We were all under her spell.

The car went over a few bumps, and Zara jostled in my arms. Beau, Cassian, and I stiffened, worried she'd wake up and freak out. Thankfully, she didn't. She shifted her weight, draped one arm around my neck, and stretched her legs out over Cassian's lap.

"Bro! Watch the bumps!" Cassian scowled at the back of Patrick's head.

The car evened out, and I relaxed with the princess resting in my arms. No one said anything else; luckily it wouldn't be a far drive. Along the interstate highway was a small dirt road that would allow us to drive across the border dividing the human realm and ours. Humans would drive right by it. The kingdom recognized our magic allowing us to enter. The car rolled right through the border and since Zara was with us, she'd be granted access as well. It made me sick that she had been exiled the way she had been. And now we were bringing her back against her will.

I was certain the princess would not be pleased when she woke up. Unfortunately, we didn't have a choice. Our kingdom was dying because the royals were abusing their power and draining the source. Cassian, Beau, Patrick, and I had been cast out by our chiefs; we were the rejects of our clans. And yet our people had come to us for help when clan chiefs sided with the royals to save themselves while leaving our people and our lands to die.

When Patrick revealed he had met her in the human realm, we formulated a plan with the help of her father, the former king.

Her father was sure he'd be able to sway his daughter into the fold. Kidnapping the princess wasn't the smartest idea but the only one we had. We needed her help. She had the power to overthrow the reigning king and her sister, the queen. The throne was rightfully hers even though she had been exiled for fourteen years. We desperately hoped she would be willing to help us. She was our last hope and the only person in our realm and the human realm that could save us all.

I pressed my lips to Zara's forehead and dozed off until we arrived at my lair in the kingdom.

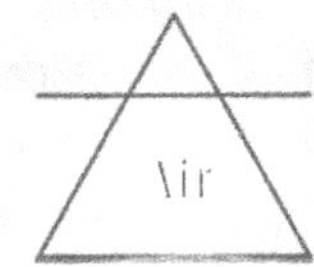

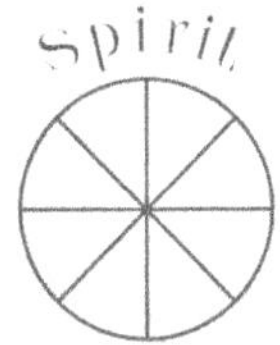

Chapter Four

ZARA

My magic swirled in my belly, and a contented sigh escaped my lips. I stretched on the soft mattress and snuggled into the satiny sheets. Satiny sheets, what?

Muffled voices reached my ears.

"She's waking," someone said. "Should we tie her up?"

"No, she's not a prisoner," a different male voice said.

"Zara?"

Something brushed my hair from my face, and my heart rate galloped in my chest at an alarming rate. Who were these people? Where was I? What happened? I lay there completely still.

Until it all came flooding back to me - the intruder on my doorstep.

I snapped my eyes open, and I kicked my leg out and swung my fists at the man closest to me. He grunted then pinned me on the bed with his body weight and restrained my hands above my head.

"Zara, stop, it's me. Cassian. We were friends when we were kids. Do you remember me?" he asked in a soft voice.

I bucked and rolled him off me, putting as much distance as I could between us. Cassian? My eyes blinked rapidly as the man before me came into focus. It had been years since I'd last seen him, but I would recognize him anywhere.

"It's ok, princess, we're not going to harm you. Here, drink some water." Cassian picked up a glass of water from a table near the bed.

I glared at him as he got closer. Cass was no longer the chubby boy I remembered. He regarded me with cautious blue eyes and his cleft chin tipped downwards in deference. His round face had morphed into a strong jaw and high cheekbones. He wore jeans that fit snugly around his thighs, and his T-shirt molded to his torso. He had the body of an avid swimmer. Wow, Cassian Brooks had grown up hot.

I used my water magic to dump the glass of water on his face. "What the fuck, Cass?! Why did you kidnap me?"

"I'm sorry, Z! It was the only way. We didn't know what else to do." Cassian sputtered and wiped the water off his face. "I highly doubt drugs and kidnapping were your only choices. You couldn't have sent an email or a text message like normal people?" I rubbed at my temples to stave off a headache I knew was coming, then swung my legs off the bed.

I swooned when I stood and then slumped back down on the mattress. He'd used fairy dust, which was like chloroform, to knock me out and bring me here. The drugs were still in my system, but something else had made me swoon. The power of the kingdom, the home I had been exiled from, seeped into me as soon as my feet touched the stone floors.

With a deep breath, I braced myself for the onslaught of magic and stood again. Magic surged up through the soles of my feet and I paused to give my body a moment to adjust while I took in my surroundings.

It wasn't a typical room of any sort. It was more like a cave, the flooring and walls had varying shades of gray limestone. The base of the bed was made up of the same natural rock. Deep red satin sheets draped over the mattress. Lanterns had been placed around the bed and floated above us. If I hadn't been kidnapped, I would have thought the space was romantic.

"Zara, please, give us a minute," Cassian said.

"You have some nerve, Brooks." I scowled, then looked down at my body. I was wearing a T-shirt that hung down to my thighs.

"Where the fuck am I? Where the fuck are my clothes? Did you undress me?" I rounded on my childhood friend, and then noticed another man on the opposite side of the room watching me warily. Two of them. Oh shit, this wasn't good.

I reached for my magic and was pleased to find it thrumming through me stronger than ever. I readied myself for an attack.

"Relax, Z. And no, I didn't undress you. I would never. We thought you would be more comfortable, and we laundered your stuff. It's in the bathroom." Cassian pointed to an open door behind me.

I marched into the bathroom and braced my hand on the counter. I was certain this was my biological father's doing. Fuck the royal family. They'd disowned me fourteen years ago and I had zero interest in hearing what they had to say now.

I used the bathroom facilities and even brushed my teeth with the unopened toothbrush that was sitting on top of my laundered jeans, T-shirt, and hoodie. Like the palace, this place had modern-day plumbing and electricity all powered by mage magic. The bathroom was beautiful, but my foul mood circumvented any admiration I would have normally had for the all-natural stone and pewter finishes. I glanced at the water-fall shower and frowned.

Damn kidnappers had ruined my fantasy of having an outdoor shower, that looked just like it.

My purse was amongst my clothes, and I rummaged through it and pulled out my phone. There was no signal, and the battery was running low. Figured.

Cassian and the other male stood shoulder to shoulder as I came out of the bathroom and stared at me. I stared back and took a moment to study the stranger's appearance.

He was just as tall as Cass and had honey-blond hair that brushed the back of his neck. His light green eyes regarded me with curiosity. He had full lips and wore joggers that left little to the imagination. I swallowed hard.

"We're not here to harm you, princess. We need your help." His voice slid over me like velvet.

I glared at Cass, then glanced at the stranger, and then back at Cass.

"No." I walked away. It was a dumb response, but I needed to get away from the two handsome men before my lady bits decided sticking around might be fun.

"Princess, wait," Cassian said behind me.

"Don't call me that. I'm not your princess. I'm leaving." I followed the path of lanterns out of the romantic bed chamber, which led into an open cavernous space.

I stomped along the path with determination, but my steps slowed as the rest of the cavern came into view. I was awestruck. The room outside of the bedchamber resembled a living area. The natural formations of the mountain provided functional furnishings and artistic design elements as well.

Stalagmites created an intricate interior design of shelving, tables, and seating areas that were made comfortable with fluffy light-colored cushions. A few plants seemed to grow out from the stone itself, which wasn't possible. I leaned over one plant and bent to touch the damp soil. There had to be an irrigation system of some sort. I continued along the path and admired the scenery brushing my fingers on the plants as I passed by.

The natural limestone striations flowed throughout the entire cavern and created a masterpiece. Fairy lights floated twenty feet above and illuminated the space in a soft golden glow that highlighted the curtained ribbons of stalactites that hung artistically along the cavern ceilings and walls.

The Goddess built the entire space herself. No mortal artist human or elemental could design such beauty by hand. Something in my heart stirred. It felt like I had come home.

"Z, let's talk. Please." A familiar voice startled me out of my musings. I turned to face the man I had said goodbye to over ten years ago. Silver eyes rimmed with black stared back at me, and a mix of emotions overwhelmed my brain. In that split second, I wasn't sure if I was angry, surprised, happy, or disgusted.

Perhaps all of it applied.

First a ghost from my childhood in the kingdom, and now a ghost from my time at the youth home. Patrick Lockwood had been my savior, my love, and like everyone else I once loved, he'd abandoned me. And now he was a part of this kidnapping scheme?

Fuck him.

"I'm sorry we had to do this, Z. Letters were sent to you and, well, you never responded. Your father desperately wants to speak with you. We need your help." Patrick said. The scrawny kid I had met as a teenager filled out nicely. His muscular arms flexed as he extended his hand to me.

I stepped out of his reach.

"No, Trick. I can't believe you're a part of this. Whatever it is you need from me, the answer is no. You all can fuck right off." I walked backward. These fuckers had the audacity to ask for help after kidnapping me. And damn them all for looking so good.

"The kingdom is in trouble, Zara. We need your help. Please hear us out," Cassian said.

"Hear you out? Seriously? You kidnapped me. I'm certain that has to be the absolute worst way to ask for a favor, assholes." I was pissed. I sent a force of air magic, slamming Cass and Trick into the stone wall several feet away.

The blond guy stepped in front of me with his hands out and said, "Princess, please just a few moments, and we'll get you back to Silk City. Please, I don't want to hurt you."

Several thick vines crept up through the cracks in the stone flooring. I gave him a wry look. *Please, as if that's going to hold me back.*

"If you love your plants as much as you should earth elemental... back the fuck off." I created a ball of fire and let it hover above my palm.

"Enough, Zara," an authoritative voice said behind me and he covered my hand with his, extinguishing my fireball. Great, a fire elemental. I turned to face him.

"You?! You're the asshole who drugged me on my doorstep. Get out of my way." I recognized his voice from earlier and snarled.

"No." His golden eyes pierced mine. "Not until you hear us out. As Beau said, we will take you back to Silk or wherever you want to go whether you decide to work with us or not. Please, angel, let us explain."

"No!" I held my fingers out and counted them for added effect. "One, I don't appreciate being brought here against my will. Two, I was banished by royal decree and shouldn't be here in the first place. And three, my mother needs me. She is sickly, and she needs my help to administer medication. If you need my help, make a fucking appointment."

He glanced behind me and nodded at the other three men. "I...we didn't know she was ill. Come on. I'll take you home now." He held onto my hand and led me out of the cavern.

"I'm Phineas Strait by the way," the fire elemental said. Phin's body was hot. Not just in the physical bulging muscles sense, because he had plenty of those. He also had waves of heat pouring off him, indicating he was a powerful fire elemental. Like my biological father. I looked up at him, and his golden gaze locked on mine.

"And that's Beau Duray." He tipped his chin to the blond walking on the opposite side of me. "And you already know Patrick and Cass."

I didn't respond as I assessed the four men. Although I was considered tall for a woman, the top of my head barely grazed Phin's and Beau's shoulders, which meant they were at least six and a half feet tall. Their large muscular bodies had me blocked in, while Cassian and Trick were directly behind us.

The reality of my situation began to sink in. I was surrounded by four large, powerful elementals, and in an unfamiliar place. I started to get nervous.

Phin squeezed my hand and offered a small smile. The slight movement caused his coppery brown hair to fall haphazardly on his face, covering his stunning eyes.

Beau also smiled down at me. He ran a hand through his blond hair, and the hem of his shirt rode up, revealing a lean, muscled abdomen. A large tattoo covered his torso and if I wasn't mistaken, it was a mage rune or a cluster of runes. Hmm...

Great, four hot as fuck elementals. Too bad they were asshole kidnappers.

We kept walking through the cavern, bypassing a kitchen and dining room, and into another living area that had three separate hallways carved out of the cave itself. The natural beauty of the space was incredible, and my elemental blood longed to explore my surroundings.

I had been there all of fifteen minutes and I already loved the place. Stockholm syndrome was already setting in. Goddess help me.

The path we were on seemed never ending and the incline became steeper. I must've been completely out as I had no recollection of being brought here.

"How long was I out?" I asked.

"You were asleep for a few hours." Beau looked down at his watch. "It's almost 9 a.m."

We finally came to a vast open space that could only be described as an airplane hangar even though there was no airplane in sight. Several vehicles occupied the space and there was plenty of room for more.

Phin walked me over to a white SUV. The royal family and palace guards had SUV's just like this. They were powered by water and magic and not easy to come by in the kingdom. It made me wonder what Phin's connection to the royal family was. Most elementals didn't drive. They traveled by air, water, or horse.

He opened the front passenger door and placed his hand on the small of my back, guiding me into the car. He was so close his smokey cinnamon scent drew me in, and I inhaled before sliding into the front passenger seat. *I'm such a weirdo.*

Cassian climbed into the backseat and Phin got behind the wheel. Trick and Beau kept their gaze on me as we drove away.

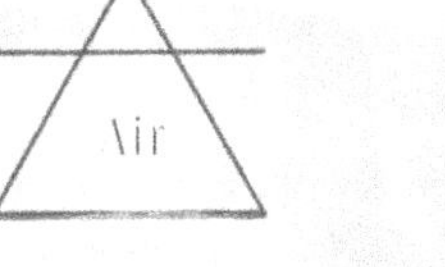

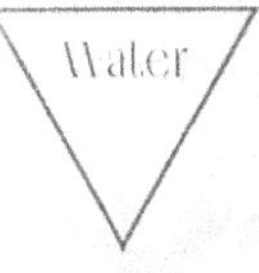
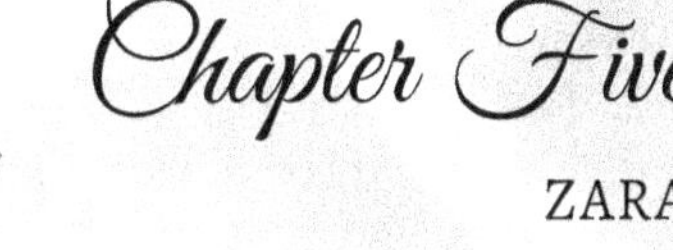

Chapter Five

ZARA

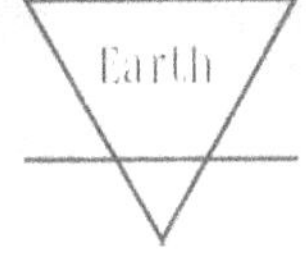

Phin and Cassian were utterly silent as we drove away from the cavern. The area they had brought me to was on the far west of the kingdom, an area I had never visited. That wasn't surprising though. I had been a child when I'd left, and aside from family excursions, I hadn't done much in terms of exploring.

The area we were in was not well traversed or populated. Elementals tended to live as close to the Source as possible. I suppose things may have changed in the last fourteen years.

Based on the location of the cavern, it was obvious to me that the guys were hiding out. A part of me wanted to know why, but I was more interested in soaking up the kingdom's magic.

Everything about the kingdom was different from Silk City. The air had a magical essence to it that seeped into my pores. Even the rays of the sun seemed to dance on my skin.

We drove down a winding dirt road. Pine and fir trees soared high above us, a hundred feet in the air, and in the distance, a crystalline turquoise body of water came into view. I sat straighter in my seat and gawked at Transcendental Oasis, the most sacred waters in the entire kingdom. I gaped at the lake, and a large part of me wanted to stop and go for a swim.

"It's amazing, isn't it?" Cassian said his face close behind me. "I love it here. It's too bad this is all about to go away."

His statement was troubling. I was about to ask when Phin reached for my hand and garnered my attention. "We can stop if you want for a couple of minutes. I need to make a call anyway. Would that be, ok?"

I nodded, then focused my attention back on Transcendental Oasis. As a child, this had been one of the places I wanted to see, but my parents had forbidden it. It was a special oasis they told me, only to be visited on rare occasions. For my fourteenth birthday wish I had asked to spend a day at Transcendental Oasis with my family. Supposedly, my mother had planned it, but it didn't work out that way. Instead, that was the day I was banished. And now, fourteen years later I was at the one place I had longed to visit when I was a little girl.

That day had served as a recurring nightmare for so many years. It had taken an emotional toll and yet, oddly enough, sadness didn't overwhelm me as we drove closer to the oasis. At that moment, all I felt was a sense of peace capped with a tinge of excitement.

My fingers grazed something soft, and I turned to see Phin's hand enclosed around mine and my fingers pressed against his lips. I frowned as my kidnapper casually placed a soft kiss on my hand and was more shocked that I hadn't pulled away. What was wrong with me?

I was at a loss for words and continued to stare at Phin. Like the other men, he was a looker and that was downplaying his appearance. His sharp angular features were perfectly proportioned over olive skin that was slightly darker than Thadd's. I could see the outline of defined muscles under his white button-down shirt and his dark gray slacks strained over his wide thighs.

He parked alongside the dirt road and turned off the engine. My door opened and Cassian held out his hand to me. I glanced back at Phin. He placed another kiss on the back of my hand and released me. Cassian grasped my other hand and helped me out of the car.

The entire exchange with Phin had been so strange, but I didn't give it another thought. Transcendental Oasis became the center of my attention. It seemed to beckon me.

I went straight to the shore. Unlike most freshwater springs, the sandy shore was grainy and white. I took off my shoes and rolled up the hem of my jeans as far as they would go.

The cool waters tickled my toes, and I couldn't help but smile. I took a deep, cleansing breath, spread my arms wide, and thanked the Goddess for all the beauty that surrounded me. My spirit soared. It felt so good to be home.

"Zara," Phin said behind me.

I turned to face him. Despite the way I had been brought here, I couldn't wipe the big smile from my face.

He smiled back and said, "You have a phone call."

My brows scrunched up as I took the phone out of his hand and answered. "Hello?"

"Zara, honey? Are you ok?"

"Mama? I'm good, I'm on my way home. Are you ok?" Nervousness held me in its grip, and my gut clenched.

"I'm fine. That old friend of yours is here, the handsome one with the silver eyes. He said you were needed in the kingdom, but you were concerned for me so he's bringing me to you. He also brought an elemental healer to help with my disease. She's very sweet but said she'd be able to care for me better if I went to the kingdom. I just wanted to confirm with you, before going with them."

I narrowed my eyes at both Phin and Cassian, not buying it.

Then I said into the phone, "Mama, I'm switching to video call right now." I pressed the button, and Gigi flashed on the screen.

She was still at home.

"Did they hurt you?" I asked her.

"Of course not, honey. I'm fine. The healers are nice, and I am looking forward to seeing the place where you were born. Are you ok?" Gigi smiled and looked perfectly at ease.

"I'm better now that I know you're ok. Did they say when you were going to get here?" I ground my teeth.

Gigi asked someone off camera, and I heard a muffled voice. "Patrick said in an hour. I packed some of your things. I'll be there soon. I love you."

"I love you, mom. Can you hand Trick the phone?" "Hi, Z." Trick's face appeared on the screen.

"Harm one hair on her head and I will boil the blood in your veins and rip you apart." I hung up the phone.

Phin and Beau looked at me with their mouths agape.

"Don't look at me like that. That was a dirty thing to do, you little shits." I tossed the phone to Phin, and he caught it easily.

"Turn around and give me some privacy." I sneered.

Once their backs were turned, I stripped out of my hoodie, T-shirt, and jeans, and then I jumped in the lake. Transcendental Oasis was the largest natural geyser in all the realms. The temperature was perfect and felt like a welcoming embrace, washing away all my sorrow and cleansing my soul. I swam leisurely, taking my time until I heard a whistle. Cassian waved at me from the shore with a towel in his hand.

I swam with my underwear on, a pink lacey bralette, and a matching thong. I took the towel from Cass and motioned for him to turn around. I wasn't shy about my body, but he didn't deserve a free show.

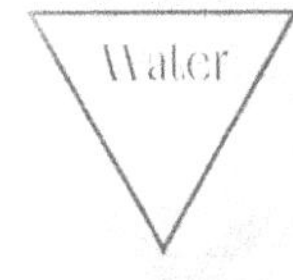
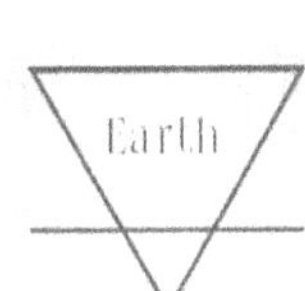

Chapter Six

CASSIAN

My heart rate sped and my jeans got tighter as she sauntered out of the lake. The little chubby girl had grown up to be a gorgeous woman. I'm not going to lie. I had hoped she'd be completely naked when she walked out of the lake, but the tiny lingerie set she wore was sexier and made her even more alluring than she already was. I couldn't stop staring at her curves and those perfect breasts with those hard nipples sticking up at attention.

She held my gaze as she took the towel from me and twirled her finger in the air. I smiled and turned. Then I caught Phin sitting in his car staring at her openly. So unfair.

A few moments later she walked by me, fully dressed and I followed behind her like a love-sick puppy.

Phin grinned at her and asked, "Enjoy your swim?"

She nodded and smiled. She wasn't very talkative, which was not at all what she was like when we were kids. Perhaps living alone amongst the humans had made her shy or maybe she just didn't want to hear anything we had to say. It was probably the latter.

Phin, the smooth operator, held her door open.

I sat in the back seat and slid behind Phin, allowing me to stare at the princess. I was at a loss for words myself. We had been so close when we were kids and I missed her. Seeing her after all these years sparked a different feeling in me though. I was eager to get close to her again.

"How much longer till my mom arrives?" she asked.

Her mom, wow, she'd formed a true bond with her foster mother. I looked down at my phone. "Thirty minutes or so. We figured you may want to settle in, and we wanted to fill you in on everything."

She glanced at me over her shoulder with narrowed eyes. "I don't care about what's happening here and have zero desire to help you."

She had that same stubborn streak just like when we were kids. Oh, how I had missed her.

"Well, umm...that's understandable. Beau's mom is a healer. She went with him and Patrick to do a medical consult. From what I understand, she has the sugar sickness?" Phin looked at her for confirmation.

"Yes, diabetes," Zara replied.

He continued, "Calla, Beau's mom, is confident she can help her. We'll make sure your mom is cared for and healthy. And possibly, while she is being cared for, you'll hear us out and hopefully you'll agree to help."

Phin was a smooth motherfucker. He even grasped her hand and kissed her knuckles. I was envious, and I needed to step up my game.

"I have no desire to hear about your problems. My mom and I won't be staying long." She turned to look out the window, but she didn't pull away from him. That made me want to hold her other hand.

"That's fair, Zara," I offered. "We went about this all wrong. The least we could do to make amends is care for your mom."

This time when she glanced back at me, the corners of her mouth tugged up. She was trying to hold back a real smile, so I flashed my pearly whites at her and turned up the charm. "We'll make sure your stay is comfortable for as long as you wish to stay."

That earned me a real smile. Yes! Point for me.

We did have pressing matters to speak about and time was short. Zara's sister and her sister's husband were complete gobshites. The greedy assholes were draining the kingdom's magic. As soon as Queen Amina and King Issac took over the crown, they went after the Source. It was a sacred mountain where the Goddess resided; it was her temple.

At the base of the Source was the Sanctuary, hallowed ground, a place for worship and paying homage to the Goddess.

Everyone in the kingdom was a born elemental. Some were more powerful than others. Without access to the Source, our people began losing their innate connection to the Goddess and their powers were waning. Low to mid-level elementals were losing their magic rapidly, and some had succumbed to illness.

Without our people, the imbalance the kingdom had been experiencing would have been catastrophic. Little by little, the people of this land, the ones responsible for keeping Mother Earth balanced and abundant, had been cast aside and left to perish. And thus, the land was falling ill as well.

The royals were either enslaving people or killing those that defied them. Those that had managed to escape came to us for help.

Phin, Beau, Patrick, and I were on top of the power scale. Even though we had been rejected by our clans, we all felt a sense of responsibility to the people.

I was born a water elemental. A couple of years after Zara had been banished my secondary magic kicked in and I'd had my first shift. I could shift into any animal on land. My clan chief and uncle hated me for it and thus tossed me out.

The other three men had similar issues with their clans. That rejection helped the four of us create a brotherly bond, and we had been living on the outskirts of our people. We made a home in Torch Mountain away from our clans and the royal family. As far as we were concerned, the rules the royals enforced didn't apply to us.

Still, we weren't about to turn our backs on the people of the kingdom. We needed to right the wrongs before the imbalance became irreparable. These were desperate times and desperate measures had to be taken.

Zara's father had been trying to contact her for well over a year now, and she hadn't bothered with a response. We had someone deliver messages to her in person, one with the royal seal and one without. From afar, we watched Zara open her front door for the messenger. As soon as she'd seen the royal seal, she'd torn up the envelope on her doorstep and left the pieces of paper to fly off in the wind. Our second attempt was with an unmarked envelope that had been delivered to her at work. We witnessed her opening the letter, glancing at it for two seconds, and then she lit it on fire right there at the bar. When the bar patrons asked her about it, she replied, "*No one tells me what to do.*" The bar patrons had cheered, and the princess smiled.

And so her father had come up with this brilliant plan to have her kidnapped. The four of us did as he'd asked because we didn't have a better solution. Now the beauty sitting in the front seat of Phin's car was our last hope, and I crossed my fingers that she would help.

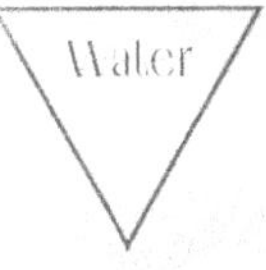

Chapter Seven

ZARA

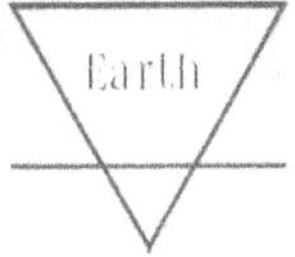

Phin took a different route to the cavern he called Torch Mountain, his lair. I gave him a sidelong glance, and he didn't offer more. Our fingers were intertwined as though we had an intimate relationship. Oddly enough it didn't make me cringe, but the situation was just too awkward, and I drew my hand away.

He reached over and placed his hand on my knee, which was even more intimate. Before I could argue my point, he started speaking.

"I was banished by my clan, the Pyres. When they banished me, I made myself a home here. I've lived on my own since I turned twenty-five. My father lived here before he passed, so I just moved in, made a few upgrades, and over the years it has grown."

"And now the four of you live there?" I glanced at Cassian.

"In the lair, yes," Cassian answered. "We - Patrick, Beau, and I- needed to find a place to live after being banished by our clans. Phin offered his man cave, and we've been roommates for what? Four years now?"

Phin nodded. "Four or five. Patrick was the first to move in. He found me as he was flying overhead, and we became friends. Then Beau and Cassian moved in a year or so later. And now our little community of exiles is growing. Not that you want to hear about that, princess."

The entire situation did sound intriguing, but I wasn't about to get suckered into their issues whatever they were.

"I'm not your princess. I keep telling you that." I turned to stare out the window again and placed my hand on my lap which landed on Phin's hand. He laced his fingers with mine and squeezed.

Phin drove up a steep road that led to the massive hangar door that opened as we got closer to it.

Once parked, Cass opened my door for me again and helped me out. "Thank you," I whispered.

He placed a kiss on my cheek then stepped away from me and averted his eyes. "Forgive me, Zara. I overstepped." He stared at the ground.

"Um, it's ok," I stammered then shook my head. I should have slapped him in the face. If I was still the princess, it would have been expected of me. I wasn't a princess anymore, and I wasn't even slightly annoyed by his gesture. The peacefulness I felt from being back in the kingdom was messing with my head.

"This way," Phin said, and I followed him and Cassian.

"Your mom should be here shortly."

We passed through a metal door and went down a pathway that was different from the one we'd taken earlier. The path led us to a large open living space. There were leather mismatched sofas surrounding a stone coffee table and a colorful Persian rug covering the stone floor. On one wall was a television. I tilted my head and frowned.

"Satellite." Cassian turned it on with a remote in his hand.

"Phin has all the modern conveniences of the human realm."

"What? How?" I asked as I looked around and noticed two archways on opposite walls, leading to places I hadn't explored.

"Magic tech. I have a business in Silk City. During my visits I've picked up a few things," Phin said beside me.

"Well, that explains all the cars. How long have you had this business?" I asked.

Occasionally powerful elementals left the kingdom for education and supply runs, but having a business there was unheard of.

"Several years now. I'm a blacksmith. We make custom iron pieces, and I have a crew of humans that handle the day-today business. I created all the metal pieces here myself."

"Nice," I replied.

Impressed, I looked around. There were metal accents throughout the cavern, from furnishings, fixtures, and décor, all of which complemented the mountain. He was a talented craftsman. And an ironworks business made sense considering he was a fire elemental. With enough firepower, he could easily manipulate metal.

Voices floated in from the hallway we had come from, and Beau with Patrick and Gigi appeared. I ran up to my mom and gave her a bear hug.

"I'm happy to see you." I knelt beside her wheelchair. "You look good!"

She looked well-rested and healthy. "Did they give you something?" I asked.

"Yes, some herbal concoction. I haven't felt this good in years, and I could have walked, but these boys were being overprotective." She got up from her wheelchair, and I stood with her, then looked around for her cane.

Trick handed it to her, and she waved him off. I was in shock. She hadn't walked without her cane for years.

"This is lovely, Zara. Is this where you grew up?" She gazed about the cavern.

"No, Mama. This is Phin's place." I replied, then both Phin and Cassian introduced themselves.

She looped her arm in Phin's, and he led her to the dining area where lunch was being prepared.

Beau cleared his throat. "Zara, this is my mother Calla, and my sister Rosemary. They are gifted healers and have agreed to look after your mother."

The two almost identical women stood behind him, carrying large satchels. They both had light brown hair and deep brown almond eyes. I glanced back at Beau and then back to the mother-daughter duo. He didn't look like them, and I didn't look anything like my biological family either. Elemental bloodlines were weird that way. Physical traits varied while magic was inherited. If both parents had the same elemental magic, the child would inherit the same. If parents had different elemental magic, their children would manifest the strongest of the two. My father was a fire elemental while my mother was earth, and somehow, I ended up with all.

I introduced myself to the mother and daughter team and thanked them for offering to look after Gigi. "We are earth healers, princess. We are happy to help. I've given her a tonic that will sustain her, but we'd like her to stay with us where we can monitor her condition and ensure her care," Calla said. She stood close enough for me to see the gray hair at her temples and the fine lines around her mouth and eyes.

"I'm not your princess," I blurted. That would be my default answer to everyone in this damn place. I realized how rude my tone was and quickly apologized for my outburst.

"I'm sorry. That was rude of me. Please, just call me Zara. And thank you for caring for my mother. I am happy to pay you for your services and whatever else you require."

"No payment is necessary; it is our pleasure. We are just happy to have you home. We will prepare her quarters and be back to check on her in a few." Rosemary and Calla bowed and walked out the way they entered.

Elementals had great power and skill that could help Gigi, yet I was reluctant to trust the entire situation. I knew they were going to ask something of me soon, and I had no intention of helping them. Would a cure for Gigi be worth helping these so called rejects? For the mother of my heart, I would do anything, but I wasn't going to let the guys know that yet. At some point, I would have to hear what they had to say.

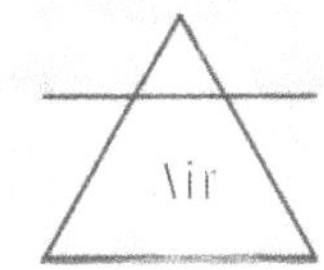

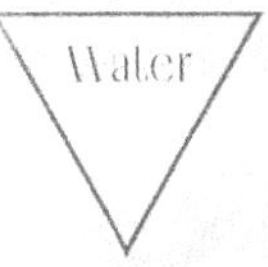
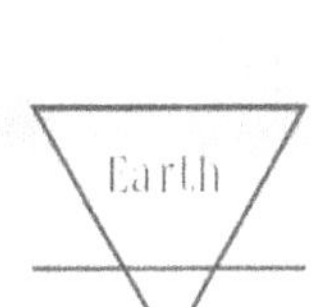

Chapter Eight

ZARA

While I was speaking with the mother-daughter team, everyone aside from Beau went to the dining area. After the women went to do whatever it was they needed to do, Beau placed my hand in the crook of his arm and led the way.

"Thank you for helping my mom." I looked up at Beau as we walked to the next room.

"Of course." His sea-green eyes sparkled when he smiled. "I'm sorry we didn't know what you were dealing with when we came up with this plan of ours."

His cheeks flushed and it made me instantly like him.

"We failed you and hope we can make amends," he added.

"I'm not interested in sticking around or hearing about your problems," I said.

He stopped walking and turned to face me. "That's fair, Zara. Just... keep an open mind. Ok? We won't force your hand."

His tone was sincere, and I felt my body relax. He was one of those salt-of-the-earth types. The kind of person that was genuinely good-hearted and trustworthy.

I met his gaze and nodded, "For Gigi's sake, I can keep an open mind."

He flashed me a bright smile and guided me to the next room, which was a modern kitchen, sectioned off from the dining area, by a large stone counter. The delicious aromas made my mouth water, and I realized I hadn't eaten since the day before.

"Princess! I'm so happy to see you!" A robust gnome shuffled towards me and shook my hand. His smile spread across his round, pink-hued face.

Although I didn't recognize him, his warm greeting chipped away at the walls I had in place around my heart.

"My name is Linc. I was an apprentice at the palace when you were just a little girl. And now I am here and am looking forward to cooking for you. Come, come, lunch is ready."

He motioned for me to sit at a large round table where Gigi was already sitting as well as the three other men.

"Thank you, Linc, but I'm not a princess anymore. Please, just call me Zara."

"Nonsense! You will always be a princess to me. But perhaps, now that you have grown, I shall call you, Lady Zara." He gave me a flourishing bow.

As far as monikers went, it wasn't much better than princess, but his cheerful behavior was infectious. I shook my head but couldn't help smiling at the gnome.

The round table was large enough to fit more people but there were only six place settings.

"Won't Rosemary and Calla be joining us?" I asked, and I looked towards the way we had come from.

"Umm...no, they have their work, and we thought you'd want to dine with just us," Beau replied.

"Why would I want that?" I stood and walked to the hall we'd come down to find the healers.

"Where are you going?" Trick flashed to my side.

Startled and annoyed, I glared at him. "To invite the healers to join us. Is that ok, Linc?" I directed the question to the gnome, realizing he may need to prepare more food.

"Of course, my Lady! The more, the merrier!" Linc smiled.

"I'll find them, please, sit." Trick placed his hand on my back and guided me to my seat.

"I can do it." I moved towards the hallway, but Phin grabbed my hand and tugged me into my chair.

"You don't know your way around yet, Zara. Patrick will use his speed to find them and ask them to join us. Please, sit."

In moments, Trick returned with Calla and Rosemary. Both women smiled and thanked me for the invitation.

I insisted Linc join us for lunch as well. He was taken aback by the invitation but reluctantly agreed.

He'd prepared a wonderful feast. Rather than having him plate each dish for everyone, I helped him bring platters of food to the table, for us to serve ourselves family-style. No one liked the idea of me helping Linc. But I didn't care. I wasn't helpless and I wasn't going to sit there and wait for one gnome to serve nine people. As I brought over a pitcher of water, I realized what had everyone in a tizzy.

I stood at the table with the water pitcher in my hand and cleared my throat. As soon as everyone gave me their undivided attention, I said, "I am not your princess. I do not expect or want any of you to wait on me. If we are to coexist together for the next day or two, please just treat me like the normal elemental that I am."

Everyone nodded their understanding as I went around the table and filled their glasses.

After that, the conversation started off awkward. The healers were incredibly quiet and barely nibbled. And the four men were reluctant to say much.

It was just too weird to have that many people together and not have a conversation going. Everyone seemed uncomfortable, and perhaps it had been my fault for asking Linc and the healers to join us. I knew the four men wanted to discuss more serious matters, but I wasn't ready for that, so I sort of steered the conversation and kept it on lighter matters.

"This is delicious, Linc," I said to the gnome.

He'd prepared a scrumptious lunch of salads, fruits, and my favorite tarragon chicken with a white wine butter glaze. The delicate flavors blended well and exploded on my taste buds. There was nothing better than freshly harvested produce and herbs.

"I'm glad you like it, my Lady. I am looking forward to cooking for you. You always had a sophisticated palate even as a youngin'."

I laughed. "I was a little chubby kid and ate everything. Wait…I still eat everything. Right, Mama?"

Everyone laughed.

"Oh child, yes, yes, you do have a healthy appetite, and you're quite a good cook, too." Gigi smiled at me.

"I learned from the best, but I could probably learn a few more tricks from Linc here." I bit into the savory chicken and moaned a little.

"You're not wrong. This dressing is delicious. We need to recreate this one." My mother nodded, and then she placed a fork full of veggies in her mouth.

"Now, now, ladies, let me do the cooking for you. It's what I'm good at."

We laughed, and the conversation flowed with ease from there.

I was impressed with Linc's cooking skills and for remembering my strange palate from when I was little. For the first time in years, nostalgia didn't feel like a punch in the face.

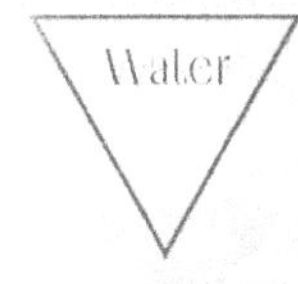

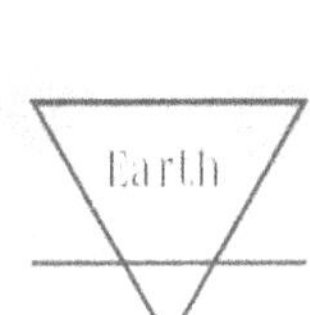

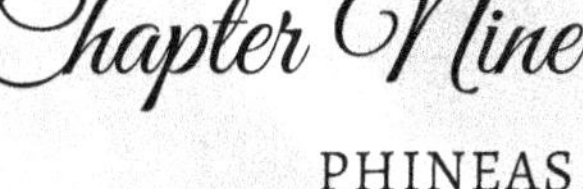

Chapter Nine

PHINEAS

After lunch, I showed Gigi where she would be able to rest. Zara followed. She was concerned, and she wanted to speak with the healers and Gigi.

I left them to it and went back to find the guys. Patrick and Cassian were in the living room and Beau was in the kitchen. We needed privacy to come up with a plan, so we decided on meeting in my office. A secret panel opened behind the television and we entered.

Cassian said, "She is more amazing than I could have ever imagined."

We all nodded in agreement; he wasn't wrong. She'd surprised me by inviting the healers and Linc to join us for lunch. And then she got up and helped Linc serve us. She had insisted we stop treating her like a princess. She most certainly wasn't like any royal I'd ever met before.

"Although, she is as stubborn as I remember her. Once she sets her mind to something, there's no changing it." Patrick plopped in one of the chairs across from my desk while Beau and Cassian sat on the sofa.

"Well." I took a seat behind my desk. "That's why I wanted privacy. We need another approach. I was hoping to use Gigi as a way to convince her to help, but we had to play that card earlier than anticipated."

"My mother said it would be a few days to get Gigi's blood sugar stabilized. After that, she can be placed on herbal remedies which she can use at home." Beau offered while placing his dirty shoes on my coffee table. I scowled at him, but he ignored me and made himself comfortable.

"Considering she's not supposed to be here anyway, we may not have that much time. Her father wants to see her though. We need to do that today," I told them.

"That's going to suck. I hope he is ready to do some groveling." Patrick shook his head. "She has no love lost for that man."

"What's our other option, if her father is unable to convince her?" Cassian asked. "Like Phin said, we can't use Gigi."

The four of us remained quiet for a few minutes thinking over our options. After seeing how down-to-earth she was with everyone at lunch, it became obvious to me that the best way to solicit her help would be for her to witness what was going on for herself. This wasn't the best option though; it was too dangerous. The fewer people who knew about her presence the better.

"I hate to say this, but I'm thinking she needs to see the refugees," I said.

The guys didn't like this idea any more than I did. We didn't want to expose her. If her sister found out she was here, she would be out for blood. We needed to formulate a plan to deal with the royals before we could risk that.

"Fuck." Cassian got up and paced.

"I don't like this either. But what other options do we have?" I shook my head. Not only would we risk exposing her too soon, but taking her to see the refugees was another manipulative move.

"Let's take her to her father first. If that works then we're good. If not, we'll take her to see the refugee camps. We'll have to," Patrick said.

"I hate that idea." Beau took his feet off my coffee table and sat upright.

"She's done," I said. On the surveillance cameras, I watched as she left Gigi's room and came down the hallway. I got up from behind my desk and the four of us filed out of my office.

We all sat casually on the sofas in the living area as though we had been there since she had gone off with the healers and her mother.

"Is your mom ok?" Cassian asked her.

"She is resting right now. The healers said she is taking to the magical remedies rather well so it should only be a couple of days." She smiled.

"That's great news," I said, even though it wasn't. We were hoping for more time. "I hope she is comfortable and has everything she needs. I put your things, the stuff she packed for you in your room. I can show you around if you're up to it."

She nodded and followed me out of the living room. We headed farther down the pathway, and I pointed things out so that she could find her way around. She wasn't a prisoner and secretly it was important to me that she liked the home I'd built.

The room I designated to be hers was mine. It was the largest and most comfortable space and I liked the thought of her sleeping in my bed. It was farther away from where her mother would be staying, but once she learned the layout, she could use her magic to fly around the place.

When we entered the room, she sighed. "Whose room is this?"

"Mine. But don't worry, I'll stay on the opposite end of the lair with everyone else. This is all yours, for as long as you want to stay," I added. "Feel free to make yourself at home."

She smiled as she walked around my private space. "This is incredible. Your entire lair is." Her voice was soft.

Her approval pleased me. I was hoping she liked it enough to stay. The mountain carved out nooks here and there that served as shelving and storage plus a bed massive enough to accommodate my beast jutted out from the limestone wall.

I had earth elementals create the mattress from the softest and sturdiest cotton and silk. And then I infused all the linens in here with magic, making them flame retardant in case my beast belched fire in his sleep.

There was a bathroom on one end that had all the modern conveniences the human realm had. Not every home in the kingdom had electricity and plumbing, but I wasn't like anyone else. Because of my business ventures, I had contacts and money which afforded me a comfortable lifestyle.

I also had a small kitchenette built in the room for little conveniences like java for early mornings or wine for nightcaps. It was a perfect spot for entertaining the ladies, yet I never brought women up here. It was too personal.

The bed chamber was saturated with natural light that shone through one open wall. I had kept it closed when Zara was sleeping in case she'd be tempted to escape. Outside of the opening was a large balcony, carved out to accommodate the size of my beast. He liked to sit out there and soak up the sun. At the very edge of the balcony was a mid-sized infinity pool, a natural oasis I could heat with my magic.

Beyond that showcased a spectacular view of the valley. Torch Mountain, my home was across from Glacial Mountain. It was midsummer, but Glacial Mountain was always snowcapped. Melted snow-fed waterfalls streamed down the mountain and flowed into Ethereal Lake below. Elementals called this area the Valley of the Goddess. According to legends the Goddess and her sisters, Sun and Moon, were born here. And now it was mine. When I had been rejected by my clan, this mountain had called to my beast. I had flown here, and the mountain had transformed to my needs. The mountain itself was sentient. It spoke to me and me with it.

As the others joined me, it changed to accommodate them as well. But the mountain would not speak with them, it had said to me it was mine. Elementals had zero access to it unless I allowed it.

Earlier, when Zara was brought here, I expressed to Torch my desire to make the princess feel at home and keep her safe. It purred, happy to comply.

We were four hundred feet from the base of the mountain. From this access point, it seemed like we were sitting on top of the world.

Zara had a curious gleam in her eyes as she walked through the opening. Once outside she gasped, her beautiful lavender sparkled like polished amethyst. On the far right of the balcony was a massive day bed draped with blankets. A couple of end tables had hidden compartments which held nothing but cups and elemental wine.

"I'm speechless, Phin. This is the most amazing room I have ever seen. How did you find this place?"

"Zara." I sighed. "I'm afraid you would hate me once you learned the truth"

She tilted her head and narrowed her eyes. "Umm, well, the only way that could happen is if you...were the cause of my banishment. Somehow, I find that unlikely."

I smiled at her. "No, I had no part in that." I pulled out two cups and a bottle of earth wine from a cabinet behind me.

"This is hard for me to say for some reason," I said while pouring the wine and offering her a glass.

"Thank you." She clinked her cup with mine and took a sip. "You don't have to tell me if you don't want to. I respect your privacy," she said but kept her eyes on thc valley.

"Thank you, angel." I placed a hand on her arm and guided her to sit next to me on the ledge. It was a four-hundred-foot drop to the valley floor, but she wasn't bothered by it. Nothing would happen to her while she was with me anyway.

"Before I was banished, I served under your father as one of his personal guards. That's how me and the other guys met, except for Patrick. But umm...yeah we were all in the royal guard and then my parentage came into question when it was time for my father to name his successor." He cleared his throat.

"My mother had two husbands and only one child. By rights, I should have taken over the clan and had been groomed to do so. The issue was, one of my fathers' umm...went crazy." I glanced at Zara. Her purple gaze didn't have a trace of judgment in it and gave me the courage to continue.

"Long story short, he lost his mind trying to connect with his beast and left the clan. He lived here for a brief period long before I moved in. Anyway, when we had concrete evidence that crazy Dad was my sire, we - my parents and I - hid that information from everyone except your father. My fathers and yours were friends. My not-crazy dad served on the high council for a time. We were able to hide my little secret for a few years.

Once it was discovered, the clan wanted me out. No one wanted a crazy clan chief. I lost touch with my parents. They had turned their backs on me. I don't blame them really. It was either disown me or leave the clan. Your father was the one who insisted I go west and so I did. I settled here, and he and I stayed in touch."

I gulped my wine. "He was very kind to me, Zara. He helped me get through a very difficult time in my life. I'm sorry."

"Huh?" Zara frowned at me. "So you're saying the man that banished me, saved you? And that's why you thought I'd hate you?"

I nodded and drank more wine. She didn't say anything for some time, and I honestly didn't know what to say either. Zander Cavendish was more of a father to me than the man who had raised me and the one that sired me. If our roles were reversed, I'd have issues with this information. Perhaps I shouldn't have told her. "Is he the reason I'm here?" Zara asked.

"Yes, he'd like to see you, today if possible." I kept my voice calm and neutral.

We drank our wine in silence. I finished my cup and motioned to refill hers. She shook her head and said, "Can you take me to him? Now?"

"Yes, if you like. He's not far and he's waiting. He'll be able to explain things."

"Well, fuck." Zara exhaled. "Let's go then. May as well get this over with. And thank you, for being honest with me. I am sorry that your....that the man you thought was your father was such an ass and am glad you had support from someone to guide you through that difficult time in your life."

"Really? You're not mad?" I blinked at her in surprise.

"At you? No, not in the slightest." She stood, and I rose beside her. "My relationship with Zander Cavendish is between he and I. However, just because he showed an act of kindness to you, it does not excuse what he did to me."

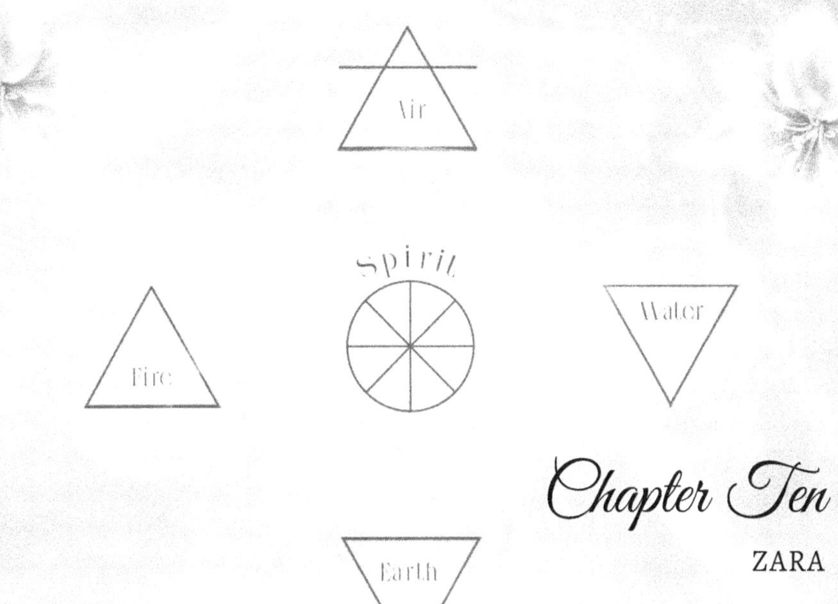

Chapter Ten

ZARA

Phin had created a luxurious home, and it was generous of him to offer his bed chambers to me. I knew he and the other guys were doing what they could to convince me to help them with whatever it was they needed help with. At some point I'd have to hear them out. They were caring for my mother, after all, and there was a part of me that was curious. I had planned to ask Phin about it, but he'd dropped a bomb on me.

He had a special relationship with Zander. My biological father. I stopped thinking about my biological parents as mom and dad a long time ago. And I considered Gigi and Leon to be my real parents.

Still, hearing Phin's story left a twang of jealousy in my belly with a dash of envy. It was surprising I hadn't fallen apart in a puddle of emotions. I had to credit Phin for the way he broke the news. He loved Zander and respected him. Yet he didn't rub my nose in it. Instead, he treaded the topic carefully. Plus, he did not insist that I visit my father or forgive him. I appreciated the way he handled things. After hearing Phin's story, I wanted to hear what the former king had to say for himself.

Before leaving, we stopped to check on Gigi, who was still asleep. I was grateful for the healers. Even with all the medication and weekly doctor visits, her condition had gotten worse. Elemental magic and herbal remedies would hopefully make her feel better and maybe prolong her life. Elementals lived long lives. Humans, on the other hand, were so delicate. At some point, I would have to let her go. The mere thought of it hurt, and I was determined to delay the inevitable as long as possible.

Beau and Cassian offered to stay behind to keep an eye on her while Phin drove me and Trick to visit Zander.

As he drove, I hung my head out the window and admired the landscape. I missed this place. Everything about the kingdom was different from the human realm. The colors of nature were more vibrant, and the crisp, clean air had a slight fragrance. And aside from the hum of the vehicle, it was peaceful.

Phin explained that Zander had been ordered to leave the royal grounds shortly after my sister and her husband were crowned. That was a shit thing to do considering my mother had passed mere months prior, but perhaps my sister had a reason for her actions. Although the men hadn't had a chance to explain what they were dealing with here, I assumed the new king and queen were making loads of changes.

That made me curious. Everything about this adventure had piqued my interest. Phin's reclusive lair, not to mention his business in the human realm, was intriguing. Beau's and Cassian's royal guard stint, then banishment. And Trick. What was he doing here? He sat behind me and I could feel him staring at the back of my head.

Memories of my time in the youth home resurfaced, and I squirmed in my seat. Trick and I had been children when we'd met and fallen in love. Well, I'd thought it was love, but as I got older I realized I was clinging to him because we had so much in common. He had been abandoned by his family, his caretaker died, and he ended up in the youth home. I had no one else at the time, and I was vulnerable. One day he disappeared. Luckily, I had Gigi and Leon. Their love and support helped me mend my broken heart and eventually, I moved on. Somewhat. I still had trust issues, but I couldn't blame that on Trick. It was a self-defense mechanism I shrouded myself in to keep my heart protected.

I sighed, and then Phin nudged my arm with his elbow.

"We're here."

I looked out the window and wrung my hands together. Phin placed his large hand over both of mine and gave me a reassuring squeeze.

We parked in front of a small cottage in a heavily wooded area. Both men got out of the car, and I just sat there. Butterflies fluttered in my belly.

Trick opened my door and knelt beside me. "Zara, if you'd rather not do this, we'll take you home. But if you do, we promise to be right by your side."

A lump caught in my throat and prevented me from speaking, so I nodded and got myself moving. Phin came up beside me and grasped my hand. He stood in front of me and met my gaze, "We're right here, angel."

I thought I was prepared for this, but I wasn't even close. There were too many emotions swarming through me. I wanted to stomp in there and demand answers. And I wanted to run into my father's arms like a little girl and cry on his shoulders.

With a deep inhale, I clung onto Phin's hand like a big sissy and allowed him to lead the way. He opened the door and walked through the cottage, clearly familiar with Zander's home.

The house looked small on the outside but on the inside it was huge. Beyond the foyer was an archway that led deeper into the cottage. Just on the other side of the archway, a pathway split three ways. Phin explained, to the left, led towards the royal suites, the right, guest suites. We took the third option, walking straight through to the kitchen and dining area that opened into an exquisite arboretum.

My biological mother, the late queen, had been a powerful earth elemental. This had her magical signature written all over it even after all these years. Yet, there was something not right about this. After she passed, her magic should have passed with her.

Unless there was a stasis spell of some sort woven into her magic.

The beauty of the garden called to me and aggravated me at the same time. As much as I wanted to meander through the arboretum, I fought the pull of the earth magic that surrounded me. After all these years, the wound from being wrenched from my home was still raw and gnawed at my gut. I needed to get out of this place. The former queen had done absolutely nothing on my behalf when I'd been banished from these lands, and I wanted to be angry with her.

Phin led me through the arboretum following the path that rounded out to a seating area. My father sat at a table sipping from a teacup. His once vibrant blue eyes looked bleary and his shoulders sagged. He had aged and appeared to be battling some sort of illness. My heart cracked to see how frail he had become, but I refused to allow sentimentality to cloud my judgment. His last words to me fourteen years ago had imprinted into my memory, my heart, and my very soul. *"Zara Angelique, you are hereby banished from the Elemental Kingdom and are no longer a member of the royal family."*

"Welcome home, my daughter. I'm happy to see you, it's been so long." Zander stood and walked forward to greet me.

I stepped away from him. "Considering you had me kidnapped, I don't carry the same sentiment. But since I am here, what do you want, Zander?" My voice quivered, and I fought the tears threatening to pool in my eyes. I would not cry in front of this man. I would not.

Zander grimaced, and he drew back his shoulders. He was about to admonish me for being disrespectful. His jaw clenched and he squinted at me. Oh boy, he was pissed. For a brief moment, the insecure fourteen-year-old I had been resurfaced, and I almost apologized. Before I could lose myself in the past, I straightened my spine and stared back at him. Anger sparked within me, and the sad little girl stepped to the side as the woman I had grown up to be took over.

"Do you have something to say? Because I don't have all day." I raised my chin.

"We need your help." Zander collapsed in his chair. "There is an imbalance within the realm. We need to right the wrongs before it's too late."

"So? Have your only daughter, the queen deal with it."

Zander succeeded his throne to my sister after my mother passed.

That was three years ago. "She has a royal army that can do her bidding. And this is not my home anymore. In case you forgot, I was exiled. Deal with your own mess."

"It's not that simple, Zara. There are many dark forces in play.

Please, sit down and let me explain." Zander slouched in his chair and blew out an exhausted breath.

"Zara, please sit." Phin held out a chair for me.

Reluctantly, I sat across from Zander and stared at him expectantly.

Zander wouldn't meet my gaze; he stared into space and then started to speak. "The kingdom is dying Zara. The reigning king and queen have blocked off the Source. Our people are weakened and some have lost their powers and have become ill. We even have reports that some people have been killed. If this imbalance is not corrected the people and the land will die."

King Zander Cavendish had been a powerful elemental, tall and sturdy. He'd had a commanding presence about him, and he had united the elemental tribes maintaining peace for well over a hundred years. It broke my heart to see him frail and weary and to hear about the kingdom falling to pieces after all of his hard work.

As a child, I'd loved and respected him. I wanted nothing more than to make him proud of me, but I'd never gotten the chance. And I'd never received an explanation as to why I had to be sent away. After all these years he was asking for help from me, well demanding actually, since he had me kidnapped. And he hadn't bothered to apologize for any of it. He didn't even offer an explanation.

I stared at him for a while, waiting for more, but he said nothing. A frown creased his forehead and a part of me wanted to comfort him. But the walls I had built around my heart were solid, impenetrable under the circumstances.

It dawned on me that he wasn't at all sorry for what he had done to me. And that made me sad. A tear trickled down my cheek, and I swiped it away with the back of my hand. I'd never get the explanation I wanted and deserved. Nor would I ever get an apology.

Perhaps he had more pressing things to deal with than apologizing to me, but damn it, he had a shit way of asking for my help, not that I could. To have me kidnapped and then dismiss a long overdue apology was just another kick in the teeth.

"Thank you for taking care of my mother. The healers are doing incredible work." The tears I had tried to suppress streamed down my face, and I hated myself for it. This man did not deserve my tears. "Good luck with dealing with your daughter and son-in-law."

I stood up and walked out. Phin followed me. "Zara, wait. There's more you should know."

I needed to get far away from everyone before someone got hurt. "I...I need some space. I'll be back." I ran out the front door.

I sprinted down the dirt path as fast as I could. My magic bolstered my movements, giving me more power and strength. Wind surged all around me until it lifted me off the ground. My body soared with my magic high into the sky. I let my magic envelop me and surrendered to it. I had been born with a connection to all the elements. Air magic hadn't been my most prominent. Yet here in the kingdom, it poured out of me with so much power. It had never felt so exhilarating; it was bursting through me.

I floated above the kingdom and called the wind to my fingertips amassing a storm, fueling it with all the anguish and hurt that had festered in me for the last fourteen years. A wind funnel formed in the sky, and I wanted to pour all of my magic into it and unleash it on the world. The surge of power was intoxicating.

"Zara," Trick said behind me. I turned around but no one was there. "You really should work on those anger management issues," he whispered in my ear.

I'd always known he was an air elemental. I just hadn't known he was powerful. Not every air elemental could fly, just like not every fire elemental could withstand lava.

The storm I had amassed winked out and my anger with it.

Trick and I circled one another while we floated a hundred feet in the air. The midday sun warmed my body as we soared high above the clouds.

"What are you doing here, Patrick? I thought you didn't know your elemental parentage. Was everything you said about yourself all lies?" I asked. My long white locks streamed behind me.

"Don't call me that, please. I like the nickname you gave me when we were kids. I missed hearing you say it." He hung his head for a moment, then raised his face to look at me. "No, Z, everything I told was the truth. I was dropped off in the human realm shortly after I was born. Like you, I had a nanny for a time. After she passed, like you, I ended up in the youth home. My father came to Silk City and found me after his wife passed away."

"Why did you leave? One day you were there and the next you were gone."

"I...I'm sorry, Zara. I did come back, years later. And you were upset, rightfully so. A vampire bit me. I had to leave you. I didn't know what was going on with me. I spent a few years with my sire adjusting to my new life and then found out about my father looking for me. My sire released me, and I came here. When the Zephyr clan learned that I was a vampire, they kicked me out.

Sort of."

"What are you talking about? How are you a vampire? You're walking around in the sunlight, and I just witnessed you eating normal food." I narrowed my eyes at him as we floated in the sky.

Trick held up his hand, showing me a gold ring on his right pinky. The setting was in the shape of a flaming sun with a topaz sitting in the circle.

"It was a gift from my father. It's a druid heirloom, which makes me immune to the sun. And vampires eat food if they want to. It doesn't sustain us as blood does though."

"You could have said all that when you showed up years ago. Instead, you showed up at my house acting as if nothing happened and we could pick up where we left off." I swiped a stray hair away from my face. "A text or an email inviting me to lunch would've been more effective. I was worried, but I would've understood. And what the hell does "sort of" kicked you out mean?"

"I know. I know. In my head, you were waiting for me. I didn't expect that you'd move on. That was wrong of me." Trick took a deep breath. "I told my father right away what I was. He was ok with it. We had some blood stored at his place, and someone found it and that someone told four others. They threatened to tell everyone in the village."

He paused while we drifted. "My father pleaded with them and offered to pay for their silence. The five men took my father's money and killed him anyway. And then they threatened to tell everyone in the village, so, I killed them."

Whoa! Patrick the sweet protective man I met at the youth home, had admitted to me he'd committed murder. The weight of his words felt like an anchor dragging me toward the ground. I didn't know how to respond.

"Talk to me, Zara," he said while wrapping an arm around my waist.

I tried to pull away, not wanting to be so close to him, but he wouldn't release me. "You were sinking too quickly, Z. I didn't want you to hurt yourself."

"Trick, I'm sorry that happened to you, but damn it, if you had just told me what you were dealing with I would have understood." I smacked his chest.

"I know, Z. I realize that now. But at the time, I didn't know what was going on. I was afraid of hurting you, so I left. I haven't stopped loving you Z. I've thought of you every day," Trick admitted.

"I'm overwhelmed with information, Trick. I appreciate your wanting to keep me safe. And I'm sorry about what happened with your father but also glad you got a chance to meet him."

I realized then that Trick had been affected by our untimely separation even more than I expected. Although he could've handled things differently, I couldn't hold it against him. Becoming a vampire wasn't something to take lightly. To say he had a lot to deal with was the understatement of the century. Was I ready to pick up where we left off? Absolutely not. But at least that chapter of my life had closure and perhaps we could begin a new one.

"Do you hate me for what I did to those men?" Trick asked in a soft voice.

"No," I replied as my feet touched the ground. "You avenged your father and defended your life. I don't hold that against you."

He reached out and caressed my cheek. "Thank you, Z. It means a lot to hear you say that."

I gave him a small smile and allowed him to lead me through the woods.

As we walked, I pondered the messed-up situation. Everything here was rather fucked up and I had zero information about what was happening with my father and my sister. Not that I'd allowed him to explain. Seeing Zander conjured a multitude of different emotions. There was anger, sadness, and most of all, confusion.

Why was he living alone like a recluse? Amina loved our father just as much as I did. Why would she kick him out? Or perhaps it was his doing? No, that didn't make sense. He would have wanted to remain at her side as part of her high council. What did Zander mean by dark forces?

And then there were Phin and Trick with their stories of being banished by their families. Trick was on the run for murder. Yikes. Did Cassian and Beau have similar stories? Earth elementals like Beau and his family were often cherished for their powers. Why were they on the run? Plus, Cassian's parents were friends with my parents. I couldn't imagine they were cast out as well unless Amina got rid of everyone which did not seem right. What was she up to?

I followed alongside Patrick, lost in thought until he came to an abrupt halt.

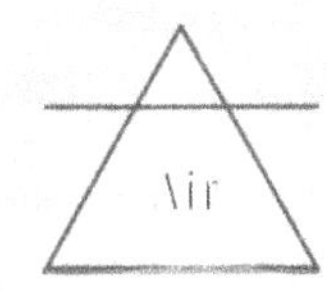

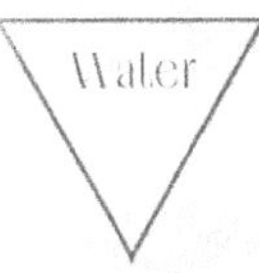

Chapter Eleven

ZARA

"Something's wrong," Patrick said as he pulled a phone out of his pocket. Did elementals use human technology now? I looked over his shoulder and noticed it was similar to the type of communication device the royal guards used.

"Phin got someone to modify human tech with magic so that he can stay in touch with his business, and he hooked us up so the four of us can communicate with one another. It's not as sophisticated as a smartphone, but it has basic phone, video, and text capabilities." He answered my questions before I could ask.

I was about to ask more but a lion burst out of the trees behind us, startling me. Defensively I called my fire magic to my hands. Trick placed a hand on my shoulder and stopped me from doing anything rash. "Don't. It's just Cassian."

The monstrous lion stalked towards us and transformed into a familiar man with blue-black hair. Cassian approached us with his muscular naked body on full display. His chest was heaving and coated with sweat.

Wow, just wow. The lion thing was new. And the body was...all man. It took me a moment to avert my eyes from Cassian's nakedness and focus on the conversation the men were having.

"There's trouble, we have to go," Cass said. "Royal guards have been seen in the area."

"I'll go up and cause a diversion," Trick said. "See you soon, Z." He placed a kiss on my cheek and floated up into the sky.

"I'm going to shift, Zara, then you need to climb on my back," Cassian said to me.

"Wait, why? I can fly," I replied.

Cassian grasped my hand and shook his head. "No, they had scouts in the air, and they may have spotted you and Patrick. It's better that you stay low for now. Come on, hope on."

He shifted into a lion again and then laid down on his belly so I could climb onto his back.

I held onto his mane, and he loped into the woods at breakneck speed.

Everything around us became a blur as Cassian sped through the woods. The effect was dizzying. Although he was running full out, his strides were graceful. Horseback riding was certainly more jarring. Still, I tucked my face into his mane and held on.

His fur was soft, and he had a briny ocean scent that was so Cassian. I could feel the solid muscles of his large back between my legs.

Cassian skidded, kicking up dirt and pebbles all around us.

My stomach lurched from the abrupt stop. He laid on his belly, and I rolled off his back, placing the palm of my hand on his flank to brace myself as I stood.

Cass shifted and said, "Zara, get behind me."

He placed his body in front of mine and walked backward.

"Who is she?" a female voice asked. "New girlfriend?"

Cass's much larger form blocked me from whoever was speaking.

"What are you doing here, Dahlia? Don't tell me you're still working for the royals?" Cass said in a menacing tone.

I stumbled on a rock and Cass turned, extending his hand to keep me upright.

"Of course I am. You should be, too. If you ask nicely, I am sure the king and queen will forgive your..." she paused.

"Whatever you want to call your magic. Wait, is that?"

Footsteps approached closer, and I peeked around Cass to see a beautiful blonde-haired beauty walking towards us. Her blue eyes pierced me with the points of a thousand daggers.

"It can't be. Why is she here with you?! Are you two? NO." She paced. "This can't be. I won't allow it."

"Dahlia, I don't want to fight you. Let us go and you can report whatever you want to your queen," Cass said in an even tone that barely restrained the temper that flared under his muscles.

"No! Don't even try to sweet-talk me. The queen will have your heads!" Dahlia clenched her fists together and punched the dirt with a force of earth magic.

The earth rumbled, and the ground beneath our feet caved in. We fell into a sinkhole. Rocks and dirt followed our descent. I clawed the upturned earth all around me trying to grip something, but the soft soil provided nothing for me to hold on to. We tumbled at least forty feet and came to a stop with a thud.

"Zara? Are you ok?" Cass stood over me, naked as the day he was born.

I nodded and stood up with his help. My body ached. We both had scrapes and bruises but at least nothing was broken.

A sliver of light from high above cast shadows in the small sinkhole. Shit, we'd have to climb and dig our way out. Or perhaps I could fly us out.

"Who was that?" I dusted myself off, thoroughly annoyed with the earth elemental.

"Crazy ex," he muttered.

"Don't call me crazy, you jerk!" Dahlia shouted from a few feet away.

I turned to face her, and she sneered at Cass and me.

Cassian had the nerve to laugh. "Got caught up in your little temper tantrum, did you? Now, what's your plan? Wait, don't answer that. You're working for the tyrants that are killing our people. Your decision-making skills are obviously sketchy so just sit in the corner and let the adults do the talking."

Oh, dear. That was not the right thing to say to a disgruntled ex. The second Cass turned to face me, Dahlia shot out her earth magic again.

Cass held me close to his chest, bracing for the next impact, and then he ducked bringing me down with him as a boulder punched through the air where his head had been.

"I hate you!" Dahlia screamed.

Damn that woman. She was trying to kill us. The boulder she threw slammed into the dirt-packed wall. The ground rumbled and shifted while rocks tumbled down on us.

Our little sinkhole dimmed even more, and all went quiet, and then something hissed like a spring coming loose.

"Aww fuck," Cassian cursed.

"Z, hang on to me and do not let go. Understand me?" He hoisted me up into his arms, and I locked my legs behind him as water sprayed my back.

"Is that what I think it is?" I turned to see where the water was coming from, and my heart rate sped.

"Yep. We're about to be flooded," Cass said in a grave voice.

"Maybe I can fly us up to the top. It's not that far. And then use my earth magic to widen the hole?" I looked up where the light was coming through.

"You think you can carry me?" He smiled. "I'm much heavier than you, Z."

Cass had a point. I hadn't flown much in the human realm and when I did, I'd needed a running start. Plus, I'd needed to consider his weight and Dahlia's.

"It's ok, we might be able to ride the rise of water to the top and punch our way out, but if not, plan B. Just hang on, ok?" He kissed me, his lips soft and covered in dust, but I didn't care. If I was about to die, I'd do it knowing I had at least one kiss from my childhood love.

"You would save her and leave me here to die!" Dahlia was still alive and more pissed than ever.

She threw a barrage of earth magic again, which loosened the dirt wall increasing the flow of water. The sliver of light above disappeared, casting the sinkhole in complete darkness. Rocks tumbled all around us, and one slammed into my shoulder.

A loud thud followed by an audible crack came from behind Cass. I peered over his shoulder but couldn't see a thing.

"Dahlia?" I called out.

"She's gone." Cassian's voice was grim.

His arms tightened around me, and I squeezed him back, ignoring my aching shoulder.

The water level had reached my waist and was rising quickly. With my water magic, I could hold my breath much longer than any human, but I couldn't hold it forever. Fear pierced my spine like daggers made of ice.

"Cass? If we don't make it out of here, I'm glad I got to see you again," I murmured.

"Shh. Don't talk like that, sweetheart. We're getting out of here, I promise," he whispered in my ear.

The wall behind me broke free and a force of water slammed into us. Cass dug in his heels, and he used his magic to split the flow of water to move around us.

"Plan B. Climb on my back and when I tell you, take a deep breath and hold it," Cass said in a decisive tone.

"Wait, what's plan B?" I spun around him and tucked my face into his neck. The water level reached my shoulders.

"I'm swimming us out of here. Deep breath."

I took a deep breath and hung on. Murky water surrounded us as Cass swam straight into the blast of water, swimming upstream. His muscular body fought against the current, his magic helping him against the force like he was going head-to-head with a thirty-five-foot wave. He swam against the tide for an eternity, and it seemed like we weren't getting anywhere. I hung on to him helplessly while his arms and legs pumped through the water, slowly making progress.

My magic waned, and my lungs were desperate for oxygen. I willed myself to fight, to hold on longer, but my body spasmed, and my grip around Cassian loosened. I wasn't ready to die. I had so much life to live but the lull of the water was hypnotic. And all my worries and troubles disappeared.

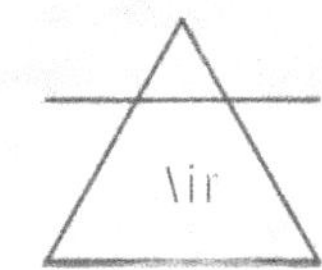

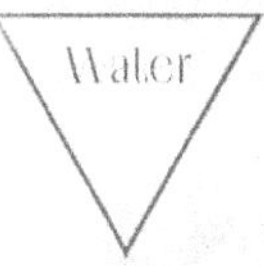

Chapter Twelve

ZARA

I felt a surge of magic pulse through me. Cass's strong body gripped me as he moved us through the water. His lips fastened to mine, and he breathed into my mouth.

Oxygen filled my lungs, and I sucked in the precious air greedily until I choked.

"Zara?" Cass's voice was urgent. "Zara!"

I rolled to my side and coughed up water, realizing then we had made it to dry land.

Once I caught my breath, I threw my arms around Cassian and hugged him tightly.

"You saved me. Thank you." I kissed his cheek.

He drew away from me, then cupped my face. "I will always do everything in my power to save you, my princess."

When we were children, in Cassian's eyes I wasn't *the* princess I was *his* princess. It used to make me giggle every time he called me his. And although I was no longer a princess, my insides turned warm and gushy.

He leaned in for a kiss and I met him halfway. Our lips collided, and I ran my hands up and down his muscular back. He was naked on top of me, and I felt him harden, his length pressed on my belly.

Something about being in a life-or-death situation had me in a frenzy. I wanted to strip naked for him and feel all the pleasures of being alive.

A loud screech reverberated through the sky and brought me to my senses. Cassian pulled away from me, and we both looked up. The last traces of sunlight faded into the horizon. How long was I out?

"It's ok." He kissed my neck and my collarbone. "It's just the guys looking for us. Are you ok?"

"I'll live," I replied.

I was a sopping mess. My clothes, down to my shoes, were saturated with lake water.

"The guys will be here soon. I have to go." He tilted his chin towards the lake. "I need to find Dahlia."

"Do you think she's alive?" I asked, hopeful. Although she tried to kill us, I didn't wish death on the poor girl.

"No, her heartbeat stopped after the boulder crushed her. Shifter hearing." He tapped his ear. "In close quarters I can hear a pulse. Anyway, I want to retrieve her body, and give her a proper burial."

I stood up with him and hugged him. "Go, I'll be right here."

While Cassian went back into the lake, I stripped off my wet clothes and used my air magic to dry them. After swimming in Transcendental Oasis earlier that same morning, I was able to dry off and warm up with my magic almost immediately. Nearly drowning in whatever lake I sat beside, had zapped my strength and my magic was weak. It barely provided a puff of air. Even my fire magic, which had always been my strongest, did nothing to warm me.

Perhaps it was my body. I felt exhausted and my shoulder ached. Determined to do something to better my situation, I wrung out my clothes as best as I could then set them on a nearby rock. Next, I searched the area and gathered a few twigs in hopes of starting a fire. My teeth chattered, and gooseflesh pebbled my skin.

I placed my meager findings of dried twigs and leaves on the ground and called my fire magic. The expenditure proved fruitless and left me panting with exhaustion. I calmed my nerves, closed my eyes, and pulled on my magic but nothing came.

Well shit, guess I was doing this the old fashion way.

Using two stones and dried leaves as tinder, I got the fire going at the same time as Cass emerged from the lake carrying a limp Dahlia. Seeing his grim face cracked my heart. I walked over to him to offer some support as he lay her crushed body on the muddy shore near the fire. I reached down and closed her eyes and said a silent prayer to the Goddess.

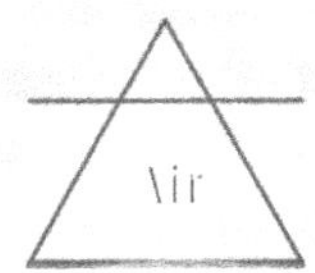

Chapter Thirteen

ZARA

"I just need to rest a bit, then I can shift and get us out of here. Unless the guys show up first." Cass sat wearily by the meager fire. He was exhausted from using so much magic.

"I'm sorry, Cass. Do you want to talk about it? About her?" I finally asked. I wasn't sure what their relationship was like, but I wanted to give him the option to talk about it in case he needed to.

"Not much to say, Z. I haven't seen her for years and things didn't work out between us." He glanced at me. "Ask me anything else, please."

He wanted to talk, but that topic was off-limits. I was ok with that.

"Ok, how are you a shifter? And what happened to your parents?"

There were so many questions shuffling around in my head, but I decided to start with the easier ones first.

"Honestly, I have no idea about the shifter part. It happened one day about seven or eight years ago. There must be a shifter in my lineage somewhere. As far as my parents, my biological father passed away, and although my mom has three other mates, she didn't deal with his death very well. They all moved to the Pacific," he said, staring into the fire.

"Oh, I'm sorry to hear about your dad, and I hope your mom is ok," I told him. His family was the best. His mother always had a big smile on her face and his dads were tough as nails, but they were kind to me.

"Thank you. I'll pass on your greetings. My Uncle Valyn, not sure if you remember him, but he took over the clan after my dad died, and he banished me because of my shifter abilities."

"What? That's ridiculous." I looked over at him.

It was always surprising how single-minded people were.

"People are afraid of things they don't understand." He shrugged. "I'm fine with it, honestly. I'm glad I'm not working for your crazy sister, I mean, the royals."

I smiled at Cass. "It doesn't bother me if you call her crazy."

The sound of beating wings got my attention. I looked to the sky to see where the noise was coming from, but a rush of wind sent leaves and debris flying in all directions. I shielded my face with the crook of my arm, and then a terrifying roar disturbed the peacefulness of our surroundings and my flight instincts kicked in.

I wanted to run, but Cass held me still.

Several feet away, a mighty dragon landed gracefully. The dragon turned his massive body in a circle and caught sight of me.

I shuffled backward, but Cassian blocked me from running away. My heart raced as the dragon got closer. I wanted to flee, but I couldn't take my eyes off the beast as it unfurled itself, rising an easy thirty feet in the air. Black opal scales shimmered creating a kaleidoscope of varying metallic colors. He bent towards the ground, his neck snaked down to stare me in the face. I stepped closer to him, taking slow cautious steps. There was something oddly familiar about him. His reptilian red eyes stared back at me and in a split second his eyes flashed gold.

I reached out and his nose met my palm. Holy hell.

"Phineas," I whispered. His massive head leaned into my hand, and his scales were warm and smooth like glass.

I ran my hand up his long neck, and then his leathery wings. He was magnificent and scary, but still an incredible beast.

A portal opened a few feet away, taking me by surprise, and out walked Patrick and Beau. *Who put up a portal?*

The dragon arose to his full height and spread his wings. Magic swirled around him like smoke, and he transformed into a tall naked man. Solid muscles flexed under bronze skin. Phin's coppery brown locks were disheveled on top of his head, and his intense golden gaze traveled up and down my body.

Between him and Cass, there was just too much naked skin around, and I became self-conscious about my lack of clothing as well.

"You're shivering, angel." Phin wrapped me in his warm arms.

I sighed and snuggled closer to his naked body. Sensual heat rolled through me, and I became keenly aware of every hard ridge of his torso and his swollen manhood pressed up against my bare skin.

"My magic is spent," I muttered.

"It's ok. I've got you." He made circular movements up and down my back. When his hands ran over my injured shoulder, I winced. He frowned at my bruised skin, then kissed it gently.

"Here, Zara, I dried your clothes." Trick handed me my jeans and T-shirt.

Reluctantly, I stepped away from Phin's heat and dressed quickly.

My gaze switched back and forth between Cass and Phin as they walked towards their friends who handed them a bundle of what I assumed to be clothing.

While I laced up my shoes, the events of the day came flooding back to me, and I started to panic. I wrung my hands together and paced.

"Princess?" Beau broke the silence. "Are you ok?"

I snapped out of my momentary shock and glared at the four men. Survival mode gave way, and exhaustion, fear, and anger hit me all at once.

"Don't princess me! What the hell happened? And what is the meaning of all this? A vamp, a dragon, and a lion? And what the hell are you? Did you open a portal?" I pointed at Beau. "And where is my mom? Is she ok?"

"Your mother is fine, Zara. She's with my mom, sister, and the others at the healing village. They're safe. Calm down," Beau answered me with a soothing voice.

"Calm down?! The last twenty-four hours have been less than ideal. Someone start explaining." I rolled my neck, trying to dislodge the tension that had settled on my shoulders.

"She's injured, Beau. Tell us what happened here." Phin glanced at the dead body lying a few feet from the fire.

Cass explained running into his ex and everything that had happened while Beau ran healing magic over my scrapes and bruises. His soothing touch calmed my nerves, and his magic zinged through my minor injuries like a wakening elixir.

"Thank you, Beau. I feel much better." I gave him a small smile. "Someone explain, please."

"The king and queen sent the royal guard to ambush a nearby refugee village which is why we had to get you to safety," Phin said as he shimmied jeans over his thick thighs. "They are going after anyone that has enough power to pose a threat to their rule. And as you can guess, there's a threat in numbers. This particular camp was one of the largest."

"I interrogated one of the guards and learned Issac, the supposed king, has recruited powerful elementals as his guards, and their directive is to dismantle all refugee camps. This is the first we've heard of this, and we need to regroup and take action." Patrick stood off to the side slightly away from everyone.

"Why is my sister doing this?" I pressed.

For a moment, all four men stared at me in silence. I threw my hands up. "Fine, yes, I am ready to hear all about your problems here. So, please, I am all ears."

Cassian let out a deep exhale. "Well, long story short. Amina's husband is a complete blowhard. He is a powerful earth elemental, but has no family to speak of. His status began to rise through the ranks, and he set his sights on your sister. Your mother was all for it. Your father had his reservations. But your sister insisted on marrying him. She pushed your father for his blessing for more than a year. Finally, he gave in. They got married, your mother took ill a few months later, and then your father abdicated the throne. As soon as your mother passed, your father was forced into retirement. Then they went after the Source."

"Wait, my sister sent Zander away from the palace? Why?" I asked.

"Within days after your mother passed, the new king and queen dismantled the royal army. Issac got rid of anyone loyal to your father. King Zander stood up to him, and that's when he was told to leave," Phin replied, a solemn expression shadowing his face.

I shook my head. "The queen died five years ago. Why all of sudden is all this blowing up?"

Beau sat on a nearby rock and said, "After King Zander and his loyalists were uprooted, it seemed as though the new king and queen were content. That lasted for a year...give or take and then the real problems started. Little by little, their hand-selected royal guards moved into the sanctuary until one day the devout were outnumbered. They were told to leave. If they resisted in any way, they were killed. And then the entire mountain was closed off to visitors."

"As you can imagine, Z, once the Source was closed off, the land started to change. We can feel the disconnection. But elementals with less power to begin with, are getting weaker and weaker by the day. With elementals unable to maintain balance in this realm, storms are breaking out here and in the human realm."

"In some parts, lakes have begun to dry up at rapid rates. The Brooks clan worked with other water clans, and we cannot seem to figure out why or where the water is going. To make matters worse, some water clans have left to live in the human oceans," Cassian added.

"Farms are not as abundant as they had been. Harvest seasons have been producing lower numbers every year since Amina and Issac took over," Beau, the earth elemental, stated while randomly throwing rocks into the distance.

Phin focused his gaze on me. "Between the chaos your sister has created and all the storms and food shortage, our people are dying alongside the land. As the magic wanes here, the people will soon covet the magic for themselves just to survive, thus leaving all of the other realms that depend on us for stability to fend for themselves. And I think you know what happens if the kingdom does that."

"The human realm will suffer and slowly deteriorate to extinction. Fuck," I said in a soft voice.

The humans would call it climate change when in fact it was my sister and her husband abusing their power as royals and hoarding the Source all to themselves.

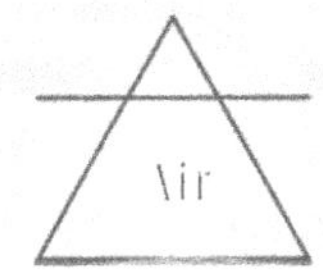

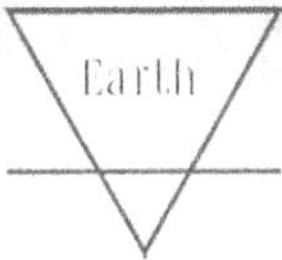

Chapter Fourteen

BEAU

"I know this is a lot to take in, all in one shot, Z, and there is more to discuss, but we should go and check on Gigi and my mom. They're at the healing village. I want to make sure they're safe," I said to her while putting up a portal that opened on the outskirts of the healing village where my mother lived.

Cassian picked up Dahlia and strolled in, Patrick right behind him. Phin extended his hand toward Zara, and she accepted it absently.

I had to admit I was envious but also glad she was at least giving us a chance. Whatever it took to keep her with us was a win in my book.

"That's a neat trick," she said as she glanced at me over her shoulder.

I quickly caught up with her and Phin and smiled. "My mage abilities manifested at eighteen. Kind of like theirs." I waved a hand toward the other guys. "I studied for years with the palace mage. We, -my parents and I-, kept my abilities secret. Somehow it was discovered, and my tutor was killed and I was banished from my clan."

"Killed by who?" Zara asked.

"Umm...your sister ordered it, and the king had me banished." I ran my hand through my hair.

"This place is so messed up." Zara shook her head. "I'm sorry that happened to you."

She looked deep in thought like she was trying to wrap her head around all the craziness her sister was up to.

"It's fine, Z. I'm ok. We all are." I grabbed her other hand.

She didn't pull away, which made me sigh in relief, then she looked up and gave me a genuine smile. I was a goner. At that moment, I fell hopelessly in love with her.

The healing village came into view. It was quiet, and people hid in their houses. That was expected after the news of the attack on a nearby refugee camp.

Cassian and Patrick went towards an area where Dahlia could be prepared for burial. While Phin and I lead Zara through the village where the healers were set up.

I caught a glimpse of Gigi's curly salt and pepper hair near the campfire at the same time Zara did. She released both me and Phin and ran to her foster mom.

Gigi was a rotund, dark-skinned woman of African descent. She spoke with a southern drawl and had the kind of smile that made the shittiest day brighter. I could see why Zara loved the woman.

Phin and I stopped to stare at the mother-daughter duo. The love and care they had for one another were clear. It made me happy that the banished princess found family after her own carelessly cast her aside.

She had made a life for herself amongst the humans, a humble and simple life. But one she enjoyed from what we could tell. We had watched her for some time from afar the same way we were doing now, and she'd always had a smile on her face. It was as though she was both the sun and the moon, and everyone couldn't help but want to be within her orbit.

Cassian and Patrick came up beside us. We all admired the princess.

"I think I'm in love," I said.

"Me too," Cass, Phin, and Patrick said at the same time.

We all chuckled.

A few weeks ago we all discussed what was to happen if she chose one of us as her mate. We all fancied the idea of being chosen and knew if we weren't, we'd have to let her go. But we all agreed that no matter whom she chose, we would not allow that decision to break our brotherly bond. Neither of us wanted that. In our dreams, she would choose all four of us and we would be ok with that.

"Uncle Beau!" My niece's voice brought me out of my musings to the present moment.

"Hi Ivy, shouldn't you be in bed?" My sister Rosemary's daughter was six years old, and it was way past her bedtime.

She jumped in my arms. "Yes, but I heard Mom say the princess is here. Can I meet her?"

I chuckled and set her down on her feet. "Yes, on one condition." I gave her a stern look and she nodded enthusiastically.

"Do not call her princess."

"Why not? She's still a princess isn't she?"

"Well, sort of. But she's all grown up. Maybe you can call her Lady."

Happy with that, she scampered away, picked a night blossom, and ran back over to me. I strolled up to Zara with Ivy clinging to my hand.

She was laughing with Gigi and stood when she saw me approaching.

"Hi, um...this is Ivy, my niece, Rosemary's daughter. Ivy, this is Zara and her mother Gigi." I smiled at her.

Gigi said hello. Zara extended her hand to my little niece.

"Nice to meet you, Ivy."

Ivy curtsied and bowed then said, "Nice to meet you, princess lady Zara. This is for you."

She held the flower out and Zara accepted it. "Thank you, this is lovely. Almost as lovely as you, Ivy." Ivy giggled, and Zara kissed her forehead.

"Ivy?!" My sister called out from behind me.

"Ooops, I better go. Nice to meet you, princess lady," Ivy said then ran towards her mother.

Zara laughed. "Nice to meet you too, Ivy."

"Thank you, Beau, for making sure my mom was safe. She said it was ok for us to stay here?" Zara asked.

Gigi cleared her throat. "I said it was ok for *me* to stay here, Zar, not we. They've got medical equipment set up, and it will be easier for me to be here near the healers. You don't have to sleep on a medical cot just to hover over me." Gigi shuffled to her feet without the use of her cane.

Hmmm...as my mother thought, the medications she had been taking were doing more harm than good.

"Mama, it's not safe to be here," Zara argued.

"Nonsense, child. It's not safe for you to be here. Calla said I only need another day, two max, to adjust to the herbal remedies, and then she can release me to home care. I'll be fine. Go make amends, Zara, and we'll go home together."

The tears in her eyes felt like a gut punch.

She grabbed her mom in a fierce hug and sniffled. "If something happens to you, I will never forgive myself."

Gigi patted her back. After a moment, she released Zara and said, "Come, I'll show you where I'm set up. It's lovely here. These elementals sure are crafty."

Zara turned to look at me, and I nodded. We weren't leaving without her.

While Gigi showed Zara around and introduced her to people, me and the three guys sat by the fire pit and got comfortable.

The village elders talked to us for a moment, and they told us their plans, which were nothing. Earth elementals didn't like confrontation. They were farmers and healers. After two to three years of roaming the kingdom to avoid the royal guard, they were done.

I couldn't blame them.

Zara walked toward us. A swarm of people followed behind her, asking questions. She smiled and answered them politely.

"I feel like I should save her from all those people." Patrick stood up.

Zara noticed and shook her head slightly. It was her way of saying she could handle it. I couldn't stop grinning at her.

Before too long, she made it back to us. Sage, one of the village elders and my mother walked alongside her.

"Thank you both, for looking after my mother. I promise we will be out of your hair as soon as she's well." Zara shook Sage's hand and embraced my mother.

"Are you sure we can't offer you anything to eat or drink?" Sage asked Zara. He stood too close to her for my liking. The other guys didn't like it either as we all stood and created a protective circle around her.

Zara smiled sweetly, and I wanted to smash Sage's face in.

"No, Linc promised to have a delicious meal prepared, and I'm afraid we're already late. Thank you though. I plan on visiting again tomorrow."

"Perfect, and if you'd rather stay here, both you and your mother may have my quarters as long as you need it." Sage placed a kiss on her hand.

Son of a bitch. Phin tensed beside me. This was not going to end well.

Zara nodded, drew away her hand, and stood closer to Phin. His body immediately relaxed. Thank fuck. His beast could be a surly asshole.

"Bye, mom, see you tomorrow." I reached over to grab Zara's hand, and we all headed back to the lair via a portal I put up.

Chapter Fifteen

ZARA

By the time we reached the lair, I was exhausted. Linc was his usual bubbly self and had prepared a feast again. After everything I had learned about the elemental men's personal history, seeing Zander, almost drowning, and leaving Gigi with the healers, I wasn't hungry. My emotions were a bundle of knots that sat at the bottom of my belly, but I couldn't refuse Linc. He wasn't the cause of my problems, and it'd be unfair to take out my poor attitude on him.

He cooked up a delicious steak dish, and the five of us ate heartily. Linc asked me about my favorite foods which I both appreciated and regretted at the same time. I had no intention of staying, and I had made that clear to the guys. It seemed like they forgot to clue him in. I played along, and the guys chimed in about their preferences as well. It was a joyous meal but before too long, I started to yawn.

Linc refused my help with cleaning up and shooed me out of the kitchen. Me and the four guys ended up in the living area. I was ready for bed, but more questions needed to be answered.

"Should we continue our earlier conversation, or do you want to get some rest?" Trick asked as the guys sat on the couches in the living room.

"I'm exhausted, but I have a couple of questions. Well, no, I have a lot of questions. I don't know where to begin." I paced in front of them.

"Why are they doing this? There has to be a reason," I finally asked.

"We don't know. I met Issac at one of the earth elemental rallies, and he was always power-hungry. He has some sort of hold on Amina, not sure what it is, but she is enthralled," Beau answered.

"Ok, so they want power. Which they have. There's more to it," I said thinking out loud.

"I agree, but we haven't pieced that together, yet." Trick rubbed his chin.

"And what do you want from me? How am I supposed to help you with this?" I asked.

"You're the rightful heir. You could rally the people and give us the numbers we need to storm the palace and take over." Cassian propped his elbows on his knees and looked at me.

I laughed. "You think people will follow their banished princess? That is just ridiculous. Why isn't my father rallying the people? They loved my father, or that's how I remembered it."

"Your father's power is waning and he's weak." Phineas kept his gaze on the floor. He didn't want to meet my eyes.

I stopped in front of Phin and stared at him. "Is he dying?" I asked even though I already knew the answer.

"Yes. The healers have not been able to figure it out," Phin answered in a low voice.

"Zara, your mother's death...we suspect foul play. And your father's illness is suspicious as well. My family has worked on him and I looked into it also. It seems like dark magic." Beau explained.

"How long does he have?" I asked. My body felt numb.

Through the supernatural grapevine, I'd gotten news of my mother's death. Despite everything I had been through, I was devastated. I'd asked Zander for permission to attend her funeral but was denied. His refusal wasn't a surprise, but it still hurt.

Hearing that Zander was ill and dying created a well of despair deep in my gut. After all that he had put me through, I still didn't want him dead.

"We're keeping him stable. But a couple of months maybe." Beau gave me a compassionate gaze. I appreciated his sincerity.

I moved to sit between Cass and Phin and slumped, tipping my head up to stare at the cavernous ceiling high above. I had no idea how I could help. Or if I wanted to. Gigi and I could go home and live our lives in peace. Life in Silk was carefree and simple. All this drama wasn't worth the effort. Or was it?

I stood up from the couch and looked around for the way to get to Phin's room. "I need to get some sleep."

"I'll take you to your room." Phin stood next to me.

The rest of the guys stood as well.

"Do you all sleep in the guest rooms?" I asked. When Gigi was here, she'd taken a nap down the corridor, which had several spare rooms. I imagined they all had their rooms somewhere in this massive lair.

"Sometimes, yes. But most of the time I go to the lake," Cassian said.

I nodded, understanding his need to be in his element.

"And I go up." Trick pointed upwards. "I have a nest near the top."

"I'm an earth elemental so this cavern is perfectly comfortable. Sometimes I sleep in the woods if I need more plant life." Beau smiled.

Phin grasped my hand and pulled me closer to him. "I have my room, but sometimes my dragon likes to be near the fire. There's a lava pit deep in the mountain."

"This mountain?" I quirked an eyebrow at him. *Did he make his home in an active volcano?*

He smiled and nodded. "It's dormant. The lava pool is shallow and way beneath the surface."

For some goofy reason, I leaned into his chest, and he kissed the top of my head.

Cassian pulled me away from Phin and held me close. He released me and tipped my head up to look at him. "Good night, sweet Zara, I'm happy you're here."

"Thank you, Cassian, for everything. You saved my life today. I don't know if I could ever repay you." I stood on my tiptoes and placed a kiss on his lips.

"No repayment necessary. Holding you again is enough of a reward." His strong arms crushed me to his chest, and he kissed my hair. My poor water elemental, he must've been exhausted. We stood together for a sweet moment, and then he released me.

Beau enveloped me in his arms next and said, "I'm happy you're here too, Lady Zara. Sweet dreams." His smile lit up his face. I reached up and caressed his cheek.

Trick drew me away from Beau and snuggled against my back. He wrapped his arms around my chest and nestled his face in the crook of my neck. "I missed you, Z, and I'm so sorry for leaving. I hope you can forgive me. Good night."

I placed my hands over Trick's arms, not ready to let him go. To be honest, I wasn't sure there was anything to forgive. It took me a long time to get over him, and for a while, I didn't think I'd ever get over it. But I did. To see him after all that time had passed made me feel something, and I didn't quite understand it. I wasn't harboring any grudges or ill will, but I had to admit; a part of me was drawn to him.

I turned in his arms to face him. Once upon a time, Patrick was my world. His silver eyes had always captivated me; something tugged in my chest. He pressed his forehead to mine.

"I won't hurt you again, Zara," he whispered, and then he released me.

The three men left me in the living area with Phin, who linked his hand to mine and led the way to his room. I followed, lost in thought. I was physically exhausted, my emotions were a turbulent mess, and my attraction to the men in the lair confused me.

When we reached the room, Phin stopped at the door. "Do you need anything?" he asked, our hands still linked together.

He had been openly affectionate with me all day, and yet at the moment, it seemed like he was pulling away. It was as though he waited for permission to come in and a part of me wanted to give it. But it had been an exhausting day. There were too many emotions swirling through me. I was not in the best state of mind to make hasty decisions.

"I...I don't think so," I answered, even though truthfully I didn't want to be alone. I wanted him to stay. "Thank you, Phin."

"Ok." He ran his fingers gently up and down my arms, causing me to shiver. "I won't be far, angel. Just call out for me and I'll come running." He tilted my head up to meet his gaze, and paused. His eyes bore into mine searching for something I could only speculate on. After what seemed like a long drawn-out moment, he leaned down to place his lips on my forehead, and then he turned around and left.

Lust warmed my belly from the simple, innocent kiss. And despite how exhausted I was, I sighed with disappointment.

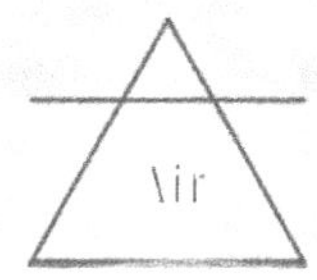

Chapter Sixteen

ZARA

After Phin left, I went straight to the shower. The first time I'd used the bathroom I had just found out I had been kidnapped and I wasn't in the mood to appreciate it. This time I marveled at all the modern conveniences crafted with natural materials. There were no plastic containers on site, aside from the shampoo, conditioner, and my other beauty products, packed amongst the things Gigi had brought for me.

Closer inspection revealed a furnace made up of lava rock, which heated the water and the flooring. By elemental and human standards, this place was fancy.

After my shower, I tossed and turned on Phin's comfortable bed. My body was physically exhausted, yet my mind raced.

What was my sister up to? Who spelled Zander and why? Would the people rally behind me if I asked? Did I want to get involved? Why was I attracted to these four men?

The ramblings in my head would not shut up. Frustrated, I got up and snooped. I wasn't proud of myself, but I was curious to see how Phin lived in this beautiful lair.

As soon as my feet met the floor, the fairy lights came on. I went to his closet carved out of the same limestone. It was as though the mountain changed itself to create a space specifically for this purpose. Well-appointed shelving and drawers along with metal fixtures created a walk-in closet any woman would swoon to have. Elementals were often simple people with meager belongings. But Phineas Strait had a decent wardrobe of suits, jeans and tees, and other casual menswear. It made me wonder how often he spent time in the human realm. Disappointment fluttered through me. I would've liked to have met him in Silk City where none of the royal drama existed.

I decided to explore the outdoor space next which was closed off by sliding metal doors. The closer I got to the door, I realized it was made of copper and had an engraved intricately designed dragon. Wow. Phin had added his craftsmanship to what nature created. I traced my finger over the dragon, and the door opened.

A rush of wind entered the room, and then I gasped as I took in the mighty dragon before me. Phin rested comfortably, his large body encompassing the entire balcony.

He lowered his enormous dragon head right in front of my face.

"Hi." I reached out and pet his snout.

He tilted his head, then a shimmer of magic vibrated around his body, and a naked Phin took its place.

"Are you ok?" Naked Phin asked me.

I focused my gaze up toward the sky and said, "Mmm hmm, yes, sorry for intruding. I couldn't sleep."

"It's ok, you're not intruding. I just wanted to be close and not invade your space."

He towered over me and frowned. "Are you sure you're ok? What are you looking at?"

He tilted his head up to look up at the star-filled sky. His body heat enveloped me, and I almost reached out to touch his bare chest.

"Zara?" Phin's forehead scrunched up, and he placed his hand on my waist.

"Umm, yep, I'm good, but do you mind covering up?" I bit my lip and kept my eyes on the stars.

He chuckled. I heard him shuffle around then he said, "Ok, you can look now."

Phin wrapped a blanket around his waist and smiled at me.

My cheeks flushed.

He patted a cushion on the daybed, took a seat, and motioned for me to sit with him.

I settled between his legs, my back to his chest, while he reclined and wrapped his arms around me. The night air was chilly, but Phin's body heat felt like snuggling with a warm blanket.

"I should have asked before you sat down if you wanted something to drink." Phin's breath brushed my neck.

My body tingled, and I snuggled closer to him. "No, it's ok, this is perfect."

"Do you want to talk about what's on your mind, Zara? This can't be easy for you," he asked.

"Did you know my mom, Gigi, was sick when you kidnapped me?" I had a feeling they did a background check which meant they had to know.

"Yes, but we didn't know what type of illness. We asked Beau's mom to remain on standby in case it was serious, and you made it a condition to stay."

"Were you at The Convent, the night you kidnapped me?" I asked.

"Yes. And before. We've been watching you," he replied as though it was completely acceptable behavior.

His candor surprised me, and I sat up to look into his eyes.

He didn't flinch.

"This is important to us, Zara. Our people, this land. We won't force you to do anything. But we had to use everything at our disposal to sway your opinion."

"Wow, your honesty is something." I turned around and leaned my back against his chest.

"Are you angry with me?" His lips grazed my shoulder.

"No, surprisingly I'm not. I appreciate your passion to try and save everyone. But…" I paused and let out a deep breath. "I don't feel the same way. There was a time when this kingdom meant everything to me, and I wanted to protect it. That's no longer the case. It's been so long, and I've built walls."

"Understandable. It's unfortunate but I do understand. I wish I had known you back then. I was a kid myself and on a different path. If I could have saved you, I would have."

I turned, straddled his lap, and gazed into his golden eyes.

"Phin, I want to go home, back to Silk City in the morning."

He closed his eyes for a moment, then he pulled me against his chest. "Ok, Zara, ok. I won't force you to stay. I will take you and your mom home myself. I'm sure Calla will continue to help Gigi."

"You're not mad at me?" My voice sounded muffled.

"No, angel, I couldn't be mad at you ever. I'm so sorry for kidnapping you. Perhaps if we had approached this differently, we would have had a more desirable outcome."

"Thank you, Phin." I burrowed my face in the crook of his neck.

He ran his hands up and down my back in soothing circles. It felt like a million pounds had been lifted from my shoulders, and I immediately fell asleep.

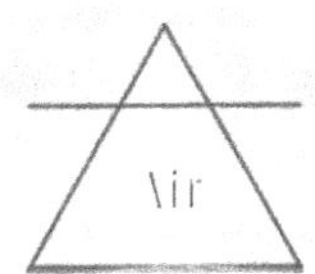

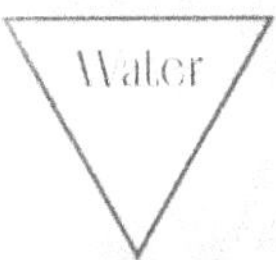

Chapter Seventeen

PHINEAS

As gently as possible, I stood with Zara in my arms. I didn't want to wake the sleeping princess.

I needed to stop thinking of her as the princess. She hated that.

I laid her down on the bed and slowly unwound her arms from my neck.

"Don't go," she said in her soft sleepy voice. I paused, not sure if I'd heard her correctly. "Stay."

There was no way I'd ever refuse her. I climbed into bed, stretching out a bit to make myself comfortable, and smiled as she molded herself to my body.

I lay awake for some time thinking things through. She wanted to leave and that sucked for all of us. This world would perish and the human realm right along with it. The elemental kingdom was responsible for maintaining environmental balance throughout several realms. The magical realms could sustain themselves for some time without us, so that wasn't an immediate concern. The humans were the most delicate. Their lives were temporary, and they had zero magic. Plus, their lifestyle was wrecking their planet at an extremely fast pace. Their demise was approaching, and if we didn't get a handle on the problems here, that would happen much quicker than they could ever imagine.

But none of it was Zara's fault nor her responsibility. I couldn't blame her in the least for wanting out of this clusterfuck. Especially after being banished. If I had been in her position, I likely wouldn't want to help either.

We wanted to take her to see the refugee camps as a last resort in hopes of playing on her sympathy. People were ill and dying. It was heartbreaking to see that and it would work. But I couldn't do that to her. The kidnapping was bad enough, not to mention her emotionally stunted father.

Damn him. I believe we would have had more time to convince her had he just apologized. I knew for a fact he regretted the decision he made fourteen years ago. He had admitted it to me more than once, but for some reason, he couldn't find the words when she was right in front of him.

And now, I get to tell him and the other three guys that she was leaving tomorrow morning. Beau, Cassian, and Patrick had fallen for her. And so had I. It was more than physical attraction; it was something deeper. There was something special about Zara. It was as though she had a magnetic pull that drew us in. I'd noticed it from afar, and being around her for even just a day had only amplified my need to be around her and make her happy. But as much as I wanted to keep her close, I'd never force her, and neither would the guys. None of it mattered though. Even if she felt the same attraction to us as we felt for her, it wouldn't be enough for her to take on a responsibility of this magnitude. We were asking too much.

As though my thoughts summoned them, they walked in through the open balcony door. Patrick approached the bed, Beau and Cass following closely behind him.

I pressed a finger to my lips, telling them to be quiet.

"Everything ok?" Beau whispered.

"No, not really. She wants to go home. Tomorrow morning. And I said yes." I replied.

"What?!" Patrick asked in a loud voice.

Cass smacked his arm. Beau and I fixed them both with irritated looks.

Zara squirmed and murmured something unintelligible. Her leg curved up around my torso, and I ran my hand up and down her bare thigh. Her skin was silky smooth, and I felt myself harden.

Down boy. Not the right time.

I looked over at the guys. "She's not happy here, and I won't force her to stay."

"What about the camps? Shouldn't we swing by first?" Cass asked as he sat on the edge of the bed.

The pain in the ass was making moves to climb into bed with us. She was his first and maybe, only love. Sure it was puppy love. They'd been kids after all, but he had been heartbroken when she was banished. And after what they went through today, he'd be crushed having to say goodbye again.

"No, we've manipulated her enough," I said and that was final. I won't do it again. It was unfair to unload all of this on her as it was.

"Fuck. There has to be another option." Patrick let out a frustrated sigh.

"So, what? We're just going to pick up Gigi and take them back to Silk City? Just like that?" Beau asked.

It was a good thing we were having this conversation while Zara was asleep. In any other situation, it would have been a shouting match rounded out with a spectacular cuss fest.

"Basically, yes," I replied.

Beau teleported out, then returned moments later with a blanket and a pillow, and he laid them out on the floor beside the bed.

I quirked an eyebrow at him. Was he planning on sleeping on the floor?

He shrugged. "If this is the last time we ever see her again, then I'm not leaving."

"Good idea." Patrick flashed out with his air magic, leaving a gust of wind in his wake.

Lucky for him, Zara didn't stir. If he'd awaken her, I'd have to hit him.

As suspected, Cass slid under the covers on the other side of Zara. I shook my head, almost waking her. She shifted her body so she was right on top of me. The tip of my cock pressed against her core. I groaned. If it weren't for the thin panties she wore, I'd be tempted to try my luck.

"Dude, you can't have sex with her right now. That's just not fair." Beau sat up from his makeshift bed which had to be uncomfortable as hell.

Patrick walked in with a bed roll. He, at least, was thinking.

Cassian whispered, "Goodnight, princess." He held her hand and placed a kiss on her knuckles.

This was so freaking weird. I gazed up at the ceiling and realized Beau had the right idea. If this was indeed the last time she was with us, I needed to savor every moment.

I wrapped my arms tighter around her and sighed.

Please, Goddess, do not let this be the last time she'll be in my arms.

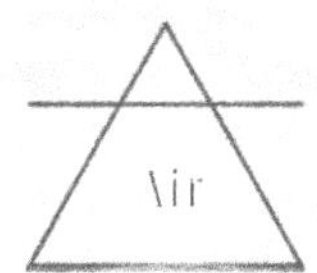

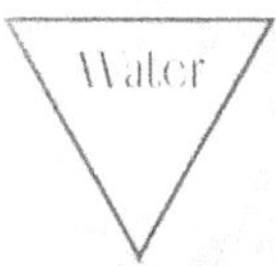

Chapter Eighteen

ZARA

I stretched out, fully extending my legs, then my arms.

"Oohmpf," someone said beside me. I startled awake and turned toward the sound. *Cassian?*

"Good morning, angel," Phin said from the other side of me. He had a sleepy smile on his handsome face.

I traced the sharp planes of his cheek. "Morning."

Something landed on my foot, and I sat straight up.

Beau and Trick were lying head to foot at the bottom of the bed, still, fast asleep. As was Cassian. Trick had a hand draped around my ankle, and it made me smile.

Phin sat up to drag me back down against him.

"Sorry, you fell asleep on the balcony, so I carried you in here," Phin whispered.

"I remember that." I looked up at him and he smiled. "Do the four of you um...you know?"

His brow shot up. "Sleep together. No. Never, this is a first."

"Oh, sorry ,I didn't mean to offend. I just thought...with this big bed and all, maybe you were a foursome or something like that."

He barked out a laugh. "That's just too funny. But no, angel, we don't swing that way, not that there's anything wrong with that. But no.

The guys came in to talk about things. I told them you were going home today, and they wanted to stay close to you."

"Hmm." That was kind of disappointing. The four elemental men were seriously hot. I felt feverish just imagining them together, naked, muscles flexed, washboard abs tense, sweat glistening on their skin.

"Zara." Phin tilted my head to face his and kissed my lips. "I don't know what you're thinking about, but my beast can feel your lust."

I leaned in to continue our kiss and brought my leg up around his bare waist. Oh my, he was still naked. Phin gripped my ass, and his hard length pressed up against my thigh.

Someone shifted on the bed, and I stopped myself before things went further. What the hell was my problem? He was my kidnapper. And I was leaving in a few hours, maybe less. I couldn't start something with him. Or could I?

Cassian rolled over and pressed his chest to my back. He slid his hand around my waist, placing it between my body and Phin's.

Oooh, this was interesting.

Phin gripped my chin and tilted my face to meet his. His golden gaze held mine, then he lightly brushed my lips with his, while Cass's lips grazed my shoulder.

I gasped and rocked my hips. Every nerve in my body came alive. This was wrong. They'd kidnapped me and although they may have had a good reason to do so, that didn't make it right.

But they felt so good. Phin's heat created waves of heady excitement in my core, while Cass explored my neck and shoulder with his mouth. I moaned.

I wanted to get lost in the pleasure they were offering me, but something in my brain pumped the brakes and brought me to my senses. I sat up and covered my face with my hands. Both men sat up with me.

"Sorry, Z, we're not trying to take advantage of you." Phin ran his fingers along my spine.

It took everything in me to prevent myself from arching into his touch.

"We went too far, Zara. Forgive us." Cass rested his chin on my shoulder. "If you want this, we'll give it to you. If you don't, that's ok too, we'll just fantasize about you from afar. You always get the final say."

I tilted my head, giving Cass access to my neck. Closing my eyes, I relished the feel of his soft lips against my skin. Phin leaned over and captured my mouth with his. My legs spread apart, kicking someone at the bottom of the bed.

Afraid I woke up one of the other guys, my eyelids fluttered open, and Beau had been openly staring, his gaze glazed over with lust. He liked what he had witnessed, and if not mistaken, he wanted to see more.

"What's going on?" Patrick muttered. He raised his head and rubbed his sleepy eyes. I almost felt bad for waking him, but I caught a glimpse of his bare chest, and my mind went into the gutter again.

Aside from Phin, all men were naked from the waist up. Phin was hard and pressed against my thigh. Oh boy, I wanted this. So much. But I knew if I did, I'd wind up wanting more.

"I need a cold shower." I moved to get off the bed, but Cass pulled me to him for a chaste kiss, and then he gently released me.

The other men looked at me expectantly, so I bent over and crawled the very short distance to peck Beau and then Trick on their cheeks. I knew full well both Phin and Cass were staring at my ass and could probably see how wet I was through the skimpy panties that covered my sex. The thought of them staring sent a thrilling rush through my body.

With a groan, I climbed over Phin, but he wasn't going to release me without a kiss. His large hands encircled my waist, and he held me close. I brought my lips down to his to give him a chaste kiss but his hands ran up my body and he grabbed a fistful of my hair to keep me in place. His mouth devoured my lips, and I was just about to give in when he released me.

I sank against him breathlessly while his hold on me remained light as though he was giving me space to think.

With a force of discipline I didn't know I possessed, I climbed off the bed and walked toward the bathroom. Before I closed the door, I glanced back at the four gorgeous men who were openly staring at me.

"You guys are killing me," I muttered, then closed the door.

After a long shower, the guys and I had breakfast in the kitchen. Linc prepared a light, yet delicious meal. He noticed me carrying my overnight bag and frowned.

When I told him I was leaving, he sniffled. As sad as that made me, I held onto my resolve and said goodbye and thank you.

He gave me a tight hug, then walked away wiping at his eyes.

Even though the drive to pick up Gigi was short, all four men insisted on accompanying me all the way to Silk City. I sat in the front seat between Phin and Beau. Cass and Trick sat in the back.

As soon as Phin backed out of the driveway, I reached out for his hand. He laced his fingers with mine and kissed my knuckles. In truth, if it hadn't been for all the drama with my father and sister, I may have stayed. No, not true, I would have stayed.

I stared out the window the entire time questioning my sanity. Perhaps it was a sex thing. I was with Thadd a night or two ago and as good as it was, I wanted more. Needed more. Maybe I needed professional help. Nah, I was more than comfortable with my insatiable sex drive. I just couldn't remain in the kingdom amongst the bullshit my sister was causing. All the sex in the kingdom was not enough for me to stick around and deal with that nonsense.

Phin parked the truck on the outskirts of the healing village, and we all followed Beau inside to find Gigi.

It was dark when we had been here the night before and I hadn't been able to appreciate how unique it was. Hyperion trees surrounded the village, providing seclusion and protection. Bamboo huts were neatly placed in rows along the dirt path. A large structure served as a makeshift clinic where Calla tended to her patients. Some ground-floor huts were used as dwelling units for families and had attached bathrooms. Most of the villagers' housing was constructed in the trees themselves, rising twenty-five feet off the ground. The tree homes were sleeping pods, which looked like large bird nests. There were four pods per tree, each approximately one hundred square feet. One would have to climb up to the sleeping pod via bamboo ladders resembling large wooden flutes.

On the ground level, there were several bathroom units conveniently located near the bird nests that had an open-air tub and separate shower tiled with natural stone. And outhouses were strategically placed around the housing.

The communal lodge sat in the middle of the village. It contained a kitchen equipped with an underground oven and a firepit with a metal grate for grilling. The dining area was also in the communal lodge and had been the most utilized space. Villagers gathered for meals and meetings, and it was also used as a school for the little ones for part of the day.

That was where we found my mother. A couple of kids sat around her and were laughing at something she was saying. She was probably telling them a story. Gigi was a natural with children, and I knew all too well how captivated these kids were by her stories.

She waved when she saw me approaching, and the kids turned to see what she was looking at. I smiled and waved, and then the kids rushed me. I separated from the guys as three children no older than seven reached out and hugged my legs.

"Well, hello." I smiled and patted their little heads. "Has Mama Gigi been telling you stories?"

"Yes, princess lady Zara. She's very funny," Ivy, Beau's niece, said.

The kids giggled and hung onto me while we walked.

Rosemary, one of the healers, gave me a big smile and then ushered the children to wherever they needed to be. They grumped in protest but did as she asked.

I hugged Gigi. "We're leaving, Mama. We need to grab your things."

"Right now?" she asked.

I nodded. "We'll be able to maintain the same level of treatment at home. Beau's gathering the remedies and the protocols. And he will bring them to us as needed."

"Ok, honey, if you're sure." She nodded hello to the guys, and then linked her arm with mine while we walked towards the hut where she had stayed.

As soon as we were away from the guys, she asked in a low tone. "What happened? Did they hurt you, Zara?"

"No, no, quite the opposite, actually," I assured her. Aside from kidnapping me, all four men were above reproach.

"Did you have sex? Please say yes. It wouldn't be right if you didn't have sex with at least one of them." She gave me a teasing smile.

I laughed. "Aren't you supposed to say things like, 'wait until you're married or at least make them buy you dinner first?'"

"I'm not that kind of mother. You know that."

We both laughed. When we reached her hut, I heard hurried footsteps and screaming. "Stay here, Mom." I opened her door and all but pushed her in.

The village erupted in chaos. People ran to and from, everyone running for cover. A frantic elemental ran up to Cassian and Sage, the village elder I'd met the night before. Cass's face twisted into an angry scowl, and he immediately shifted. His clothes torn to shreds, he loped off. Trick and Phin strode past me, their body language tight with rage. What the hell?

Beau appeared beside me and said, "Z, you should probably hang back with your mom."

"Why? What's happening?" I asked. "Is it, my sister?"

"Well, not her exactly, but she is the cause of the chaos." Beau frowned.

"I'm not going to hide. I could be helpful." I pushed him away from me, but he didn't budge.

"I don't think that's a good idea." He stood in front of me blocking my view.

Someone let out a gut-wrenching scream, and he turned. I moved around him and ran toward the scream which led me to the opposite edge of the small village.

The scene before me was disturbing. People stumbled into the village sobbing and wounded. Some were also bleeding. I found Calla, who struggled with a distraught woman. As I got closer to her, the mother was wailing over a wounded child.

Shit.

"Calla, how can I help?" I knelt beside her.

"I need to see the child, but she won't let me!" Calla tried desperately to calm the woman.

"Hi." I cupped the woman's face with my hands. "Look at me. Let us help you. Is this your child?"

The woman nodded, then released the child to Calla's care.

"Princess?" She looked at me with a pleading gaze. "Please help us."

"I'm Zara. What's your name?" I patted her arm.

"I'm Raven and this is my son Rocko." She sobbed.

"I'm not finding any wounds. It might be a concussion," Calla said beside me.

But the child had been covered in blood.

"Raven, are you hurt?" I asked and looked down at her body. Her torso down to her hip was soaked in bright red.

"I tried to protect him. But he fell." Her voice sounded weak.

"Why don't you lie back and let Calla take a look at you? And I'll hold onto Rocko, ok?"

I switched places with Calla.

I did a quick check, not that I needed to because Calla had already confirmed no wounds, but it made me feel useful. The boy was passed out, but he seemed fine.

"Bullet wound. We need to get her to surgery," Calla said then waved one of the village men over and he carried a limp Raven to a makeshift clinic.

Bullet wound? Why are they using human weaponry? Where did they get a gun? Swords, daggers and magic were the typical weapons of choice, but not guns.

"Zara, take Rocko to Rosemary and find Beau, please." Calla hurried after the man who carried Raven.

I did as she asked and left a sleeping Rocko with Rosemary who was busy herding all the other children. I found Beau patching up a man with burns on his arms and torso.

"Your mother needs you in surgery," I said to Beau. "There's a gunshot victim."

Beau cursed, and I followed him out. The village didn't have an operating room. It was just another hut with a few more medical supplies. The healers made do, using their magic along with a few surgical tools.

I worked alongside Beau, helping him remove bullets, stitch up flesh, and wrap up the wounds. He was a gifted healer and he worked tirelessly. Magic for all elementals was not infinite.

After his third patient, he started to sway on his feet.

Sweat coalesced on top of his brow, and I dabbed his forehead. We were working on a victim with multiple gunshot wounds.

"Guide me, Beau. I can help," I said. I was no healer, and earth magic wasn't my strongest magic, yet I was learning to do things alongside him.

He nodded.

"Place your hand over his chest, and use your magic to locate the metal. It will feel like something foreign is lodged where it shouldn't be."

I did as he advised, and felt a foreign object lodged in the middle of his chest near his heart.

"Got it," I stammered. "It's so close to his heart."

"It's ok, steady. Call it to you, Zara, call the metal to you.

Think of your hand as a magnet calling the bullet to you."

I pulled on it with my magic, and the bullet slid out. Blood spurted everywhere.

"My turn." He stated.

Beau's hands hovered over his chest and glowed with magic as he repaired all damages to the tissues and arteries. Once he was satisfied with the outcome, he nodded.

"Now, Zara, I'd like you to cauterize the wound using your fire."

I did as he asked, and the man on the table screamed in agony. Beau held him down as I sealed off the wound.

"Good, next one. Quickly, he's losing too much blood." Beau's mouth fixed in a grim line.

We worked side by side for hours. Beau was an excellent teacher. I couldn't help but marvel at his skill.

After the last gunshot wound, Beau and I did what we could to help the others. We administered basic first aid care and water.

There were so many people coming through. Most of them were injured. My magic roiled under my skin, begging to release retribution for all the innocents that had been harmed. There was no time to be angry though; there was too much to do.

We went to find his sister to offer assistance with the children. Beau kept surprising me with his skill and the way he handled every patient.

He was gentle with the children, and he beamed at them, putting them at ease while healing minor cuts, bumps, and bruises.

"What can I do for you, Beau? Do you need a break? Maybe some food." I wrapped my arms around his waist.

"No, thank you, Zara, I'm fine." He tilted my chin up to face his. "I'm going to check on the surgical patients. Do you want to come with me?"

"I'll stay with the children." I looked into his emerald eyes. Gently, he pressed his lips to mine. The innocent kiss quickly turned into something more. I suckled his bottom lip and swept my tongue through his mouth.

He tasted of earth and summer. I wanted more, but the timing was horrible. I sighed when he released me and watched him walk away.

Hours upon hours later, Trick found me rocking a little one to sleep. "Z, we're taking off."

"Wait a minute, where are you going? What's going on?" I stood with the child in my arms.

"We gotta go." Phin looked at the kid then at me, the corner of his lips turned up a little. "We'll be back."

"No. Tell me what's happening. Did you find the men responsible for this?" I demanded.

"Possibly, but it's not safe, Zara. Stay here," Cassian said as he stepped up beside Phin.

"I'm coming with." I placed the little girl in Trick's arms.

He gaped at me, then said, "Hold on." He handed the little girl to the nearest healer and returned to us ready to head out.

"Zara." Phin scrubbed a hand down his face. "You need to stay hidden. Either stay in the sky or ride with Cass. I don't want anyone to see you."

I nodded then followed him and Trick as they floated upwards into the air while Cassian shifted into his monstrous lion form.

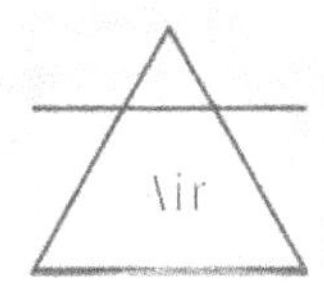

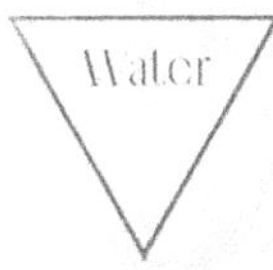
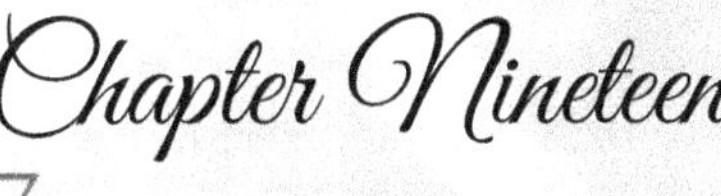

Chapter Nineteen

ZARA

Phin's dragon flew like a rocket ship. He soon became a black dot in the distance, heading straight towards a plume of smoke a few miles away. Trick and I sped through the air as fast as we could to catch up, and then Phin's form swooped towards the ground.

I nodded at Trick, encouraging him to follow. He surged forward, and I struggled to keep up. I needed to practice using my magic more.

As I got closer to where Phin had landed, the chaotic scene was worse than the last. People screamed as the forest around them went up in flames. The fire spread from tree to tree, surrounding the village and trapping villagers. We needed to put the fire out and get everyone to safety.

Phin transformed into his human form while I landed on the scene. Cassian leaped over a wall of fire and shifted before his feet touched the ground. Trick strode up behind us with two pairs of sweats and handed them to the two shifters.

"I'll contain the fires. Get as many as you can to safety." Phin pulled up his sweatpants as he walked into the middle of the village. He extended his arms wide and called his fire magic. The nearest fire shot straight toward him, and he absorbed the flame into his body. Whoa. His skin glowed like molten lava and my fire magic wanted to reach out and rub up against him like a cat in heat. I mentally slapped myself for the inappropriate thoughts and got my head back in the game. As much as I wanted to admire the fire elemental in all his glory, I put my overactive libido on pause. There was work to do.

Phin walked around claiming fire like it was a part of him.

Cass, Trick, and I went into each hut looking for survivors. Like Trick, I used my connection with air magic to clear the smoke as we went through the village making sure we weren't stoking the fire. Luckily, the village was small, and everyone survived.

Beau arrived via a portal to tend to the wounded. Trick and Cass were in charge of organizing the people and getting them to safety. I went after Phin as he ventured deeper into the woods where more smoke rose into the air.

I jogged to catch up with Phin, and he turned to me frowning. "Zara? You should be with the others."

"I want to help. And if it's too dangerous, I'll fly away."

"Come here." He tugged me to his chest and left a quick scorching kiss on my lips.

He released me with a groan and held my hand as we came to a smoky clearing. I looked around perplexed. There was smoke but no flames. It was a magical smoke screen, and we had just walked into a well-planned trap.

"Long time no see, Strait. And who do we have here?" A red-haired male with bushy eyebrows looked me up and down.

"You brought me a present. Wonderful."

"Chas Wheeler, of course. I should've known. Still tormenting women and children, I see." Phin sneered and angled his body in front of mine while keeping Chas in his sight.

"You won't get away from me this time, Phineas. Kiss your girl goodbye and give her to me. I'll treat her real good, or I can burn her alive with you." Chas's hands became flames that stopped at his wrist.

"Fuck you," Phin growled. He turned to bring me in front of his body and smashed me to his bare torso. "Stay close, angel. Do not move."

"Have it your way." Chas grinned like a psycho.

With my chest against Phin's torso, I braced myself for Chas to throw fireballs at us. Instead, he punched the ground, and a circle of fire lit up around me and Phin only a few feet away.

Chas stood there laughing while the wall of fire shot up ten feet into the air and crept closer to us. I had an affinity for fire magic like Zander. It had been my dominant magic all my life. I'd never absorbed fire as Phin had, but for the most part, fire rolled off my skin.

Phin had his arms out, and his magic vibrated against my chest. A dozen rocks the size of golf balls rose in the air. They glowed a fiery red, infused with searing heat. He shot them at Chas like rapid-fire bullets.

Chas's eyes widened as the scorching stones punctured his flesh, burning him alive from the inside out.

With his death, the circle of fire went out of control. It shot fifty feet in the air and kept coming towards me and Phin. Sweat trickled down my back. Despite my affinity with fire, my heart thundered in my ears.

Phin turned me around to face him. "I'm going to shift, duck, and then stand close."

His hot hands felt good on my arms, and I glanced at them and tilted my head to the side. His skin had that molten lava glow from before, yet my skin remained unharmed.

He ran his finger over the sleeve of my shirt, and it turned to ash, but my skin had not been affected.

"How is this possible?" Phin shook his head. "Ok, hang on."

With one arm around my waist, he crushed me to his side.

He extended his other hand towards the circle of flame and pulled.

The fire kissed his fingertips and seeped into his body ever so slowly. As Phin absorbed the flames, his skin glowed from his fingers to his hands, up his arms, and to his shoulders.

He exerted his will over his magic, straining to control it from going any further up his body. Sweat dripped down his temples. He clenched his jaw with determination, his muscles taut.

I stayed glued to his side and slid my hand over his chest, moving up to his shoulder.

Phin jerked away from me, but I kept going. He was absorbing too much fire, and something in me was certain I could help. He didn't need to take on this burden alone.

With the tips of my fingers, I traced his shoulder and my skin glowed like his. Heat consumed me like a lover's caress. I wanted more and I pulled.

"Zara," Phin gasped.

The flames sank into our bodies. Phin absorbed the brunt of the impact, and his torso, neck, and shoulders glowed like lava. My T-shirt burnt to ash where his skin made contact, but my magic held, keeping me protected. I tilted my head to face him. He clenched his jaw and pulled hard at the fire, like cracking a whip, and he extinguished the flames.

His chest was ablaze with fire magic, and I caressed every muscular plane. He leaned down and pressed his lips to mine. His hot tongue swirled through my mouth, and I arched into his body. Heat licked up and down my spine, sending tantalizing tingles through me and straight to my core.

Gunfire startled Phin and me, and we abruptly released each other.

"Damn it." I cursed. My hormones were all over the place.

First Beau and now Phin. Ugh. I needed an intervention.

"To be continued, angel." Phin chuckled.

My T-shirt was now a crop top, and my jeans had holes in them, which helped to conceal the blood that had stained them earlier. Phin and I ran towards the sound of the gunfire where Trick, Beau, and Cass faced off against palace guards.

There were two SUVs and eight guards, their guns raised, and they barked orders at the three elemental men. They hadn't sensed Phin and me creeping up behind them, so I blasted a wave of heat directed at their weapons. They dropped their guns and clutched their burnt, blistering hands.

"Nice," Phin said beside me. I gave him a wink.

With unimaginable speed, Cass pounced on the guards that stood next to the vehicles closest to him, cracking bones and tearing off limbs.

Trick in his vamp form was ripping out throats, while Beau was taking out guards with his bare hands.

"Is anyone alive?" I asked, as Phin and I arrived. The three guys looked at me as though I was crazy.

"We need to question someone, maybe they'll have useful information," I explained.

Cassian shifted back to his human form. "Here, Z."

He knelt next to a man who was sprawled out on the dirt road. The injured male's arms and legs rested at odd angles.

I stood next to a naked Cass and did my best to keep my lustful thoughts to myself.

The man on the ground was breathing and barely able to speak until he saw me. "It's true," he sputtered. "You're real."

I knelt next to the injured man. "What was the purpose of your mission?"

"Princess. You're...you're..." he muttered.

"Real, yes. I'm real. Answer my question." I wanted to slap him.

He groaned. "I only did what I was told. Don't kill me. I have a family."

I looked over his injuries. From what I could see, a broken leg and elbow would be the worst of it. "Sure. Why not? We'll get a healer to mend your broken bones, but first, we need answers."

"We were looking for Firestarter. Small boy. He has dual powers."

"Where were you taking him?"

He griped pathetically. "I need a healer. You promised."

I smacked his face and he sputtered. "The Sanctuary. That's where we take all of them."

And then he passed out.

Our enemies were dead except the injured man who was now my prisoner. I was determined to get more answers out of him, so we agreed to keep him detained at the healing village. The SUVs were hidden in the forest. And the villagers insisted on staying in the place they had called home. They wanted to rebuild.

Beau opened the earth, and the ground swallowed up the dead bodies. Then he put up a portal for us to get back to the village.

I left the men to sort out our new hostage and went looking for my mother. She was telling a large group of children a bedtime story. The sun had gone down hours ago, and I hadn't even noticed. I walked up behind my mom and hugged her. "I love you, Mama."

She patted my arm and released me. I glanced at the bundled children, looking for Rocko. He didn't seem to be amongst the crowd and I panicked a bit. I went straight to the hut I had last seen him, and he was sitting beside his mother.

Calla was checking Raven's sutures and gave me a grave nod. Oh no. I patted Raven's arm. Her breathing was shallow, and her skin was pale and cool to the touch. Tears pooled in my eyes.

Rocko sat silently staring off into space.

"He hasn't moved or eaten anything. Maybe you can try?" Calla asked me.

I nodded, then knelt in front of the little boy. "Hi, Rocko. I'm Zara."

"Hi." He sniffled.

"Would you like something to eat? You must be hungry." I wiped away his tears.

He shook his head.

"Ok. How about a bedtime story? My mama is telling bedtime stories to the other kids. Would you like to listen?"

"My mama's hurt." He started crying and tears welled in my eyes.

I gathered him in my arms and held on tight.

After a moment, I released him. "The healers are doing everything they can for her. For now, I need you to be a big boy and at least have a little something to eat. Can you do that for me?"

He shook his head and whispered, "I made a mess in my pants."

"It's ok, we'll get you cleaned up."

Calla thankfully overheard and was pulling clothes and a towel out of a drawer.

"There's a bath through here, Zara." Calla pointed to a door.

"Thank you." I picked up Rocko and took him to the bathroom.

Thankfully, it was a lovely bathtub made of bamboo. The water from the spout was cold, but I showed Rocko my magic and heated the water.

He smiled at my use of magic. "You have fire. Like me."

He snapped his fingers and a tiny flame ignited on his little fingertips.

"Oh! That's impressive! How old are you?"

"Almost seven. But Mama said I have strong fire. But not so strong earth." Rocko dunked his head under the water.

Wow, his magic was indeed strong for someone of that age. Most powers didn't manifest until ten or so unless the person's magic was powerful.

After his bath, Rocko and I checked on his mother, then went in search of food. He ate, and soon he started yawning. I carried him back to his mother. Her condition hadn't changed. Beau was in the room, and he smiled brightly at the kid who was curled up in my arms sound asleep.

Calla walked in and whispered, "Ah, there you are. Did he eat?"

"Yes." I kept my voice low. "Is she getting better?"

"Only time will tell. He can rest here." Calla motioned to a small cot on the other side of the room.

I placed Rocko on the bed, tucked a blanket around his little body, and kissed his forehead. Then I said a silent prayer to the Goddess to heal his mother and keep them safe.

Outside of Raven's room, Calla and Beau waited. I told them about Rocko's powers and about him being the target the king and queen were probably looking for.

Calla ran off to speak with the elders about assigning a guard.

Beau wrapped his arm around me, and I leaned into him, grateful for his strength. "Have you eaten?" He asked.

"No, not hungry. Do you know what time it is?" I replied, my voice sounding as weary as I felt.

"Almost midnight. You haven't eaten since breakfast. Let's get you fed."

I shook my head. "I need to get Gigi home, please."

Beau almost stumbled. "Ok, anything you want."

Gigi was already sleeping when we went to her hut. I sighed, it'd be cruel to wake her. I found a paper and pencil and wrote her a note asking her to be ready at first light.

It wasn't safe here; we needed to get home.

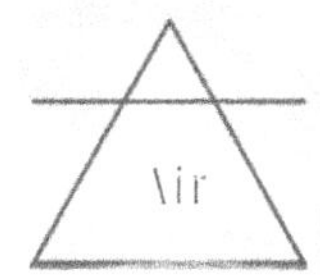

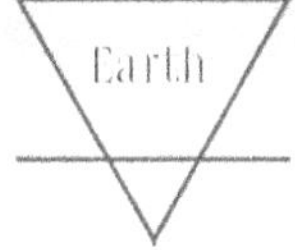

Chapter Twenty

ZARA

After everything that had happened the day before, I slept like the dead and still felt exhausted. I couldn't shake the images of all the injured people and the scared children. It broke my heart to witness the turmoil of this realm. What was this kingdom coming to? What was my crazy sister doing?

One of the guys tried to get me to eat last night, but I had been too tired. I took a quick shower and then fell on the bed face first. As requested, Phin woke me up at the crack of dawn to pick up Gigi. We were going home.

The guys were disappointed, but they didn't make a fuss. I needed Gigi to be far away from this place. Funny how the ghetto of Zone 7 was safer than a kingdom full of elementals. Of all the magical species, elementals were the most peaceful. We were raised to appreciate all elements because the only way to survive was for all of us to work together. Creating balance was essential and it was the elemental way of life. How and why did that change?

At the healing village, the four guys got out of the car and waited for me.

"Do you mind getting Gigi while I wait here?" I asked Beau who held my door open.

He frowned and then nodded.

Although, I'd wanted to leave the day before, I couldn't. Many refugees needed help, and I'd hoped my efforts had made a difference. I was worried for all of them, but I was too chicken to face them. I needed strength to do what I planned to do.

Gigi and the guys approached the SUV. With four muscular men, it would be a tight fit in the vehicle, but we only had an hour's drive. We'd make it work. I loved how my Mama always had a smile on her face. Despite everything going on, she had a way of maintaining a positive attitude. Someday, I hoped to emulate her demeanor.

I got out of the car and hugged her as one of the guys loaded her belongings in the back. I took up my usual spot in the middle of the front seat, between Phin, our driver, and Beau, while Gigi sat between Cass and Trick.

"How'd you sleep, Mama?" I turned to ask her.

"Relatively well, all things considered. Are you ok?" She asked me, her eyebrows pinched together with conccrn.

"Yes." *A little anxious.* I turned in my seat.

Cassian explained things to my mother as we drove through the kingdom, and then Gigi pointed out things in our neighborhood. It made me smile as she told them about where I used to play and where I went to school. It was funny how much she remembered.

Phin parked on the street in front of our house, and we all got out of the car. I exited on the driver's side and looked up at him. He had sad eyes.

I caressed his face. "You're coming in, right?" "Of course." His voice was hoarse.

I wrapped my arm around his waist, and we followed Gigi and the other guys inside.

Gigi offered refreshments, and the four men gathered in the small dining room. Their large bodies made the entire home feel as though it had shrunk.

I left them to it and went to my room. By the time I returned to the living area, the guys were seated and Gigi sat comfortably on her rocker.

"Mama, did you put your remedies away?" I asked.

"Yes, and Beau already went over the protocol. Be still, Zara. You worry too much," she chided.

I smiled and knelt next to her. "Well, as your daughter, that's my job. Especially since I'll be gone for a little while."

"What? Where?" She sat straight up.

"Mama, I have to go back to the kingdom. I don't know if I can help, but I have to try." I pressed the palm of her hand to my cheek.

"That's my girl. I knew you wouldn't let that sister of yours continue her shenanigans without a fight. But you could have said something earlier instead of having these nice boys drive all the way here for nothing." She moved to stand, but I shook my head.

"It's not safe there, Mama. You have to stay here. I won't be able to focus if I'm worried about you."

"Oh, Zara, come give Gigi a hug then." She stood and pulled me up and into her arms.

She released me, then looked into my eyes. "Zara, I am so proud to call you my daughter. You are the light of my life."

She hugged me again and I sniffled.

"Now go! Teach those fools a lesson."

That made me laugh. I wiped my face with the back of my hand and nodded. "I'll be in touch as often as I can. And umm...maybe you should take Phin's number."

I turned to look at him. He had a business phone that worked in the realm.

"Of course, I'll program it into your cell, Gigi. And I can also give you my office info." Phin stood and reached for Gigi's phone which was on the table next to her rocking chair.

After he stored his info, he showed it to Gigi and said, "I will call my staff now, and they'll know to come running if you ever need anything. Even if it's a trip to the grocery store, ok?"

My heart swelled.

"Aww, such sweet boys." Gigi batted her eyelashes and smiled at him. Then she reached out and hugged him.

I stepped away as the guys said their goodbyes to Gigi and grabbed a suitcase of clothes that I had packed. My phone was still dead, but I pulled it off the charger anyway and packed it with my other things; hopefully, I could recharge it at the lair somehow even though there would be no reception.

I snuck out and loaded my things in the SUV. I wasn't anxious to leave. I just wanted to get going before I changed my mind.

Gigi and the four guys came out as I finished loading my suitcase. She approached me and I gave her another hug.

"I love you, Mama, so much."

"I love you, too." She kissed my forehead, and I got in the car.

Thankfully, the guys didn't dally. The urge to change my mind was so strong. I knew what I had to do, but I was reluctant to leave the only safe haven I had ever known to run straight into shark-infested waters.

We waved at Gigi as Phin backed out of the driveway. As soon as she was out of sight, I sobbed.

"Do you want me to turn back?" Phin slowed to a stop.

"No. No, I'm doing the right thing. But perhaps we can make one stop if we're not in a rush." I rubbed my eyes and took a deep breath.

He nodded. "Sure, where to?"

I directed him to Thaddeus Sloane's place.

Thaddeus was a well-respected businessman in Silk City and a powerful mage. His business was a mystery to me. It was one of those situations that were best left unsaid. I knew he was financially well-off, judging by all the expensive cars he drove and the several real estate properties he owned. The brownstone we were heading to was his most modest property, even though it took up an entire block.

"Park here and I'll walk." I pointed to a side street.

"Why?" All four men asked at the same time.

"Entrance to his place is on a busy street without much parking, and I need to ask him a favor. It might be best for me to go in alone," I explained.

"We're coming with you," Trick said. "I for one would like to meet this friend of yours."

The other guys in the car murmured their agreement.

"Fine." I rolled my eyes. It wouldn't be the first time I introduced Thadd to someone I was dating. Not that I was dating any of the men in the car, but a few of those kisses weren't exactly innocent. Still, I was certain Thadd wouldn't have any problems with it. He was confident like that.

We parked on a side street near Thadd's brownstone on the edge of

Zone 7. The place was like Fort Knox, and I was sure he had cameras tracking me and the four elemental men approach his domain. I wouldn't be surprised if his team was already running background checks.

I pressed the buzzer at the front door and waited while Beau, Phin, Cass, and Trick created a protective circle around me.

A moment later the door opened.

"Zara." Thadd stepped out, lifted me off my feet, and smashed our bodies together. "I've been worried about you. You were supposed to call me days ago."

The four elemental men behind me stiffened, and someone growled.

"Are you ok? Have you been crying?" He drew away a bit, peering at my face, while still holding me up.

"I'm fine." I squirmed down his body until my feet touched the ground. "I need a favor. May we come in?"

"Of course." He motioned with his hands.

I introduced Thaddeus to Beau, Phin, Trick, and Cass as we entered, and he led them into the living room where the four elemental men took a seat.

Thadd took a couple of strides toward me and swept me off my feet again.

"I was a worried, babe. You haven't replied to any of my messages. And there's a huge storm approaching the coast." He pressed his forehead to mine.

I wrapped my legs around him. "Sorry. I was in the kingdom and didn't have phone access."

"Can I get you anything?" he asked me.

"No, thank you, we can't stay long. Umm...I was wondering if you'd keep an eye on Gigi for me. I'll be away for a few days and not sure when I'll get back."

"What's wrong, baby?" he asked, then shook his head.

"Don't say nothing. I know you better than that. Talk to me."

Thaddeus leaned on the back of one of the sofas and set me down in front of him between his legs. Despite our open relationship, we always circled back to one another, and he'd never pressured me for more. It was one of the reasons I trusted him. No matter what our relationship status was I knew I could count on him.

I sighed and told him everything except the kidnapping part. Thaddeus was sometimes protective, and he'd be pissed if I told him about that even though it was my father's doing.

After giving him a rundown of the last couple days, Thadd drew me into his chest. I sank into his muscular chest and the familiarity of him.

"Fuck, Zara. I'd rather you not do this, but I can tell you've made up your mind." He drew away from me and placed his large hands on my face.

"I will check in with Gigi daily and keep you posted. Will your phone work in the kingdom?" he asked.

I shook my head.

Thadd glanced behind me, nodded his head, and one of his friends came out from a back room.

"Hi, Will," I said to the burly man that worked with or for Thaddeus. I wasn't sure which.

Will nodded at me, handed the phone to Thadd, and then went to shake hands with the four elemental men.

"How do you have a phone that can work in the kingdom?" I asked Thadd.

"I have all the best toys. You know that." Thadd winked at me. He turned the phone on and programmed his info, then handed it to me. "It has the basic functions; text, video calls, camera, that's it."

He kept his hands around my waist as I looked at the phone. While I went through the settings, he placed kisses on my neck. I pulled away from him, but he held fast to my waist and buried his face in my cleavage.

I yanked his hair back to get him away from my chest while at the same time someone cleared their throat. "Behave yourself," I said to Thadd.

He laughed. "I was just curious to see what these four would do."

The four elementals stood and stared at Thaddeus with murder in their eyes.

"You're a troublemaker." I bopped him on his forehead.

Thaddeus laughed. "Just having a bit of fun. But seriously, be careful and call me if you need anything."

"Thank you." I motioned to the four elementals and led the way out, shaking my head.

The four guys went to the SUV ahead of me, and I turned back to face Thadd. "One more thing?"

I walked back to his doorstep, and he hooked a finger in the waistband of my jeans.

"Anything for you, baby," he said with too much smolder in his voice.

"Quit. Be serious for once. Would you know of someone buying or selling human weapons in the kingdom?" I had a feeling if anyone knew, he would.

Thaddeus squinted at me with concern. "Not off the top of my head, but I will look into it. Come here for a second."

He pulled me back into his house and then disappeared into an office not far from the living room. I peered out the front door to check on the four elemental men who waited at the corner for me. They seemed concerned, but not pissed. Thank Goddess. I did not want to deal with male temper tantrums right now. I sincerely wasn't trying to anger them or make them jealous. We met three days ago, and I wasn't ashamed of my sexuality or any of my lovers. And although Thadd and I weren't an official couple, I wasn't about to let him go.

I held up my pointer finger, giving the elemental men the universal one-moment gesture and then turned to see Thadd coming towards me.

Thadd pressed me against the door frame with his firm body and kissed me hungrily. I ran my hands through his hair and moaned against his mouth. I wanted him to undress me right there and get lost in his strength. It would have been so easy to forget about the problems of the kingdom.

"Baby Z, I don't want you to go." He nipped and sucked at the sensitive spot on my neck right below my ear.

"I have to, Thadd. I have to do what I can."

He slipped his hand into my jeans, reaching toward my core. I had the presence of mind to stop him from going any further.

"I want this, you know I do, but we can't not right now." I peppered kisses along his jawline.

His advancement slowed for a moment. "Just one taste, babe." His fingers squirmed underneath my panties and he plunged in.

I hid my cries of pleasure by sinking my teeth into his shoulder.

"Fuck yes, you're so wet, baby."

He removed his hand out of my jeans and sucked on his finger.

I groaned and watched him lick my juices.

"I have to go. We'll continue this soon, ok. I'll be back." I pushed on his chest, trying to create some space between us.

My body was feverish, and my breathing labored.

"You're delicious, baby. And yes, we'll definitely continue this soon, or I'm coming to that kingdom and bringing you home myself."

Thadd pulled a gun from his back pocket and placed it in my hand. "Use it if you need to."

I started to protest because I did have my elemental magic, but he pressed a finger to my lips. "I know, elemental princess, just in case. Keep this on you, for me."

He removed his finger, replacing it with a kiss. I grumped a little when he released me, and then I walked to the car. Damn it, I needed to get laid.

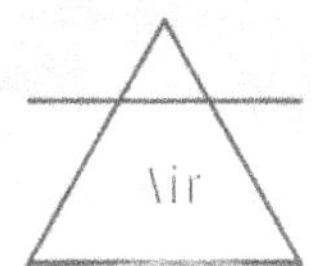
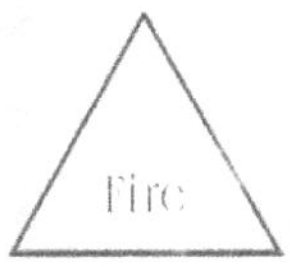

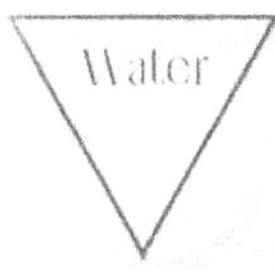

Chapter Twenty-One

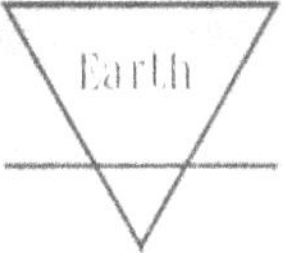

ZARA

I walked over to the car where the four elementals waited for me with scowls on their faces. I wish they would've stayed in the car.

Phin's eyes were an alarming shade of red. Oh no, he could not shift right there in the human realm. We had too many things going on; we didn't need to add more shit to the pile.

"Phin?" I stood in front of him. He didn't look at me. Damn it. I placed my hands on his face and tilted his head toward me. "Take me to the kingdom, please."

He finally looked at me. "I want to kill that guy."

"No, I won't allow it. Besides, I'm leaving with you. That's all that matters. Right?"

His eyes flashed back to their sparkly gold, then he picked me up, placed me on the hood of the truck, and kissed me hard. His tongue swept through my mouth possessively and his fang pierced my lip.

"Mine," he said with a beastly voice.

Damn these men. My eyes widened as I found Phin's dragon staring back at me. Uh oh. I nodded. "Let's go back to the lair."

We got in the car, and I turned to face the other men who were watching Phin warily.

"Sorry about that." I tipped my head towards Thaddeus's place.

"You don't have to apologize, Z. We all know you had a life before us," Cassian said.

"He's a bit of an asshole, but not your fault. He seems to care for you though, but let's hope we never have to see him again. What did he give you?" Beau asked.

I showed them the phone and the gun. "I asked him if he knew who was selling human weapons to the elementals. The guards we ran into yesterday were all armed with guns. It doesn't make much sense to me that the royals have implemented human weapons. I'm curious to find out who's selling and who's buying." Phin drove us out of Silk City without saying a word. He placed a possessive hand on my leg and the natural heat he emitted was exponentially hotter than usual. I leaned into his body and trailed my fingers on his hand. His shoulders relaxed a bit.

"What are you planning to do with that information? Buy more weapons?" Trick asked with a snarky tone.

I tucked the gun in the glove compartment and turned to face him. "Excuse me."

He shrugged. "Just wondering if you're planning to raid the palace with guns blazing. Maybe your boyfriend can help." His tone was laced with too much hostility for my liking.

"What the fuck is your problem?" I glared at him.

"Aside from the fact that your boyfriend is an asshole. What the fuck are you doing with a prick like that? Low standards much?" Trick scoffed.

The other three men spoke at the same time.

"Whoa, dude! Not cool," Cassian said.

"Knock it off, Patrick." Beau scrubbed his hand down his face.

"Apologize, now!" Phin glanced at Trick in the rearview mirror.

I wasn't going to let him off that easy. I launched over the front seat and managed to nail Trick with a right hook to his chin.

Beau yanked me back to the front seat. Cassian put his body between me and Trick, while Phin pulled off to the side of the road.

"Enough!" Phin growled. "Patrick, apologize." "Sorry," Trick muttered.

"Zara?" Phin side glanced at me.

"What? I'm not sorry," I told him.

"Zara, he apologized, let's just forgive and move on." Beau gave me a sidelong glance.

I rolled my eyes. "Sure, apology accepted."

We drove to the healing village in silence. According to Beau, healers like his mother and sister had a clinic set up at the Sanctuary. Once that was raided by the royals, they became a refugee healing camp. It was hidden and they often moved to avoid detection. It was awful, considering how badly healers were needed with all the violence that had been happening.

At the village, the guys wanted to interrogate the guard we had apprehended the day before. We had offered him healing in exchange for information. I hoped the hostage would be able to give us more information about what the royals were doing and what their goals were.

When we got out of the car, Phin said, "Patrick, a word please?"

I stayed put until Phin stepped next to me. "Go with Beau and Cass, angel. I'll be right there."

He kissed my cheek, then I looked over at Trick. He refused to meet my eyes.

Phin and Trick walked off to the side while Beau and Cassian pulled me away from them.

"Are they ok?" I asked.

"Patrick was out of line, Z. It is none of our business whom you choose to love or bed." Beau shrugged.

"Yeah, he overstepped. Phin will straighten things out." Cassian grasped my hand and steered me toward an area of the village I hadn't seen yet.

"It's not his place to straighten things out. I can take care of myself." I looked up at the two men as we continued walking through the village.

Beau smiled. "We have no doubts about your capabilities. Phin was our commander in the royal army. He was the first to go out on his own. After we all got sent away by our clans, we sought him out for guidance and shelter. He didn't refuse us, and he's been managing the chaos since."

"Phin's hot-tempered sometimes, but overall he's a good leader,"

Cassian said. "And we all know this is not the time for petty disagreements."

I thought about this information, and I didn't know how to feel about it. A part of me felt bad for getting Trick in trouble. Yet a part of me didn't. My relationship with Thaddeus or any other man was my business. I had zero intention of committing to Thaddeus, or any of the four elementals. Perhaps a discussion about where I stood as far as relationships went was in order. I was attracted to all four men, but a physical attraction in my book didn't mean love. One of the reasons Thadd and I got along so well was we understood each other. We had incredible chemistry, and we were both comfortable with our arrangement.

"Here we are," Beau said as he turned to face a hut that had been reinforced with magical wards. "I'll check on the patient while we wait for the other two to start our interrogation."

I didn't want to wait for Phin to speak with the hostage, but he turned the corner before I could say anything. Trick was nowhere to be found.

"Everything good?" Cassian asked him.

Phin nodded. "He needs to blow off some steam."

That didn't make me feel better about the situation. Trick and I had a complicated history. After hearing what had happened to him, I understood why he left and I didn't hold it against him. When he had come back years later to make amends, I was seeing someone else. I do remember telling Trick I had moved on and whatever he had to say was irrelevant. Was I with Thaddeus at that time? If I remembered correctly, it was around the same time frame. I wondered if Trick knew about that.

"Are you ok?" Phin asked me.

I nodded. "Shall we talk to the hostage?"

Beau came out of the hut. "He's ready."

Phin, Cass, and I followed Beau into the small room. Like the rest of the village, the hut was constructed of bamboo. The difference in this hut was the plain dirt floor, and the tiny windows that barely provided fresh air or light into the small space. Magical wards covered the hut to prevent the hostage from escaping or an unexpected rescue attempt.

Cassian jerked his head towards the door and said, "I'll stay out here and keep watch."

He probably didn't want to be in the tiny, enclosed space with four people. Both Phin and Beau took up so much space there wasn't much room to move around.

The hostage looked at me from the bed he had been lying on. "Princess. You are real. Oh, my Goddess. I have been praying for your return and the Goddess has answered. Blessed be."

"What's your name?" I asked while Beau held the only chair out for me to sit on.

"Grant. Thank you for saving me, princess. The kingdom is safe now that you're home." He sat up as best he could with one leg in a splint.

"Enough of that." I waved him off. "We need info on your mission. You told us you were looking for a powerful elemental. Why? And where were you taking that person?"

"The queen wants all of the powerful elemental children brought to Source Mountain. And some adults, if they comply. They've set up a camp there where the Sanctuary used to be. They are sorted and then sent to the palace."

His voice sounded weak, but his eyes were clear, so I pressed on.

"If adults don't comply?" I asked.

"We are told to shoot...if we have to." Grant hung his head.

Damn it, Amina. What the actual fuck?

"Kill powerful elementals? Why are you working for her?"

My body vibrated with anger.

"The king and queen have threatened our lives and the lives of our children. We don't have a choice. Umm...most are spelled into servitude."

"Spelled? How the hell are they doing that? Are you spelled?" I stood up, alarmed. Could this be a trap?

Phin and Beau stepped in front of me protectively.

"No, no, I'm not. I never got the rune, see?" Grant hiked up his sleeves and showed us the inside of his wrists.

"Fuck." Beau got closer to Grant and did some spell casting. A wave of magic washed over the injured man, then Beau stepped back and exhaled.

"He's clean. But we need to verify this info," Beau said.

"This doesn't make sense. Why haven't you been spelled?

And where is this magic coming from?" I stared down at Grant.

"There's a mage that is loyal to the king." Grant did his best to make himself comfortable. "Me and my cousin were trying to escape during the ceremony, but we didn't make it, obviously. We snuck back into the fold and no one asked questions. The rune doesn't change us. It makes it so we cannot use our elemental magic or weapons against the royals. The only way to break the spell is to kill the spell caster or kill the slave."

"Where did you get the human weapons from?" I asked, hoping he could shed some light on this topic.

"The king has a contact in the human realm. My cousin is on the team that collects and distributes the weapons. Most of us don't like what's happening, but it's better than starving. Can you save us, princess?"

"I'm not your princess." I snarled. Then in a softer tone, I continued. "But, I will try to right the wrongs committed by my sister. We need to know everything you can tell us about the sanctuary and the palace."

"Of course, I will help in any way I can." Grant bowed his head.

Grant spoke for a long while. He had begun working for the new king and queen when their royal guards had come into his village demanding their compliance. They were weaponized with human guns and shot anyone resisting them. They took all able bodied men and sequestered children and women of low power status. Those that were spared had been placed in some sort of role as servants to the monarchs.

His job was to hunt for refugees looking for anyone that had notable power and bring them to Source Mountain.

"How do the king and queen know who has power?" Phin asked.

"The seer. She has visions and tells us where to go," Grant replied.

"So, there's a mage and a seer assisting the monarchs. And thousands of guards. We need a way in." Phin looked off into space as though he was thinking out loud.

"I can do that! My cousin is also not spelled. He could help," Grant said excitedly.

Beau shook his head. "You won't be of any help until you heal. We'll let you rest and check back with you."

Phin, Beau, and I left Grant in his jail cell hut and found Cassian waiting outside. He tilted his chin up when he saw us.

"Patrick was here and we both heard everything. What now?"

"Where did Patrick go?" Beau asked him.

Cass shrugged, and we all kept walking.

"I need to check on the children," I said. "Meet up with you guys later." I waved them off and turned down a familiar dirt pathway.

Phin jogged up beside me. "I'll come with you. The others are going to dig up the bodies from yesterday to confirm the rune story. After you're done, we'll head back to the lair."

I nodded at Phin and continued into the village. As soon as we walked through the village center, the children came out to greet us. They were sweet kids, and it was refreshing to see so many smiley faces. Despite everything, the children maintained their innocence and had a positive outlook. It gave me hope. Even Phin's typical serious nature melted, and he smiled around them.

We spent some time with the children and then went to check on Raven and Rocko. Raven was still weak, but at least she was alive. Rocko had refused to play with the other children because he hadn't wanted to leave her side. I was concerned about the boy's safety considering the royals were after him. Phin said Beau had already taken care of that by putting a concealment-type spell on the kid, and he had been certain he would appear to be a low-level elemental if anyone came looking.

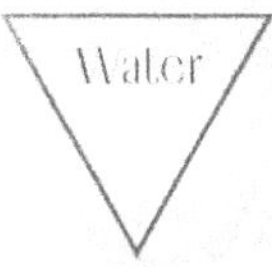

Chapter Twenty-Two

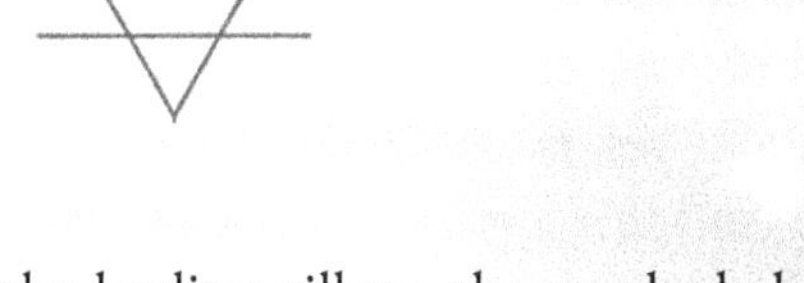

ZARA

By the time we left the healing village, the sun had already set. Beau, Cass, and Trick were still out confirming Grant's story about the runes. And I was beat. Phin and I got into the SUV and drove back to the lair.

Phin parked in his usual spot in the hangar. I took the gun Thadd had given me from the glove compartment and tucked it into the waistband of my jeans. He glanced at the gun, and his demeanor changed. His back stiffened, and the corner of his top lip lifted in a snarl. Silently, he retrieved my suitcase from the back of the vehicle, walked me back to my room and set my suitcase on the floor by the door.

"Do you have everything you need?" He glanced at the holster again, and then began to circle me with a predatory glint in his eyes. He traced a finger up and down my spine, and my body tingled.

I nodded and stepped away from him. Although, I was certain Phin would never hurt me, his prowling made me nervous.

"What's this about?" I asked.

He shrugged. "I just needed you to myself, to discuss the mage."

"What would you like to discuss?" With every step he took toward me, I took two steps away from him.

"I don't like him touching you," he snarled.

"You're not the boss of me." I kept him at a distance.

He paused, his eyes flashed from gold to red. "Don't test me, princess."

"Don't call me that." I squared my shoulders.

His voice was deep and gravely. With supernatural speed, he flashed in front of me. Up close his irises were red with gold veins in them, and he had vertical pupils.

Shit.

"Do you have a name, dragon?" I asked.

He slid his tongue over his bottom lip, and he regarded me with a predatory glint.

"You may call me Beast if you like." His voice was deep and gravelly.

"Great to meet you, Beasty. May I speak with Phineas?"

He chuckled. "Do I make you nervous, Lady Zara?"

"Actually, yes. But that's only because we haven't spent much time together. And this is probably not the right time considering we have a kingdom to save," I said, trying to remain calm.

In a blindingly fast movement, Beast tore my top and my jeans clear off my body, then he threw me on the bed.

The fast movement made me dizzy, and it took me a moment to get my bearings. He knelt between my legs, studying me while removing his clothes.

Nope, not like this. I scrambled off the bed, kicking him as I fell to the floor. My attempts at saving myself were futile. Beast picked me up from the ground and slammed me back down to the mattress.

"Zara, cooperate, please. I won't hurt you," Phin said in his normal voice.

I relaxed a bit, and he sniffed me from my head to my crotch. I shuffled backward on the bed trying to get away from the odd encounter, but his hands held me in place.

"Mine." He wasn't asking me a question; it was a statement.

All right, two can play this game.

"No, you are mine." I hooked my legs around his neck and flipped him over. I pinned him to the mattress keeping him trapped between my legs.

"And I am the one that chooses." I slid down his body and called my fire magic to my hands and gripped his neck.

His skin heated against my hand, meeting my fire. His eyes were red, and fangs protruded from his mouth. "Yes, mistress. I am yours."

Phin's eyes returned to their golden hue, and I released my fire.

I pushed him away to see whom I was dealing with. "Phin? Are you back?"

"It's me, angel. I apologize." Phin stood up abruptly, and then he bowed his head and left the room.

I blew out a breath of air. What did I get myself into? I should escape or at least feel terrified, but no, I felt intrigued if not a bit aroused. What the hell was wrong with me? I shook my head and carried my suitcase to the closet. I slipped on my bikini, and then I went to the balcony to decompress and make a few calls. Thaddeus sent a text stating Gigi was ok, but I called her anyway to check in and gave her my new number. She was doing well and had been diligent with her new remedies.

I settled into the infinity pool outside of Phin's room. The sun dipped below the mountains and painted the sky in vibrant shades of pink, orange, yellow, and blue, casting the valley below in a brilliant glow. Nature in all its glory was on display before me, and I inhaled deeply.

As beautiful as Valley of the Goddess was, I couldn't shake the ominous feeling that niggled at the back of my mind. The conversation we had with Grant only fueled my frustration. What was my sister up to? I had hoped to give her the benefit of doubt, but everything Grant had said sounded like she was just as culpable as her husband.

As a child, Amina had always been beautiful, smart, well liked, and well-behaved. I on the other hand was the complete opposite. I had been the mischievous one getting into trouble and running amuck like a wild child.

I couldn't fathom why she was behaving so out of character. But, I suppose I had changed since I'd been away. Perhaps she did as well. Still, I retained the glimmer of hope in my heart that the chaos was her husband's doing and not hers.

The water rippled around me, alerting me to Phin's presence. I hadn't heard him approach but I knew it was him. The natural heat of his body increased the temperature of the pool a tad, and his smokey cinnamon scent warmed my insides.

I inhaled deeply and turned my head toward him. "Hi."

"Hi," he replied. "I'm sorry about earlier, Zara...about my beast. That must've been horrifying."

"It wasn't," I assured him. "It was different. I am certain you and your beast would never hurt me. I suppose if I am staying here for any amount of time, I should get to know the both of you better."

"He's never done that with anyone before. I can't apologize enough." His face was shadowed with remorse, his brows scrunched.

"I'm ok, Phin. Your beast is a bit bossy, but I can handle it. Although you may want to reiterate what I told him. I choose whom I want in my life and in my bed, not him or anyone else for that matter." I turned back to gaze at the valley below.

Valley of the Goddess was picture perfect as the sun slowly dipped behind the mountains. My favorite fairy tales as a little girl had always been about the Valley of the Goddess. The stories didn't do this place justice. Not in the least. The valley was a hidden treasure.

Phin leaned against the edge of the pool next to me. "This is my favorite time of the day. And my favorite thinking spot."

I smiled. "Am I intruding?" This was his bed chambers, not mine.

"No, I like having you here." His shoulder brushed against mine. The contact made my skin prickle.

Phin slipped behind me and massaged my shoulders. I sighed as he kneaded away the tension that had begun to exacerbate over the last few days.

His warm, strong hands slid down my back, like a hot stone massage. I groaned as he massaged my lower back and pressed his lips to my shoulders, creating a path of hot kisses to my neck.

I ground my hips against his groin and rubbed his hard cock in the process. I tilted my head back against his shoulders as his hands snaked around my belly. A warm, sensual wave unfurled inside me. I reached behind me to run my fingers through his hair.

His nose grazed my cheek and his hands traveled up to my breasts. I was wearing a white two-piece bikini, and my hard nipples protruded against the fabric. He pinched the taut buds while he sucked and nipped at my neck.

"Phin," I said in a low breathy moan. "Maybe we should talk first."

"Perhaps," Phin whispered. "But first let me take care of you. It's been a rough couple of days. Let me make you feel good. May I do that for you? Make you writhe with pleasure until your voice is hoarse from screaming my name?"

What woman in her right mind would say no to that? I was well aware I was treading in dangerous territory. Especially after the encounter with his beast. But the only response I could muster was a lust-filled whimper, and all thoughts of discussing our intentions moving forward disappeared, leaving nothing but want in its wake.

He undid the straps of my top and he fondled my breasts with deliberate intent. I gasped and angled my face toward his. His lips sought out mine, and he ground his hardness on my ass. Phin's hands moved down to my hips, and then he untied my bikini bottom straps. He slipped his hands around to my pussy. Warm thick fingers slid down from my clit to my tight hole. I gasped and rocked back and forth on his digit.

"That's it, angel. Does that feel good on your clit?" Phin purred in my ear.

"Oh yes, Phin," I moaned. "More."

He slipped a finger in my cunt while maintaining firm pressure on my clit. Every stroke was slow and deep, prolonging my pleasure.

Phin squeezed in another finger. My entire body vibrated, and I gyrated back and forth, crying out his name. My body began to tighten as my orgasm crested through me.

Then Phin turned me around to face him and hoisted me out of the pool. He sat me down on the ledge, spreading my knees apart.

"I want you to come in my mouth, angel. I want your juices dripping down my tongue." Phin dove in face first, keeping his eyes on me.

"Oooh, fuck yes." I cried out.

My hips bucked against his mouth. His tongue laved between my folds, then circled my entrance. Every swipe tingled my sensitive nerve endings.

In no time at all, I was at the precipice of pure bliss. My walls clenched, and my orgasm burst out of me.

I was coming down from the high of my climax, panting, as he climbed out of the pool, and he wrapped me in a towel. He picked me up with ease, and then he laid me on the bed.

His hands roamed all over my bare flesh, his lips following the trail. "Every inch of you is exquisite, angel. I want to spend the rest of my days worshiping your body."

"Phin." I writhed under his touch. "I need you inside of me. Now."

He chuckled then suckled my clit. My body quivered. I was at the pivotal point of pleasure again, but I wanted more. I wrapped my legs around his neck and flipped him over, keeping my cunt fastened to his mouth. I rode his face until I climaxed all over him.

Phin's face was drenched with my juices; his tongue ran across his lips.

I smiled then kissed his jaw, then his neck. When I got to his nipples I suckled them and grazed them with my teeth. He hissed and his hips bucked. I took my time sucking and nipping at his nipples then trailed kisses down to his hard thick cock.

I took him in my mouth, and he gasped. "Fuck, Zara, that feels so good."

He bucked, shoving his cock down my throat. I sucked at him greedily, and then he pulled me off him and flipped me over.

"Is this what you want?" He asked and rubbed the head of his cock between my folds.

"Mmmm...yes please," I begged.

He nudged himself at my entrance and plunged in. "Oh fuck, Z. You feel incredible."

The sharp pain from being stretched made me gasp. His hips did slow deep thrusts making my toes curl. He placed my legs on his chest and pumped faster.

Our body temperatures began to rise along with our passion. His skin took on that fiery glow like it had when he'd consumed flames at the refugee village. Before I could panic about being burnt alive, my fire magic surged and collided with his. Streams of red, gold, and orange lava swirled under the surface of our skin. He looked like a fire god and me his goddess. An all consuming heat filled me with intense carnality. Phin continued to pump into my hot, drenched cunt. Our combined fire heated me from the inside and melded us together making it impossible to know where I began and he ended. At that moment we were one being made up of passion and flame.

A slick heat rolled over my clit, and I came all over Phin's cock with a rigorous spasm. He hammered my pussy until he shot a river of cum in my womb.

His body collapsed on top of mine and we caught our breaths and brought our body temperatures back to normal.

Phin's softening cock slipped out of me, while he turned us over on the bed. He brought me to rest on top of him, and I nestled my face on his chest.

"What just happened?" I asked my voice hoarse.

"I'm not sure. I've never experienced anything like that before. My fire takes over sometimes. And I have never known anyone that can match my fire. Your magic is like mine." His voice was raspy as well.

We probably needed to hydrate, so I raised my head.

"Are you ok? What can I get you?" He propped himself up on one arm.

"I'm fine. I was just looking for water," I replied.

A knock made me turn my head toward the door.

"Rest, angel. It's probably Linc. I told him earlier that I would bring you down for dinner. He was very excited that you hadn't left," Phin wrapped a blanket around his waist, and went to the door.

I perked up at the mention of dinner. "Oh, I could eat." I smiled at him sheepishly then buried my head under the pillow.

Phin muttered something, and then I heard some shuffling around. I sat up to see what was happening and found Phin wheeling in a cart filled with food. Linc respectfully stayed outside the door.

"Thank you, Linc!" I yelled.

"You're welcome, my lady. Sorry to disturb you, but you must eat. I'll not bother you again." Linc walked away before Phin shut the door.

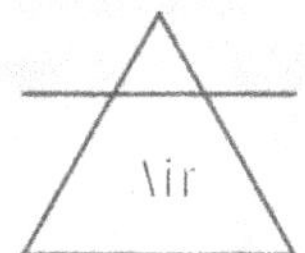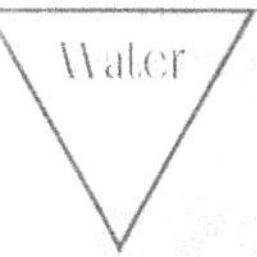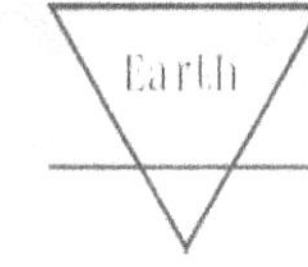

Chapter Twenty-Three

PHINEAS

I closed the door and wheeled the food cart closer to the bed. Zara was sprawled out and looked like an angel. Her creamy, tanned skin was absolutely perfect, and her white hair sparkled against the dark red sheets.

I climbed onto the bed and placed kisses on her knee and along her thighs. My beast rose to the surface, and I snaked my head between her legs and inhaled.

She is exquisite. So delectable and insatiable. Her needs are great. My beast purred.

I peppered kisses up and down her thighs, and Zara spread her legs wide for me. She made a soft mewling sound; arousal shot through my body.

She's fertile, almost ripe.

Do not impregnate her! I almost verbally shouted, which was unnecessary and a bit weird. It was weird enough having a conversation with the magical being that lived in my head.

Don't be daft. I said almost. Pay attention.

He was such a cantankerous shit sometimes.

You need to take better care of her. She needs to feed. She's hungry.

I will as soon as she wakes. Leave her alone, let her rest.

No. I'm not done.

My beast guided my movements, and I didn't fight him. He wouldn't hurt her. He was possessive, but that was because he claimed her, there would be no other female for us now or ever.

I slid my tongue through her folds and parted her pussy lips. She moaned for me, and my dragon took its time savoring her taste.

My beast purred and caused a hum of vibrations on her cunt. She pumped her hips up and down, fucking my mouth.

She propped herself up, resting on her elbows and watched me feast on her pussy. Our gazes met, but to my surprise, she didn't startle. My dragon was present, and I knew she saw it in my eyes. My golden eyes were now red with gold striations in the iris.

Her skin heated, and her rocking became more fervent. She loved being licked by my dragon, and my dragon enjoyed pleasuring her. I slammed two fingers into her tight entrance, and she came all over my tongue.

The aftershocks of her pleasure had her writhing under me, but my beast was not done with her yet.

"Mine," my beast growled. And I stalked up her body.

"Phin?" her tone was even and curious.

"He's here." And I was, but my beast was riding point at the moment, and I was ok with that. He had never shown an interest in any of the women in my bed, but it felt right to share her. Still, it was probably best for me to set her mind at ease.

I shook my head and spoke in my voice. "I won't hurt you, Zara. My beast just wants to savor you like this as well. If you are uncomfortable, I can stop him."

She cupped my face and brought me down on top of her body. "I want both of you." She held my gaze as my beast roared and speared her with my cock.

She kissed me savagely and kept her eyes on me as I fucked her hard. I had her coming for me over and over again.

Our mate needs to be cared for. Give her a warm bath and food. My beast purred in my head.

He was content, but completely useless in terms of providing her basic needs.

Zara was a boneless heap next to me. We were completely sated and both could use some pampering. But that was my job. I slid out of bed and got the water going in the bathtub, then went back to collect her.

I gathered her in my arms and placed her gently in the tub.

Zara jerked awake when her skin hit the water.

"Oh!" she said. "This is nice."

"Relax, I'll be right back." I walked out of the bathroom as she settled into the tub, and then I returned with two glasses, a bottle of red wine, and a small platter of fruit.

We sipped and nibbled while I told her about my connection to Torch Mountain.

"Are you serious?" she asked as we got out of the tub. "The mountain is sentient? And it responds to you?"

"It communicates with me and I with it."

Zara placed her hand on the wall. "Hi, I'm Zara."

The mountain purred, and I felt it rumble a bit under her hand.

"That is so cool," she said with a big smile.

We returned to the bedroom, and I pulled the cart of food Linc had prepared closer to the bed.

She stood by the bed and stared at it with a frown on her face, then she looked at me. "Did you clean up?"

I looked at the clean sheets and laughed. "No, that's Lulu's doing. She's Linc's wife. They live here, and she somehow knows when things need cleaning. You never see or hear her. She's just always there. Don't ask how she knows; she just does. The guys and I made a mess in the living area once, and we all fell asleep there. When we woke everything was spotless."

She gave me a look that said she wasn't buying it.

"Check the closet if you don't believe me."

She went to the closet and gasped. "What the?? She unpacked my suitcase and hung my clothes. This is amazing!"

"Wait a minute." She walked back into the room. "Was she in here when we were, you know?"

"When we were what...fucking?"

Her cheeks flushed, and I chuckled. "No, she wasn't in the room. My beast would have alerted me of any presence and she's, I don't know, shy."

I had already placed a tray of food on the bed and climbed up being extra careful while Zara followed. "Plus, I umm." I watched her recline as I handed her a plate of food.

She took the plate and asked, "You 'umm'?"

"I told them to be extra nice to you, so that you'd stay," I whispered.

She giggled. "I'm staying, not forever. But at least until the realm rights itself."

Zara tilted her head at me and frowned. "I probably should've said something before all this. But, Phin, I'm not good at relationships. I have trust issues and I plan on going home. To Silk City."

My beast grumbled something I couldn't make out. I shook him off and nodded at her. "I understand, Zara. I'm not thrilled with that news, but I am thrilled you're willing to help us. It's a blessing for the entire realm to have you here."

"Well don't go counting your blessings just yet. I'm not sure how I can help," she said between bites of pasta. "This is so good." She groaned.

"Speaking of, what's our plan?" She asked after swallowing a big bite of food. She had a hearty appetite which made me smile.

I swallowed some pasta and chased it with a gulp of wine. "We need to first see what the guys dug up, then we'll move the vehicles and have them modified. Then I'm thinking we need to speak with Grant about the layout at the sanctuary. Several refugee camps need to be rallied together. Also, we will need numbers if we're going against the royal army."

She sipped her wine and then said, "That's where I come in, right? Do you think these elementals will come together if I ask? And where are the guys anyway?"

I nodded while I chewed. Zara bent over and crawled to the cart on all fours to pick up a bottle of wine. My cock twitched. She sat back on her knees and refilled our cups. I stared at her barely clothed body. She noticed me staring and placed a kiss on my lips.

"What was the question again? Sorry I got distracted." I said as she reclined on the pillows. I set my plate down on the tray and scooted closer to her.

I knelt between her legs and pushed her knees apart. She placed her foot on my chest and shook her head. "Phin, be serious for a moment. I was asking about rallying the refugees."

I grasped her foot and massaged it, then slid my hands toward her calf. Her satisfied moan made me smile.

"To answer your question, the answer is, yes, they will. Once we spread the news that you're back, people will gather together instead of separating and hiding. But like I said, we need to know what's going on at the sanctuary. I hope the info from Grant will be helpful. If not, we'll go on a stealth mission to gather intel. Either way, we'll organize the people for an attack."

I grabbed a plate of dessert from the cart and handed it to her.

Her eyes widened. "German chocolate cake?!" She squealed and stuffed a huge bite in her mouth. "Delicious!"

She sliced a piece and held it up to my lips. I accepted the morsel of sweetness and she smiled. We continued our light chit-chat for some time, then we tidied up a bit and got ready for bed.

Zara fell asleep in my arms, and although she was set upon leaving the kingdom, I was also determined to keep her by my side.

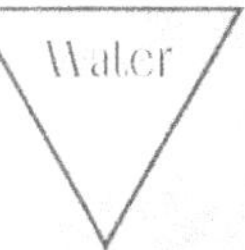

Chapter Twenty-Four

BEAU

My gut twisted into knots when I heard Phin and Zara's voices coming down the hall. He was making her laugh, and a part of me was jealous. Then she rounded the corner and gave me a dazzling smile. Every trace of jealousy evaporated. At that moment she was beaming, and that smile was just for me.

"Good morning, Zara. You look well rested." I smiled and pulled her into my arms as she got closer to me.

"Good morning, Beau." She kissed my cheek. "How did it go yesterday?"

I maneuvered her body to stand between my legs. "Ok, it seems Grant was telling us the truth."

"That's good. Perhaps we'll be able to get more from him to infiltrate their base camp." She drew away from me, but stayed between my legs and turned to pluck a grape from my plate and pop it into her mouth.

"The other guys still asleep?" Phin took a seat next to me at the kitchen counter.

I nodded and repositioned Zara so she was sitting on my lap.

"Thank you, Linc," she said to our in-house chef as he handed her a cup of java, a plate filled with fruit, and a breakfast sandwich.

She moved to get off my lap, probably wanting to sit on her own chair, but I held her in place.

"We'll need another chair in here," I muttered, looking over at the two empty chairs on the other side of Phin. "For now, you can stay right here."

She shrugged and started in on her breakfast.

Cassian walked in and frowned at me. Then Zara noticed him and smiled brightly. He smiled, bent down, and kissed her cheek.

"Where's Trick?" I asked.

"I passed him in the hall. He said he needed to check on something and to contact him when we need him," Cass replied.

Phin growled. Patrick needed to get over his ego if he wanted this to work.

"I guess the first stop is the healing village, then we can formulate a plan. I also think we need to get Zara over to one of the refugee camps."

Cass nodded at Linc as he was passed a much larger plate of food. "We should do that together. Show a united front."

"Sounds good to me. Healing village first, then a camp. I'm thinking of the one closest to King Zander's place. Is that ok with you, Zara?" I asked the beauty sitting on my lap.

"Yes, to all of it, but I'd also like to see my sister." She bit into her breakfast sandwich.

The three of us elementals and the gnome froze in place.

"What?" She stood and turned to face us.

"No," Phin said.

Zara narrowed her eyes at him. She insisted she was no longer our princess, but sometimes she sure had a stubborn streak like one.

"Z, it's not safe," Cassian said in a soft tone.

"Maybe I can send a letter asking for a meeting. I think that would be better than me just storming in and dismantling her reign, don't you think?" She looked at each of us.

We stood there silent not wanting to drop yet another bomb on her. Linc disappeared in the pantry somewhere. Phin stared off into space with a deep scowl. Cassian hid his face in his hands. And me, I couldn't look her in the eye.

"Ok, what's going on? You're obviously hiding something." Zara crossed her arms over her chest.

"What they're afraid to tell you, Zara," Patrick said as he strolled into the kitchen. "is that your sister doesn't want to see you."

She gasped.

"If you guys aren't going to be honest with her, I will."

Patrick looked at us with contempt in his eyes. He had a point, but I did not appreciate his attitude. Whatever problem he was harboring needed to be dealt with or things would turn ugly real quick.

"Talk to me Trick." Zara met his gaze.

"Well, this is second-hand info, but from what I understand, your father had written a royal decree rescinding your banishment after your mother passed, but your sister used her Queen status to override his decree and reenacted it." Patrick relaxed in his chair and sipped his coffee.

He was being an asshole. His words were hurtful, and he was so callous about it. I wanted to punch his face and from the glaring looks, Cass and Phin had felt the same way I did.

Zara's lip trembled a bit and tears glistened in her eyes. She moved away from me and stood behind us.

We all turned to face her, not sure what to say.

Finally, she faced us, her eyes red, but when she spoke her voice was strong. "Do any of you know why?"

Cass spoke up first. "Zara, I hate to say this, but what Patrick said is mostly correct. As to why, I think she feels threatened. Kingdom law states that you could take the throne from her. You are older and the rightful heir. Had King Zander's decree been held, you could have waltzed in and taken it back no questions asked. Now, I'm afraid it won't be so easy. I was there when she burnt the king's decree and when she enacted the law reenforcing your banishment."

"You were there?" Her voice wavered.

Cass and I nodded. "I was there as well, Z. She is not the sister you remember. When she met Issac, things changed. She became entitled, demanding, and downright unpleasant. We assume it's his influence, but it's hard to say. Right now she has all the power. She could imprison you which would not be ideal. It is best that you stay away from her. For now."

"What did my sister say, exactly?" Zara clutched her middle like she was having a tummy ache.

I was hoping she wouldn't ask this, and I was reluctant to answer. But perhaps knowing the details would give her the resolve she needed to deal with this situation.

"I don't have a sister. The kingdom is mine," Cassian muttered with a pained expression.

Zara's gaze softened after hearing those words. She knew how difficult it was for Cass to tell her the truth.

She turned to face me, and I knew she wanted to know if there was more. Fuck. I wanted to punch Patrick in his vampire face for bringing this up.

"I won't hesitate to have her killed if she takes one step into the kingdom." I couldn't meet her eyes. We knew how her sister felt and kidnapped her anyway. But we had no intention of her getting hurt. We vowed to keep her safe and we would not fail.

Zara started to giggle. Then she started to laugh.

We all looked at her as though she had gone insane. Maybe she had. I was worried. She didn't seem to understand the severity of what we were dealing with.

"So my sister wants to kill me, and you all thought it was a great idea to kidnap me and bring me here?"

"Zara, we will keep you safe. We will end Amina and Issac's reign, and you will never have to worry about this ever again." Phin got up to approach her.

She held out her hand, halting him in place. "I have zero intention of becoming queen. You four and my father can figure that part out. My goal is to stop this nonsense. Elementals are supposed to be peaceful people, not power-hungry tyrants. Freeing our people from those tyrants is all I care about, so let's get to it."

"How many villages do we have to visit?" She paced.

"Hard to say exactly. When the royals took over, people scattered all over the realm trying to get farther away from the palace and the Sanctuary. Some have remained hidden. From what I can tell from flying around, there are about a dozen within fifty miles of here. And the last time I checked on the eastern side of the palace, there are about the same in each quadrant," Phin offered.

"The powerful water clans are either in the ocean or lakes. The not-so-powerful are in the coastal villages." Cassian chimed in.

"How many people are in each village?" Zara asked.

"Nearby, three dozen at the most. That includes women and children. Not all fighters," I explained. There were many skilled female fighters, but more than half were mothers.

"Are the villages segregated by innate magic?" she asked.

"Yes," we all said at the same time.

Zara stopped pacing and pinched the bridge of her nose. I had witnessed her father doing the exact same thing more than once. It almost made me smile.

"All right, we have work to do. Change of plans. Let's start with the two largest villages nearby. After that, we can visit Grant. We'll meet back here in ten minutes." She spun on her heel and walked out of the kitchen.

The four of us did as we were told.

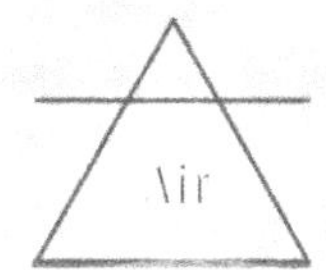

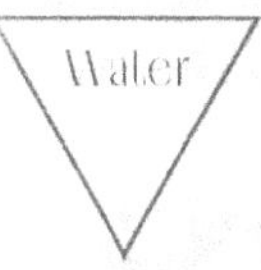

Chapter Twenty-Five

CASSIAN

After Zara gave us our orders, we all fell in line. I scarfed my breakfast, went back to my room, changed, and returned to the kitchen with three minutes to spare. Zara was already waiting.

She hadn't noticed my approach, so I waited in the hallway and watched her from afar. She was speaking to Linc and his wife with a big smile on her face. They were smiling and chatting as though they were old friends. In some ways they were, both Linc and Lulu had worked at the palace when we were children. She may not remember them, but they remembered her.

Earlier when she came up with her plan, she reminded me of her father. She analyzed the situation and made swift decisions. Her intelligence and confidence were inspiring. She would make a great queen, even though she didn't want to be one.

Beau came up beside me. "She is incredibly beautiful. And so smart."

I nodded. "She also has the same leadership style as her father. The people will follow her."

"Are you two ogling the princess like creeps?" Patrick asked from behind us.

I turned to face him. "That was a shitty thing you did earlier."

"What? I only did what you three wimps should've done in the first place. Besides, she had a right to know how much danger she's in." Patrick's haughty tone grated on my nerves.

"Are you trying to push her away, asshole? What's your problem?" Beau snarled.

I've never heard him sound so aggressive. He was an excellent warrior, but like most earthers, he always erred on the side of peaceful resolution.

Patrick didn't answer right away. He rubbed his forehead as though he was trying to figure out what his problem was. We all knew it had something to do with Zara's lover in Silk City. But we couldn't help him if he kept pushing us away.

I patted him on his shoulder. "You need to keep it together. If you need alone time with her to speak about your relationship, do it. We all need to keep a level head right now." As long as he'd be able to stay on task and keep his personal shit in check, we'd be ok.

We walked into the kitchen area at the same time as Phin.

Linc and Lulu gave Zara a bow and scurried off.

"We'll take one vehicle and head to Smokestack. There were thirty fire elementals last time I checked. It's close and I figure it would be good for numbers," Phin stated, and we all filed out to the hangar.

"I can open a portal," Beau offered.

Phin shook his head. "No, we'll approach all villages that don't know about your magic on foot. Once we have their allegiance, then we notify them of your magic and tell them that you may teleport in and out for expediency's sake. I don't want anyone to think they're under attack."

Beau nodded in agreement. It would take longer, but his reasoning was sound, so we all piled in the SUV.

An hour later, we were at the fire elemental refugee camp.

The camps were all the same. These were temporary living situations. Villagers were vigilant and ready to pack up and move out if the royals came stomping through. The villages were mini communities where all residents had a part to play. Powerful elementals served as elders in charge of organizing the chaos. Everyone in the community protected and provided for each other and cared for those who couldn't care for themselves.

Without access to the Source our powers weakened and for those who did not have as much, to begin with, it created a much greater concern. It was as if they practically became human.

Illnesses were commonplace and death followed quickly. Here at Smokestack, the numbers weren't as staggering as some, and I had a feeling Phin chose this village because of that. He didn't want Zara to become overwhelmed.

As suspected, they greeted Zara as though she were the Goddess herself. She handled the attention with aplomb and within fifteen minutes of being there, the entire village of thirty-two people was swearing loyalty to her.

Zara was a natural leader. She gathered necessary intel on power level, non-fighters, and any exotic strengths. She established a means of communication so they would be ready when the time came. And she even took note of their needs, which were mostly food and healing. The reluctant princess had promised to do what she could, and I saw the determination in her eyes to keep her word.

After leaving the fire elementals, Phin drove down a dirt road and stopped at a fork. "We have two choices. Drive down the mountain to an earth elemental camp." He pointed left.

"Or drive up to an air elemental hideout." He pointed right.

"Let's pay a visit to the nearest air elemental village. We need flyers. Then the earth elementals. We need to stabilize our ground troops," Zara said.

"Bad idea, princess. Air elementals hate me," Patrick said with a roll of his eyes.

"Perhaps we need to change their mind about that." She kept her voice light and turned to offer him a friendly smile.

Patrick scoffed. "I'd rather not." He tapped on the back of Phin's headrest and said, "I'll get out and meet you back at the healing village."

"No. If there's a problem, let's deal with it. Right now." Zara gave him a hard stare.

Shit.

"Pffttt." Patrick tried opening the door, but it wouldn't budge. "Unlock the damn door."

The door was unlocked, and Patrick got out.

"Seriously guys, what is his problem? It's me, isn't it? Let me out," Zara said. She was sitting between Phin and Beau in the front and neither was willing to let her go.

"Let's go to the air village. He can meet us there or not. You're right, Z. We need air flyers, so let's just get the process rolling." Beau's tone was calm, but I could see the frown that marred his face through his reflection on the window.

"He's right. Patrick will come around," I offered, although I wasn't sure what his problem was.

Phin turned the SUV right and made the slow trek up the mountain. No one uttered a single word for a bit until Zara broke the silence.

"Wait, no. This is not right. We have to do this with him." She looked at Phin, and he slowed the car.

"Don't worry about it, Z. He's just got some issues." I shrugged even though she couldn't see me. I wasn't sure what to do about the situation, but his attitude had turned sour ever since Silk City. We'd have to confront him soon before things got out of control.

Zara turned in her seat to face me. "No. I will not, not worry about it. We all need to work together, and he's a part of this, isn't he?"

The three men in the car offered grunts and nods in response.

"Stop the car, Phin. Please? I just need a minute," she asked the fire elemental behind the wheel.

"I won't fly off. I promise." Her voice was soft, pleading almost.

He stopped the car and we all got out.

Zara paced around the SUV, then stopped to face the three men.

"I feel like Trick has a problem with my being here. Has he said anything to either of you?" she asked.

We all shook our heads. Patrick could be reclusive, and it had always been a chore getting him to communicate.

"I'm not sure what to make of this situation with Trick, but, as I said earlier, I have no intention of becoming queen or staying here in the kingdom. Whatever my sister and her husband have been up to is not right. My goal is to help free the Source so that our people can thrive. But I am leaving." Zara continued.

"We talked about this, Zara. I am ok with whatever you're willing to give," Phin placed a kiss on her forehead.

"I agree with Phin, Zara. I'm happy that you're here and wouldn't want it any other way." Beau wrapped her in his arms.

Once he let her go, I stepped up to face her. "Zara." I blew out a breath. "You may not want to hear this, but the truth is, I lost you once and I will not lose you again. I am staying by your side through this fight to save our people and after that...I will follow you wherever you go. I don't even care about staying here."

Her eyes glistened, and she threw her arms around my middle. I kissed the top of her head. She was my first love, my only love. I was ok to share her with whomever. But I refused to let her go ever again.

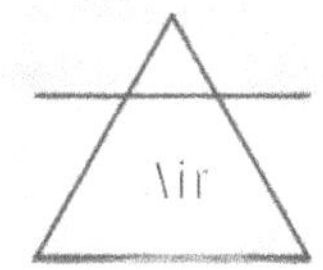

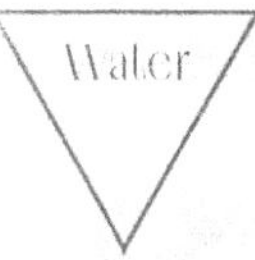
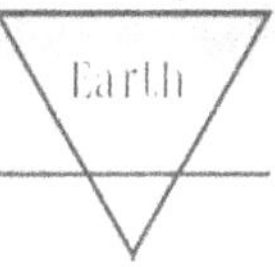

Chapter Twenty-Six

ZARA

Cassian's revelation made me misty-eyed. As children we were inseparable and out of everything in the kingdom, I had missed him the most.

I held him tightly and hid my face in his chest. I didn't want to cry in front of the guys.

"We've got company," Phin said behind me.

I released Cass and turned to see Phin and Beau looking up at the sky. I raised my hand to shield my eyes from the sun and noticed a cluster of black dots heading our way. From the distance, it seemed to be a flock of birds, but they were moving too fast.

Within minutes, eight powerful air elementals reached us and floated gracefully down to the ground. The tallest of the group approached us with a scowl on his face. Beau and Cassian stood on either side of me and slightly in front. Phin strode closer to meet our visitors.

As the air elemental got closer, my eyes widened. He was the spitting image of Trick. They could have been identical twins.

"Storm, just the man I was looking for." Phin extended his hand.

The air elemental shook his hand and the corner of his lips turned up in a slight smile. "Phineas, I thought maybe my brother was finally coming to make amends, but I see he's not with you."

Storm glanced behind Phin, and then his eyes met mine. He tilted his head, and his expression softened. "Zara Cavendish," he whispered. "Is it really you?" He walked around Phin and came towards me.

"Princess." Storm knelt and bowed his head. "Storm Lockwood, at your service."

The formality in his tone and gesture made me uncomfortable. Everything about his demeanor indicated he had been a loyal guard to the royal family. "I'm not your princess," I muttered.

"You are the true heir. I dedicate my life to yours and will dispatch the usurpers that have unjustly taken your throne."

Oh brother. That was a bit much. It took everything in me to refrain from rolling my eyes. I had to handle it with some grace.

"Your life is your own, brave loyal warrior. Rise, please. If we are to dispatch the usurpers together, treat me as your equal." That was the best I could come up with.

Gently, I tugged his hand until he stood, but he kept his chin to his chest. If I had to guess he had been one of Zander's knights from way back when the warriors of the kingdom bowed constantly to him. I tipped his chin up to meet his eyes.

"I appreciate your loyalty to the former king, Storm Lockwood. However, you don't need to treat me with the same deference." I smiled at him, and he visibly relaxed.

He was about to say something, but I held up my hand. "Before you say anything more, do not call me princess. Zara will do just fine."

His face bunched up as though he ate something sour, and it almost made me laugh.

"Pleased to meet you again, Zara. I remember you and this one, running around the palace halls as children." He jutted out his chin toward Cassian. "It is good to have you back. These are my men."

He introduced us to the seven airmen behind him. We walked a short distance into the woods to sit under shaded trees, and Phin proceeded to tell him of our plans.

"We are happy to assist you prin...Zara. But, keep my half-brother far away from my people." Storm scowled.

What is with these Lockwood men and their drama? Trick explained what happened with his father and the council that ordered his banishment from their clan. He had acted severely, but it didn't warrant this kind of animosity. At least not to me. I decided to allow Storm to speak his peace.

"Explain please," I implored.

"My father was killed because of his second nature." Storm stood from the rock he had been sitting on and paced in our small circle.

I waved my hand at Beau, Cass, and Phin, and then said, "We're all two-natured, Storm. You will ally yourself with us, but not your kin?"

"That's not it. He retaliated and killed good men. He should have come to me before acting so rashly." With a defeated look, Storm sat back down on a rock.

He'd lost his father, and someone close to him had died as well. Shit.

I got up and sat on a rock across from him. "Your father was killed for protecting his son. Protection he shouldn't have needed from those supposedly good men. Amina and her husband have been using human weapons against our people. We need every available elemental, two-natured, or four in my case. We have to set our differences aside and work together. That has been the way of this kingdom since its inception. These are hard times, Storm. Find it in your heart to forgive him so that we can fight together and win."

"You are a true leader, Zara Cavendish. I will do as you say. After all, if you can forgive your father, then I too can forgive my brother." Storm stared into my eyes.

Aw, shit.

"That's a different issue," I muttered. I couldn't flat-out lie and say I forgave my father. I wasn't even close to forgiving him.

Storm quirked an eyebrow at me.

"My situation is different from yours." I raised my chin.

"He killed my wife's father and left our clan leaderless then he took off and hasn't been by once to check on our people." He met my stare.

Aw shit, this elemental was going to challenge me every chance he got.

"I was a child when I was banished, then kidnapped to help save the kingdom, and my father hasn't apologized for any of it," I retorted.

"Forgiveness is forgiveness, Zara." Cassian chimed in.

Ass. I glared over my shoulder at him. Whose side was he on, anyway? And to think just a few moments ago he was my favorite. If he wasn't so hot I'd punch him in the nose.

Cass gave me his boyish lopsided grin. I bit the inside of my cheek to keep myself from smiling back. There was no way I could stay mad at him.

Storm gave me a genuine smile that reminded me so much of the Trick I had loved when I was fifteen years old.

I sighed. "My father and I have a long road to forgiveness, but I am trying. At some point, I'll get there. But I won't lie to you or make false promises. And I wouldn't expect that of you either."

"Patrick is the only family I have left. Shortly after my father's death, the current royals killed my wife and my two children. I would also like to make amends with him." Storm placed his hand over mine and squeezed.

Storm left to speak with what was left of the Zephyr clan, a total of twenty-six people with twelve avid flyers. The king and queen had killed more than half of his clan. They were ready to avenge their loved ones.

As we had done with the Smokestack clan, we planned on meeting again at a neutral location to discuss how we'd take back the kingdom, starting with the Source.

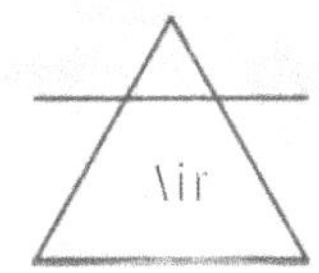

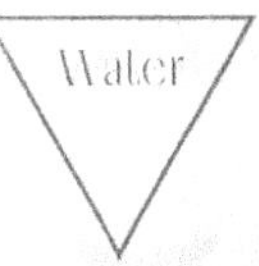

Chapter Twenty-Seven

ZARA

I t was well past midday, but I had insisted on stopping at the earth village. We were near enough, and the village Grant was in was on our way back to the lair.

The Terra village was a sizable farming community. According to Beau, the people had founded this village not even a year ago which was impressive considering the abundance of food they had been able to cultivate from the lands. It seemed this part of the kingdom was not affected by whatever had plagued the villages nearest to the Source. Before Amina and Issac had taken over, the land nearest to the Source had been more fertile. Now it was the opposite.

The people of Terra were wary of us at first until Beau and I showed them our earth magic. We used our gifts to help stimulate their crops of wheat, corn, and newly planted fruit trees. And Cassian helped by using his water magic to direct the flow of water, and Phin used his fire to meld metal tools to make harvesting much easier.

These were simple people, and there were many children, even more than in the healing village. When I asked the elders where all the parents were they informed me that most had been killed or captured.

The able-bodied men and women were not fighters, but they knew the lay of the land and would be essential to help us find the most suitable route for the army we had hoped to amass. Most importantly, they had offered to open their doors to anyone needing a new home and were more than willing to supply food should any clan need it.

We stayed longer than intended, but left with another ally, and we made our way to the healing village. The drive was long. It would have been quicker to fly, but that was something Cassian hadn't tried yet. According to him, he was comfortable shifting into two animal forms, a lion or a wolf. He transformed into other animals but was most comfortable in those two. And as of yet, he hadn't chosen an animal that could fly. He'd have to give that a try, which he was excited to do.

Beau on the other hand could put up portals, but not one large enough for the SUV. At least not yet. Both he and Cass had some studying to do. And I could use more training with my magic as well. Having been exiled at fourteen, my magic training had been incomplete. And with the passing of my nursemaid, there were no other tutors available to me. Magic usage for me was solely based on instinct.

It wouldn't hurt for me to do a little homework of my own. I rarely used my magic in Silk. There was no need and, moreover, my magic weakened over the years. Here in the kingdom it was spewing out of my pores, and restraining it could be disastrous.

Once we reached the healing village, we went straight to see Grant. Beau's sister Rosemary had been checking on him regularly and reported that he was healing up quickly. She also insisted that he be let out for some time to get exercise.

Grant gave us every detail of the encampment at the Source. It was well-guarded, and they had far more numbers and weapons than we initially thought. The royals were expanding their reach far into the eastern quadrants. It was ascertained the best way to find the refugees would be to go in search of them ourselves. The fastest way to the eastern quadrant was going straight across, right through the palace. Going by sea would take months. Beau would be able to put up portals, but as Phin pointed out, we didn't want unsuspecting villagers to think they were under attack.

After speaking with Grant, we went in search of the elders to convey what we had learned. I let the men handle those discussions while I went to check on the other villagers.

Raven was feverish and pale and not faring so well. Beau's mother said she was fighting an infection, and they were doing all they could for her. Rocko stayed by her side, refusing to eat or play with the other children. I was able to coax him out for a time, but he seemed content to stay by my side.

Ivy sat next to us while he ate, and I hoped he found a new friend.

The children were gathered in the communal area for storytime. I stayed with them until Rocko started nodding off. I set him down on the cot beside his mother, and then went to find the men.

I was beat. It was time for us to go home. As we drove, I kept thinking about Trick. He and his brother were so different, just as Amina and I had been. Now even more so. I wondered what he had been up to all day. I needed to figure out a way to make amends, even though I had done nothing wrong. It just didn't sit well making all these plans without him.

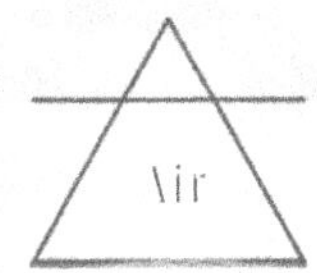

Chapter Twenty-Eight

ZARA

Phin helped me out of the car, then swooped me up in his arms. "I can walk," I said wearily.

"Yes, you can. But this way I can hold you close." His voice was tired. We'd had a long but productive day.

He set me down on the ledge of the bathtub and then left, giving me privacy to bathe and get ready for bed.

Feeling refreshed after taking a hot shower, I found Beau, Cass, and Phin waiting in the bedroom. A table had been brought in and was covered with delicious-smelling food.

"Oh, I didn't know you were all waiting," I said.

"We weren't waiting long, angel. We all freshened up as well, and Patrick should be joining us soon," Phin replied. "Come here, Z." Cass held out a chair for me. "You must be starving. You haven't eaten much all day."

That was true. The Terra villagers had fed us fruit, but we were all so busy doing what we could to help them we hadn't eaten an actual meal since breakfast.

Cass placed a kiss on the top of my head when I sat. A moment later Phin leaned over and kissed my neck while Beau grabbed one of my hands and kissed my knuckles.

I blushed at their sweet gestures and reveled in the feeling of being cherished until Trick entered. He leaned against the doorway, scowling at the three of us. I stood, concerned something bad had happened and approached him warily.

"Is everything ok?" I reached out to touch his hand.

Trick jerked away from me and staggered a bit. He seemed drunk. Had he been drinking all day?

"I'm fine. Seems like you are doing more than fine. Three men, huh? Is that your thing now? One's not enough so you need to take three between your legs. Well, news flash, I won't be the fourth." He sneered down at me.

Did he just slut shame me? Fuck that noise. I punched him in the face. "Get the fuck out, Patrick. And never speak to me like that again."

"I'm sorry, Zara. I...I'm not myself." He pressed his hand to his cheek.

I turned my back on him, walked back to the table and braced a hand on the back of the chair where I had been sitting.

He muttered more apologies, and then I heard footsteps leading out towards the hallway.

"I'd rather be alone," I said in a small voice. "Please."

Trick's' words cut deep. I didn't have the strength in me to keep the tears at bay. But Beau, Cass, and Phin didn't say a word.

From behind me, Cass wrapped his arms around my body. Beau knelt in front of me and rested his head on my belly. Phin stood beside me and stroked my cheek.

"We'd rather not leave your side right now. We won't. You don't have to speak. Just come sit, and have some wine," Phin said.

The other two men released me, and I numbly followed Phin's lead. He moved past the table, and he grabbed a bottle of wine and led me to the balcony. Beau and Cass followed.

Phin climbed on the day bed and guided me to sit between his legs. I leaned back against his chest and stared absently at the night sky. Sparkly stars danced around the crescent moon and a soft cool breeze caressed my skin. I sighed and allowed the peacefulness of the valley to wash over me.

A blanket was draped over the front of my body, bringing me back to the present moment. "Thank you. You guys don't need to stay. I'm good."

"No, Z, you need to eat, and besides this is where we want to be." Cass handed me a cup of wine.

I took a huge gulp of wine, and another. Then I reached for the bottle and refilled my cup.

"Do you want to talk about it?" Beau asked as he settled on the day bed. Surprisingly, it was large enough for all of us with room to spare.

I shook my head, polished off my second cup of wine, and poured another. Cass eyed me then said, "I'll go get another bottle."

Cass returned with more wine and a cart filled with food.

"You need to eat, angel," Phin whispered in my ear.

I shook my head. "I'm not hungry. But you should eat." I moved out of his way so he could get a plate of food.

Phin fixed himself a heaping plate then he sat back, and I snuggled against his side. Cass and Beau assembled their plates, and we all sat on the daybed. As the men ate, we went over what we had learned thus far. We had allies and had formulated a tentative plan.

It felt wrong to discuss all of this without Trick present, but damn it, he had gone too far. Every time he entered my thoughts, I drank more wine.

"I don't think we have enough time to head east no matter which route we choose. From what Grant had told us, the royals are picking up momentum," Beau said between bites.

"Is there a way to relay a message to someone on that side of the kingdom? Someone we can trust?" I sneaked a bite of steak from Cass's plate. Mmm...Linc did good work.

"Honestly, Storm may have contacts. He was in the royal guard before me and has more connections," Phin replied.

"I agree, he may also have a way to reach his brothers in arms. And we should do the same." Beau added. He buttered a slice of soft freshly baked homemade bread and handed it to me.

I smiled at him gratefully and took a bite.

"I can also go down to the coast and pass on missives through the ocean. I have cousins that would happily help. I don't think anyone would believe that you're with us though." Cass looked at me. "Unless they saw you in the flesh." He fed me another bite of steak. I really needed to get my own plate of food.

I stood to get up and do just that, but Cass blocked me. "It pleases us to care for you, Zara."

Oh no, this was weird. But the men around me all just shook their heads.

"Just for tonight, angel. I promise it won't be weird." Phin held out a fork full of veggies, and I bit into it. All the wine had made me hungry and well, it felt good to be pampered.

"Thank you, all of you," I said with my mouth full.

"Excuse me."

The guys chuckled.

"I love how casual you are." Cass laughed. "You're so different than when we were children."

"You are certainly not like any royal I've ever been around." Phin kissed my cheek.

"I especially love how much you curse," Beau added.

"Thank you for noticing. I made it a point to establish an unrefined vocabulary since I am no longer a princess." I giggled and guzzled more wine.

It was rude and very un-princess-like behavior. The former queen would roll over in her grave if she saw how uncouth I'd become. It made me want to behave even more unseemly.

"Seriously though," I said as the wine worked its magic. "I know we need numbers, but perhaps, we can send in a small contingent and take out the mage. That should release the spell everyone is on."

"It's worth a shot. We just need a way in," Beau added.

We had finished eating but sat outside and continued drinking. The business talk subsided, and we spent the rest of the night getting to know one another. The guys were openly affectionate with me, which I returned in kind. The wine had lowered my inhibitions. Despite what Patrick had said earlier, I was proud of my sensuality.

At some point I was sitting between Phin's legs with my back against his chest, his fingers trailing up and down my arm. Now and then his lips grazed my shoulders. Cassian sat opposite us and massaged my foot. Beau lay on the bed, using Phin's leg as a pillow.

I reached out and ran my hand through Beau's thick locks and accidentally dribbled wine down my chin and chest.

"Oops." I sat up and raised my hand to wipe away the wine, but Cassian leaned over and licked up the mess I'd made.

I closed my eyes while Cass rolled his tongue over my jaw, then my neck, and my chest. Phin stiffened beneath me, and Beau moaned.

Cass's lips found mine, and I leaned into his kiss, savoring the taste of wine from his tongue.

"You've had plenty to drink." Cass drew away from me.

I nodded. My nipples were hard, and moisture pooled between my legs.

Someone took the glass of wine I was still holding and set it aside. I opened my eyes to see Beau on his knees, staring at me with half-hooded eyes. Phin ran his hand down my back, his natural heat seeping through my tank top, and I arched into his touch.

"Angel," Phin purred in my ear. "We all want you. But perhaps not tonight. It's been a long day, and you've had a lot of wine."

I shook my head, wanting to seduce the three men, and the world around me swayed a little. Maybe Phin was right.

But they were all so hot. It was practically criminal to let all those muscles go to waste. I just had to see them all naked.

Phin chuckled behind me. *Did I just say all that out loud?*

No, of course not. I'm not that drunk.

Cass laughed. "She's definitely had too much to drink."

Beau stood up with a boyish grin and offered me his hand.

"Come on, beautiful, time for bed."

I stood up and wobbled. Beau braced a hand on my waist and helped me walk a relatively straight line to the bed, which gave me the giggles.

The three men followed me into the room, and I gave them my seductive walk, swaying my hips suggestively. Wine sloshed around in my brain, muddling my thoughts, and had me stumbling onto the bed ungracefully, sending me into another fit of giggles.

Sexy walk, epic fail. Drunk walk, perfect ten.

I made it onto the bed without falling over, still determined to get some. I tore off my top and unclasped my bra, freeing my breasts. The men groaned. I sat at the edge of the mattress, resting my butt on my heels and beckoned them to join me. They were so beautiful, all three of them.

Cass stood in front of me at the edge of the bed. I slipped my hands into his T-shirt, running my fingers over the hard ridges of his stomach. I grazed over his nipples, and he drew in a sharp intake of breath. He leaned down and captured my lips with his. I pulled at the hem of his T-shirt desperate to get it off.

I want to lick every inch of those hard abs. I thought to myself.

I kissed Cass from his navel to his chest and somehow got my head tangled in his T-shirt. He chuckled, lifted his shirt, freeing my head, and released me into Beau's arms.

Beau was shirtless and wearing sweats that did nothing to hide his erection.

I love sweatpants.

The men chuckled. I rubbed my cheek over the swollen member straining to be free of the material. Suddenly I was hungry. I pulled on the drawstring which would not budge. The darn thing was giving me trouble. It was kind of like a damn constrictor knot. *What the hell is he keeping so secure in there?* I fumbled with the stupid knot.

"I got this, Z." Beau placed his hand over mine and stepped away letting Phin take his place.

I stared into Phin's golden gaze and licked my lips.

Damn this man literally lit my pants on fire without using his magic.

He chuckled.

Shit did I say that out loud? Have I been voicing my dirty thoughts out loud this entire time?

"Yes," Cass mumbled behind Phin. I shrugged and moved to unbutton Phin's jeans. He cupped my face with his warm hands and lightly brushed my lips with his.

"Lie back, angel," Phin gently pushed me away from him, and I slowly reclined on the mattress.

Yeah, that's what I'm talking about. I did as I was told.

Once my head hit the pillow the room started to spin, and I bolted straight up.

"I think I'm going to be sick." I hopped off the bed and ran to the bathroom.

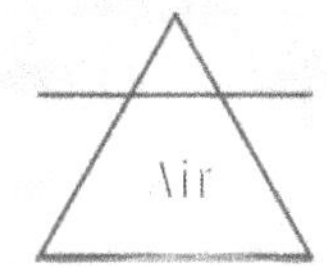

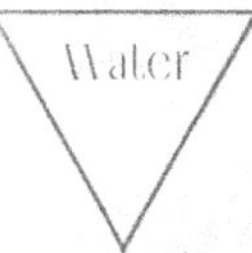
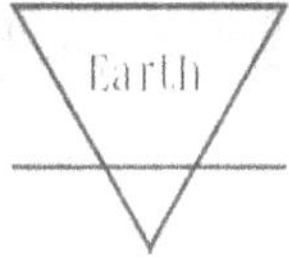

Chapter Twenty-Nine

ZARA

I woke the next morning with a headache. Slowly I sat up, massaging my temples, and cursed the wine gods.

"Wine and I are no longer friends," I muttered to myself.

Cassian chuckled, and I glared at him with one eye.

"Not funny," I grumped, then the events of the night before flooded my consciousness. "Oh my Goddess, I hope I didn't embarrass myself."

The smell of coffee gave me hope, and I was grateful to see Beau at the foot of the bed with a big grin on his face.

"You didn't embarrass yourself." Beau handed me a steaming cup of coffee. "But you do make one sexy drunk."

He kissed my forehead as I blew into the coffee mug.

"You were adorable, Z. We need to get you drunk more often." Cass leaned over and kissed my temple as I sipped my coffee.

"And all the guys have decided to wear sweatpants and only sweatpants from here on out," Beau added.

I coughed, choking on my coffee.

Cass gently patted my back, while he and Beau got a good laugh.

"Remind me never to get drunk around you all ever again," I said when I recovered. My cheeks flamed hot.

I remembered clearly stating how much I loved sweats and everything else I did. I wanted to burn those memories from my brain, and I wanted to savor them as well. Despite my shameful display of seductive drunkenness, they had been complete gentlemen. They'd held up my hair and cleaned up my mess. You know a man loves you when he takes care of you as you puke your guts out and then wakes the next morning to tell you were adorable and sexy. And I had three of them. My heart swelled like a big ole happy balloon. I practically floated off the bed.

Beau chuckled. "Drink your coffee, Zara, I figured you'd need it. It's a special brew guaranteed to cure hangovers."

"Thanks." I smiled at both of them over the rim of my coffee mug.

Beau leaned over and planted kisses from my elbow up to my shoulders, while Cass moved my hair and kissed my neck. Goosebumps blossomed all over my flesh. I tilted my head, allowing them to kiss away my hangover and my embarrassment.

My coffee cup tilted but Cass braced it before it toppled over.

"Drink, Zara, it will help you feel better." Beau's voice was low and raspy.

I took a big gulp, and then Phin grunted and rolled over.

"Time is it? Is that coffee?"

"Time to get up," Cass said. "And you need to get your own coffee. Beau made something special for Z."

I smiled at the sleepy fire elemental and leaned over to peck him on the cheek.

"That's all I get?" He frowned as I climbed off the bed.

"For now." I blew him a kiss and went to the bathroom.

By the time I finished my morning routine, my foggy brain had cleared, and the guys weren't in bed anymore. I grabbed the phone Thadd had given me and went to the kitchen while reading his text asking me to call him.

Beau, Cass, and Phin were sitting at the kitchen counter drinking coffee and having breakfast, but not Trick. I frowned at his empty seat. My happy mood turned sour. Was he still pouting? I stomped out of the kitchen and went in search of his room.

It wasn't hard to find. Down the hallway that housed guest rooms one door was closed with a note tacked to the door. My name was scribbled on the parchment.

I snatched the note and then knocked on the door. There was no answer and so I opened it and peered in. It was empty. No Trick and no personal belongings. Odd. I sat on the bed to read the note.

Dearest Zara,

I thought I could do this...be around you again without expectation. I thought I could be ok if I had to share you with the others. But I can't. I love you so much. I want you all to myself. As always. I shouldn't have left you when I did. I blame myself. And I will regret that decision for the rest of my days. You deserve to be loved Zara. You are truly a treasure. I just don't want to witness you being happy without me. I know that you will succeed in freeing the Source. I wish I were man enough to see you through this, but I am not. I am sorry for the harsh words I left you with and for leaving you again. I hope you can forgive me.

Yours forever, Trick

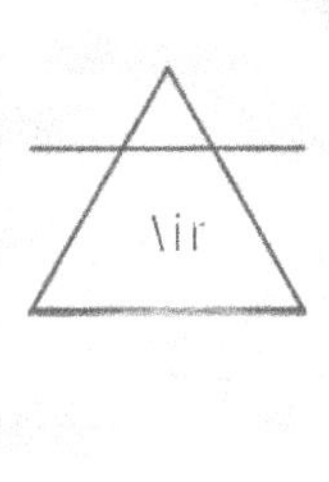

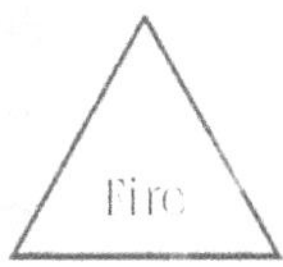

Chapter Thirty

ZARA

S on of a bitch! Fucking Patrick Lockwood left via note...again. He didn't even have the balls to tell me to my face.

I clenched my fist, crumpling the note, furious with how Patrick had left things. Was it too much to ask for him to be upfront with me once in his life? Tears pricked my eyes, but I refused to let them fall.

Beau, Cass, and Phin came in and found me pacing.

"Zara?" Phin's voice was laced with concern. "What happened?"

I threw the note at him and continued pacing while the three men read Trick's goodbye letter.

"What can we do Zara? How can we make this easier for you?" Beau asked.

"I cannot believe he did this to me, again! He has the fucking nerve to say he loves me, and then walk out. You know what? That's not love!"

The three men said nothing as I continued ranting.

"Who says I love you and I never want to see you again in a fucking note! Couldn't he have the decency to at least say it to my face? I gave him a pass the first time; we were kids. But now, he's almost thirty years old! After all this time, did he expect me to wait for him? Did he expect me to run into his arms, begging to pick up where we left off thirteen years ago? No! Just no!" I blew out a frustrated breath.

"I was more than willing to put the past behind us and do this mission. I was even willing to forget the nasty shit he said to me yesterday. But this...this is unforgivable." Anger, frustration, and hurt rolled through me.

This place had turned out to be one emotional roller coaster after the other. Why was I putting myself through this? Was it worth the drama? Deep down I knew the answer, which was why I chose to drop off Gigi and return. But damn that man.

I shook my head. Was it my fault? I felt a physical attraction toward all of them. Was that manipulative? The last thing I wanted was to break up their brotherhood. In my book that was just as bad as breaking up a marriage. I stopped pacing and faced the three men.

"Answer me honestly. Is my being here causing a divide between the four of you? Would this mission be better without me?"

"No," the three men said at the same time.

"Perhaps I should go back to Silk, so that Trick can come home and work on this with you," I said ignoring their response. "Zara." Phin scrubbed a hand down his face. "The truth is, before we brought you here..."

"Kidnapped," I corrected.

Phin grimaced. "Before we kidnapped you, the four of us watched you for a few weeks. The more we watched you the more smitten we became. We confided in one another about how we felt. Patrick had told us of your relationship and how you refused him when he tried to make amends years later. He made it clear that he had let you go and would never stand in the way of your happiness. And that included us. If you wished to be with one of us or all of us or none of us, we were all in agreement that we'd be gentlemanly about the situation and give you whatever you wished."

He paused and then patted the bed for me to sit. I plopped my butt down next to him.

"As far as the mission goes," Phin grasped my hand and continued, "you are more essential to its success than any of us. We all know this."

"Zara, I know you don't want to be the Queen, but you inspire people without even trying. We won't win this without you. And if one or all of us need to go, so be it. But not you, never you." Cassian sat next to me and draped an arm over my shoulder. "As far as our brotherhood, when it comes to you we all agreed, just as Phin said."

Beau knelt in front of me and placed a hand on my knee. "Patrick has had a hard life. And he is often as hard on others as he is on himself."

"I've had a hard life as well, Beau." I interrupted. "That doesn't give me a license to take out my abandonment issues on everyone else. I'm not making light of everything he has gone through, but he can't keep using it as an excuse to walk away every time things don't go the way he wants them to go."

I rubbed the bridge of my nose. "I am well aware of my commitment and trust issues, which is why I'm always upfront when going into relationships. I wasn't lying to you all when I said I don't do love. That doesn't make it right, but at least I'm not stringing any one of you along and then leaving you high and dry with nothing but a shitty note."

"You're right, Z. I believe he will come around when he's ready. Right now, for whatever reason, this is too hard on him. Let's give him his space," Beau replied in a soft tone.

I let their words sink in for a minute. We were a team and Trick was a part of it. Although I knew Beau was right, if it were up to me I'd drag him back here by his hair. That would probably make things worse.

"Isn't he essential to our plans?" I asked. We needed him, and regardless of everything that had happened, I wanted him with us.

"Honestly, yes, but Storm could possibly fill in. I'll head over to see him," Phin offered.

I took a deep breath and then pressed the palms of my hand to my eyes. "Does he even have somewhere to go? This room looks empty to me."

As far as I knew the four men lived in this lair, and from what Storm had said they weren't on good terms, and they had no other family members.

The three men looked around the room, realizing it was empty.

Cassian opened what I had guessed was a closet. "Shit. He cleared out."

"Zara, we'll get to the bottom of this. I'm sure I'll be able to find him. For now, don't give it another thought," Phin told me.

"Why don't you take some time off, Z? It's been a rough couple of days." Cass rubbed my arm. "Maybe visit Gigi for a few hours?"

"That's a good idea. I can portal you in, then we," Beau pointed at Phin and Cass, "can visit Storm and the coastal villages."

"Shouldn't someone speak with Trick?" I asked.

"Yes." Phin nodded. "We'll go looking for him first. I think if we split up, we'll have a better chance of finding him. Go to Silk City, angel."

"Ok, Thadd did send a text this morning saying he wanted to talk. I'm guessing it has to do with the weapons thing I asked him about," I told them.

"Good. You can work on that angle, and we'll pick you up in a couple of hours." Cassian placed a kiss on my forehead.

"Just to be clear," I stood up and faced the three men. "I would rather leave than come in between your friendship. He's out there somewhere alone. That's not right."

"You're not coming between us, Zara. But I will bring him back so you and he can work this out." Phin gave me a small smile.

Before going to Silk, Beau and I stopped at the healing village to pick up more herbal remedies from Calla. I checked on Raven and Rocko. Thank Goddess, Raven was feeling better, and the infection had abated. She was awake, and her skin had a healthier hue. Rocko was also behaving more like a little boy than a distraught child.

Gigi was elated to see Beau and me. He checked Gigi's blood sugar and restored the remedies. She was also on the mend.

The earth healers were performing miracles and I couldn't be more grateful. After tending to my mother, Beau told her he had to go.

I knew he and the other guys wanted to search for Trick before going to see his brother. They figured it was best to bring him back into the fold before asking Storm for help.

Before putting up a portal, Beau asked for some privacy so I pulled him into my bedroom.

He had a somber look on his face, and I started to get nervous.

"Beau, is my mom ok? You look, dreadful," I asked.

"She's fine, Zara." Beau gave me a weak smile, which didn't reach his eyes.

"I thought something was wrong with my mom." I breathed out a sigh of relief.

This time his smile was genuine.

"I'm just reluctant to leave you here. I'm worried you may not want to come back because of Patrick. We all want you in our lives, even if it means sharing with each other and with your mage friend. We would rather share you, than chase you away. I don't want you to give up on us."

"Thaddeus? You guys have talked about Thadd?"

"Phin mentioned your insistence on keeping him in your life," Beau admitted. "I understand and would never expect you to choose between him and us. I know you love him."

"That is correct. I don't have any intention of sending him away. I miss him, and I plan on seeing him today," I said honestly. I wasn't ready to admit to loving Thadd, but the rest of what I said was the absolute truth.

"You don't have to explain or tell us every time you're with him." He twirled a strand of my hair between his fingers. "I saw you two together the night at the bar. You were standing between his legs, kissing, his hands on your ass. It was hot." He had a faraway look in his eyes that said pure lust.

"That didn't bother you, seeing me like that?" I asked.

"No, not at all. I haven't stopped thinking about you naked since." Beau's voice dripped over me like warm honey.

I stepped in closer, my nipples brushed up against his torso. His big hands roamed over my body from my shoulders down my arms. He slid them around my waist and inched up towards my breasts. My breath hitched.

Beau's hands slid under my shirt. He palmed my breasts, then bent to take my nipple into his mouth. I gripped his hair and did my best to stifle a pleasure filled moan.

His lips found mine, his tongue hot and urgent. I was hungry for more, but he suddenly released me.

"Someday, beautiful. Someday soon." He whispered in my ear.

He set up a portal and winked at me as he walked through to the other side.

I flopped on my bed. Beau's revelation gave me the fanny flutters, and I couldn't wait to explore his fantasies.

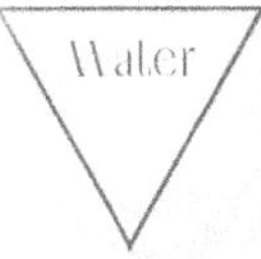

Chapter Thirty-One

ZARA

After Beau left, Gigi and I did some house cleaning, and then we went out to do some shopping. I even stopped at The Convent to give Magz a heads-up on what I was doing. I still had almost a week and a half off, but he was like a surrogate uncle, and it was only fair to keep him posted.

Thadd picked me up when Gigi went to her room for a nap.

We got some Chinese take-out and then headed back to his place.

"So, sounds like this vampire is the jealous type. What are you going to do?" Thadd asked after I told him the story about Trick.

We were in his living room in front of the television, our usual spot when we were at his house. I was sitting cross-legged on his sofa while Thadd sat next to me on the floor, with his back pressed up against the cushions.

Linc's cooking was delicious and healthy, but I had picked up a few bad eating habits from all the years living amongst humans. And after drinking my weight in wine, I needed the calories. At least I wasn't feasting on take-out burgers. Although that didn't sound so bad either.

"I'm not sure there's anything I can do. I don't like that he's out there all alone, and a part of me feels as though I should step away from them and the situation so he can go back home." I tipped my head back and slurped chow mein noodles.

"Hit me with some of that." Thadd leaned back, and I fed him some noodles.

After swallowing his food he said, "Well, I for one would love it if you forgot about that bullshit and come home. But you're needed there, and that guy needs to get over it. If he can't, fuck him."

"Hey, don't be mean," I replied.

"Baby, the guy is being a selfish prick. If he and the other guys talked about it and came to an agreement, then he should honor his word. Him skipping out like this means his word is worthless. He's letting his personal feelings keep him from completing a mission that affects count-less lives."

"Open." Thadd held a bite of orange chicken in front of my mouth. I bit into the sweet and sour goodness.

"Don't feel bad about him being on his own. He doesn't need to be. He chooses to be by himself. If he loved you, really loved you, he would be happy to see you happy." Thadd was facing me and I leaned over to peck his cheek.

Huh? I thought about Thadd's words for a moment, and he wasn't wrong. But for some reason, I still felt like a home wrecker.

"Give." Thadd pointed his chin at the container of food I was hold-ing. "You're not done are you?"

I shook my head and fed Thadd more noodles as requested.

Thadd spoke as he chewed. We were so comfortable with each other that it was hard not to smile. "Anyway, I don't like you being around that guy. A vampire with a ring that allows him to walk in sunlight is dangerous."

"Well, if he's truly gone, then I won't have to worry about it." I shrugged and continued eating.

"Not good enough, baby." Thadd wrapped his hand around my leg and kissed my knee. He glanced up at me for a second as I chewed.

I reached for a glass of water that was sitting on the end table beside me and sipped. "What?" I asked. He was staring at me with an odd look on his face.

Thadd knelt between my legs and unbuttoned my jeans.

"Umm...excuse me? I'm eating," I said.

"Lift," he said as he attempted to tug my jeans down.

I raised my hips too stunned to reply and too curious to stop whatever he had planned.

He shimmied my jeans off my legs, then sat back down, settling between my legs, and continued eating.

"What was that all about?" I asked, totally confused.

"I miss your skin." He popped a bite of orange chicken in his mouth and then rubbed his cheek on my bare knee.

"You're so strange," I pecked his cheek, and set my container of noodles on the floor beside him.

Thadd smiled back at me. "As I was saying, you need to be protected, baby."

"From Trick? How?" I asked and scratched his scalp with my nails.

He almost purred. "Not sure, but I will think of something. In the meantime, the weapons drop-off is in three days. As you can probably imagine, weapons dealers are unsavory characters, and they will expect their money. But if you're interested maybe we can hijack the weapons after the exchange."

"Oooh, I like that idea. Once the royal guards drop off the money and pick up the weapons, we'll take the weapons from them. Actually that could work. We'd have a way to get into the

Sanctuary since the guards there would be expecting a delivery."

"Good idea. You'll just need intel on how many guards and vehicles are expected to be here and info on where the weapons are supposed to be delivered." Thadd ran his hands over my calves to my knees.

"Are you done eating?" I asked.

"No, but I'm distracted." He peppered kisses on my knees.

I reached down and picked up a container of Chinese food and began feeding him while he was content with running his hands over my legs.

After our fill of takeout, Thadd knelt between my legs, facing me. He kissed the inside of my thighs sending a stream of shivers up my spine. I closed my eyes and let myself get lost in the sensations that buzzed all over my body.

"Thadd?" I moaned his name. "We um...probably shouldn't."

"Why not?" He pushed up my T-shirt and kissed my tummy. "Are you in love, Zara? Are you leaving me for good?" "Never." I leaned into his touch. It was the truth. I'd never tire of Thaddeus and could not imagine a life without him.

"Then why not? I'm willing to share." Thadd's deep voice slid through me like fine wine.

I didn't have a response for that. If he was willing to share and the elemental men were willing to share, who was I to argue with their reasoning? I pulled my T-shirt off completely and unclasped my bra.

"Beautiful." Thadd palmed my breasts, pinching each nipple. He suckled my breasts, then slid up to kiss my neck.

"Have you had sex with them?" Thadd whispered in my ears.

"No." I shook my head. "Not all of them."

"Mmhm. Let me guess. Fire." He kissed my jaw and I felt him begin to harden against my pelvis.

"How'd you know?" My voice was low and breathy.

"I know things." He shrugged. "Did you like it, baby? Did you like having his hot cock, in your pussy?"

My clit started pulsating. Thadd always had the best pillow talk. Desire rolled through me and I wanted him in me.

"Yes," I replied, my voice low and husky. "Does that turn

you on? Knowing someone else is fucking me?" Thadd groaned, his rock hard cock between my legs.

"I love it. You deserve to feel good, baby. I just wish I could watch." His teeth nipped my ear lobe.

I tangled my fingers through his hair and yanked, searching for his mouth. My tongue forced its way between his lips and swirled with his, over and under. Imagining Thadd watching while one or all of the guys used my body for their pleasure had my core slick with need. I dragged his T-shirt over his back, and he pushed his joggers down over his hips.

His cock bounced free, thick and veiny from restraining his passion. I fisted him with both hands and slathered his precum all over his head. He felt hot and heavy in my palms.

"I think you like the idea of me getting fucked by those men just as much as I do," I whispered in his ear and his cock jumped in my hands.

He tore my panties, shredding the lacy fabric. My pussy juices smeared all over the chair beneath me. He grabbed my hips and speared me with his hot length. My back bowed, jutting out my breasts. Thadd latched onto a nipple with his teeth while he plowed into me with intense thrusts. I clawed his arms, my pulse raced, my breathing ragged.

Thadd reached down to massage my clit and I shattered. My orgasm shuddered through my body. I gasped, trying to suck air into my lungs as Thadd pulled me off the couch. He brought me to my knees, flipped me around, bending me over the chair. I looked at him over my shoulder watching him stare at my exposed pussy while smearing my juices all over my legs. He sank two fingers in my tight entrance, and I moaned, rocking back and forth on his digits.

Pleasurable tingles escalated within me as I imagined he was watching me get fucked by another dick.

"Your cunt is so beautiful, Z. I want to see it being filled by a big cock, while you take another one in your mouth."

He replaced his fingers with his cock and shoved his slick fingers in my mouth.

"Just like that, baby." Thadd wrapped my hair around his fists while his thrusts became more and more fervent. He slid his fingers down my throat.

"Yes!" I screamed around his fingers, my body tightening, my second release not far.

An audible pop and hiss came from the entryway. Thadd covered my body with his and sent a blast of magic at the intruder.

"What the fuck? Dude, I almost killed you." Thadd started

moving his hips again. "You can either watch, join us, or get the fuck out."

What the shit? I raised my head to see who Thadd was talking to, and a portal winked out behind Beau.

"Beau?" I licked my lips.

His gaze fixed on my body and his cock stirred under his sweats. He didn't say a word, but he didn't leave either.

"I think he wants to watch us, baby. Maybe he'll even join us." Thadd cupped my breasts while I moved my hips over his cock.

Thadd kissed my jaw, and I angled my face to capture his lips. "You want him to watch, don't you? You want him to come closer."

"Yes." I kept my eyes on Beau, my entire body feverish.

"Closer."

Watching him watch me writhe under Thadd was a greater turn-on than I could ever imagine and I wanted more.

"She wants you closer, Beau." Thadd rocked back and forth gently.

Beau placed one foot in front of the other, keeping his eyes on me. I extended my hand as he got close. He grasped it and knelt beside me and Thadd.

I leaned back, sitting on Thadd's cock and ran my hand over Beau's chest up to his neck and brought his face close to mine.

"Is this ok?" I kissed along his jawline up to his ear.

He swallowed hard and nodded. His mouth found mine, and Thadd growled. His hips bucked pushing me up.

"You're ok with this, Zara?" Beau asked.

I nodded as Thadd kept fucking me with slow deliberate strokes.

"Yes. I want this. I want you to want this too." My voice was breathless. I was ready to come again.

"You're so beautiful, Z. So fucking gorgeous." Beau drank me in, his eyelids growing heavy.

"It feels so good. Thadd's cock feels so good." I hooked an arm around Thadd's neck.

"Your pussy feels fucking amazing, baby. And so beautifully wet." Thadd drew away from me a bit, and Beau hesitantly tracked his eyes toward my hips.

"You can look," I said to Beau. "I want you to." He leaned closer to Thadd.

"Oh fuck," He said in a low sultry voice. "You're drenched."

I grabbed his hand and pushed it between my legs. Massaging my clit with the heel of his palm. I cried out in pleasure, and Beau released his inhibitions.

He crashed his mouth to mine while his fingers ran along my pussy lips, grazing Thadd's cock that pumped in and out of me.

I tugged at his sweats and freed his cock. I smeared his precum over my hand, using it as a glide, to stroke over the velvety taut skin.

"Suck his cock," Thadd demanded as he moved our bodies so that I was on all fours and at the perfect angle for Beau to feed me his length.

His sweet, salty shaft slid through my mouth and tapped the back of my throat. I braced my hands on his thighs while Thadd gripped my hips and he continued to pump into me.

I felt so full, complete. Suckling noises accompanied our groans.

A warm trickle of magic slid down my spine to my ass. I startled and released Beau with a pop and glanced back at Thadd.

"Does my magic feel good, baby?" Thadd asked me, as his magic massaged the forbidden hole.

I gasped and dug my nails into Beau's legs. My body began to shake, my climax just moments away. I held back, not wanting this moment to end too soon.

Beau fisted my hair and fed me his cock. I was completely filled again, and Thadd's magic massaged and prodded, making me buck against him. Beau wasn't about to be outdone. His magic slid around my throat, down to my breasts, kneading and pinching at my nipples.

Thrilling sensations of pleasure overwhelmed me. I shook all over. My pussy clenched, everything went taut, and I shattered into a million pieces.

Thadd didn't stop nor did Beau. Both men pumped, relentlessly chasing their release. Thadd lost control and came with a guttural grunt. His thrusts didn't stop, and my body rocked fucking Beau with my mouth. I looked up at the earth elemental, peering at him through my lashes and he let go. His warm seed hit the back of my throat and leaked from my mouth.

His chest heaved as he released me. I licked my lips, swallowing every trace of cum, and both men groaned.

Thadd pulled me up to sit on his lap. He kneaded my breasts. "I love you," he whispered.

He kissed my shoulders, my neck and he consumed my lips. Licking, and sucking the last traces of Beau's seed.

Beau hissed, and I opened my eyes while kissing Thadd, gauging his reaction. He gripped his cock mesmerized by what he was witnessing.

I wasn't done. And neither were my men.

Beau gently cupped my knees and spread them apart, placing my legs on the outside of Thadd's and giving him a full view of my filled pussy. He traced small circles around my clit making me quiver.

Thadd moaned with me, his cock hardening again as my walls squeezed him tight.

Beau licked my nipples as Thadd palmed my breasts, then trailed kisses down over my belly and he kept going lower. His lips hovered over my clit, and I quivered.

Both Thadd and I stared down at the earth elemental with anticipation.

"I want to lick your cum." Beau looked up at me and his tongue darted over my sensitive nub.

I raised my hips, allowing him to nibble my swollen clit while exposing Thadd's shaft and Beau's tongue laving over my clit and brushing against Thadd's hard cock.

My nails dug into Thadd's arms, and my writhing became more frantic. Thadd hissed. His grip on my breasts tightened.

Beau slid his tongue over my pussy lips, grazing Thadd's shaft, and sending us into another frenzy.

"Not yet, beautiful. I want you to come in my mouth." Beau pinched my clit.

"I'm ready." I panted.

Beau pulled me off Thadd, laid me on the floor, and devoured my pussy. His tongue traced every sensitive nerve ending with exquisite pressure. He moaned, creating a perfect vibrating sensation on my clit.

With my head in Thadd's lap, I angled my face and sought to stuff him in my mouth. He moved my hair out of my face and brought his tip to my lips. I rolled my tongue over his head, savoring the taste of our essence. And then I exploded all over Beau's tongue.

My body spasmed, the aftershocks rocking through me, and I thought I had enough. But Beau pulled my face away from Thadd's cock, saliva dripping all over my face, and kissed me hard, while he threaded his cock into my pussy.

"Fuck," Thadd grunted.

Beau released my lips and kept fucking me. "Zara, you're so damn tight. I won't be able to last long."

I locked my mouth over Thadd's cock and sucked his tip while stroking his length.

My body was overwhelmed with pleasure. My cunt tingled, my clit pulsed, and my entire body trembled. There was so much all at once and I was there for it. I wanted these men to provide me with endless pleasure and for them to use my body for theirs.

Beau growled with a final thrust at the same time as Thadd spurted all over my face and chest.

Our breathing was ragged. My body was completely useless. If it were possible to sink further into the ground, I would have.

Beau peppered me with kisses, murmuring sweet adoring words. When he released my body, Thadd picked me up and carried me to the bathroom to clean up. Both men had to hold me upright in the shower. I leaned on one while the other soaped me, then leaned on the other while the other rinsed me off. They toweled me dry and placed me in the middle of the bed where I passed out.

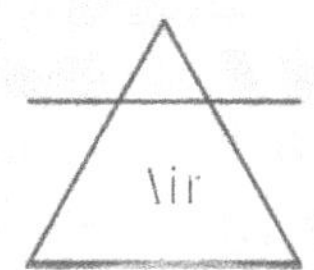

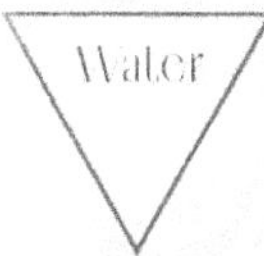

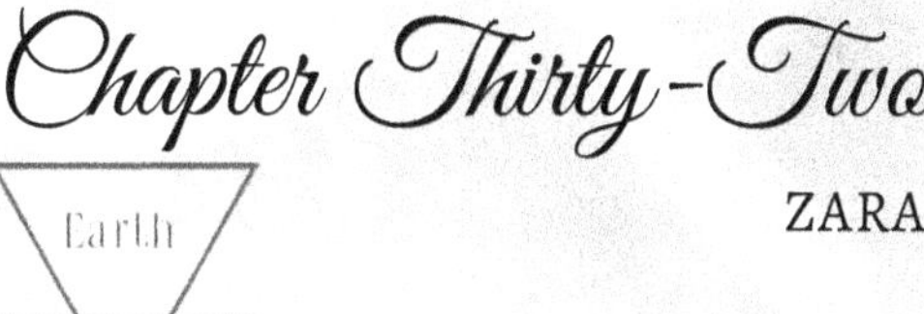

Chapter Thirty-Two

ZARA

The sound of voices coming from downstairs woke me. I was completely useless after my sex marathon with Thaddeus and Beau and had curled up on Thadd's bed for a short nap. Who would've thought the two magic wielders in my life would be into group sex? I was the luckiest woman alive.

I took my time getting myself together and walked downstairs to find Thadd, Beau, Cass, and Phin lounging in the living area.

"She wakes." Cass stood and greeted me with a kiss.

I returned the gesture and asked, "Why didn't someone wake me?"

"You haven't been sleeping long, baby," Thadd said.

"And we just arrived," Phin said as I pecked his cheek.

"Beau put up the portal for us about thirty minutes ago."

I kissed Beau on his temple as I passed him and then sat on the arm of the chair where Thadd was sitting.

"Any news from Patrick?" I asked.

Phin grimaced. "No, sorry, Zara, we couldn't find him."

My shoulders sagged. "Ok. What did I miss?" I couldn't go on worrying about him.

"I told them about the weapons delivery and your idea about using it as a way to get into the sanctuary." Thadd slid me over to sit on his lap.

"It's a good idea, Z. We just need to get more details from Grant." Cassian smiled at me.

"If you need help, let me know," Thadd offered.

"We may take you up on that," Phin told him then he stood. "We need to get back to the lair and start planning. You're welcome to join us, Thadd. This way you'll see the lair and be able to teleport in whenever you need to."

Mages and their teleporting gifts. They were so lucky. I had access to all four elements of air, fire, water, and earth. It was a unique gift amongst the kingdom as a whole but not so amongst my Cavendish ancestors. I had a great, great, great grandsire that had access to all elements as well as druid magic.

In the kingdom, the fifth element often referred to as spirit or universe was rare. It was said mage or druid magic had come from the fifth element. I never tried accessing spirit magic. It was something worth looking into.

I glanced at Thadd to see how he'd react to Phin's offer. It pleased me to see the elementals accepting him, and we could surely use his help.

"Thank you, but I have some business to take care of. Call me later, babe." Thadd tipped his head up to me.

"Yes, of course." I kissed his temple and rose to stand near Phin.

When we returned to the lair, I went to my room to freshen up and went to the kitchen, where Linc was placing platters of food on the dining room table. I picked up a large bowl of salad and a matching bottle of salad dressing and took them to the table. Linc scowled at me, which I openly ignored.

"Lady Zara! It is my job to serve you." He placed his hand on his hip.

"Perhaps, and no one would deny that you do incredible work. But around me, family always helps each other out, even if it's just bringing food to the dinner table." I flashed him a sweet smile as I moved past to grab a side dish of some sort.

Linc stood in my path blocking the table, his eyes watery.

Uh-oh. What did I do now?

"Family. You, you think of me as family?" he asked with a soft watery voice.

Oh my. Living with Gigi had rubbed off on me. She had a way of treating everyone as though they were family. How do I say this without leading him on to think I was staying for good? Damn it.

"You and Lulu have made my stay welcoming. Your kindness warms my heart, and I will always look upon the both of you as family, no matter which realm I'm in." I smiled down at him warmly, and he dabbed his eyes with his apron.

"Thank you, Lady Zara." He bowed his head, sniffed, and then shuffled past me.

Phin sat next to me, and Beau was on my other side. Cassian hadn't made it into the dining room yet, and that's when I noticed the table had been set for four. A lump formed in my throat as I thought of Patrick. *He should be here.* I blinked the thought away and reached for the bottle of wine then hesitated. I'd drunk too much the night before and awakened with a wicked headache. I didn't want to repeat that again; we had an important mission tomorrow.

"It's ok, Z, I have more hangover remedy." Beau winked at me and poured me a generous cup of wine.

I smiled back at him and took a deep drink.

Voices floated into the dining room, and I turned to see who was coming. Half of me had hoped Trick was back and we'd have a chance to resolve our differences.

Cass strolled in wearing a big smile, laughing at something the man next to him had said. And although the man was the spitting image of Trick, it wasn't him. It was Storm, his older brother. My shoulders sagged.

I turned in my seat, bringing the cup of wine back to my lips. Phin draped an arm around my shoulders, and Beau squeezed my knee, reassuring me.

Cassian stopped behind my chair, and I tilted my head up to accept the kiss he placed on my nose. Beau and Phin greeted Storm.

"Zara, you remember Storm," Cassian said. "We will need a flyer to finish this mission, so he volunteered."

Storm smiled at me. "Hi, Zara. Thanks for having me."

It didn't feel right to do this without Trick, but I suppose he had made his choice. And we needed a strong air elemental. I smiled back at Storm and sipped more wine.

Linc placed a bowl in front of me first, then he served the guys.

Phin leaned into me. "Are you ok with this?"

"Yes." I nodded. I had to be ok with Storm's presence. We needed an air elemental, and Patrick had bailed on us.

The lobster bisque in front of me smelled delicious, but I'd lost my appetite. My mind kept tripping over itself, trying to move past the absence of Trick and the addition of his brother, who looked so eerily similar. This place was fucking with my head.

"Try this, it's delicious." Beau held up a spoon of steaming bisque to my lips. "Blow."

I did as he asked and sighed. It was delicious.

"Eat, angel," Phin whispered.

He was right. If I didn't eat, the guys would shovel food in my mouth, and I didn't want that. The last thing I wanted was to look like a spoilt princess that needed to be fed, especially in front of Storm. I gave myself a mental shake, picked up my spoon, and began feeding myself.

Cass looked over at me as we began the second course.

"Tell Storm about Thadd's info, Z."

I dabbed my mouth with the napkin that was on my lap.

"Thadd found the arms dealer that has been supplying guns to the royal army. They ordered one hundred to start and another five hundred to be delivered in a couple of weeks. The transfer will take place right outside of Silk." It was a risky situation, but we couldn't waste the opportunity.

"Who's Thadd?" Storm asked.

"A friend," I said and didn't offer more. "He can help us intercept the shipment if we want. I'm thinking we do that. And then we hitch a ride back with the guards straight to the sanctuary," I replied.

"Grant said his cousin is part of the crew that picks up the weaponry. Perhaps we can use that to our advantage. We can take out the other guards if they are spelled then head back with Grant's cousin," Beau added between bites.

"The problem is, we have to be prepared for an all-out war. Once we get into the sanctuary, the king and queen will be pissed, not to mention the mage and the crone," Cassian chimed in.

"Without their weapons, we'll have an advantage. We'll need to move in fast and take out the mage and the crone." Phin rubbed his chin. "We can do this. I am sure of it."

"We need to speak with Grant first. Get more details out of him. And hopefully, his cousin will be there at the pick-up so that we can confirm his findings. Hell, maybe we should just take him with us. Has he shared any details about how many guards there are? What element of magic do they hold?" Storm asked.

"He couldn't be precise, but we estimate over a thousand spread out between the sanctuary and the palace. And if the intel Thadd gave us is correct, only one hundred are armed. Still, that's a lot considering elementals are losing their magic more and more each day the Source is cut off," Cassian replied.

The magic in the kingdom was weakening at an alarming rate. We needed to act fast or soon our people would be utterly defenseless. They'd become humans. For powerful elementals like the five of us at the table, that would happen as well, but not as quickly. I didn't need my magic much in Silk City, but it was always there. Taking it away completely would be like robbing me of my breath.

Linc and Lulu worked around us to clean up after our meal while the five of us moved into the living area to continue our plotting. The guys suggested we ask Thadd for more details, so I got him on the phone. Bless his big mage heart. He was happy to drop whatever he was doing to assist.

With a plan in place, I bid the men goodnight. It had been another long day, and the realization of facing my sister created an uneasiness in my belly. I knew it would come to this, but despite everything I had heard, I loved her and wanted to believe she was innocent.

"Zara," Storm's voice halted my steps as I walked down the hallway to my room. "May I have a word, please?"

I slowly turned to face him. The resemblance between him and his brother hurt my heart. Why did Trick have to be such an asshole? I scrutinized Storm's appearance, searching for something that made him different from Trick.

They were equal in height and stature. Storm's black hair was a bit longer and it had a slight wave. His skin was pale, so white he almost looked like he was chiseled out of alabaster stone. Storm's nose was perfectly straight, whereas Trick's had a slight slope to it. And Storm's lashes were something to behold. They were long and thick and made his silver eyes appear opaque. And I was grasping for straws.

"Hi." He gave me a shy smile. "Can we sit?" He motioned to the sitting area outside of my room. Well, Phin's room. I wondered if I was sleeping alone. The thought of doing so made my tummy gurgle, and I looked toward the way I had left them.

"It's ok, I won't harm you, but if you feel more comfortable with the other guys present, I'll go get them," Storm offered.

"No, it's fine." I smiled and moved towards a comfortable looking lounger.

Storm sat across from me and rested his elbows on his knees. "So, I just wanted to thank you for including me in this. It feels good to be actively doing something about this mess. Since my wife and children... it's been rough. Being busy is the only thing that is keeping me sane. And now I finally feel like I have the opportunity to avenge them."

"I'm sorry for your loss. And yes, of course, we're happy to have you."

"Are you really though? Happy to have me? I can understand if you aren't. I was told you and Patrick had some history and the way he left things was a dick move. Not that that's any of my business. I just want you to feel comfortable having me around. And if you're not, I hope you give me the chance to change your mind."

Although older, Storm, reminded me of the Trick I used to know. The boy I remembered had been smart, thoughtful, and introspective. Damn it, this wasn't easy. But I had to get over my personal issues because if Trick wasn't going to help, we needed someone else. Lying to Storm would be the easy route. It would put him at ease, but fuck me I couldn't do it. If I wanted this to be a success, honesty would be the way to go.

I sighed. "Storm, I am happy that you're working with us. But it is awkward for me. I feel like we- the group of us are cheating on Trick in a way. We've replaced him so quickly and it unsettles me. And to top that off you remind me of the boy I used to know. I'm not sure what to do about all of that, but I assure you I will not let my jumble of emotions interfere with us working together."

"Well, I don't know him well or at all, actually. We met shortly before my dad was killed. After his death, my wife and daughters were taken from me, and that marked the beginning of this shit storm. We all scattered trying to get away from the tyrants. So Patrick and I never got a chance to bond and admittedly, I probably would have killed him because fuck, I was pissed. I'm not sure how I can ease your mind about things, but I promise you this, I will see this through till the end. I won't abandon the mission or you." He stared at me with those arresting silver eyes.

"Thank you, Storm." I got up and moved toward my room.

"One more thing." He grasped my hand before I got too far, and I glanced over my shoulder to face him. "If it is ok with you, may I stay here at the lair? Just for the next few days. I'd like to be close and would like to reserve my strength, rather than flying back and forth."

"Oh, umm, I don't mind, but I'm a guest here as well. I think Phin would be the one to ask."

Our fingers were intertwined and it felt...natural. He stood up and stared down at me while remaining contact. Uh-oh. I smiled at him and reluctantly walked away.

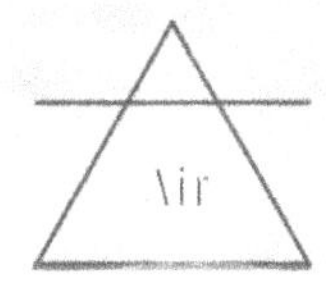

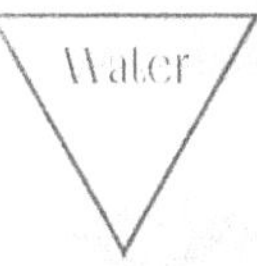

Chapter Thirty-Three

ZARA

The next morning I was off to the Coastal Villages with Cassian while Beau, Phin, and Storm went to speak with Grant about the weapons drop off and to get a layout of the Sanctuary.

Cassian had relatives at the nearest Coastal Village, which was along the southwest border of the kingdom. The drive took over an hour, but he was good company and he made me laugh. It was like we were children again and no time had passed.

The coastal village was unlike any of the villages we had visited. Colorful cottages dotted the coastline surrounding a harbor called Siren's Cup. At the very end of Siren's Cup stood a lighthouse painted in bright red. It was charming and reminded me of something that would be found on the East Coast of the human realm.

The briny scent of the ocean washed over me, and a cool breeze ruffled my hair as we walked through the village. The sun sparkled against the azure harbor as houseboats bobbed, swaying in tandem with the rhythm of the waves.

"You like it here," Cass stated. It wasn't a question. It was a fact and he wasn't wrong.

I smiled at my water elemental. Holding Cass's hand while walking through the village made it feel like we were on vacation.

Marlo Brooks, Cass's aunt and the chief of the village, gave us a tour.

The villagers were cordial and agreed to help us in any way possible. They all seemed to be in good spirits and in good health. It wasn't all that surprising as we were at the far southwest corner of the kingdom, thousands of miles from the palace.

"You have a well-run village here. You're self-sufficient and seem to operate autonomously. And the villagers are healthy. Have you experienced any negative effects since the royals took over?" I asked Marlo.

"Our numbers have increased because of them. People that were close to the Source or the palace migrated here, putting as much distance between them. It creates a bit of strain on our resources, but we're making do." Marlo's long, wavy blue hair whipped behind her in the breeze. "Besides, no one wants to be ruled by the tyrants."

We finished our tour and said goodbye to Marlo.

She hugged Cass and said to him, "You children need to visit your parents more often. Take the tide. From here it won't take long. And besides, I'm sure your mother would love to see the princess."

"I'm not a princess," I muttered.

"Nonsense." She scoffed. "You'll always be our princess, lovely, until you're crowned queen."

I gave her a hug, and then Cass and I went back to the car.

"When was the last time you saw your mother?" I asked him.

"A year. Maybe more." He said in a soft voice. "Would you like to visit? It's not far."

"Sure," I replied, and he led me toward the shore.

I kicked off my shoes when we got to the beach, and we walked up to the water. The gentle waves tickled my toes. It was a beautiful day and yet a feeling of dread crested up my spine. Flashbacks from nearly drowning days ago made me hesitate to get in the water.

"What's wrong?" Cass asked, his brow furrowed.

"Um, on second thought. I'll just wait here." I replied.

He stared at me a moment, then nodded.

"I promise to keep you safe, Z. But if this is too soon, I understand." He stroked my arms.

I'd always loved swimming and was good at it. Water was my friend, and I didn't want to run from my fears.

"How does this work?" I clenched his hand.

"Well, first I will go in and get some Ogonori. I will imbue it with my magic and place it on the bridge of your nose so that you will be able to breathe. It's perfectly safe, I assure you. From there we will hitch a ride on the North Equatorial Current to my family's place."

I bit my lip. The very idea of being underwater made me nauseous. I blew out a deep breath like a boiled-over tea kettle. I didn't want to do it, and I didn't want to back down either. At some point, I would need to face my fears and get back in the water. And who better to help me overcome my fear of drowning than a water elemental? I nodded at Cass.

"I'll keep you safe. Wait here ok." Cass stripped down to his boxers and then disappeared under the ocean surface.

A few minutes later, Cass sauntered out of the water. Droplets sparkled over his skin, highlighting every muscular plane of his defined torso.

"Hey," he shook out his hair, sending drops of water flying everywhere.

I giggled and turned my face to the side as the droplets sprayed me.

"What do you have there?" I asked, looking at the purplish brown seaweed in his hand. Doubting it would help me breathe underwater.

"It doesn't look like much, but..." Cass cupped the seaweed between both hands and chanted under his breath until the seaweed glowed. "Now, it's magical."

Cass reopened his hand, and the bundle of seaweed had flattened into a strip resembling a purplish band-aid. He placed it over the bridge of my nose.

"Now you're ready." Cass smiled.

I shook my head. "Nuh-uh. This is not going to work." I lived and breathed magic, but this did not convince me of its magical powers.

"We'll take it slow. If you feel uncomfortable, I'll bring you back to the surface. I promise." Cass stared deep into my eyes.

I undressed down to my bikini and laid my sundress over his pile of clothes. Cass clasped his hand over mine, and I squeezed it tight. My breathing became erratic the closer we got to the water, but I didn't let that deter me. When the water reached my breasts, I couldn't go further. The thought of being submerged underwater made me panic. I tugged on his hand, wanting to go back to the shore.

"Hey, it's ok. I've got you. Just focus on me." Cass picked me up, and I locked my legs around his back, staring into his eyes.

He fastened his lips to mine, and his tongue slid into my mouth. I lost myself in his kiss, closing my eyes. We dunked underwater. I tried to wriggle free and swim up to the surface. Cassian deepened our kiss, his strong hands groping my body as we swam, the water swirling all around us.

Afraid to let him go, I clung to him. The water temperature got cooler the deeper we went. I smashed myself against Cass's body, coveting his warmth. The urge to fight my way to the surface was strong, but Cass's confidence gave me courage and held me steady. I kept my eyes closed and surrendered to him, relinquishing any doubts and trusting him and his magic to keep me alive.

Water gurgled around us, and the ambient noise of the ocean began to relax me. The salty ocean slithered over my skin like a lover's caress, tempting, and seducing. Cass's magic unfurled and propelled us through the water. My body felt weightless.

Zara, I heard him whisper my name. I realized then that

Cass's magic had worked, and I could breathe just fine. I opened my eyes to find ocean life teeming all around us. Sea creatures of every type and color swam by like an underwater parade. It was vibrant and magical, but my water elemental had all of my attention.

Cass's lips dragged across my jaw. I groped his body, kissing him like he was my lifeline. His large hands slid from my waist to cup my breasts, massaging and then pinching my hard nipples. I groaned and ground my hips on his torso. His rigid length pressed up on my core, begging for entrance. He nipped at my neck and trailed kisses down to my breasts. His tongue flicked my nipples. He pushed my bikini bottoms to the side and slipped in a finger.

I grasped a handful of his hair which was completely blue, just like the ocean, and tugged him away from my breasts, allowing me to fasten my lips over his. His finger massaged between my folds, but I needed more. I wanted all of him. I glided my hands down to his boxers, stroking his hard cock, eager for him to fill me. After pulling out his hard length, I guided him to my aching slit.

Cassian didn't hesitate. He stared into my eyes and with one sharp thrust, he buried himself deep into my pussy, stretching my entrance. He braced his hands on my waist as he pumped in and out of me. His teeth clamped onto my nipples, his thrusts fierce. I matched his frenzy, our bodies slamming into each other.

Tingles ran up and down my skin. Pleasure swelled through my body. Everything melded together, and my climax erupted. Tiny orgasms rolled through me, making me tremble. His lips latched onto mine, his breath filling my lungs, my heart, and my very soul. Cassian's blue eyes gazed back at me, conveying undying love and devotion. He had loved me since we were children, and still did.

Our lips locked, our tongues danced, and then he released my body. He hoisted me over his shoulders all while navigating the current. I wrapped my legs around his shoulders, and his mouth consumed my core. Every stroke of his tongue left delectable shivers on my sensitive skin. My body arched, completely weightless. Another orgasm rolled through me.

Cass brought me down off his shoulders and pressed his chest to my back. He threaded his hard cock into my pussy and drove in. He gripped my hips, and pumped harder and faster, the resistance of the ocean holding up my body. He reached around and flicked my clit and then he dragged a finger down the crack of my ass and massaged the puckered hole.

I bucked against him, encouraging him to enter. He leaned over me and bit into my shoulder, slipping his thumb into my ass. The exquisite pain mixed with pleasure tore my orgasm from my body, and my eyes rolled back in my head. Cass's body tightened, and he released himself with an explosive force of magic. Both of our bodies shuddered from the onslaught of pleasure.

My body draped over his as I turned in his arms. Cass cradled me and peppered kisses all over my shoulders. I dozed off, trusting him with my life completely.

"Zara, sweetheart, we're here." Cass shook me a little.

I woke up and found myself in a room awash with Pepto Bismol. The floor felt spongy and the walls were smooth and shiny. If it weren't for the different textures, it'd be difficult to tell the difference between the floors and the walls.

My wet hair was plastered to my neck and back, my skin cold and clammy. Cassian drew me to his chest.

"Come on, let's get you warmed up." He led me down a narrow hallway and turned into a room with the same pink walls and spongy floors.

He pushed along a seam on the pink wall, which opened and revealed a cabinet stocked with towels, generic T-shirts, and trousers. Cass handed me a towel and a long-sleeved sweatshirt, that hung past my knees.

"Where are we?" I asked.

"This is where my mother and two of my fathers were born," he explained. "It's called Aqueous. This here is just a receiving area, for guests. We'll find my parents in the common areas of this shell."

"Shell?" I paid closer attention to my surroundings. The flooring smoothed out, and pink and white swirl patterns with flecks of silver adorned the walls in a marbling effect.

"See for yourself." He tilted his chin to his left.

The open space before us fanned thirty feet above like a scalloped seashell. We stepped down into the room that resembled the bed of a clam. It was spacious, and people milled about. The air was balmy, like in the cavern except it had a salty taste to it.

"Cassian!" a woman exclaimed.

"Mother." Cassian embraced her.

I stepped back and gave the two a moment. Mariah had long blue hair that flowed down to her knees.

"Princess Zara!" As she peered over Cass's shoulder, her gray eyes caught mine. She released her son and rushed towards me, enveloping me in a hug.

"Mrs. Brooks, wonderful to see you again." I hugged her back.

"Oh my!" She covered her mouth with her hands. "I can't believe you're here. And you're all grown up and so beautiful.

Come, tell me everything."

Cass and I spent an hour with his family, reminiscing and getting caught up. When we left, I realized there was so much to the kingdom I had missed, and I never wanted to leave again.

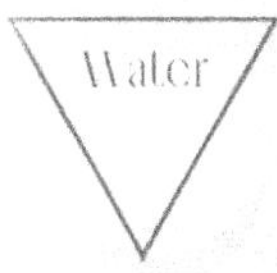

Chapter Thirty-Four

ZARA

The day before the weapons mission, we drove out to visit Zander. He had asked to see me and had told the men it was important. I wanted to refuse. We were gaining momentum with the villagers, and I wanted to keep going before heading to the sanctuary. The men vetoed my idea, and I found myself hesitating while Beau stood outside the car holding the door open for me.

I sighed and scooted across the truck's bench seat and allowed Beau to help me out. He grasped my waist, and placed a kiss on the top of my head.

The three men and I slept together nightly. They kept me up with plenty of delicious sex and woke me with more delicious sex followed by breakfast in bed. I wasn't complaining in the least, although I did miss Thadd.

Storm stayed in the lair but hadn't pursued me on a personal level. Although he was alluring in his own way, I wasn't ready to travel down that path...yet. He was certainly helpful though. He rallied flyers to transport food to the villages that were in need and provided sound council.

Overall the team we'd assembled was well received and success was within our grasp.

I followed Cass and Phin into the cottage Zander now called home with Beau and Storm on either side of me. Although I had no reason to feel any trepidation, their support boosted my confidence as we strode through the cottage.

Zander was seated at the same table I'd seen him at the first time we came by, and he looked weary, even more so. I sighed.

"Zara, thank you for coming. I was told you have been working with these men on rallying allies. I am grateful, daughter, for your assistance. I wanted to meet with you before you confront your sister. There are things you should know."

I stood in front of him with my arms crossed and waited patiently.

"Please sit, this will take some time. Would you like something to drink?" He waved a hand at the only empty chair at the small table.

Phin pulled out the chair, and Cass went to get cups and a carafe of water. I looked at my father suspiciously then sighed. I did not want to be there any longer than I needed to be.

I sat and waited for my father to speak.

"Don't kill your sister. Please. She is not herself. I fear she may have been spelled by her husband's mage. Killing the mage should release the people from doing their bidding. However, it may not be enough to release her. The mage should have a grimoire. In it, you will find the necessary spells and how to undo the damage. You might be able to spare her."

It hadn't been my intention to kill her. She was my little sister and despite what I had been told, I loved her. I just needed her to stop this foolishness. But, after everything I had seen thus far, I wasn't about to make any promises. Refusing to show any emotions, I gave Zander a flat stare.

"The seer has her hand in this somehow. With her gift of sight, she may already know your plans." The former king looked at the men silently standing near the table then he focused on me. "Your exile shields you from her gift. Technically speaking you have been banished and are no longer considered a part of the kingdom. She can only see those that the kingdom has claimed. This should work in your favor. Plan accordingly and take nothing for granted."

Phin was about to say something, but Zander shook his head and held his hand out. "No, no details. Once Issac and his mage learn of your involvement, they will come here first. The less I know the better. Report back after the mission.”

Well, shit. We needed to brainstorm again. Fuck.

“Is there anything else?” I asked Zander.

I let the weight of the question hang in the air, curious to see if he’d have the decency to offer an apology.

He shook his head and turned away from me, refusing to look me in the eye. Coward.

“Thank you for the info. We have work to do.” I got up and moved towards the front door.

“No, thank you, Zara, for staying,” he said.

I waved a hand and kept walking. As soon as I reached the front door I heard him whisper. “I...I’m sorry, for everything.”

I paused for a moment before opening the door wondering if I’d heard him correctly.

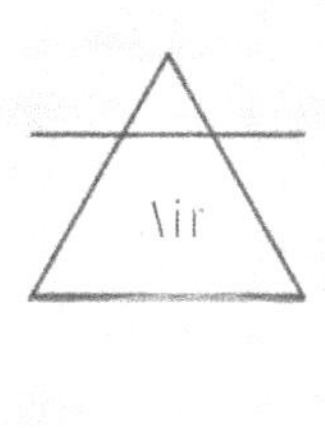

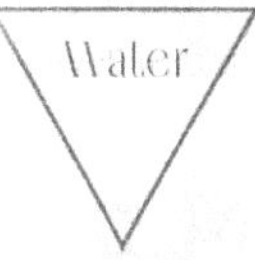

Chapter Thirty-Five

STORM

King Cavendish did not look well. His frail state fueled my determination to end Issac and Amina's reign. I had refused to call them king and queen and my family had paid the price for my arrogance.

That had been three years ago and still, my heart hurt. I shrouded myself in anger, using that vile emotion to keep my clan safe. There were so few of us left. Some were spelled by the mage and stuck in the palace or at the sanctuary doing their bidding. The pain from losing so many was a constant wound that hadn't healed, and I wanted to save them all, my clan and all the others.

Working alongside Princess Zara helped quell the anger and renewed my faith in the kingdom. She brought hope to so many and yet she was so humble about it. She got in the trenches and worked alongside the ailing offering assistance to every village to improve their situation. It was clear; the people hadn't forgotten their long-lost princess. And I needed to stop calling her that.

In so many ways she was every bit the royal. She carried herself with grace and elegance. And yet she never looked down on anyone and treated all with equality regardless of age, gender, or power level. Cassian was right. She inspired people to follow her.

I was curious to see how she would handle things with her sister. They were close as children, but so much had changed. Still, blood meant something. In many ways, I hoped she'd inspire me on how to deal with my brother's issues.

Patrick, and I never had any kind of relationship. My half-brother and I didn't even know one another until a few years ago. And even then, we didn't have an opportunity to spend much time together. Perhaps that was why anger towards him came so easily. He'd had my father killed, and it was easy to place all the blame on him.

My father hadn't died at Patrick's hands, and I knew that. Truly, it wasn't his fault. I just needed to direct my anger somewhere, and he had made a viable target.

I sighed and looked over at the silent beauty in the front seat. She was sitting between Phin, the driver, and Beau. Phin always drove and liked keeping her close. A possessive gesture his beast probably required. She leaned on Beau's shoulder napping comfortably. I envied their closeness. The other three men in the car were openly affectionate with her. They were so lucky. Not only was she beautiful, but she was kind and loving too. Why my brother walked away from her twice...was beyond me.

As though she knew I was thinking about her, she slowly opened her eyes. She caught me staring, and a flutter of nervousness cramped my stomach. But Zara smiled at me, then winked and went right back to sleep. I turned to look outside the window and smiled, content to daydream about the lavender-eyed beauty.

Phin punched the brakes and I slammed into the front seat.

Alarmed, I immediately looked at Zara, who was in Beau's arms. The big man had shielded her body with his.

"What the fuck?" Cassian cursed, rubbing his shoulder.

"Up ahead. Zara, angel, you ok?" Phin asked.

I peered out the front windshield and saw a group of soldiers lined up on the dirt road. They were far. As an air elemental, my vision was keen, and I could see them clearly. Royal guards had blocked the dirt road.

Zara grunted and tried to unwrap herself from Beau's arms.

"Sorry, angel. We need to get you to safety," Phin said then turned to look at the rest of us. "Everyone else ok?"

"We're good back here." I looked over at Cass who seemed fine as he focused on the men ahead of us.

"I'm good, Z?" Beau kept his arms around her

"I'm fine. What's going on? I can't see that far." She squinted.

"Dragon vision, angel. There are six armed men ahead. So, obviously royals. We need to get you out of here. Storm, can you fly with Z back to the lair?"

"Yep, of course," I replied and tried to open the door to get moving, but it remained locked.

"Sorry, you two will have to go out the back hatch. I don't want to risk them seeing the doors open and going after Z." Phin looked at me through the rearview mirror.

Zara didn't hesitate. She climbed over to the back seat, squeezing between Cass and I and then she continued over to the very back of the SUV.

"Unlock the hatch, Phin. See you guys at home." She blew them a kiss, opened the hatch, and then I followed suit, climbing over the seats not nearly as gracefully as she had.

Once outside, I grabbed her hand and led her into the woods. As soon as we were covered by trees and foliage, I turned and blew a gust of air along the dirt road to cover our footprints.

"Smart thinking," Zara said and grabbed hold of my hand. "I have no idea where we are and to be honest, I am not sure if I can fly that far. I've never done it."

I smiled at her, appreciating her candor. Most elementals hid their weaknesses, but not Zara. She was open about it and made no excuses.

"It's ok, we'll walk a bit further so that whoever it is, they don't see us. Then we'll fly up and head out." I squeezed her hand.

"How much flying have you done?"

"Umm...not much. Ok, only a few times, and only since I've been here. In the human realm, my magic isn't very strong. Here it's full, almost overwhelmingly so. The first time the guys brought me to see Zander, I got upset and ran and then flew for the first time. No one knows about that. Not even Trick who came to find me."

Involuntarily, I winced at how she casually called her father by his first name.

"I love that you're so open about everything. It's refreshing." I turned my head slightly.

Zara shrugged, her phone beeped, and she pulled it out of her pocket to read a text. "Phin. He said a few air elementals took flight." She showed me the message.

"Well, shit." I rubbed my chin, thinking about the area. Something in my gut said to go left, and I knew what was in that direction. It was farther out, but I gave in to my instincts and led Zara on. "This way. There's a cove nearby. We can wait it out for a bit."

We walked on silently for a while until we came upon a ravine that slanted down to a mystical silver lake. Zara stopped short and placed a hand on her chest.

"This is breathtaking." She whispered.

I forgot sometimes that she'd lived in the human realm for many years. There were beautiful places there as well, but nothing like the kingdom.

We stood atop a deep ravine, which marked the entrance to Treasure Veil. It was the halfway point between the Source and Torch Mountain. Black rock formations gave way to black sandy shores that surrounded a silver lake. The water was clear and reflected off the black sand in its depths. Legends say Torch Mountain erupted with a torrent of lava following the Goddess as she journeyed east to meet with her sister in the middle of our lands. When she and her sister met up the Source was created and that became her new home. Legends about her sister were rare.

"Is this Treasure Veil?" she asked me, not taking her eyes off the view.

"Yes, I've flown over a million times it seems, but I never dropped down to get a closer look. I know there are things to do, but we can explore if you want. Briefly. Your men will worry." I told her.

She looked positively radiant standing there with a huge smile on her face, and I hoped she'd want to explore this legendary place... with me.

"We have to explore. The magic here is singing in my veins." She turned to face me with a twinkle in her eye.

"Hand me your phone. I'll contact Phin and let him know we're delayed."

I called Phin, and he answered on the first ring. "Angel, are you on your way back?"

"Nope, not your angel. We're at Treasure Veil. She wants to explore. Everything ok?"

"Ok, good. Yeah, keep her away. We're dealing with it. Keep me posted and stay out of sight. The flyers are still roaming around looking for you."

"Get names if you can. We'll be in touch." The idea of the flyers working for Issac made my skin crawl.

"Everything ok?" Zara asked.

I nodded. "They're dealing with it. He wants us to stay out of sight."

She grabbed my hand and tugged me along. "Does anyone live here?"

"No, not that I am aware. From what our teachings say, the land doesn't provide much in terms of food. The black rock is not the best for plant life. My guess is no one wanted to try to cultivate the area. Umm, pardon me, prin...Zara. This is faster." I slipped an arm around her waist and then floated us down the ravine towards the black sand. It was either that or hike two miles downhill. Plus, it gave me an excuse to hold her close.

She wrapped her arm around my neck and stared at our surroundings until our feet touched the ground. "I could've flown." She looked up at me with a small smile.

My insides turned to mush, and the only reply I could muster was a goofy smile. She caressed my cheek, indicating it was the correct response. My face flamed hot, which made her chuckle. To her credit, she didn't call me out on my involuntary reaction.

Zara stepped away from me, then bent over to remove her shoes and roll up her jeans.

I stood still for a long moment, admiring Zara in her element. Her natural beauty glowed from within as she skipped along the shore allowing the lake to lap against her bare toes. She tipped her face up to the sun and spread her arms out wide. The land was welcoming her home, and she was soaking up everything it wanted to give her. And I...I was finding it hard not to be mesmerized by her.

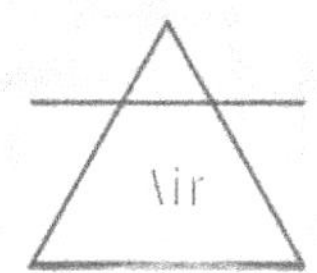

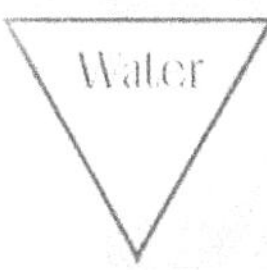

Chapter Thirty-Six

ZARA

Treasure Veil was even more mystical to me than Transcendental Oasis. The land not only spoke to me, but it also enveloped my entire being. Every inch of me buzzed.

Storm sat on the black sand with a faraway look in his eyes. He didn't seem to notice me as I got closer until I said, "Hey." I knelt in front of him. "Are you all right?"

He cleared his throat and blinked. "Sorry, yeah, I was lost in thought. You looked so peaceful I didn't want to disturb you."

"You're not disturbing me, but if we have time, I'd like to explore the cove."

"Sure." Storm stood, dusting himself, off and I rose with him.

We walked along the black sand shore until we came to a grotto comprised of the same black stone which surrounded the cove.

The rock was jagged and sharp, jutting out in haphazard ways. Between the dark rocks all around us and the black sand below our feet, the tenebrous cave seemed like an endless void.

I called on my fire magic and released several tiny, flaming balls into the grotto, revealing a large cave. Storm and I gave each other the same mischievous grin. We were both intrigued and moved further inside.

Storm walked ahead of me, moving forward in the middle of the cave, following the fireballs that lit the way.

I called up more fireballs and wandered closer to the cave wall to the left. Shimmering silver and gold veins covered the black rocks. Mesmerized, I traced a vein that seemed to be liquid but only traces of glittery dust remained on my finger. I held it up to show Storm.

"Stay close, Zara."

I nodded and walked towards him, staying alongside the cave wall, until my feet were swept under me. I gasped as I plummeted into the void; my stomach lurched, wind whistled past my ears. I was falling fast.

Something hard gripped me, slowing my descent. Storm held me close to the muscular planes of his body, his strong arms reassuring.

"Damn it, Zara, you scared the shit out of me. Are you ok?" His breath fanned my cheek.

"I'm fine. I panicked," I muttered, as shame rolled through me. I should have called on my air magic and saved myself.

"It's ok, I got you. Can you release more fireflies?"

I did as he asked and a dozen fireflies lit the dim space. We continued to float down toward the cavern floor. In no time light shone below us and Treasure Veil, the *real* Treasure Veil came into view.

Our feet hit the ground and my jaw dropped. Storm and I stayed in each other's arms as we gazed about the cavern we stumbled into.

"You're seeing this right?" I asked Storm.

"Umm...yeah, I just, wow. I have no words."

The black rock that encased the entrance above was long gone. We were surrounded by a garden of precious gemstones. Rows upon rows of purple amethysts, pink and green quartz, and aquamarine in every shape and size sprouted from the ground.

I stepped away from Storm, and he grasped my hand as we ventured deeper into the cavern walking along a soft dirt path. Diamonds, rubies, sapphires, and emeralds sparkled from the cavern walls, casting a colorful glow that pulsated with magic.

The kingdom had an abundance of priceless natural stones and gems. Children were required to learn about stones and what healing or magical properties they held. All the Goddess's creations were lovely. However, elementals were taught to appreciate and admire their beauty in their natural form. And we never took from the earth for our enjoyment or coveted natural resources as assets to be traded.

Polished erythrite, a blood-red stone as tall as me, gave way to a mound of shimmering labradorite, a multihued stone of greens, blues, and orange. Calcite and tourmaline of every color created hedges along the path, leading us on a mesmerizing journey deeper into the unknown. Rods of heliodor, almost opaque, added a hint of mystery to the colorful patterns created by the crystal hedges.

Curious to discover what other wonders the cavern held, we ventured along the pathway and followed the sound of rushing water. Storm held onto my hand as our eyes feasted on the myriad of colors and precious stones.

Soon we came upon clear waters that led around the cavern to a waterfall, that ascended fifty feet into the air. Spires of aquamarine glowed around a white stone which served as the backdrop for the waterfall giving the water a two-dimensional illusion. Mist sprayed while steam rose from the river below.

"Moonstone." Storm said as he eyed the white stone behind the waterfall. "Does your phone have a camera function?"

I nodded and handed it to him.

While he took pictures, I got undressed, down to my panties. I wore a sports bra which I had no intention of swimming in. I arranged my white, wavy locks to conceal my breasts and knelt along on the shoreline.

Smooth moss agate, a stone colored in varying shades of greens, reds, black, brown, and yellow covered the ground like sand creating a shoreline. Ripples of water licked my skin, warm like a natural hot spring.

"Zara?"

I glanced over my shoulder to face Storm who was taking pictures of me.

"The guys are going to be so jealous." He strode closer to me, with the phone pointed at me.

I turned away rolling my eyes, then stood preparing to dip in the water.

Storm came up behind me, linked our hands together and rested his chin on my shoulder.

"Going for a swim are we?" He asked.

"It'd be a travesty if we didn't." I grasped his hands, guiding him to splay his fingers over my belly.

"I agree. Go ahead. I'll catch up." He pecked my cheek then stood back and undressed.

I strode into the water and dunked my head diving a good twenty feet before touching the floor of the hot spring, covered by Dragonstone. I grabbed a stone, and then I swam back up to the surface. I turned the stone over in my hand marveling at the blood red and green marble pattern and its completely smooth surface.

Storm took that precise moment to sneak up behind me, scaring me out of my skin.

"Goddess help me! Storm! You scared the shit out of me." I splashed him with water.

He chuckled and sputtered. "Sorry, I couldn't help myself. What's that? Dragonstone?"

"From the surface below." I nodded handing him the stone, while he floated around me.

"It's perfect. You're perfect Zara." He stopped in front of me and floated closer.

"Hope that wasn't too much," his cheeks flushed red.

I wasn't sure if it was my royal heritage that made him so polite around me or if he was a shy guy. But the way he flushed red all over his face, neck, and even his ears endeared him to me.

"It's not. It's umm...I'm not sure. I do appreciate the compliment. It's an awkward situation, because of my history with Patrick."

"Do you still love him?" He asked.

"No." I shook my head. "I thought I did when we were kids. That was a long time ago."

It still bothered me that he wasn't with us, and no one had heard from him. I sighed.

Thankfully, Storm didn't press the conversation. We swam up to the waterfall.

Upon closer inspection, the white stone surrounding the waterfall was a mixture of white moonstone and selenite. The difference was the color. Although both were white, the moonstone was solid white to its core while selenite had a hint of grey and white and almost looked opaque.

We swam for a while then walked back to the shore where we'd left our clothes. I covered my breasts with my hands as I got out of the water and had planned to use my air magic to dry off and get dressed right away, but Storm had other plans.

"Here." He separated my long wet hair and brought the two strands forward to cover my breasts. Once my hair was rearranged he released my hair and pulled my arms down to my sides. "There, you're perfectly decent."

I looked down at my chest and laughed. The outline of my breasts was visible, but my nipples were concealed.

We sat comfortably on the smooth stone shore. Storm propped his head up with his jeans and offered his stomach for me to use as a pillow.

He told me about his wife and children. His voice was full of love as he recalled fond memories. He was an excellent storyteller, and I found myself drawn into his love story. I could see why he was still heartbroken after all these years but right then the only emotion he emitted was pure joy.

"Tell me about you, Zara. Tell me about your life in Silk City." Storm bent his knees, and I sat up, then leaned against his legs to look up at him.

"It wasn't easy at the beginning, but I had Nan, my nursemaid. She died one year and two months after my exile. Being underage I ended up in a group home where I met your brother. He was the only elemental there and we became friends. I was young and found comfort in him because we had something in common. But to be fair, it was a short friendship. Four months after getting into the youth home, Gigi and her husband became my foster parents. Trick and I remained friends until he disappeared. I think our entire relationship lasted ten months. As a kid that seemed like a lifetime," I said.

"Was it serious?" He made small circles on my knee with his thumb.

"As serious as it could be for kids that age, although your brother is two years older. But we didn't have sex or anything." I shrugged.

"When did he come back? I was told he tried to mend things and you sent him packing."

I laughed. "Well, I don't remember being that harsh about it, but perhaps I was. I was pissed. I believe it was six years later. I was already out of college. I had done some traveling and had just started dating someone else."

"Are you still with this someone else?" His hand rested on my leg.

I stared off into space. "Umm...That was Thadd. He's helping us with the weapons mission. You two haven't met yet, but you will soon."

I looked back at Storm, who was gazing upon my exposed bosom. He licked his lips, and I curled in on myself, trying to cover up.

He sat up and placed a hand on my arm. "Sorry, Zara. I didn't mean to make you uncomfortable. I was...admiring. I apologize. Forgive me please."

"It's ok. We're adults, right?"

"Yes. I promise I won't do anything unseemly. I hold you in the highest esteem. If you wanted to walk around naked, I wouldn't think any less of you and will always treat you with the utmost respect." He stared at me intently and I blushed.

He leaned back with a smile and asked. "So why aren't you and Thaddeus more? It seems like you are pretty close."

"Thadd has secrets. After all these years I have no idea what he does for a living. He is crazy wealthy and a talented mage. But he has always been kind to me. We have great..." I tried to find the right words. "Chemistry. We have great...chemistry."

I sat upright. The movement caused my hair to fall away from my chest, and I didn't let it bother me. My breasts were on full display, and the way Storm licked his lips again made my nipples hard.

"Truthfully, though, he isn't to blame. I have my issues. And he doesn't seem to mind. We both like things the way they are. We have sex without commitment. He dates other women. I date other men, and it works. He's special to me though. I do love him. He is my closest and oldest friend. He has been a constant in my life, and I'm not willing to let him go, even now with the others in the picture."

"It'll work out. Cass, Phin, and Beau seem to be ok with the arrangement, right?"

I nodded. "I'm always honest with my expectations upfront. The three elemental men understand me. I plan on going home after this issue is dealt with."

"Will you miss them?" He sat up, focusing his silver eyes on me.

"Absolutely. I will miss all of this. You too." I smiled at him.

Storm leaned towards me. He stroked my cheek, then ran his fingers down my arm, his gaze following the trail and stopped at my nipples.

He was so close, his warm breath fanned my lips. "We should explore a little more before it gets dark."

I quivered under his touch. It was too much. I had three other men waiting for me. And Thadd was in Silk City. Although we weren't committed to one another, it felt like I was asking and taking too much. I should have moved away from Storm, but my lady bits had different ideas.

"What kind of exploring?" My voice was low, and I bit my lower lip.

With his fingers, he pulled my lip, releasing it from my teeth. "I want to explore your body with my mouth." He whispered.

I closed the distance, our lips clashed with intense heat. Storm's tongue glided along my bottom lip. My tongue met his and delved into his mouth. Our kisses became feverish. He slid his hand into my hair and pulled me onto his lap. His cock was stiff and swollen. I ground my core against him.

"Oh, fuck, Zara." His mouth moved to my neck while he palmed my breasts.

I tipped my head back, moaning and rocking my hips while he clamped his mouth on my nipple.

"I want you, Zara, so much." He flipped us over on the smooth stone sand.

I spread my legs wide to make room for his broad frame.

"You have me so hard I won't be able to stop. If you want to slow down, now would be the time to tell me."

He kept kissing me, and I didn't stop him. It was too fast.

Sort of. I had known Phin for maybe two days before we had sex.

After that night, I couldn't get enough. And right then, with Storm between my legs, I was in the zone of feeling and savoring every sensation. Rational thought left my brain.

"Are you ok with my situation?" I asked.

"Of course. It is the way of elemental women, Zara," he whispered against my neck. "I wanted to take this slow, but my body has other ideas."

His hard cock strained against his boxers.

Then my phone chimed beside my ear. Storm and I drew apart a bit and chuckled.

Phin texted; he, Beau, and Cass were already at the lair. I messaged back, stating that we'd be there shortly.

Storm stood and brought me up with him, and we dressed quickly.

I took one last look at Treasure Veil. It was a shame to leave and I sighed. But, Storm came up behind me, placed a kiss on my cheek, and whispered, "We'll be back, Zara. I promise."

With that, we followed our way back the way we had come, to the beginning of the path, and soared up towards the surface.

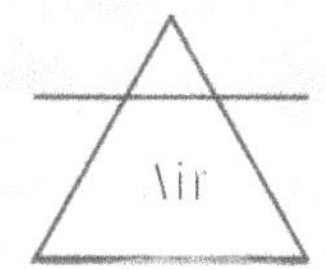

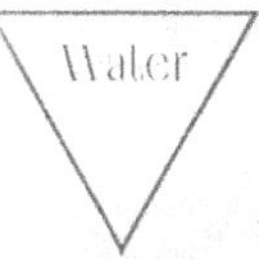

Chapter Thirty-Seven

PHINEAS

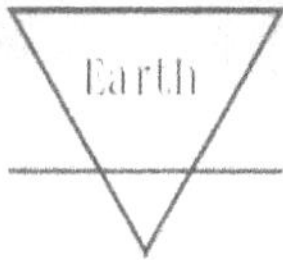

My beast was restless. Zara had been gone for a few hours with Storm. He wouldn't harm her, and I wasn't jealous... not really. I just wanted, no needed, her near. I paced in the living area, creating a path in the stone flooring.

"Relax, Phin, she's fine." Beau held out a cup of mead. "They'll be here soon. Besides, it's good they get to know one another."

I accepted the cup and kept pacing. He was right, but my beast was anxious.

"Incoming!" Cassian shouted from the hangar.

I shifted to my shadow form and arrived at the hangar entrance beside Cassian. Beau arrived a minute later.

Cassian was startled by my sudden appearance and shook his head at me. My shadow form was a side-effect of my fire magic. It allowed me to move quickly without having to shift into my dragon. It came in handy in small spaces. With the Source, being cut off, we tried to reserve our magic, and using my shadow form wasn't necessary for this instance. I shrugged. Seeing my angel right then; was more important to me.

Zara and Storm landed a few feet away from the entrance.

Her cheeks were pink, and she was breathless.

"You did well, Zara. I can't believe you haven't traveled that distance before," Storm said appraisingly.

"You're a good teacher, but I have to say I'm spent. I feel like I ran a marathon," Zara replied, her chest heaving with exertion.

"You did, that was close to a thousand miles," I said to them.

"What? Why would you let me do that?!" She smacked Storm's arm.

"I would have caught you if you faltered, Z. You did fine." Storm chuckled.

"Fuck, I'm exhausted." Zara bent over, her palms resting on her knees.

I walked up to Zara and drew her into my arms.

"Come on, you'll feel better once we get some water and food in you." I kissed the top of her and let her lean into my body for support.

We walked leisurely to the kitchen, Cass and Beau leading the way. Storm filled us in on Treasure Veil although I had a feeling there were a few details he left out.

It was dinner time, but Zara was exhausted. I took her into the bathroom and joined her for a hot shower. Two orgasms later we entered the bedroom and found the other guys setting up the table for dinner.

"Thank you." Zara smiled. "I'm starving."

"We thought you might be," Cassian pulled her in for a passionate kiss.

Once he released her, she walked up behind Storm who was seated at the table, and wrapped her arms around him, kissing his cheek and neck. He closed his eyes and leaned into her.

She moved away from the air elemental and then sat on Beau's lap. Their kiss started out sweet and tender, then grew as she began to moan.

Linc knocked on the door and wheeled in a cart. "Excuse me, sirs and my lady. I don't mean to disturb. I'm delivering your entrees is all."

"Thank you, Linc," Zara said.

The gnome kept his head down and waved behind him as he exited.

"So, what happened earlier?" Zara asked as we began filling our bellies.

"They were royal guards out on patrol. Two airmen and one water and one earth. The air elementals were Glen and Chris. We didn't get what clans they were from, but we detained them and put them in the cells." I looked over at Storm. He might know them. "You're welcome to talk to them, but Beau has good news."

"I was able to remove the runes," Beau said with a twinkle in his eye.

"You've been able to undo the spell?!" Zara squealed.

It was big. On top of all the things we dealt with daily, Beau had been diligent and had worked all hours to figure out the spell that enslaved our people.

"So far. We won't know for certain until they're in front of the royals and that is risky. But from what I can gather, it is permanent. We just need to monitor them. They are far away from the other villages, but we can get to them quickly to check up on them. And I installed a magical alert system if something changes," Beau said modestly.

"Well, done earth mage. You did good," Zara leaned over and gave him a smooch.

"Thank you, beautiful. But let's not get too excited. We need to test it," Beau told us.

"I have faith in you." Zara winked.

"I do too," Cass said and lifted his cup of wine. "Toast to making progress."

We clinked cups and continued eating.

"On to more pressing matters," I said between bites. "We have the crone and her foresight abilities to deal with."

"We have to assume she will know when we're coming," Storm said. "And if I remember correctly, her sight kicks in when the royals or herself are in harm's way."

"That encompasses our entire mission. How do we fly under her radar?" Cassian muttered.

He was right. We wanted to take out the crone, the mage, and then dethrone the king and queen. The queen might be spared, that was Zara's call. If the crone was working with them, she'd see us coming.

"Where is the map? The one we created according to Grant's info," Zara asked.

"In my office. I'll go get it," I said.

I shadow-walked to my office, got the map, and returned seconds later. Cass helped me tack it on the wall in the living room where we gathered after dinner.

Zara stared at the map. Her brow scrunched up in a frown.

I pressed my chest against her back and wrapped my arms around her chest. "What are you thinking, angel?"

"We need a distraction. That's the only way." Zara replied with a deep exhale.

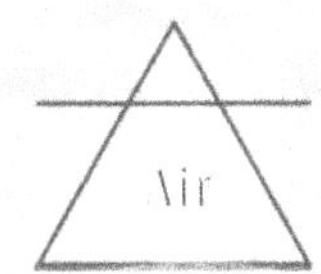

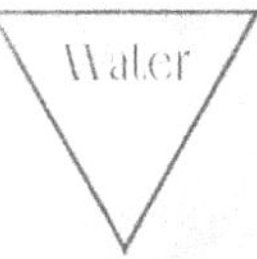

Chapter Thirty-Eight

ZARA

"Zara!" My mother opened her arms, greeting me on the front porch of our humble home.

"Good morning, Mama." I gave her a squeeze. "I've missed you."

She ushered me and the four elemental men inside. Phin introduced Storm and he explained Trick's absence. It still bothered me that no one had heard from him since his letter. Phin and Storm traveled by air often looking for him, and they'd even stopped at his nest. It was almost as though he disappeared. According to the guys, Trick was always a loner, and they weren't worried about it.

Gigi had breakfast ready, and the four men sat in our tiny dining room to eat, while I fired up my tablet and returned emails.

An hour later we went to Thadd's. He opened the door and shook hands with the guys as they came in. After my last visit here, the elemental men were more accepting of my relationship with him. The images of that afternoon with Beau and Thadd flooded my brain, and I found myself eyeing our host.

"Good morning, Thaddeus." I greeted him with a hug. It was just before 9 a.m. and Thadd was not a morning person. I had insisted on getting an early start. I wanted to visit my mother and a part of me was a nervous wreck about our plan today.

"Good morning, beautiful. You're the only person in the world that can wake me this early, you know that?" He draped himself around me.

I smiled. "Thank you for doing this for me. I appreciate you more than you know."

We gathered in the living area and reviewed the plan. With Thadd's help, we were going to intercept the royal's purchase of human weapons here in Silk City. Once we confiscated the weapons, me and the four elemental men would drive back to the Sanctuary in the royal guard's vehicles. It was the perfect cover.

"We have a couple of hours. Help yourself to anything in the kitchen or the bar," Thadd offered. "A word, Zara."

I moved to follow him, and the four elemental guys stood with me.

"It's ok guys. I'll be fine," I said.

Thadd placed a hand on the small of my back guiding me out of the living area.

"You guys are welcome to watch if you want. We'll leave the door open," he told them.

I tilted my head up to glare at him.

"I wasn't planning to seduce you. Unless that's what you wanted." Thadd winked.

I smacked his stomach and went upstairs to his room.

Thadd's room was masculine, with dark grays and sharp lines. He was always organized and tidy, and I loved teasing him about his anal-retentive nature. Everything had to be in its proper place.

I hopped on his bed, pulled a pillow onto my lap, and ruffled up the covers.

"You're doing that on purpose." He gripped my ankles and drew my body towards him.

"And I thought you weren't going to seduce me," I replied.

He removed the pillow and gave me a hungry kiss. I tangled my fingers in his hair, pressing him closer to me.

"I missed you," he said between the kisses he peppered all over my neck and chest.

"I think you meant to say you missed sex with me."

He laughed. "Yes, babe, that too. Are you ok? The guys treating you well?"

I nodded. Thadd and I had talked every day since he'd given me a phone that worked in the kingdom. Still, it was nice to be missed.

He pushed me back on the bed so that I was lying down, and he laid on top of me, resting his body weight on propped elbows.

"Good. Are you planning to live there when this is all done?" he asked.

I spread my legs further apart for his wide frame and shook my head. "No, I won't leave Gigi."

He let out a sigh of relief.

"Or you," I admitted.

He gazed into my eyes, and a broad smile spread over his face.

"Good, I'll be happy to have you home." He placed a tender kiss on my lips. "I did want to give you something." He sat up and paused. Thaddeus, successful businessman and badass mage, looked nervous.

I straddled his lap. "What's on your mind?"

"I don't want to scare you away." He ran his hand through his hair and tried to avoid my gaze.

"I love you, Zara. So much. I'm not asking you for commitment or to choose me and only me. Nothing like that." Thadd's voice got soft. "These last few days, you've been in so much danger. It's driving me insane. I feel helpless because I want to keep you safe. The only way for me to do that if I'm not at your side is by sharing my magic with you. By...marking you with magical runes."

I sat there speechless for a moment while Thadd bowed his head, reluctant to meet my gaze.

I tipped his chin to face me and went all in. "I love you too, Thadd. But..."

He pressed a finger to my lips, wearing a wide grin. "No 'buts,' just let me enjoy this for a moment."

I gnashed at his finger with my teeth, and he snatched it away before I could chomp it.

"I was going to say, but I'm not sure about this rune business. What does that entail?" I asked.

He smiled brightly and rolled us over, bringing his body on top of mine again. "Nothing to it. I umm... I tattoo the runes wherever you want, embed them with magic, and then it's done. We'll be finished in less than twenty minutes, unless, you know...we get distracted." He wiggled his eyebrows at me.

I laughed. "All right, what do these look like and what do they do?"

Thaddeus set up a simple tattoo gun, sterilized my skin, and got to work. As soon as the tattoo gun started to buzz the four elemental men entered the bedroom, and Thadd explained what he was about to do to me.

I took off my top, giving Thadd access to my skin. Beau stood next to Thadd, a determined and curious gleam to his eyes. My earth elemental was curious to learn all about the magic he was casting. Cass and Storm got on the bed and took up spots on each side of me. Phin sat behind me and offered his body as a pillow, but Thadd shot that idea down, stating no skin-to-skin contact was allowed.

The rune was a beautiful sun and moon design, which he placed on my upper arm. He used a golden ink imbued with magic. The golden color shimmered against my bronze skin and would glow when activated. He had designed it to shield me from vampire magic and give me a boost of magic if I needed it. Thadd was concerned about Trick's unhealthy obsession with me, and the other men agreed. They were certain; Trick would come back for me at some point.

As promised, it only took him twenty minutes. After placing the tattoo, he chanted and waved his hand over it. A rush of magic seared my skin for a few seconds and that was it.

I wasn't sure if it'd work as designed, but it made Thadd feel better about my safety, and that made me happy.

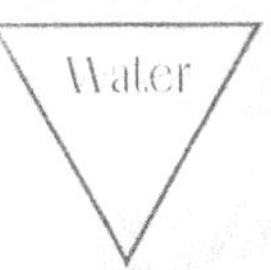

Chapter Thirty-Nine

ZARA

We left Thadd's a couple of hours later and drove to the drop-off location. Thadd provided more manpower to ensure everything went off without a hitch. His men surveilled the area before either party showed up, and he provided us with fake weapons to deliver. Phin, Cass, and Storm were going to detain the royal guards. After that, they would stash the real weapons and then head to the Sanctuary to cause a distraction. In the meantime, Beau and I were going straight in to deal with the mage.

Once all parties arrived at the drop-off location, everything went as planned. The weapons dealer got their payment and took off. Amongst the four guards sent by the royals was Grant's cousin Grainger. The two could have been brothers. They had the same red hair, green eyes, and were covered with freckles.

As Grant had said, Grainger didn't have the rune and he was eager to help us. The guys trussed up three guards while Beau along with Thadd's help, dealt with the runes which enslaved them to the mage. Thadd was confident the runes weren't going to come back, but we were being extra cautious, and they'd stay captive until the mage was dealt with.

"The easy part is over, now let's get to the Sanctuary. See you soon, Z." Cassian kissed my forehead.

Phin took his place. "Be careful, Zara, stay close to Beau."

"We got this, Zara. Soon this will be all over." Storm pecked my cheek, and then he, Cass, and Phin drove off with the trussed-up guards.

"I love you, baby Z. Check in when you get a chance." Thadd drew me into his body for a moment, breathing me in.

I watched him get into his car, wishing he didn't have to go. But this wasn't his fight.

Beau and I got into one of the vehicles which contained the fake weapons, and Grainger came with us. He confirmed everything his cousin had told us about the layout and what we'd be dealing with. It seemed nothing had changed at the Sanctuary.

At the healing village, we stopped while Beau went to release a healed-up Grant. He and his cousin hugged, and just like that, we had ourselves another ally. Having the cousins with us would make it easier for us to get as close as possible without being detected.

We drove for a time in silence, tension gnawing at the back of my neck. A few miles from the Sanctuary, we pulled over. Grant took the wheel, Grainger sat in the front passenger seat, and Beau and I slumped in the backseat keeping our heads down.

As we drew closer to the Sanctuary, I couldn't believe what I was seeing. Several round stark white buildings did not belong in what had been hallowed ground. Each structure was constructed with prefabricated materials such as plastics, fiberglass, and cheap laminated wood. Elementals celebrated nature and paid homage to the Goddess in everything they did. This was a slap in the face.

Grant parked somewhere discreetly before letting Beau and me out, and then he drove around to deliver the fake weapons. The two of us crept around the sanctuary grounds until we came upon the largest, windowless atrocity.

Nervous tension clawed at my spine. Beau reached back, grasped my hand and led the way to the main building which Grant had called the mage's domain. "No one goes near that place if they can help it." He had said with a shudder.

As we got closer to the main building, a feeling of dread threatened to swallow me whole. Living in the poorest part of Silk City, I was familiar with violence and death. But the closer we got to the mage's domain, I sensed an evil presence radiating from the round building, and a strong desire in my gut warned me to leave.

"I won't let anything happen to you, Zara," Beau said in a low voice. "Come on."

Hand in hand we crept along the outside of the building until we came upon a side door. A wave of darkness washed over me when we entered. The air was thick and heady, incense burnt the hair in my nostrils, and my eyes blinked rapidly as my vision clouded over. There were no windows. I wanted to turn back and prop the door open.

"Breathe, Zara. I'm right here with you." Beau's strong stable presence grounded me. I leaned into him for a second and inhaled his comforting earthy scent of pine and freshly cut grass.

Ready to deal with the dark forces present in the building, I squeezed his hand.

We stuck to the shadows as we entered the empty open space.

"Watch your step," Beau whispered and pointed at the floor.

Dim lighting from a few candles allowed enough illumination to make out the arcane symbols that had been drawn on the floors and walls. It became clear to me that more travesties were occurring than I had imagined.

Beau reached into his pocket and pulled out black chalk and swiped through a symbol on the wall nearest us and bent to do the same on the wall, cutting through the magic those symbols held. He broke the chalk in half and handed one to me. "These are power amplification spells. We need to break them. I'll go high, you stay low. Hurry, the mage will sense it."

I was never so happy to have this man at my side. We moved through the room as quickly as possible, breaking circles and disrupting every spell we came across. There had to have been twenty of them, the biggest one in the middle of the room on the floor. I moved straight toward the largest symbol and Beau halted me mid-step. "That one will take more than chalk to undo."

I nodded and kept working alongside him. Halfway through the room, the main door blasted open. Shards of wood went flying.

Beau and I ducked out of sight.

A tall, bald man stalked into the room, his black tunic billowing behind him. "I know you're here. I will flay your skin when I find you."

He sent a pulse of magic in the opposite direction of where we had been standing, shattering shelves and tables. We scampered to our left just missing another wave of magic.

"I can smell you, earth elemental." Another wave of magic shot through between Beau and me, separating us.

The mage followed Beau who went in the direction we had entered. I drew my gun from my holster and pulled the trigger. My bullet ricocheted off a magical shield. I ducked and used the opportunity to dismantle the symbols on the other side securing us an exit. Almost there.

The mage sent a pulse of magic, which had been much weaker. Frantic, the mage sent pulse after pulse, each one weaker than the next. He screamed in frustration.

Gunfire from outside caught his attention, and with his back turned to me, I sent a wave of magic straight at him. He sailed across the room, slamming into the wall where all his arcane symbols had been destroyed.

Beau stood and gave me a nod. I strode up to the mage lying on the floor.

"You! It can't be." He stared at me with wide eyes.

"Oh, it's me alright. Your time is done." I pulled at the water in his body, flooding his lungs.

"Wait!" He gasped. "I can help you. I can heal your father and release your sister."

Release my sister? I cocked my head to the side and eased up on my magic, allowing him to breathe. He coughed and sputtered, then a force of magic hit me in my gut. I was thrown across the room, and my body skidded over the largest symbol on the floor. I clutched my stomach and gasped for air.

"Stupid girl. You will never get your kingdom back. I may have lost my hold on your people, but now I control you!"

Before he could hit me with his magic again, Beau sent an electrical pulse, tripping him. The mage got up and shot two streams of magic. One sailed over my head. The other was aimed at Beau who erected a magical shield blocking the mage's assault. The two mages were at a standoff, their magical forces slamming into each other. Both dug in their heels, pushing each other back.

"Zara, the symbol!" Beau shouted.

The largest arcane symbol was but a foot away from where I knelt. I looked at the chalk in my hand and remembered Beau's words. This won't do.

I shot a pulse of magic at the mage which bounced off his shield. The mage's face was scrunched up with fury, and then he pushed more dark magic back at Beau.

A sheen of sweat covered Beau's forehead. He braced against the assault with all of his body weight, his muscular arms and legs flexed under the strain. His magical shield was waning, and I had to do something, quickly.

I called on my connection to my earth magic and felt it rise within me. Power swelled through every particle of my being, and the ground rumbled under my feet. I stretched my arms up to the sky then slammed my fists into the ground.

The concrete flooring split, and fissures spread through the ground, breaking the arcane symbol in several places. Both the mage and Beau collapsed to the ground. The mage screamed, then he turned towards me and started chanting.

Oh hell no. I pulled my gun out of the holster on my hip and fired, shooting him square in the chest.

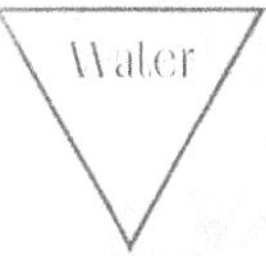

Chapter Forty

ZARA

All was quiet outside after we'd dealt with the mage. Beau went to check on things while I searched the room and found his grimoire. I found an empty satchel to put the book in and slipped it over my neck.

"The other guys are on their way here. You ok?" Beau approached me, and I nodded. "You did amazing, Z."

"I found this." I opened the satchel for him to see the grimoire.

"Good find. We'll go through it when we get home." He grasped my hand and led the way out to the front of the building.

"Zara!" Phin rushed up to me and held me tight. "I was worried."

I hugged him back and then greeted Cassian and Storm.

"Wow!" Cass peeked into the building. "Whose handy work is this?"

"Zara's." Beau grinned and tilted his head towards me.

"She split the ground with one hit."

His adoring smile made me blush.

"How did everything else go? Any sign of the crone?" I asked.

"No, she's probably at the palace," Phin answered me. "The people are all free, and we sent word via an airman to notify the people at the palace to head this way. Storm and I have delegated tasks to a couple of lieutenants we recognized. They'll rally everyone together and meet up in about an hour. Grant and Grainger are waiting to show us around. Should we get you home, Zara?"

"Oh no, not yet. I'd like to make sure the Source is reopened."

We left the destroyed mage building behind and walked the grounds of the sanctuary. The people greeted us with grateful smiles and nods. People had questions and the men promised to answer them all in due time.

The Sanctuary was approximately five acres at the base of Source Mountain. Just closing off the Sanctuary would have wreaked havoc on elemental magic. That alone could not have affected the kingdom and its people as severely as I had witnessed. Taking out the mage was one problem, but there had to be more to it.

As Grant and Grainger had explained, people were expected to serve the royals in whatever capacity they were told. Strong elementals were given the rune and forced to comply with the king and queen's demands. Those that defied them were immediately killed or imprisoned in the dungeons. Powerful children were sent to the palace, for what purpose no one knew. Average to low power wielders whether male or female were required to serve in the palace or the mines. The mining had been my biggest concern.

They were digging into Source Mountain and had tunneled a good way into the mountain's depths. Their actions had defiled the Goddess's temple and she'd withdrawn her power. Men, women, and children had died trying to claw their way to its core.

It was as if the Goddess herself turned her back on her people.

Phin found the person in charge of the mines and brought him over to us for questioning. The man whose name was Brennan fell to his knees in front of me.

"Princess, I am so sorry. I didn't mean for this to happen. I was enthralled." The man wept.

"It's ok, that part is over now. But we need to fix this and restore the Sanctuary and the Source. Can you tell us more about what the royals had planned?" I knelt in front of Brennan and held his gaze.

He scrubbed his face with a dirt-covered hand and nodded. "The mage kept us under control with the runes. But it's the seer and the king calling the shots. They didn't say what they wanted, they just wanted us to keep going. Anyone with earth magic was called upon to whittle down the rock with their gifts. Everyone else used pickaxes and shovels until their hands bled." Brennan started weeping again.

"Have the royals or the crone been here recently?" I asked.

He nodded. "All four of them on the full moon. They've been coming to the mines every full moon since we started digging eight months ago. We dug all day and all night. The full moon was the only night we had a break. They sent everyone away, but the last time I followed."

His body visibly shivered, and he fidgeted uncomfortably in his seat. "They were chanting all four of them. It was dark and evil. It scared me. I couldn't stay so I ran out."

"Thank you, Brennan. I hate to ask this, but is someone available to take us down there?" I asked.

He sobbed. "I...I will do it. One last time. I'll take you."

Damn it, I didn't want to put him through this, but we had no choice. I needed to see for myself what was happening. The Source needed to be cleansed and the only way to do that was to see what we were dealing with.

"Thank you, Brennan. We'll give you a few minutes." I patted him on his shoulder then turned to face my men and glanced over their shoulders.

"We all don't need to go. There are things that need to be done here." I jutted my chin out to point at the crowd gathered behind them.

The four men turned. "Me and Beau will go with Zara,"

Phin said. "Storm and Cass can deal with the crowd."

We all nodded, then both Storm and Cassian headed out.

At the entrance of the mines, we grabbed a couple of torches and followed Brennan in single file, Phin behind him, then me, and Beau was at my back.

The mining tunnels were shrouded in an oppressive dark magic. The hair on my arms stood on end, and a lump in my throat nearly constricted my breathing.

I reached out to grasp Phin's hand and extended my other behind my back for Beau's. Both men gave me a squeeze which quelled my anxiousness...somewhat.

A few miles in the tunnel became darker. "The sun is setting," Brennan said in a soft voice.

Phin released my hand and conjured several tiny fireballs. They floated ahead, illuminating the space a few feet in front of us and above our heads.

The tunnel opened up ahead, allowing all four of us to walk side by side, and that's when I noticed it. I slowed and glanced at the walls as the little fireballs floated by. The walls were covered in arcane symbols. Fuck me, not this again.

"Hold on guys," I said to Phin and Brennan, not wanting them to get too far ahead.

Beau held up his torch to examine the walls and cursed.

"Hold onto this, Z."

I grabbed the torch and held it close to the wall while Beau took a closer look. "Shit. Do you have your phone on you? We need a picture."

I shook my head as Phin handed him his. Beau took a video while Phin and I held up the torches. Once he was done, he said, "We need to turn back. Brennan, lead us out." He stuffed the phone into his pocket, took the torch, and grasped my hand.

Brennan set a fast pace out of the tunnels, and we practically jogged back the way we came.

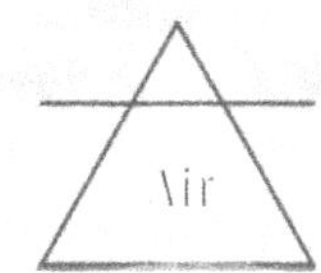

Chapter Forty-One

CASSIAN

Storm and I spoke with our people who were grateful but concerned the crone and the royals would come back with a vengeance. According to the villagers, the mage, the crone, the king, and the queen were all cruel but the mage was least cruel than the others.

We established a perimeter, took stock of food and supplies, and made sure anyone that was ill, was tended to. And then, we assigned guard duty and delegated lieutenants that would be in charge of keeping things organized and calm.

Our people were anxious about Zara being in the mines. Several elementals had told us the mines were evil, and no one wanted to go in there. She'd left with Phin, Beau, and Brennan hours ago. The sun had set, and still, they hadn't returned. The air elemental and I glanced at one another; we were both getting anxious.

To appease our people, we allowed them to trash what was left of the mage's building, turning it into a bonfire. It seemed to be cathartic. And it also provided a lot of light which helped ease tensions. The elementals here were afraid of the dark.

Hours after they had gone in, Brennan, Beau, Zara, and Phin appeared outside of the mining entrance. All four of them were breathing hard as though they'd run the entire way back. Storm and I rushed toward them.

Luckily, most of the villagers were already asleep. We didn't want to scare them any further than they already were.

I went straight to Zara. "Are you ok?"

She gave me a small smile and nodded, still trying to catch her breath. I gathered her in my arms, which wasn't a good idea because she could hardly breathe. But I was just so happy to see her.

I released her and Storm took my place.

"You were gone for hours. What the hell happened?" I asked the men.

Phin nodded. "Yeah, we got about halfway down and decided to haul ass back up here."

Beau bent over at the waist and braced his hands on his knees. "Dark magic. I didn't want to stay longer than we needed to. And I didn't want to open a portal either. Unless properly warded, activating any magic in there will adversely affect the caster. We need to prepare before we go back in. We'll need to shield ourselves in protective magic, and we'll need to figure out how to cleanse it, or the Source will never be free."

Well, fuck.

Phin clapped Brennan on the shoulder. "Thank you. Get some rest. We'll block off this entrance. Make sure no one goes back down there again."

Brennan nodded then shuffled away.

Once he was out of earshot, I addressed the guys. "The people here are afraid of the crone and the royals. We established some order, but most are reluctant to stay. I'm guessing they'll move out until those three are gone."

"I expected as much. How many people left the palace?" Phin asked.

"From what we were told, almost sixty percent," I replied. It wasn't good news but some people had given in to the fear. Despite being free of the spell, they were too afraid to rise against their captors.

Zara shook her head. I almost suggested we needed to parade her outside the palace and give them hope, but I knew she didn't want to take over the throne. That would be an unfair ask.

Plus, dark circles marred her pretty face, and she needed to rest.

"We found a place for us to sleep here, Zara. Or would you rather go back to the lair?" Storm asked her.

"Umm...I, I think we should stay. I don't want the people to freak out if they see that we're gone," she replied.

We all nodded, then Storm linked his hands in hers and led the way. Beau, Phin, and I stayed back while we barricaded the main entrance to the mines. After that, we walked the grounds and checked in with people. We also got our overnight bags out of the car we'd driven, found some food, and then made our way back to Zara.

There was a building that hadn't been used. It had showers, a small kitchen, and a couple of comfortable beds. We were told that it was one of the newer buildings that had been reserved for the royals, but they never stayed. When they visited, they went into the mines at sunset and didn't come out until dawn.

"What's with magic in the mines?" Phin asked Beau.

Beau shook his head, disgust shadowing his features. "It's bad. From what I can tell, the sigils were meant to exhaust the Source's power and redirect it to someone or somewhere. I couldn't tell where or who. There were also entrapment spells woven into it. Meaning if you tried to dismantle the spell, you'd be trapped, and your power would drain right along with it. Plus, it was fueled with blood. All those people who worked in the mines and bled...fed the spells unknowingly of course."

"Fuck me. Now what? Can we get rid of it? Please tell me there's a way to fix this." I wanted to hit something.

"Off the top of my head, I've got nothing. I need a second opinion. I may need to ask Thaddeus for help." Beau stared straight ahead.

Phin turned to face us. "Zara's Thaddeus?"

Beau nodded. Phin glanced at me, and I shrugged. We loved Zara, and Thadd was part of the package. As much as Zara liked to say she didn't do love, she had feelings for the guy, and he turned out to be a real asset. His help with retrieving the weapons was beyond tremendous. Everything had gone smoothly, and he was a cool guy when he wasn't trying to get a rise out of us over Zara. He loved her, that much was clear. They acted like their relationship was a casual friends-with-bene-fits situation but the rest of us knew better. Zara needed her space. She had commitment issues which made sense all things considered, and Thaddeus was more than ok to give it to her. It was a smart move on his part. He wanted her to be happy more than anything and like me and the other elementals, if that meant sharing her with the others, we were ok with it. Plus, I was certain something had gone down between Zara, Thadd, and Beau. My earth brother got a weird look on his face when those three were in the same room. He hadn't shared anything, at least not yet.

We walked into the building where we'd be spending the night, and Zara had just gotten out of the shower. She wore an oversized T-shirt and greeted us with a weary smile.

"We found food and brought a change of clothes," Phin told her and set the bag down on the floor near the bed.

"I'm too tired to eat," she said and climbed onto the bed.

"You must, Z." I kissed her head.

"There are multiple showers, guys." Storm ran a hand over his wet head, drying his hair.

Beau, Phin, and I grunted then headed out to take a shower.

When I got back, Storm and Zara were snuggled up on the bed. She lifted her head and gave me a wink.

"Did you eat, babe?" I snuggled against her other side.

"No, I wanted to wait for you guys." Her voice was soft. She was bone tired. From what we found in the mage's building, I wasn't surprised. She used a lot of magic, and we'd gotten up early.

"Come on then, let's eat." I tugged on her hand bringing her up to a seated position on the bed. Phin was already back and warming up food with his fire.

Beau sauntered into the room with his hair still wet. Storm got up and sent air magic over the top of his head and dried his hair.

There was a small table with enough chairs for four. We pushed the table closer to the bed and then laid out our collection of bread, soups, and salads. Phin also managed to produce two bottles of wine. We had cups for water and that was it. So, we just passed around the bottle.

Zara and I sat on the bed while the other guys sat in chairs around the table. We were famished. We hadn't eaten since we left Gigi's place. I looked over at the reluctant princess and made a note to take better care of her.

Halfway through the meal, Zara's eyelids started to droop. She lay her head on my lap, the rest of her body sprawled on the mattress.

After we ate, I picked up the princess, laid her down on the bed and snuggled next to her in the middle. Soon enough, the rest of the men found a spot on the mattress around her and fell fast asleep.

Chapter Forty-Two

ZARA

The smell of coffee and freshly baked bread woke me. I stretched my arms overhead and arched my back.

"Good morning, angel." Phin crawled up to me and kissed me proper. I kissed him back, wanting more, but loud footsteps and voices interrupted our intimate moment.

Beau, Cass, and Storm walked in speaking emphatically to one another.

"Good morning, Zara." Cass plopped on the bed beside me and gave me a wet kiss.

"Good morning, what's going on? Everything ok?" I asked, then forced myself out of bed before I got too comfortable.

Beau snagged me around my waist, and I kissed his cheek and I greeted Storm as well.

"The villagers are much better today. Spirits are high and they're making plans to defend themselves and to start anew."

"Oh, that's good news," she said.

"We certainly can't leave the Sanctuary unattended. We need to figure out the mine situation and make sure it's well guarded," Phin said.

"Then we need to regroup with the other villagers to go after the palace," Cassian added.

I went to the bathroom while the guys planned out our next moves. Our? Hmm, I wasn't sure there was an "our." My goal was to free the Source which we had, sort of. Getting rid of the dark magic was a mage's job; there wasn't much I could do there. A big part of me was eager to get back to Gigi.

After I pulled on clean clothes and finished up in the bathroom I went in search of my phone.

"What are you looking for, babe?" Cassian asked me.

"My phone. I need to check in with my mom. Oh and Beau I know you have a lot going on, but perhaps there's something in that grimoire that will cleanse the mines and help Zander."

I found the satchel, dug out the book, then turned the satchel upside down hoping my phone would fall out.

Beau took the grimoire out of my hand while chewing on some fruit.

Storm stood behind me and handed me my phone and my gun. "We may have dropped these on the floor before we took a shower," he whispered in my ear.

My face flushed, and I leaned over to kiss his jaw. Despite being exhausted, Storm and I had an intimate moment in the shower last night. We hadn't gone all the way, but hugs and kisses were the perfect remedies to remove the stain of darkness from yesterday's events.

I strapped on my gun holster and then tried to turn on my phone, but it was completely dead, and I huffed.

"Dead," I muttered.

"Mine too," Phin chimed in.

"I'm heading over to the lair. I'll get your chargers and anything else we need," Beau offered.

"We should get the weapons and update the king." Phin sipped on his coffee. "I don't want to leave here. I need to be sure we're ready for whatever the royals have in store."

"I would appreciate a lift to the lair. From there I'll fly over to my village and head back here with more flyers," Storm said.

"I'll update the king. Zara, you want to come with?" Cassian asked me.

"Umm...sure." I shrugged. I wasn't going to sit around while the guys did all the work and seeing my father wasn't the worst assignment.

Beau nodded. "Eat first, Zara. We'll teleport to the lair, then you and Cassian can drive to the cottage. Storm will head to clan Zephyr while I head back here with the weapons. Wait, no, I won't be able to carry all of that myself. Cass, you'll have to drive that back, unless..." Beau looked at Phin.

"Cass, you and Zara drive to the cottage with the weapons. I'll head over there, and my beast will fly it back," Phin said.

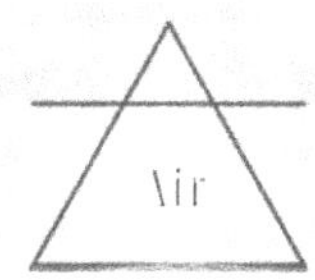

Chapter Forty-Three

ZARA

Cassian and I drove to Zander's cottage. It was a good thirty-minute drive from the lair, which I hoped would be enough time for my phone to charge.

It was interesting how the thought of seeing Zander didn't fill me with anxiety as it once had. Perhaps I was over it. I don't think I'd ever forgive him, but it felt as though I'd moved past my grief and resentment.

Besides, he needed to know what was going on. We were freeing the kingdom so that he could get back in the palace and rule. Plus, the guys had so much more important work to get done.

I was grateful to at least have Cass with me.

Another thought entered my mind and I turned to face Cass.

"Has anyone heard from Trick?" I asked.

Cassian's dark eyebrows drew together. "No. Beau and I went up to his nest on Torch Mountain, and it's been cleared out."

"I...I like having Storm around. Is that a problem?" I blurted, not even sure why I brought up Storm. I made it clear from the start that who I chose was my decision and that I didn't need permission.

Cass smiled. "No, not a problem, Zara. Not for us. We're glad you two are getting along. He's a bit of a reject as well. His father rejected him because he'd married a powerful water elemental; she was my

283

cousin. Their oldest daughter showed a strong connection to air magic though and that thawed his father's heart towards their union. They reconnected but that was short lived due to his father's untimely demise. Shortly after that, the royals went after his clan and his wife and daughters...well, I'm sure he told you. He's had a rough few years. I for one am glad he has someone to make him smile."

"Patrick on the other hand, might have different feelings about the two of you." Cass continued. "He was a bit envious of his brother. And even though Storm tried to reach out a few times, Patrick's automatic response was to avoid him at all costs. Unlike you who confronted your childhood traumas head-on, he harbored a lot of resentment and couldn't find a way to move past it. I wouldn't worry about it, Zara. He made his choice."

"How can I not worry about it? If he hated the idea of having to share with you, Beau, and Phin, he'll despise me if he finds out about Storm."

"Possibly, but as you know, it is common for powerful female elementals to have more than one mate. He knew that and accepted it. And we accepted him and loved him like a brother. He didn't just leave you with nothing but a note. He left all of us. With or without you, Z, we were a family. He rejected his family. It's kind of like if you rejected Gigi after all the years of being a familial unit. It's not right." Cass's gaze turned solemn, the pain of losing a brother casting a shadow over his handsome face.

I reached for Cassian's hand and stared out the window, thinking about the situation. Both Trick and I were discarded by our families and yet we turned out so differently. How could two people with so much in common turn out to have completely opposite ways of thinking?

Cassian pulled into the driveway of the former king's cottage.

We got out of the car, and I held onto Cass's hand. The front door opened, and Zander stood there staring at us. He motioned us inside without saying a word. We followed him through the cottage towards the arboretum.

"Sir, we are here with an update," Cassian said.

Zander remained silent. He walked straight into the kitchen and grabbed a bottle of scotch and poured himself a generous glassful.

I couldn't believe he was ignoring us. I may not resent him the same way Trick resented Storm, but Zander was being downright disrespectful.

"As Cass was saying, we are here with a quick update. We took back the Sanctuary and now we're going to take back the palace. You should be back on your throne in no time," I said.

Zander drank his scotch and still hadn't responded.

"Ok then, consider yourself updated." I tugged Cassian's hand and moved towards the front door.

"Zara, stay, please. I...I just had a flashback. Seeing you two together holding hands brought back memories," Zander whispered.

"Sit, both of you. Please." He placed two empty glasses on the table along with his glass and the bottle of scotch.

Zander and I would probably never have the father daughter relationship we could have had, had I not been banished.

But it was time to let pent-up bitterness go.

"I know you're busy, but just sit for a moment. Have one glass." Zander poured the scotch into the empty glasses and motioned with his hand for us to sit.

"Fine." I sat and sipped the scotch. Thankfully, Cass carried the conversation.

"Thank you, sir," Cassian said. "We also intercepted the weapons transfer with the help of Thaddeus, a friend of Zara's from Silk City. And she took out the mage that was enslaving our people. On top of that, she found his grimoire. Beau is looking through it to find a cure for your illness."

"You did all that for me?" Zander asked me.

"For you?" I shook my head. "No, I did that for the people of this kingdom. As far as the weapons, I didn't do that alone. And yes, I found the book. But Beau is doing the spell work, not me."

"Are you two a couple?" Zander asked. Cassian squirmed in his seat, and I gave my father a flat stare.

"My love life is none of your business," I told him. Sharing my personal life was asking too much.

Zander bristled.

We sat in comfortable silence and sipped our drinks. The scotch was good, but we needed to get moving. I drank the rest of the amber liquid and set the empty glass down. I was about to say let's go when my father poured more scotch into my glass.

I shook my head. "We need to go. There is more to do at the Sanctuary."

"Damn it, Zara." Zander placed his face in his hands.

Cassian muttered something about giving us a minute and he disappeared.

"I'm sorry. For everything. I shouldn't have banished you. I should have allowed you back in the kingdom for your mother's funeral. If I could go back in time, I would undo all of it. Do you want me to beg for your forgiveness?" He said in a soft voice.

The conversation I had with Cassian in the car clicked in place and I sat straighter in my chair to address the former king.

"The first time I came here when you had the guys kidnap me, I desperately wanted to hear those words. But I didn't get them then or the time after that and it wasn't until the drive here that I realized, I don't need your apologies. The truth is Zander, despite what you did, I found love and happiness. I made a good life for myself and have surrounded myself with amazing people who care and love me." A heavyweight I hadn't realized I'd been carrying was lifted from my shoulders. I felt free.

"I am helping your men free our people because it is the right thing to do. I made sure to save the grimoire which could help heal you because it is the right thing to do. And now I will deal with your daughter and remove her and her husband from the palace so that you can rule again because it is the right thing to do.

Aside from banishing your daughter, you were a good king. The people loved you. Putting you back on the throne is the right thing to do." I got up, and on my way out, I waved my hand and said, "Thanks for the scotch."

"Zara, wait." Zander stood and moved towards me.

I stopped a few feet in front of the door but didn't turn around.

He came around to stand in front of me.

"I don't deserve you. I am so proud of the woman you've become." He wrapped me in a hug, and I just stood there.

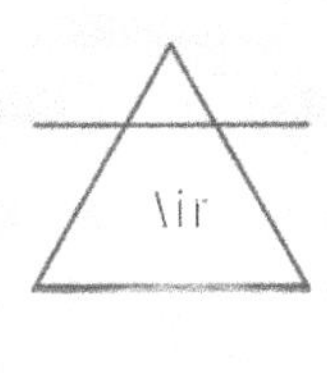

Chapter Forty-Four

ZARA

I walked out of my father's cottage confused. He'd hugged me and apologized. I had been waiting for that apology for so long, and now I didn't know how to feel about it. I decided to unpack that emotional baggage another time.

Outside of the cottage, the four men stood at the end of the driveway, staring at me. They must've seen the exchange with my father through the picture window.

"Hey." I looked up at them. "Is everything ok? I thought I was meeting up with you?"

"Hey, angel." Phin drew my body to his and gave me a salacious kiss, making me forget all of my worries.

I smiled at my fire elemental when he released me.

"Everything's on track. We're expecting company so we need to get the weapons back to the Sanctuary via a portal. Plus, I, we missed you." Phin added.

I caressed his cheek then released him to greet the rest of the guys. They gathered the weapons and a bag of my personal things that we had picked up from the lair, and we went through the portal.

The royal guard was on their way and yet the four elemental men didn't seem stressed at all. I wondered if they were putting up a front for my benefit. I couldn't really tell but decided not to question them or get panicky about the situation.

"Go relax for a bit, Zara," Storm said. "We'll come to get you shortly."

Yep, they were trying to shield me from what they were dealing with. The silly boys thought they could tuck the princess away in her ivory tower. Not this girl.

"How can I help?" I shook my head. "Don't tell me that everything's fine, and that there's nothing I can do. I'm here to see this through and if the royal guards are on the way, well, it seems like we should be planning."

"Zara, there is something." Beau gave the guys a nod, which was code for something I hadn't figured out yet, and he guided me to a secluded spot so that we could speak in private.

Once he was satisfied no one would overhear us, he spoke softly. "The sigils in the cave will take a lot of power to take them down. The five of us can work together to get it done but...it won't be enough. Elemental power won't be enough. Thaddeus seems to be a powerful mage. Do you think he would be willing to help?

I'm sorry I don't know of anyone else with his kind of magic."

"Oh, don't be sorry, I am sure he will be happy to help." I pulled out my fully charged phone. I had been distracted dealing with Zander, so I hadn't had a chance to call Gigi yet. I powered it on and noticed there were dozens of missed calls and texts from Thadd. I frowned, thinking about my mother who was under his care.

"Everything ok?" Beau asked.

"He's been trying to reach me." Uneasiness clenching my gut, I dialed his number and Thaddeus picked up on the first ring.

"Zara! Fuck, where have you been? I've trying to reach you!" Thaddeus shouted into the phone.

"Sorry, I've been dealing with a lot and..."

"Is Gigi with you?" He interrupted me.

"No. I've been at the Sanctuary like we planned. Why?"

"I've got a bad feeling, Z. My guys checked on her last night before she went to bed and this morning, she was gone." "I'm on my way." I hung up the phone, my hands shaking.

"My mom is missing. I have to go."

Beau wrapped his arms around my waist, and we teleported to my house in Silk City. Thadd was there pacing in the small hallway.

He took two long strides toward me and clutched me to his chest.

"Fuck, I was worried. Sorry I let myself in. Gigi has a daily routine, and she usually lets Will in every morning. He brings in the paper, and she makes his coffee and some healthy oatmeal shit. This morning she didn't answer, so he called me. I came straight over, and walked right in. The lock was busted. I looked around but didn't touch a thing. I found the place like this."

Her pillows and blankets were on the floor. One house slipper was in the living room, the other was nowhere to be found, and the chairs were overturned.

"I've done a sweep of the place with my mage sight, and I didn't find spells or a magical signature anywhere," Thadd added.

Beau popped out then returned moments later with Cass, Storm, and Phin.

"Zara," Phin said in a steady voice. "Breathe, angel, how can we help?"

"I...I don't know. It's like she vanished. Who would do this?" I stammered. My heart galloped in my chest. All her personal belongings were still in her room. Even her remedies were in the kitchen. Fuck, she was in trouble.

"I'll sniff around outside." Cass stripped in the middle of the house and shifted into a wolf.

"Did you check your room?" Storm asked me.

I hurried there and nothing was out of place. A double bed and a nightstand, barely fit in the small space. I sat on my bed, and bile swirled in my stomach making me nauseous. I propped my elbows on my knees and covered my face in my hands. This couldn't be happening right now. I glanced at the floor and noticed a piece of paper peeking out from underneath my bed.

I pulled it out and read the note.

If you want to see your foster mother again, you will surrender to your king and queen. You have until midnight or she's dead.

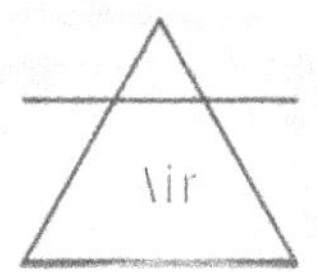

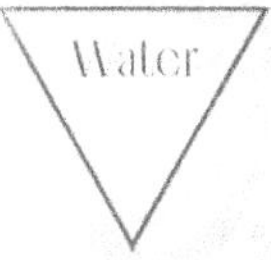
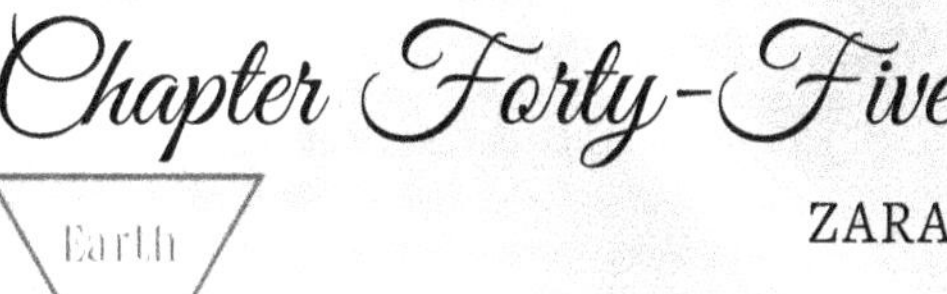

Chapter Forty-Five

ZARA

My hands shook and my body vibrated with anger. Fucking Amina. What the hell was she thinking involving an elderly sick human woman in her shit?

"Why does she hate me?" I sat on the edge of my bed clutching my belly.

"Who Zara?" Phin asked.

I handed him the crumpled note that I had clenched in my fist.

He gave Beau a knowing look and handed him the note.

Beau read it and made a disgusted face.

"I need to get to the palace now," I said to the guys and pulled out a backpack from my closet. Gigi would need her remedies and other things, so I planned to pack a few of her personal items.

"Zara, let's make a plan. They're obviously setting up a trap for you," Storm said.

I scrubbed my hands over my face. "I'm aware, Storm. But I need to get to her now. Who knows how long they've had her? She needs her meds and she must be scared out of her mind." Tears leaked out of my eyes, and I didn't bother wiping them away.

"Baby Z, come here." Thaddeus put his hands on my waist and guided me to stand in front of him while he sat on my bed.

"You're right, we need to get to Gigi right away, but Storm is right also. Give us ten minutes to formulate a plan." Thadd rubbed away my tears with his thumb.

"You don't need to get involved. None of you do." I looked over my shoulder at the other men crowded in my small bedroom.

"This is between me and my sister."

Phin stepped up behind me and pressed his chest to my back while Storm grasped my left hand. Beau squeezed in and stood on my right.

"We'll see you through this, baby. All of us," Thadd said then he pressed his face to my belly.

"Let's think this through, angel." Phin rested his chin on the top of my head.

"Give us a few minutes, Z." Storm kissed my knuckles.

I wanted to rage into that damn palace, and burn it to the ground, but they had a point. I nodded. "Ok, thank you."

Beau guided me out into the living room, while Storm and Phin went through the house looking for pen and paper. Cassian walked through the door in all his naked glory.

"Did you find anything?" I asked Cassian.

He made a face and then glanced at Phin who shook his head.

"What is it, Cass? What did you find?" I pressed. He found something and it grated my nerves that he would keep it from me.

I looked at Phin and Beau then back at Cass.

"One of you better start talking." I crossed my arms over my chest.

"Zara, it's nothing concrete, but there's something about that note." Phin glanced at the crumbled paper on the coffee table.

"That's Patrick's penmanship."

My blood went cold. I picked up the note and looked at it again. It was indeed the same penmanship as the note he had written for me when he'd left the lair. Fuck.

"And I umm...I picked up his scent outside," Cassian added.

"Motherfucker! Why is he doing this?" I started pacing.

Fucking Patrick. I wanted to pull my hair out and light his ass on fire.

Thadd got up and wrapped me in his arms. "We'll figure this out, Zara. Focus, we'll get her back."

He sat on a chair in the living room and pulled me onto his lap. I couldn't focus; my mind was running rampant with thoughts of killing the two-faced air elemental.

The other guys knelt around the coffee table, waiting for me to collect myself. I nodded at Phin assuring him I was ok for now, and he got the plans rolling.

"While Storm is drawing up a map, Thadd, if you don't mind sharing with us what kind of magic you possess, this will help us plan," Phin said as Storm began drawing up an aerial view of the palace grounds.

"I'm a master Druid. For these purposes, I can portal and I have defensive and combat magic. I have invisibility magic also, but I can't cloak all six of us. I've done four effectively, but that won't hold for more than thirty minutes," Thadd told us.

I glanced at Thadd. I hadn't known he was able to do that.

He gave me a sly smile and winked.

"That's handy. Yeah, we can make that work," Phin replied. "Zara needs to face the royals, so two of us should be with her. The other two can go in stealth mode with Thadd."

"Sounds good to me. I haven't been there before, so I'll need to follow." Thadd leaned his chin on my shoulder while peering at the map.

"Well, the closest is going to be on the northeast corner of the palace grounds. Right before coming here, there were a bunch of guards coming up from the west towards the Sanctuary." Storm pointed to a section of the palace grounds on his map.

"The guards will be distracted coming up this way, allowing us to enter here." Storm tapped the paper he'd labeled as the northeast corner of the palace grounds used for farming. "Greenhouses are here and there's an entry point, which will take us into the palace grounds. From there, we will have access to the kitchen and up towards the throne room." Storm indicated by drawing out the route on his map.

"Where would they be keeping my mom?" I asked. I had a feeling it would be in the dungeons deep in the bowels of the palace on the opposite side of the agricultural area. By foot, it would take about thirty to forty minutes.

"I want Gigi out and brought home, now. I know they said twenty-four hours, but I'm not waiting. There's no way Amina and Issac will release her without wanting something of me. I want to ensure that leverage is out of their hands." I added.

Cassian spoke up first. "The dungeons would be my first guess. But they are probably keeping her close. They sequestered some of the powerful elementals in the ballrooms near the throne room."

"We have to check both," I said.

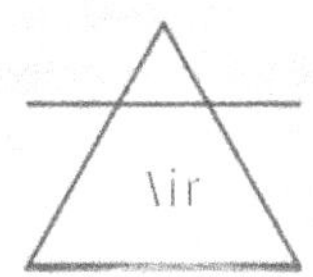

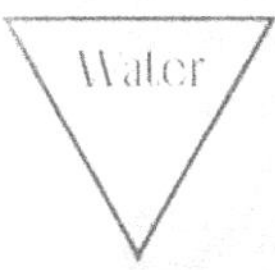

Chapter Forty-Six

ZARA

Nervous energy fluttered in my belly while I waited for the guys to formulate a plan. It was the right decision to think this through versus going in guns blazing, or magic blazing in our case, but it didn't make me feel better.

While the men debated who would go where, I busied myself with gathering Gigi's remedies and a change of clothes for her. I changed as well and was putting my hair up in a ponytail when I heard Phin say something about dropping me off at the Sanctuary. Nope, not going to happen.

I went into the living room where the men were gathered and said, "I'm going with you."

Thadd was going to use an invisibility spell, which could conceal up to four people. I was going to be one of those four. "No, Zara, it's dangerous," Cassian said.

"I agree with Cass. You are too important to this mission." Storm added.

"This is not up for discussion," I placed my hand on my hips. "This is my mother we're talking about. I'm going, so let's get a move on."

"Zara," Phin growled. "It's too dangerous."

Thadd stood and stepped up beside me. "I agree with Zara. If it were my mother, I'd want to be there. I'll do the invisibility spell; Beau you do the teleporting. And one more person would be good to have as a backup."

Phin scrubbed a hand down his face.

"Fine. We'll all go. Beau, teleport us here outside of the dungeons. From there, Z, Thadd, and I will go in to look for Gigi while the rest of you keep watch." Phin pointed out a place on the map.

"If we don't find her there," Phin continued. "We go into the meeting rooms here. From there, Thadd, Beau, and Z will remain in stealth. Cass, Storm, and I will keep watch. If you find Gigi in the meeting rooms, Beau, teleport her immediately to the healing village. The rest of us will deal with the royals."

Beau teleported us behind the building housing the dungeons. Even as a child I always hated the place. It was dark and ominous and not a place a child should ever be near. Phin dusted the only guard that was stationed at the entrance. He fell asleep in minutes. Phin removed the key from the sleeping guard's belt, unlocked the door, and he descended the long, winding staircase, with Thadd and I right behind him.

Once inside, it took us twenty-minutes to walk down the stairs. Gigi wouldn't have made it unless she was carried.

The kingdom didn't have a prison system like the human realm. If an elemental was guilty of a capital crime, it was light's out. No questions asked. Prisoners here would wait out sentencing but that happened quickly, as did execution. Especially now with the new royals in charge.

At the end of the winding staircase were three corridors. Phin pulled a couple torches off the wall and lit them. "Zara," he held a torch out to me, and I took it. "Let's split up. Holler if you find anything or run into problems."

I nodded, and the three of us ran through the halls.

"Mama?!" I called out as I peered through the small cell windows.

"I'll be your mama." A scraggly prisoner pressed his face to the window.

The place made my skin crawl, but I kept going until I was at the end of the hallway. I checked each cell again as I made my way back and came up empty.

"Nothing?" Thadd took the torch out of my hand.

I shook my head and crushed my body against his chest.

Phin met up with us with a grim look on his face. "She's not here, but a lot of good people are. I'd free them now, but we don't have a safe place for them yet."

"No, wait. If you're sure they're good people, let's free them now. They must be desperate to be freed," I told him.

Phin nodded. "Let's get back out first. I'll let the guys know."

"I'll teleport us outside." Thadd wrapped his hand around my waist, and Phin grasped my hand.

The other three men were waiting right where we'd left them. Phin shook his head. "Head to the meeting room. Storm and I will fly and notify as many soldiers as we can after we free some of the prisoners. I saw a few of our comrades in there."

"I know just the place to teleport into. See you guys in a few," Beau said.

He put up a portal and seconds later we were in one of the many banquet rooms of the palace.

Thadd grabbed my hand and said, "Whoever needs to be hidden, hold on."

Beau held my other hand.

"I'll lead." Cass tugged on Beau's hand, and then we hurried through the halls checking each meeting room. There were dozens of them. All of them were used for different events and meetings. As we jogged, I could clearly see the men to which we were linked. I was about to question if Thadd's magic was working when a group of guards walked right by us.

We kept moving as quickly as we could. My sister's voice stopped me in my tracks, and I almost stumbled. Thadd and Beau kept me upright as we rounded a corner. There she was, walking towards us, looking as stunning as ever.

A man dressed in a ridiculous outfit walked beside her. He wore navy blue silk trousers tucked into knee-high riding boots. His top was a navy and gold brocade with a ruffled neckline. He looked absurd.

Four guards flanked them, and then they stopped abruptly and turned into the Great Hall. Behind them, two guards dragged a limp Gigi.

I almost screamed and broke free of our linked hands, but Thadd gripped me and clamped a hand over my mouth.

Once they were out of sight, Cass tugged us towards the room where Gigi had been taken.

"I've done everything you've asked of me. I've even given you access to my powers. Just kill her already! I don't understand why you're dragging this on. You promised me you would kill my sister!! I don't want her here," Amina screamed at her husband.

"Stop your drivel. We needed to lay a trap. When she arrives, you're free to kill her human. And I will deal with your sister as promised!" Issac threw up his hands.

Hearing my sister speak of wanting me dead made my heart sink. The guys were right. She hated me and as much as it hurt, I couldn't let it bother me. I had to get my mother to safety. She was my only priority.

I rose on my tiptoes and whispered into Thadd's ear. "Save Gigi, get her to safety." I linked Beau and Thadd's hands together so that they could remain invisible, then I let go and went after my sister.

"Knock, knock, assholes." I strode into the throne room. My magic vibrated under my skin. I glanced at my mother, caught her gaze, and gave her a wink.

With Amina and Issac focused on me, they didn't realize Gigi was no longer where they'd left her.

"Zara! I've missed you." Amina hurried towards me with her arms flung open. My sister had long, flowing blonde hair and perfect porcelain skin. Her blue eyes sparkled like the jewels on the crown that sat on top of her head.

A part of me welcomed her embrace and longed for it. Within a few feet from me, darkness flashed in her eyes, and her lips thinned into a sneer. Instinctively, I ducked as she swung a blade aimed at my throat. I pivoted and pushed her back with a force of magic that sent her tumbling into her husband.

Issac recovered quickly and stood, taking in my measure.

"This is your sister? You said she was fat. She is anything but. She's gorgeous."

"Apprehend her!" Amina bellowed.

The guards hesitated. They recognized me, the princess that had been banished. One guard bravely raised his gun, only to be knocked out with a harsh thump to his head.

"If anyone touches her, you die," Phineas growled beside me. "This is Zara Cavendish, the true royal of this kingdom."

Beau, Cassian, Thaddeus, and Storm appeared behind me. I risked a glance at Beau, and he gave me a nod. He had gotten Gigi to safety.

I breathed a sigh of relief then refocused on the crazy royals before me.

"No, she's not! This is my throne. But with her, I might be willing to share." Issac leered at me.

He was so gross. "If I was standing closer to you, I'd hit you in the throat."

Issac laughed. "Take your best shot, sweetie."

I shot out a pulse of air magic and hit him at the base of his neck. Issac stumbled backward, gasping for air.

He got up, glaring daggers at me, and I gathered my magic.

"That's all you got?" He waved his hand around dramatically. "These six do not have the power to defeat me. If you defy me, any of you, I will kill you myself."

His voice grew louder, and a dark shadow shrouded him. He chanted something in a strange language, and a few arcane circles lit up on the walls and floors.

Afraid of picking the wrong side, the guards engaged the five men that were with me. Swords clashed, gunfire went off, and magic zipped all around me.

Using the same trick I'd used in the mage's domain, I gathered my earth magic and punched the floor creating an earthquake that cracked the walls and the floors. Issac's dark magic evaporated.

"Oooh, I like you. Your magic is strong. Come here, precious Zara. Let me make you mine," Issac hissed.

"Gross. I think I just vomited in my mouth." I made a retching noise.

Aside from his ridiculous clothes, foul temperament, and the evil oozing out of his pores, some might say he was a good looking man. Issac was tall and slender and had a perfectly symmetrical face. His hair was cropped short, and his deep-set eyes made him look mysterious.

"If you won't come willingly, then fine, I'll take you by force." He sent a barrage of fire that glanced off my body as though it was nothing more than a warm breeze.

His fire magic was too weak. I had withstood the fire of Phin's beast. Issac couldn't harm me with his paltry flames.

His face turned purple with rage. He let out a scream of frustration, and gathered a force of dark magic and sent a jolt of lightning straight to my chest.

I brought my arms up to shield my body. My skin crackled with electricity. I wound up and sent an electric bolt which he deflected. But I kept at it, sending bolts of lightning singeing his skin. The foul stench of burnt flesh permeated the air. But I did not stop and would not until he surrendered.

Amina got up and hurled a wicked ball of fire which went wide and caught the tapestries that hung from the cathedral ceilings.

"This was supposed to be your kingdom, Amina. But you treat your people like shit. Thus, you don't deserve it." I snarled at my sister.

I pooled my magic in my hands and hurled fireballs and lightning at the king and queen. They deflected each shot but were tiring quickly. The magic in my veins roared with power. I stalked closer to my sister and her husband as they cowered on the dais. They had no more power to spare. They were barely able to protect themselves.

I stood above them and sneered. "Surrender, and I'll spare your lives."

"So...so much power. I want it. And I will have it." Issac scowled. His face was aglow with sweat, his crown lay at his feet.

"I'm the chosen one!" Amina swatted her husband. "The seer chose me!"

"She chose wrong. But I will take what I must and then, I will have your sister." In the blink of an eye, a dagger appeared in his hand, and he stabbed my sister's chest.

Amina's blood bloomed on the bodice of her dress. A putrid gray smoke spewed from the wound, and Issac opened his mouth welcoming the darkness into his being. His back bowed and a soundless scream came forth from his mouth.

The sight before me was vile and dark. I was paralyzed for a split-second uncomprehending what was happening before me. He wound his arms dramatically, preparing a spell so dark the throne room dimmed.

I gathered all my magic and blasted him with my power. Air, fire, water, and earth merged and shot out at the supposed king. Issac met my attack head-on. Black fog shielded his body. My magic winked out, and I shook my head, dizzy from conjuring so much magic.

Issac didn't give me long to formulate my plan. A stream of black magic came straight at me. I ducked under his blast and shot out my special brand of magic in a ferocious pulse, slamming him in the shoulder. He stumbled to the ground. His arm hung from his body, and blood and sinew dripped on the floor.

Running on pure adrenaline I was poised to deliver the killing blow, but something barreled into me. My hair was wrenched back, and Trick's familiar voice spoke in my ear. "Sorry to do this to you."

"Back off!" Trick screamed at everyone in the room. "Zara is mine."

"Don't do this, Trick," I begged.

Phin, Beau, Storm, and Cassian appeared in front of us.

"She's not going anywhere with you, brother," Storm said.

Phin glared at Trick, with the red feral eyes of his beast.

Cassian was poised to launch. Beau clenched his fists.

Thadd was MIA.

"Bring her to me!" Issac yelled, his blood spurting all over the dais.

"Never," Trick said. "You said I could have her if I helped.

And now you are defeated and I will take her on my own."

Trick brought his fangs down to my neck and gnawed...

"What?!" Trick's face scrunched up in confusion and he bit again and again. But his sharp teeth didn't puncture my skin.

I smiled. Thadd's runes worked.

"What have you done?!" Trick tried biting my arm, over and over.

Suddenly, he dropped to the floor with a thump. Thadd wrapped me in his arms. "I'm going to kill that fucker."

While the elemental men dealt with Trick, Thadd pulled me away from the dais where Amina lay motionless on the floor. Issac slowly got to his feet with one arm barely attached to his body and started chanting again.

A menacing shadow materialized around Issac. His chanting grew louder. The hair on the back of my neck stood up and icy claws of fear gripped my spine.

I amassed my magic again, and the rune Thadd embedded in my skin zinged, lending me more power. I stood firm and unleashed everything I had. A force of magic, like a deadly meteor shower, slammed into Issac's chest.

"No!!" Dark robes billowed behind the crone as she knocked Issac's body, pushing him away from my stream of magic.

My magic winked out. I doubled-over at the waist and braced my hands on my knees catching my breath. I stared at the crone kneeling before Issac, the woman that had been essential to my banishment.

"Master!" She sobbed. "Master, please."

The room was quiet. The fighting had stopped. I didn't dare glance behind me. I couldn't stop staring at the whining crone. There was something about her that was disturbingly familiar and it wasn't the memory of our last meeting right here on this dais.

"You! I will kill you for hurting him." The crone whipped her head towards me and stabbed the air with her finger at me.

She stood and I braced myself for her attack.

"You were supposed to stay away and die." She bellowed.

Her body shimmered with magic blurring her image. In a flash, the elderly, hunched-over woman with stringy gray hair and a hooked nose transformed into a familiar blonde woman with stunning blue eyes. I blinked, and the crone reappeared. Was I hallucinating? The change happened so fast that I thought I was seeing things.

"You ruined everything and for that, I will kill you!" the crone spat.

Her image morphed again and held a moment longer, revealing my mother, Queen Anya. Her beautiful face twisted with contempt. And then the image shifted back again to the crone. I shook my head again, confused.

The crone wearing my mother's face screamed, and then she summoned a thousand sharp blades comprised of ice and hurled them straight at me.

Everything moved in slow motion. I was too stunned to move. My mind was completely devoid of all thought. And my magic was completely spent. The blades hissed through the air, their buzz deafening to my ears. I clenched my fists, ready to embrace death.

The next second, a woosh of hot air went up in front of me. A wall of fire shielded me from the barrage of magical killer blades, melting them on impact.

The wall of fire vanished, and my father staggered to the dais, his skin pale and his movements sluggish. His eyes were wide as he stared at his wife, the woman he had buried years ago. "Anya. What is this? I don't understand." His voice was but a whisper.

My mother disappeared into thin air, taking Issac's body with her, and Zander Cavendish passed out and fell to the floor.

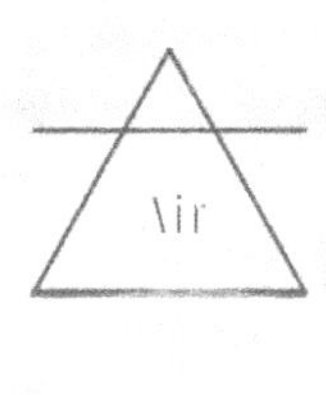

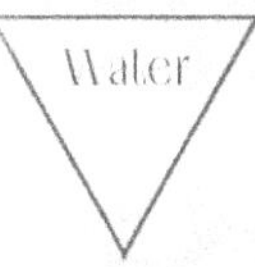

Chapter Forty-Seven

ZARA

The entire palace buzzed with energy. I hadn't had the chance to process what had just happened, which was probably a good thing. I didn't have the mental capacity to deal with the fact that my sister had tried to kill me. And to add to that incredible mess, I had seen the crone transform into my biological mother. I hoped it was my imagination playing tricks on me. Thinking about it made my stomach roll with revulsion.

On top of that, Trick, my teenage love, had tried to bite me. Storm and Beau immediately locked him up in the magically warded dungeons. We'd deal with him at a later time.

As soon as the crone and King Issac's dead body disappeared, the focus was solely on getting King Zander back on the throne.

Palace staff prepped his chambers while Thadd worked on reversing the spell that had made him ill. Until he was back on his feet, everyone looked to me for direction. There was so much that needed to be done. I operated on autopilot, delegating tasks as best as I could.

I sent the elemental men on different tasks. Phin went to deal with the army. He was a born leader, and I had been confident the troops would follow his orders. The royal guard had been on their way to the sanctuary, so he had a lot of ground to cover. Flying in his beast form helped, but he was unable to communicate with anyone in that form. It would take him a while.

Storm was sent to rally flyers that would notify the people that Zander was back and the crone and Issac were at large. I didn't want people getting too comfortable until those two were confirmed dead and their ashes buried somewhere. I was grateful for having him on our team. We needed to spread the word and make sure people were vigilant.

Beau being a mage, healer, and earth elemental had more tasks than anyone. After securing Trick in the dungeons, he had a lot of healing to do. Those involved in the scuffle in the throne room had injuries that needed tending to, including my sister. She was badly injured but the wound wasn't fatal. He tended to her and put up shielding wards in her chambers locking her in. Since Beau was the only trustworthy healer at the moment, he teleported to the healing village and popped back in with a couple of healers that set up a triage. Then he had to assist Thadd with the complex spell that had made my father ill. And I needed both men to get back to the mines to make sure it was properly warded. I had a feeling if there was anywhere the crone would run to and hide, it would be Source Mountain.

I asked Cassian to stay by my side for a bit as we set up a team to search the palace grounds. He was great with people, everyone liked him, and he helped me navigate my way around. It ended up being the worst job of all. What we found was horrifying.

We started with the crone's den, a guest villa right outside of the palace, in hopes to trap her there. But she was nowhere to be found. The evil in that place made the mage's domain at the sanctuary feel like strolling through a pleasant garden. The den was corroded with dark magic. My first instinct was to have it burnt to ashes, but we needed to confer with Beau and Thadd. I had a feeling burning it wouldn't be enough to dismantle its dark presence. For the time being, we left two men to guard it.

I had asked Cass to also deal with the prisoners. He freed the wrongly accused, and he imprisoned those that had turned their backs on Zander and their people. Unfortunately, these were all high-powered council members. It was a difficult task, but somehow Cass got it done. They were sent to the dungeons until Zander could deal with them.

And that wasn't the worst bit. In the basement of the palace, we found the children. There were over a hundred of them malnourished and scared. Some were ill.

My heart broke. After everything that had happened, I didn't bother hiding my tears. But Cass's easy-going personality made the children smile and consoled them until we could offer more.

This was the most difficult to deal with and also the most important. The royals were keeping the children sequestered in hopes to siphon off their powers. The sinister bullshit they were concocting was revolting.

I ran around the palace locating helpers to prepare food, clothing, beds, and healers for the children. A couple of members of the staff that had been loyal to Zander helped me set up a system to identify each child and locate their parents.

We worked tirelessly all day and through the night. Exhaustion seeped into my bones, and my heart weighed a hundred pounds.

I had been working in the palace library alongside palace staff management when Thadd and Phin found me. They both looked as weary as I felt.

"How can we help, angel?" Phin offered.

I gave him a small smile and shuffled a stack of papers around. It would have been so much easier if I had my tablet and did this on a spreadsheet. "Umm...not sure. The children have been clothed, fed, and given medical attention if needed. Most are asleep now, I hope. We've organized a way for parents and children to reunite, but that will take some time." I sighed. "We're opening every room in the palace for people that need it. That seems to be the most important at this point. How are the guards holding up? And Zander?"

"Zander is resting. The spell was complicated to unravel. But the worst part is over. The sickness has abated. It's just a matter of making sure he doesn't relapse." Thadd scratched the stubble on his chin.

"You think the spell can what? Reactivate somehow?" I asked.

"Yeah, unfortunately. The spell was like a parasite. It was meant to slowly eat away at the host until it consumed it. I've neutralized the spell. Frozen it out, so to speak. Only time will tell if it will hold."

I massaged my temples. "Thank you for everything, Thadd."

Phin handed me a cup of water. I accepted it with a grateful smile and downed it before he started speaking.

"The guards were freed of the enslavement spell when you dispatched the mage. They just needed to be reminded of their loyalties. I'm confident we won't have any trouble in that regard." Phin tipped his head from side to side, cracking his neck. "I split the retinue in half, sending the half closest to the sanctuary to guard the mines. They just arrived at midnight and have already organized guard duty and the encampment. And the other half are here guarding the palace."

"Have you eaten, Zara?" Thadd asked.

"Umm...I'm not sure." I paused trying to remember when I had last eaten anything. "I guess not."

"You need to eat and rest. I know there's a lot to do, but you don't need to do everything all at once." Thadd cupped my face and kissed my forehead.

"Let's take you home, Zara," Phin said.

"No, we have to wait for the other guys." I wouldn't leave any of the men behind. If they needed help, I would stay and help.

"Besides, I don't feel right leaving in the middle of all this." I sighed.

Someone cleared their throat, and I turned toward the sound. Maester Samuel Hazell, palace manager extraordinaire, had been working alongside me since Zander had been taken to his chambers. That had been hours ago.

"Excuse me, Lady Zara, but you should rest. I have gotten my four hours of sleep, that's all I require. You, on the other hand, have been moving non-stop. Rest, I can help and I will alert you of any changes. Please, trust that I can do this for you. It would be my pleasure," Maester Samuel said.

"Are you sure? There's so much to do." I told him.

Samuel had been working as the palace manager when Zander had been a boy. He was a dinosaur, but the way he hustled through every task didn't reveal it.

"I'm sure of it. Go with your men. Rest." He patted my arm with a thin hand.

I nodded and reluctantly followed Phin and Thadd as we went in search of the other three men.

We found Cassian marching down the halls. "I was just coming to look for you." He wrapped me in his arms. "The children have been accounted for and sorted, as you requested. And they're resting. You ready to go home?"

I nodded. "We're looking for Storm and Beau."

They turned the corner as soon as I said their names. I let out an exhausted breath. The adrenaline I had been running on left my body and I was ready to collapse.

"I'd like to check on my mother," I said.

"We just got back from the healing village to get some supplies and checked in on her. She's fine and was resting, peacefully. We'll take you to her in the morning, Z, after you get some rest." Beau kissed my cheek.

"Thank you. All of you." I smiled and leaned into Beau's body. He would have to carry me.

"Do you want to stay here or go somewhere else?" Phin asked.

"Oh no, I'm not staying here in the palace. I'll go where you all go." I replied.

"I'm happy to stick around and help." Thadd offered. "But first, I am beat. We can teleport home to Silk City, babe, or the Sanctuary."

"Or the lair." Phin offered. "There are enough lieutenants here to keep things safe. And calm. The elementals will sort themselves out. If we're needed suddenly, we'll portal back here."

I looked at the men surrounding me, grateful for their love and support.

"Let's go home. To the lair."

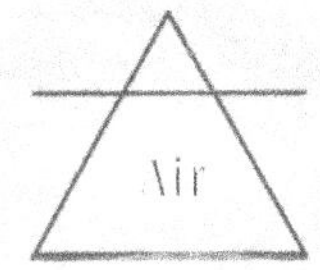

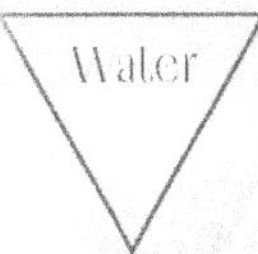

Chapter Forty-Eight

ZARA

Soft kisses roused me. Phin massaged my shoulders; his heat seeped into my skin.

A contented sigh escaped my lips. "Morning."

He chuckled, his warm breath brushing against my neck.

"Good morning. What's left of it anyway."

I jolted upright. Mid-morning sunlight bathed the room. "How long have I been asleep?" I asked as the events of the day before came flooding back.

"Almost nine hours. Don't worry, angel. After using so much magic yesterday, and all the stress, you deserved the rest. I just wanted to check on you." Phin smiled, but his eyes looked as though he didn't sleep as much as I did. Guilt stabbed at me. "You should have awakened me. Where is everyone?" I climbed off the bed and headed into the bathroom.

I left the door open, and Phin followed me. I sat on the toilet, and Phin stood in the doorway with his back turned, giving me privacy. I almost laughed at how my un-princess-like behavior made him uncomfortable.

"Umm, well, everyone is here now. Linc is preparing lunch," Phin said, facing the open door.

I flushed the toilet and washed my hands at the faucet.

"You can look now." I smiled at my fire elemental.

"We've checked on the palace and everything is moving along. We thought you may want to check on your mother." He moved behind me, his hands gliding over my back and waist as I brushed my teeth.

"Any changes as far as Zander and Amina?" I asked with a mouth full of toothpaste.

He smiled at me and nodded. "Your father is awake and asked for you. Your sister did wake up but has refused to allow Beau or anyone else in the palace to check on her wounds. He mentioned she may have some issues with her magic. But since she refuses help, he couldn't say more. Calla offered to give it a try this afternoon."

"Hmm," I murmured and rinsed my mouth.

I moved toward the shower and turned on the faucets, and then shimmied out of my panties. Phin's hot gaze fixated on me as I stood under the water.

He didn't say another word and neither did I. I knew there was much to be done at the palace and questions needed answering, but I wanted to put all of that on pause for just a little while longer. I wanted him to join me. I wanted another moment with my men before dealing with the bullshit I'd walked into. It was selfish, considering I had slept the entire morning away while they were probably up early dealing with all the problems.

With a sigh of resignation, I decided to forgo my plans of seduction and get through my morning routine quickly.

His gaze drank me in as I soaped up my body and shampooed my hair. I tried to ignore him, despite the waves of lust rolling through me. I closed my eyes, allowing the water to slide down my body, rinsing me clean.

Phin's lips fastened over mine. I hadn't heard him move. The surprise of his lips on mine, had startled me but was welcoming all the same. He hoisted me over his hips and brought me down on his hard cock. I gasped and clung to him, the delicious unsuspecting assault took my breath away. He pushed me up against the shower wall, slamming his hips into mine. Each punishing thrust was more exquisite than the last. His fire magic slid over my wet body, steam rising all around us. Heat circled my nipples and down to my clit, massaging, vibrating. I bit back my release wanting to prolong this moment, but the sweet sensations overwhelmed my body, and I let everything go.

"I tried to restrain myself, but I couldn't." He growled, his hips picking up the pace bringing me higher again.

"Your hot body is too enticing. These hard nipples." He nipped the taut buds.

"And your tight cunt always begging to be fucked. I will always want you, Zara," Phin's voice was dark and raspy.

Pleasure crested up my spine. My pussy clamped down over Phin's cock and he roared.

His body jerked, and he erupted inside me. Phin's body weight pressed me deeper into the shower wall. Our breathing was labored.

"I don't want you to go, Zara. I know you don't want to stay, but I hope we can figure this out somehow," he whispered.

I peppered kisses on his shoulder and whispered back.

"Yes, we'll figure this out."

He drew away from me, a lazy smile splayed over his handsome face. And then one of his eyebrows shot up. "Your boyfriend is here."

He slipped out of me and set me on my feet. I wobbled, but his strong arms kept me upright.

"Are you ok?" He drew me to his chest and peered over my shoulders, looking at my back. "I tried choosing a part of the wall that seemed smoother."

"I'm perfectly fine." My back felt a bit raw from being pressed up against the natural stone. But the pleasure my dragon had given me was so worth the discomfort.

"That was so fucking hot." A completely naked Thadd stood outside the shower.

I grinned and Phin smiled at me. "I can share." He kissed me and then reluctantly got out of the shower and Thadd took his place.

I wrapped one leg around Thadd's hip, and he lifted me with ease. He chuckled. "I love how much you love to fuck, but you'll have to be patient. Hold on, ok?"

I locked my legs around his hips and my arms clung to his neck. Thadd squirted hair conditioner into his palms and began massaging my scalp. I sighed as his expert hands eased away tension and left me languid in his arms. My legs and arms started to slip, but he grasped my hips and gently set me on my feet.

With my head plastered to his chest, Thadd continued his massage, then he tilted my head back and rinsed my hair.

His lips grazed along my jaw and down my neck. My leg slid up his thigh and curved around his hip.

"Patience, baby." He adjusted the faucets, and the basin began to fill.

He lowered himself into the tub and brought me down to sit on the ledge. He angled a shower jet to pour warm water over my chest, and he spread my legs. His gaze fixed on my wet, recently fucked pussy. He ran a finger down my folds slippery with Phin's cum.

He stared at it, sliding his fingers up and around my sensitive pussy lips, spreading them apart.

"You're so beautiful, Z."

He brought his mouth down to my core, suckling, and nipping. His tongue circled my entrance.

"Thadd, please." I needed more. I wanted him to fill me.

I couldn't keep still. My hips undulated, pushing my core against his face.

Thadd's tongue was relentless. He continued tongue fucking me, water splashing around me.

It was too much and yet not enough. I pushed him off me and forced him to sit in the tub. Thadd smirked. I straddled his lap and came down hard on his throbbing cock. I gasped and crushed my mouth to his stealing the taste of my cum mixed with Phin's gathered on his tongue.

Thadd gripped my hips and rocked me over his cock. I fucked him harder. My knees scraped along the tub's floor, the natural stone digging into my skin. Water splashed everywhere. I didn't care. My body vibrated with passion. I bounced on his cock over and over. I tugged his hair, pulling his head back, keeping his mouth fastened to mine. His hand slid over my ass and his finger down my crack. I felt him massage the puckered hole and it spurred me on to fuck him harder. He plunged a finger in my ass, and I unraveled into a million pieces. I tossed my head back screaming his name as he clamped onto a nipple all while he fucked me in both holes.

"You love this. Will you let me, and the other guys fill you up like this, baby? Would you like that?" Thadd rasped.

"Yes!" I rocked over his cock and finger, fucking him as his orgasm rolled through his body.

He rested his chin on my shoulder, his finger slipping out, both of us trying to catch our breath. I turned the faucets off and looked at the mess we made.

"Ooops." Thadd looked up at me with a boyish grin. I caressed his jaw and kissed his nose. "Guess we'll need to clean up."

I chuckled.

"Do you know how much I love you?" He asked me.

I nodded. Thadd had always loved me. I loved him, too. Back then I didn't realize it or maybe I had. It just hadn't been the right time.

Now with the other four men, I felt whole and complete.

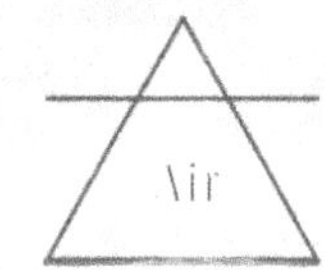

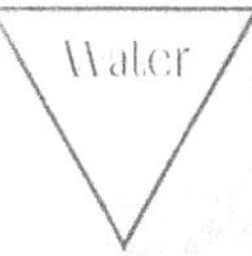

Chapter Forty-Nine

ZARA

After bath time with Thadd and Phin, I insisted on being taken to see my mother. Since Beau and Storm weren't back yet, Thadd and I traveled to the healing village via a portal. She was doing just fine and content to stay there. She was helping the village mothers with preparing meals and watching over the children.

We arrived back at the lair and gathered in the dining room for a quick bite. The men updated me on the latest news. A lot was going on, and I felt guilty for sleeping in and then taking an extra long bath.

Cassian seemed to have noticed my mood shift and patted my hand over the table. "There isn't much you could have done in the past few hours, Z. You needed to rest. Besides, you'll be happy to know that the children have been sorted. Those who had

families at the Sanctuary or in the palace have been reunited. And Storm and his airmen have been flying around to spread the news of the children that need families."

I smiled at my water elemental. The news about the children warmed my heart. At least one good thing had happened.

And perhaps my time in the kingdom was done, and I was ok with that. I'd miss the elemental men, but I was certain we would be able to continue our relationship somehow.

The crone and Issac were still at large, which was a concern, but we weren't ready to send a search party just yet. The biggest issue that needed to be dealt with was the Source. Thadd and Beau were doing the research and I was confident they'd be able to figure out how to dismantle the dark magic. The problem was that time was not on our side.

"The full moon is in less than five nights," I mentioned.

"We need to get that taken care of before then."

"You're probably right, Zara." Beau scrubbed a hand through his hair a little rougher than usual. He had a lot on his plate. His skills as a healer and a mage were in high demand. Thadd was helping with mage duties, but the actual healing was his domain.

"Well, I have a few ideas. I just need some time to work on them. Also, we can pour over the things we found in the crone's den. If we all work together on it, perhaps we'll find a way to dismantle the spell amongst her things," Thadd offered.

We all agreed to pull together on the task and put it on top of the priority list.

Shortly after lunch, the six of us arrived at the palace via a portal, and we headed straight to see Zander.

I nodded at the guard posted outside of the king's study and let myself in, my five men right behind me. "Zander? You asked to see us?"

The king was sitting behind his desk, a stack of paperwork in front of him. He had dark circles and puffy bags under his eyes, as though he hadn't slept at all, but he seemed healthier. His skin was no longer pale, and his commanding presence was back. Thadd had said he "froze" the decaying spell, and he should survive. That was good news, and I appreciated my druid tremendously for all his help. It was a lot of work to run a kingdom, and I was not interested in doing so.

He waved a hand at the chairs opposite his desk. Phin sat beside me while the other men stood behind us. There were other chairs in the study, but the men seemed content to stand next to me.

"What are your plans?" Zander fixed his gaze on me.

"I'm going home," I replied.

The men behind me shifted, and Phin reached for my hand.

Over lunch, I had been briefed on the next steps that needed to happen going forward, and it seemed to me that I was no longer needed.

Although I hadn't discussed it with the elemental men, it was the right decision.

I wanted to free the people from the tyrants and right the wrongs they'd committed. Aside from the Source being completely accessible, I'd done what I set out to do.

"I'm no longer needed. You're back on your feet.

Everything that needs to be done here you can handle on your own. The situation in the mines is critical, however, I am not a mage. I can help with the research and I will, but I don't have to be here to read. Beau and Thaddeus here will see this through." I added.

"No," Zander said in a familiar fatherly tone. "You cannot leave. You're needed here."

"Yes, I can, and I will." I gave him a flat stare.

Zander straightened in his chair and clenched his jaw. He was doing his best to stay calm. A part of me felt giddy watching him squirm. He did apologize for everything, and I held no grudges but that didn't mean he could rule over my life just because he was back on his throne.

"Zara," he rolled his neck and took in a deep breath that was meant to calm himself. "Please stay. I need your help. I cannot do this alone."

"You are back on the throne. You have a palace full of people willing and able to help you restore order. You have an army. I fail to see how I can help you," I explained, which was the truth.

"Damn it, Zara!" Zander struck his desk with a meaty fist.

"Can you have some compassion for once?!"

His outburst made me flinch. He was pissed, but I refused to back down. He wasn't my king or my father; he had no authority over my life.

"Compassion? You want compassion from me? Where was your compassion for the fourteen-year-old girl you banished on her birthday, in front of the entire kingdom? Where was your compassion for the girl that was exiled from her homeland when her nanny died and had no one to take care of her? Did she not deserve your compassion? Zander, you are no longer my king. I've done my part and now you do yours."

"I had to do those things!" Zander stood up and paced behind the desk.

The men with me shifted uneasily. Seeing their king like this must've been unnerving for them. I almost felt bad. But I wasn't about to roll over and do as I was told.

"Don't you understand? Everything I did, all of it, was done to keep you safe, Zara." He hung his head.

"Actually, no. I don't understand. Yes, you apologized. But I still have no idea why you did what you did. You've explained jack shit to me." I squared my shoulders.

Zander looked at me then walked over to a bar cart not far from his desk and poured himself a glass full of scotch. He drank it all in one go, and then he refilled his glass.

So that's where I got my drinking problems from.

"Help yourselves." Zander waved at the men and the bar cart.

Cassian stepped up to the cart, poured a glass of scotch, and brought it over to me. I accepted the glass and winked at him. He always knew what I needed without me having to ask.

Zander slumped back in his chair, sipped his scotch, and then looked at the men beside me. "We need the room."

Phin glanced at me. I nodded. He squeezed my hand, then got up and left. Cass pecked my cheek, Beau stroked my shoulder.

Storm patted the other, and then they followed Phin out.

Thaddeus knelt next to me. "We'll be right outside, ok."

I caressed his cheek, appreciating the support, and watched him move towards the door.

"Thadd," I said before he exited and held out my hand.

He came back to me and grasped my hand.

"I'm sorry I haven't introduced you." I turned toward Zander and said, "Zander Cavendish, this is Thaddeus Sloane."

Zander's eyebrows shot up to his forehead. "Sloane? And you're the druid?"

"Yes, sir." Thadd extended his hand, and he and Zander shook. "Pleased to meet you."

"Your surname is familiar. Do you know your lineage?"

"My family line has always been druids. And aside from my parents and grandparents, I don't know much about my ancestors," Thadd replied.

"Thank you for your help. You may want to look into your lineage. We have archives in our library."

Thadd nodded, then bent to kiss me full on the mouth. I smiled when he released me and turned to watch him leave. We were breaking all sorts of princess protocols.

"I'm glad you're amused," Zander said.

I couldn't wipe the grin off my face.

"So, you were saying?" I prodded.

Zander took a swig of scotch, and then said, "Do you know much about prophetic dreams?"

I nodded. It was a rare gift, one that was dreaded, and I remember him being grateful that neither my sister nor I had it.

"My mother had them. Not often, but when she did, if she ignored them, there were dire consequences. I've had them three times in my life. The first time was when I was in my early twenties. My sister was your age, twenty-eight, she wanted to take one of the stallions to Treasure Veil even though our parents told her not to. The night before she left I had a dream of her falling to her death. It was surreal. I knew in my gut I had to stop her from going. When I woke in the morning to warn her, she and her friends were already gone. I got on a stallion and took off like the wind. But I was too late. I found her body at the bottom of a ravine just like I had seen in my dream. I had to live with that for years. And luckily, I didn't have another dream until about a week from your fourteenth birthdate."

Zander pinched the bridge of his nose and drank his scotch. I gulped the contents of my glass and stood to grab the bottle from the bar cart to refill our glasses.

"In my dream, you were named heir apparent and died." He paused and pressed the heels of his palms to his eyes as though trying to erase the image.

"You died in unspeakable ways. The dream was on repeat night after night. I didn't know whom to trust or how to prevent it. And I didn't have time to prepare. All I knew was I had to get you out of the kingdom."

"So I did what I did. It wasn't until Amina sent me away that I had another dream. This time if I failed to bring you back, the kingdom would become shrouded in darkness. Storms would break out in terrifying numbers across the human realm, followed by famine and disease, and all would be lost." His voice was soft.

Well, this was some shit. There was a question that had niggled at the back of my mind, one I knew I wouldn't like the answer to, but I had to ask.

"Who killed me?" I held his gaze.

"It doesn't matter." He averted his eyes.

"It does to me." I leaned forward in my seat. "Father, if you want my help, be honest with me. I need to know."

He pinched the bridge of his nose, then blew out a breath.

"Your mother."

My heart cracked in my chest. My mother wanted to kill me. A fourteen-year-old girl. Why? Oh fuck, I almost wished I hadn't asked.

Chapter Fifty

ZARA

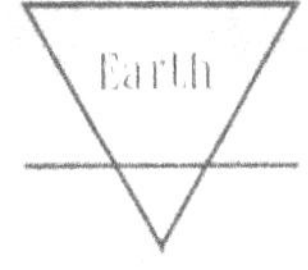

The five men were waiting outside of the study for me. I was too stunned at what my father revealed. I had no words.

"Umm, we should talk, but I need a minute to process." I waved a hand toward my father's study. "I'll be back."

I trudged down the familiar halls until I came across French doors that led to the palace gardens. Rows of colorful tulips, daisies, and calla lilies danced with the breeze, their natural beauty sure to bring a smile to anyone passing by. The sweet fragrance of gardenias and roses tickled my nose, and a flurry of sadness overwhelmed me. The garden reminded me of my mother. I jogged down the path, desperate to get away from this place. My light jog turned into a sprint, and my air magic surged, propelling me into the sky.

I soared over the palace grounds and took note of the royal guards who were practicing sword work. Others were minding the crops. On the outside, it looked as though everything was peaceful within the palace and that couldn't be further from the truth.

My mother had wanted me killed so she could have more power. She was in league with the crone. To keep me safe, my father had sent me away. I understood why he did it and maybe I could forgive him someday. But the truth still hurt my heart.

I was certain that fucking crone had been behind all of it, and now she was at large. I flew over the palace villas and found the quarters the crone had turned into her den of evil. The darkness that emanated from that place felt dirty even from thirty feet in the air.

"Zara." I whipped around, trying to find the source of that whispered voice.

Storm appeared, floating beside me. For a moment, I flashed back to my first meeting with Zander. Patrick had come to find me just like this. That had been a few days ago and so much had happened since. We still hadn't dealt with Trick, who was locked away in the dungeons. Another stab hit me in my gut.

"We were worried about you," Storm explained. The first time I met Storm I thought he and his brother were identical. After spending time with the air elemental, I could clearly see their differences. Storm had kinder eyes and he smiled more. He'd had an easier life which made him a more open and willing team player.

"I didn't mean to worry anyone. I just needed some time," I replied.

"Understandable. You need to let off some steam. I have a suggestion. If you're open to it." He had a mischievous smile plastered on his face.

"Ok, I'm all ears."

"Well, according to Beau and Thadd, our magic wielders, they have cleared out the evil den and have confiscated anything and everything that could be useful to learn more about her plans. They found her grimoire and a few diaries. Those things are now in some vault somewhere, but the den itself needs to be dealt with.

The guys were just talking about letting your father decide."

"Oh no, that place is mine." I grinned at Storm, and we sailed through the sky and landed in front of the den.

The evil energy of the place made my skin crawl and I looked forward to ridding the kingdom of it.

Thadd, Beau, Phin, and Cassian strode up to us.

"Here for the show?" I asked them.

"Wouldn't miss it, angel," Phin replied.

Beau stood next to me, and Thadd flanked my other side.

"We were talking about your magic, and Thadd had a suggestion," Beau said.

Were those two best friends now? Maybe having a threesome did that to dudes.

"Druid magic is universal or spirit magic, which is an element. You should have access to that as well. You seem to take to things easily enough, so let's give it a shot. I'm going to teach you a few arcane gestures that will channel it with the other elements," Thadd added.

He made a few gestures with his hands, and I copied them. A surge of energy flowed through my body and made me sway on my feet.

"Whoa." I gasped. "Ok, now what."

"Let it rip," Beau said.

I called on my fire and my hands flamed. "You all should step back."

A stream of molten lava spewed out of my hands and engulfed the crone's den. The building went up in flames. Black smoke billowed in the sky. I wrapped the flames in a cyclone. Whirling wind surrounded it, keeping the flames contained. The fire scorched the building, turning it to ash immediately. I summoned my earth magic, punching my power into the ground. A massive sinkhole opened under the ash and swallowed the remains of the den.

It felt like it only took minutes for me to burn and bury a building that had been two thousand square feet of solid rock. But when it was done, there was applause behind me. I turned around to see the lawn crowded with elementals and the king at the center.

Great, an audience. I shrugged and went into the palace.

Phin, Storm, Beau, Cassian, and Thadd followed behind me. We went into the library, the area I had worked in the night before, and brainstormed.

"Should we begin our research on the mines?" I asked the guys.

"We have an idea of how to neutralize it, but we need more power. After that display of magic though, you might be able to power it for us," Thadd replied.

"We can take everything we found in the den and take it back to the lair. We'll go through everything there." Beau added.

I nodded. "What about the royal guard? Are they all in line?"

"We've got good lieutenants in place, and they are keeping an eye on things. We have guards patrolling the Sanctuary and the mines night and day." Phin leaned on a chair across from me, his long legs stretched out before him.

"There were some guards that were questionable, but after that display of power, I don't think we have to worry about them anymore. Still, we're keeping a close watch," Storm said. "I think in terms of the royal guard we're good. There is a prisoner we need to visit though."

"Trick. Fuck." I grimaced. That was someone I didn't want to deal with at all.

"Well, actually he might have some intel on what Issac and the crone were up to." Beau hooked his right ankle over his knee and propped an elbow on the armrest of his chair.

"Good point." I agreed but wasn't enthused about seeing him.

"Zara," Zander said. I hadn't realized he was in the same room.

"It would also be good for you to look in on your sister. All things considered, I understand your reluctance, but she too may have news for us." Zander offered.

Shit, he had a point as well. I pinched the bridge of my nose.

"And I forgot to mention earlier, I've rescinded the banishment. You may come and go as you please, but I hope you stay. All of you." Zander turned on his heel and moved to exit the library.

"Father, wait." He stopped at the door and turned around to face me. "Thank you. Umm, would you like to visit Amina with me?"

"Yes." He gave me a weak smile.

"Is there a way we can talk to her while all of you can listen in?" I looked at my men. "She may have info on the crone and Issac's whereabouts and their plans. We need to hunt them down and start working on those mines."

"I can set up a listening spell." Thadd gave me a wink. He was so handy to have around.

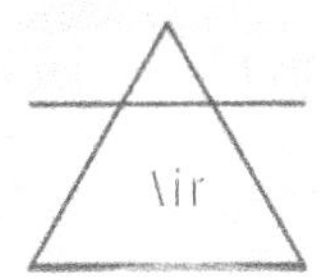

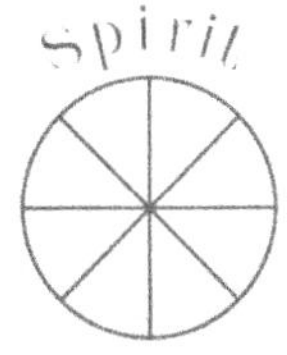

Chapter Fifty-One

ZARA

Amina had been moved to her old quarters while the royal chambers she and her husband had shared had been closed off. Beau had suggested that she be kept away from the royal chambers until we had a chance to search the place. Thadd warded it so that no one could portal in or out, and Phin assigned guards.

I thought they were being overly cautious, but when it came to Issac and the crone, we couldn't be too careful.

True to his word, Thadd set up a listening spell in Amina's receiving parlor. My father and I sat in the comfortable sitting area while the other men stayed outside and listened.

Calla helped Amina walk as they entered the parlor. After being stabbed in the chest, Amina seemed to be healing rather well. Beau had mentioned that the wound wasn't deep, but I had expected her to need more recovery time.

Amina stared daggers at me and hissed. When Amina saw our father, she looked shocked. Her gaze switched back and forth between us a few times, and then she folded in on herself and started bawling.

Zander looked pained. He wanted to comfort her, but he was holding back. He knew that she had been complicit in whatever Issac had been doing. Still, Amina was his daughter, his baby. He glanced at me, and I nodded. His shoulders sagged with relief, and he moved to sit next to her and gathered her in his arms.

Amina sobbed. I sat back and rolled my eyes. She hated me for whatever reason. She kidnapped my mother and despite her being controlled by Issac, I wasn't about to give her a pass.

Once she was done with her award-winning performance, she turned on the damsel in distress charm on our father. "He spelled me, father. I didn't know what I was doing. I would never hurt you."

"Shhh, Amina." He rocked her in his arms.

I wasn't buying it. If he wasn't going to pry answers out of her, then I would.

"Tell us everything about the crone and your husband. They've disappeared. And we need to know what they were planning," I stated.

She sneered at me, her eyes dry. "You should not be here! You've been banished. This kingdom belongs to me."

"No longer, Amina. With your sister's help, I have retaken the throne. And she is no longer banished. She will rule this kingdom should she want it," Zander said in a soothing tone.

Amina lost her shit. She clawed our father with her nails, screaming obscenities. She was completely gone. The sister I had known was no longer; she was an entirely different being.

Zander managed to restrain her. But Phin and Storm entered the parlor and trussed her hands behind her back using cuffs that neutralized her powers.

"I hate you!" She spat at me.

"Are you going to tell us what we need to know?" I asked.

"Fuck you, Zara. You've destroyed everything." Amina ranted.

"Excuse me, your highness. I may have something that will help. I just need to get back to my village. My son can take me," Calla said to my father and bowed.

He nodded, and she exited the room to speak with Beau.

Phin and Storm tied Amina to a chair, securing the neutralizing cuffs on her ankles. She hissed and bucked like a wild animal. Zander and I stared at her in utter disbelief. Whatever they had done to her was incomprehensible.

Within moments, Calla returned with a tray of tea. She offered it to

Amina who would not drink. Calla frowned and hung her head in resignation. She reached into her shift pocket and drew out a syringe. In one swift movement, she jabbed it into Amina's arm.

Amina squealed, and then her head drooped.

"Give it a minute to take effect, and she will tell you everything." Calla stood from her chair taking the tea with her.

As soon as Amina opened her eyes, my father started the interrogation. My sister resisted at first, but the truth serum Calla concocted was powerful. Sweat beaded Amina's forehead. She was in pain, and my father couldn't handle it.

I nudged him off the seat he occupied in front of her. He gave me a grateful nod and moved behind me.

"Amina, I know you hate me, but you need to start talking. Your husband and the crone have been destroying our home little by little with darkness. Why?"

"Fuck you!"

"You can cuss me out as much as you want, but you will answer my questions. Why, Amina? Why did they want to take over the kingdom?"

"Because this kingdom belongs to the crone. She and I will run this world, and we will never have to share our magic with the humans ever again." She ground her teeth, straining to keep the information to herself, but the truth serum forced it out of her.

"Share the magic with the humans? Since when have we done that?"

"You're an idiot! It's because of us the humans survive. We monitor their weather patterns and diffuse storms for them continuously. It's because of our humble lifestyle, our hard work, paying homage to the Goddess always and forever that we've been able to maintain that realm and ours. And they do not deserve it. They mistreat the earth and all its natural resources. They trample the lands with their manmade plastics and their pollution and their toxic warfare." She ranted.

"Why should we bother caring for them? Our people are weak. Always giving and giving to the humans who take so much. Those ungrateful shits. I'm tired of it." She slumped as though all the raving exhausted her.

"And how were you planning to conquer the kingdom? By forcing our people into submission?" I asked.

"Of course. That was phase one. Once we got to the Source, the crone, my husband, and I planned to harness its power and then we would decide who lives and dies." Amina had a defiant glint in her eyes.

"Please, as if you three are powerful enough to handle all that power. Besides that plan has completely gone to shit, seeing as they left you here." I scoffed.

"Don't mock me, Zara. I am more powerful than you. And they will come back for me. It's in the prophecy. They need me to complete the spell." She snarled like a wild animal.

"We already went through the crone's evil den. There's no spell. She was playing you." Ok, so that wasn't true, but I had to lead her somewhere.

"That's because I have it. It is my spell. My mother gave it to me!"

Now we were getting somewhere.

"You mean our mother? She's dead, Amina. I'm sure she wouldn't want this. She was an earth elemental after all." Come on Amina, give me more.

"Our mother is the crone, you idiot. She took over the crone's persona to deceive the kingdom. The woman we buried was the old crone who died many years ago." Amina spat out the uncomfortable truth I had known existed. Now I had confirmation.

Aww fuck. I had hoped what I'd seen in the throne room was just a hallucination.

Amina started laughing like a crazed lunatic. I glanced at my father who was sheet white.

"I've heard enough. Beau," he called out, and Beau entered the room.

"Please ward these rooms. After you're done with your interrogation down in the dungeons, I want Amina moved there. Phin, you and your men search Issac's chambers."

Zander stood and walked out. His back was straight, but he couldn't mask the pain and anguish written all over his face. Beau and Thadd went to work on securing Amina's room. Phin and Cassian were already gone. And I sat there staring at my crazy sister.

On my way out of Amina's room, Calla stopped me. "Lady Zara, I saw your mother at the healing village when Beau and I retrieved the truth serum. She's doing well with the remedies and has been helpful at the village. The children love her. She said to tell you she loves you very much, and she's so proud."

I pulled Calla in for a hug and clung to her. "Thank you, Calla. I needed that bit of good news."

She drew away from me and cupped my face. And then she hugged me again.

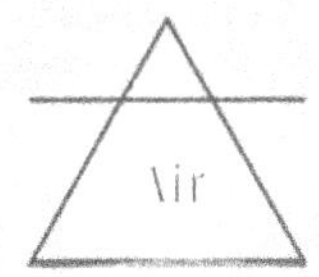

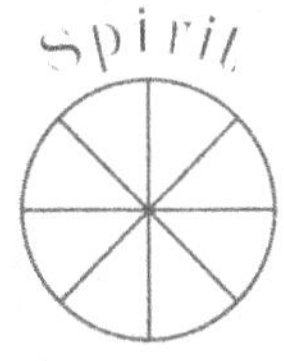

Chapter Fifty-Two

ZARA

After securing Amina in her warded room, Thadd, Beau, and I went to find Phin, Cass, and Storm. The royal chambers were suites that had been converted to suit Issac and Amina's requests and located on the opposite end of the palace. With over one hundred and twenty rooms, it would take at least twenty minutes to get there. Beau offered to portal, but walking helped me clear my head.

Zander had left Amina's room without a word, and I didn't want to question him further. I had questions, loads of them, but my thoughts were muddied and my emotional state raw. After hearing that he had dreams of my mother killing me and then Amina confessing that she assumed the crone's identity, I kept tripping over myself trying to figure out why.

Beau and Thadd hadn't said a word as we walked, and I was grateful. They were probably trying to figure things out just as I was, and really, what could we say about the matter? The crone and Issac were on our "top wanted" list and that hadn't changed. If my father wanted to accelerate the search, he'd have to pursue that on his own.

We arrived at the royal chambers, which were all sorts of weird. I walked in and walked right back out. Amina and Issac were into some dark shit. There were things in there I couldn't unsee.

I was in the room for all of three seconds and already the sight of

341

blood all over the walls and bed along with the demonic sigils were imprinted in my brain. And the goddess-awful stench.

Phin followed me out. "Zara." He pulled me into a hug. "I should have posted a guard outside the door. You shouldn't have seen that."

I held on to Phin as tightly as I could. My face smushed into his chest, and I took deep breaths, inhaling his masculine, smoky scent.

Cassian placed a kiss on my head and pressed his chest to my back.

I shivered, and a sob escaped me. There was so much darkness in the palace, within the family into which I had been born. It took everything in me to shield my mind and my heart. I felt like I was crumbling under the pressure of all the evil.

"What can we do, Z, to make this easier for you?" Cassian asked.

I wanted all this nastiness to disappear. I wanted the nightmare to be over. But that was wishful thinking, and I had to get another interrogation done before going home.

I took a deep breath and unglued myself from the safety of my fire and water.

"I'm ok." I exhaled. "I need to talk to Trick and then I want to go home."

"We'll go with you, Zara," Storm offered.

All five men stared at me, worry and concern etched on their faces. Their support tugged on my heartstrings and bolstered my courage.

"We need to find whatever Amina had been hiding in there." I pointed at the room and shuddered.

"I'd like Beau and Cass to come with me while the rest of you search," I added.

Storm shook his head. "If it's not too much to ask, I'd like to come with as well. I need to speak with my brother."

I stepped closer to Storm and intertwined our fingers. "I understand your need to speak with him, but I'm sure he'd be more forthcoming if you weren't there with me."

Trick would surely have a fit if he saw me with his brother. And Thadd's presence would have the same result.

Storm nodded and absently placed his other hand on my waist. I leaned into his body and ran my hand up his arm and around his neck.

"Ok, Zara, you're right. I will speak with him another time." He bent down and brushed his lips over mine.

I released Storm, smiling on the inside, and Thadd took his place.

Thadd crushed me to him, his hand snaked under my shirt, and he made small circles on my back. His magic slid up my spine, giving me strength. I sighed, absorbing everything he was giving me.

"Be careful, baby." He kissed the top of my head.

I angled my head and kissed his neck before releasing him.

"Are we walking or teleporting?" Beau asked as he extended his hand to me.

"Teleporting. Let's get this over with. I want to go home." I grasped both Beau and Cass by the hand and we walked through the portal together.

Cassian had released the elementals that were imprisoned unlawfully by Issac and Amina. I made a mental note to check on those prisoners. They were probably suffering from PTSD. The council members and clan chiefs that had sided with Amina and Issac were prisoners now. That was another task I wanted no part in.

Patrick was in a heavily warded cell. The door was solid wood with a small, grated window which allowed very little fresh air or light to shine through the tiny space.

Beau unlocked the door with a heavy metal key and then he made a few arcane gestures to release the wards.

Patrick sat cross-legged on the floor, a chain fastened to his ankle. His head hung low, his chin almost touching his chest. His hair covered his eyes, and his skin was unhealthily pale.

I tried to swallow past the lump that had formed in my throat. It pained me to see him like this.

"Zara, finally." His voice was hoarse.

I couldn't formulate words. My teenage love was imprisoned, and I wanted him to be free. I wanted things to go back to the way it were.

"Where are the rest of your men?" He asked, but he hadn't

raised his head. Perhaps he was peering at us through his hair. Not that it mattered, I was too shocked to respond.

"I know you're not here to set me free. So ask your questions."

I took a few steps towards him. Beau and Cass reached for me, but I shook them off. I cupped Trick's chin, raising his face, and then I combed his hair back away from his eyes and caressed his jaw.

Trick opened his eyes. They were red, swollen, and sad.

"Don't cry, Z. Please. Anything, but not tears." He whispered.

I crumbled. Everything hit me like a runaway train. I was done.

My body folded over Patrick. Clutching him to me, I sobbed. He was filthy and covered in sweat and grime, but I didn't care. He used to love me or so I thought. How did innocent teenage love turn into something so vile?

"I'm sorry, Zara. So sorry." He rasped. His arms encircled me.

"Why, Trick? Why did you do this?" My chest heaved with each sob.

He held me for a moment, rocking me like a child.

After a long moment, he finally said, "I'm not right, Z. You need to kill me. I will obsess over you forever. You will never be safe if I'm alive."

I drew away to stare into his tear-streaked face.

"You cannot mean that, Trick. I refuse to believe that you would ever harm me."

"You must!" He shouted and I stumbled back. "Zara I will never share you. I cannot. I dream of you. And I dream of killing your men. If you let me out, I will hunt them down and kill them all! And I will chain you to my room just like this so that you could never leave me."

His eyes glazed over with insanity, and his lip turned up in a snarl. I knew then the boy I used to love was gone. My heart broke into a million pieces.

I knelt in front of him, my hands clasped over his. Tears streamed down my face.

He rubbed my cheek with his dirt-crusted thumb. His gaze softened.

"If the crone and the royals have gotten away somehow, they hide in the human realm. But they will return on the full moon. The crone thinks she can harness the Source's power. The crone has a few teleporting spells, but she is not as talented as your earth elemental in that regard. They were working on another entrance to the mines on the mountain's northeast ridge. You might be able to surprise them there. That is all I know of their plans. Zara, you cannot trust them. They are not your family. Go. I never want to see you again," Trick said softly.

Patrick pushed me away, knocking me on my ass. He turned his back on me and faced the wall.

Cassian and Beau helped me to my feet and ushered me out. While Beau worked on putting the wards back up, Cass and I took the stairs in silence. I was done. I had nothing more in me; it was an effort just to take each step, let alone breathe. Patrick Lockwood was lost to me forever.

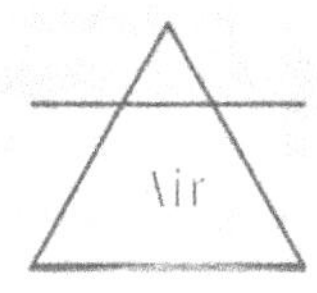

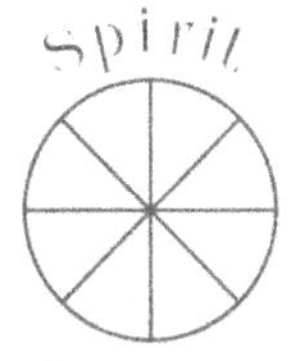

Chapter Fifty-Three

BEAU

I took my time setting up the wards in Patrick's cell, waiting for Cass and Zara to get far enough away so that they couldn't hear me.

"Why are you lingering, Duray?" Patrick asked.

He was facing me now, watching me with red-tinged eyes.

"Why do you think, Lockwood? Do you have to be such an asshole to her?"

"Yes. I don't want her to care for me. I don't deserve her. None of you do. But if she hates me, then she will not have any regrets and she'll be able to kill me."

"Is that what you want? You want her to kill you?" I asked.

"It doesn't have to be her. You'd be doing her a favor if

you killed me right now." He raised his chin, challenging me, taunting me to end his life.

I thought about it. I could easily break his neck. Then Zara wouldn't have to shed a tear over this asshole ever again.

"No, that would be too easy. You deserve to suffer for all that you've put her through. You left her twice with nothing but a fucking note, you coward. And even though you didn't deserve it, she was concerned about your welfare. She wanted us to find you, to make sure you were ok. On top of that, you didn't leave just her. You left the rest of us. It may mean nothing to you, but to us, we loved you like a brother."

"I can't do it, Beau. I can't share her." He whispered.

"Fuck that excuse. It's lame. What would happen if it was just you and her? You can't have children, you're a vamp. Do you think that's fair to her? Do you think that it's fair to rob her of that happiness just because you can't share? You're being ridiculous. If you truly loved her, everything you do would be for her. To make her life easier. To make her happy. But no, after everything she's been through and is still going through, you're worried about poor you." I shook my head at him, and then changed the tone of my voice to mimic whining. "I didn't know my parents, I was made a vamp, she moved on eight years after I left her with a note. She still loves Thaddeus."

I scoffed. "Wah, wah, wah. Those are all excuses, Patrick, and you know it."

He stared at me, his jaw slack. I was hitting a nerve or two, good.

"Patrick, she is a selfless, loving woman. And she gave you a chance, not once, but three times now. All you had to do today was apologize and offer to help her defeat her enemies. And you blew it. You will not hurt her again in this lifetime or the next. I'll slice your throat myself." I slammed the cell door, put the wards back up and made my way out of the dungeon using the stairs.

Cassian cradled Zara in her arms. She didn't appear to be crying but she was wrecked. Fuck, I should've just killed the asshole.

"Where would you like to go, Zara?" I knelt beside her.

"Home." She sat up straight. "The lair. I need some time alone. Please."

"Ok."

I opened the portal, and Cass and I were about to follow, but she shook her head. "I just need some time. Help the others and come back when you're done."

The portal winked out.

"I'm not sure that was the right move," Cass said. "I'm going back. Send me back, Beau, I'm not needed here." I walked past him towards the palace shaking my head.

"No, she wants her space," I said to him.

"Nope, not good enough. She needs someone with her." He argued.

I kept walking, taking a shortcut to the ex-royal's chambers. Those assholes were into some weird shit.

"Fine." Cass threw up his hands. "I'll ask Thadd. He won't want her to be alone either."

I shrugged. He might be right, but I didn't want to make the decision. Let the other guys handle it. I had too much on my mind. If Zara wanted us to be with her she would have asked, I think. She wanted to be alone to process everything that had happened today.

I couldn't blame her.

She'd just found out that her mother had faked her death and both her mother and sister had conspired to take over the kingdom. What a shitshow. I couldn't imagine what she must be feeling. It pained me to see her have to go through all of this. I wished to make this all go away for her. If only my magic was strong enough to make all the shit disappear.

She was tough though. She'd experienced her share of adversity, and I was certain she'd pull through it.

We walked into the royal chambers, and it felt lighter. Thadd had set up cleansing spells to dissipate the dark magic. The druid sure was helpful. He had a lot of experience, and I was learning a lot from him. My mage power would never match his in a million years, but I was ok with that. He'd make a good High Mage here in the palace. He'd never work for the king. He'd do it for Zara in a heartbeat, but we hadn't gotten that far yet.

"Where's Zara?" Phin barked at me and Cass.

"She wanted to be alone, so I set up a portal to the lair," I replied.

"I disagree. She shouldn't be alone." Cass added. Dick.

"Does she want to be alone or not?" Storm asked.

"She does," I said before Cass could get his two cents in.

"That's what she said, but that doesn't mean that's what she wants. I want to get back there right now." Cass huffed.

"Thadd? Can I get a lift?"

"Wait! Just wait, tell us what happened." Phin crossed his arms over his chest, his "'I'm the commander'" pose. I almost laughed.

Cass and I retold what transpired in the dungeons. Thadd, Storm, and Phin listened without interruption.

"I agree with Cass on two things. One, your brother is total shit..." Thadd pointed at Storm.

"Half-brother." Storm grimaced.

"Two, she shouldn't be alone. We found what we needed here. I can take this stuff back to the lair and go over things there," Thadd said.

"Excuse me, sirs." A palace squire stood at the doorway to the chamber. "King Cavendish would like to meet with all of you in his study presently."

He clicked his heels and turned to walk off.

Thaddeus chuckled. "This place is so old school. See you guys at the lair." He lifted his hand to his temple in a mock salute.

"No. He said all of us. That means you too." Phin glared over his shoulder.

"Why am I included in this summons?" Thadd waved his hand toward the hallway.

"Since you kissed his daughter on the mouth in front of him," Phin replied.

Thadd shrugged and we all filed out.

King Cavendish was looking healthier yet older at the same time. His strength was returning, but I imagined Amina's revelation had to have aged him ten years in all of ten minutes.

He motioned for all of us to sit in the chairs that surrounded the fireplace in his study. It was a mini version of the library. Tomes lined the shelves which covered one wall completely. Dark wood and dark leather furniture adorned the place. It was masculine and as Thadd put it, old school.

"Help yourselves." King Cavendish poured himself some scotch.

I shrugged. Sure, why not. I got up and poured for all the guys as they came up to the cart and picked up a glass. This was the finest scotch made by fire elementals in the north. We needed to pick up a few bottles and bring them back to the lair.

The five of us sat on the leather chairs and waited for the king to address us.

The king didn't sit. He stood by the fireplace, staring into the flames.

"Did you find anything in Amina's chambers?" He asked.

"We did," Thadd replied. A stack of books and parchments lay at his feet. "I need to read through them. But we've confiscated everything useful and I've already set up a few cleansing spells.

The palace staff was there doing the surface cleaning."

"What type of business do you have in Silk City?" King Cavendish asked the druid.

This should be interesting. Neither of us knew what he did, but we knew he was well off. Thadd arched an eyebrow at the king. Somehow King Zander found out he was a businessman. The other elemental men and I sat up straighter in our chairs and gave Thadd our undivided attention.

"Real estate investments mostly. I also have a discreet tech magic manufacturing business." Thadd answered.

It was an honest answer. Discreet was just a politically correct way of saying not exactly legal.

"I won't have my daughter marry a criminal." The king gave him a stern stare.

To Thadd's credit, he didn't even flinch under the old man's gaze.

"With all due respect, sir, your daughter has the final say in terms of whom she'll marry. If she accepts me, you'll have to go to her with that opinion of yours." Thadd clenched his jaw. "And besides, I'm no criminal."

The druid and the king had a stare-off contest for a few tense seconds.

King Cavendish tossed his head back and let out a booming laugh. It was infectious, and we all laughed alongside him.

"I like you. You have stones." The king wiped away tears of laughter from his eyes.

He cleared his throat and addressed all of us. "I asked you all here because I need your help with my daughter. I think we have cleared the air between us. We have lost so much time, but I hope to make up for it and the only way to do this is for her to stay. She's expressed her willingness to help with the situation in the mines. What I'd like from all of you is to ensure that she has everything at her disposal. If there is something she needs that you cannot give her, I want to know about it. If she needs emotional support, which I am sure she does, I don't want her dealing with it on her own. This cannot be easy for her."

"I'd like to offer you all a position here at the palace as part of the Royal Circle. Some of you know what this position entails as your fathers held the position at some point in their lives. The men and women that were on the circle during Amina's reign are currently in the dungeons, correct?" He fixed a stare at Cassian. "Yes, sir." The water elemental nodded.

"Good. I need trustworthy people around me. Zara trusts you, and that is good enough for me. I realize this might be difficult for you depending on your relationship with her, but please consider." Zander set his empty glass on the coffee table before us.

"Thaddeus, the palace requires a High Mage, who also holds a seat on the Circle. We are elementals, our lives are not nearly as flashy as what you may be accustomed to amongst the humans. But, give it some thought. I'm sure the others here will be able to fill you in." He fixed Thaddeus with a firm, non-threatening stare, but he meant business.

"The rest of you are trained soldiers and your role on the Circle is more of a political position in addition to acting as Generals in your respective fields of magic. But above all, your primary duties would be to care for my daughter. I hope she will stay and consider taking over as queen, but I fear that may take some convincing."

The five of us did everything possible to avoid the king's gaze when he mentioned Zara taking over as queen. She already told us she wasn't interested. It would take more than mere convincing to change her mind.

"If there is anything I should know in regards to my daughter, I want to know about it. I'm not asking you to betray her trust, but it is imperative that she wants for nothing and above all, she is kept safe. I'd like for you all to stay here on the palace grounds. I offered that to her, and she looked at me like I had four heads. Perhaps you lot will have better luck." He looked at each of us, and I gave him a stiff nod which I hoped conveyed nothing committal.

King Cavendish took a seat and said, "Fill me in on what you have so far."

It took us an hour to tell him what we had found and our plans going forward. We decided to take everything we had from the crone's den and what had been found in Amina's room to the lair so we could pour over the info. The king did not want any of it on the premises and wanted us to focus on this task before the full moon. We needed to find the answer to dismantle the wards in the mines first, and then we could focus on finding the crone.

Three hours after we had left Zara, we were finally ready to head to the lair. Cassian was beside himself, and Thadd was getting edgy as well.

I opened a portal into the living area near the kitchen. We carried several boxes through before the portal winked out and that was when I noticed how silent it was.

"Zara! We're home." Cassian shouted, his loud voice echoing in the cavern.

Storm smacked the back of his head. "She might be sleeping."

He shrugged and we strode off towards her room. It was empty, with no Zara in sight.

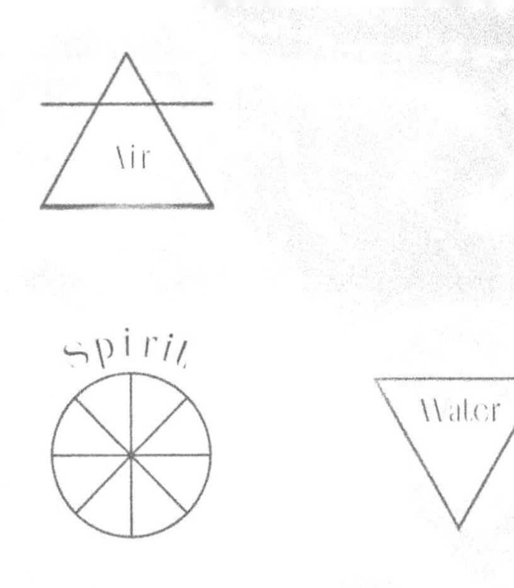

Chapter Fifty-Four

ZARA

I watched the portal wink out and let the tears fall. My discussions with Zander, Trick, and Amina felt like someone was scoring my heart with a claw made of ice. I walked past the kitchen, avoiding Linc, and went straight to the shower. The hot water cleansed the muck off my body and the darkness from my soul. Just hours ago, I had started my day in the best of ways right here in this shower. What I wouldn't give to have my men with me to do a replay.

After pulling on clean clothes I decided to sit outside on the balcony, but the beauty of Valley of the Goddess didn't calm me. I lay on the bed hoping to fall asleep, but my mind raced. And I decided then I didn't want to be alone anymore.

Well, this sucks.

I couldn't teleport and didn't have the energy to fly. Not that I could make it back to the kingdom. But Phin had a collection of cars, just sitting in the hangar. I grabbed my purse and decided to visit Gigi at the healing village. There were several vehicles to choose from, but the red sports car, which looked like an off market or custom-made Tesla made it an easy choice. The hangar door automatically opened, and I drove down the driveway. Although I didn't know where I was going, I kept an eye out for familiar landmarks, that would lead me to the healing village. Once Transcendental Oasis came into view, I knew I wasn't going in the right direction. That didn't deter me. Although I rarely drove in Silk, it felt freeing to be behind the wheel. There was something liberating about doing something for myself for once in however many days. I kept driving, thinking I'd end up at the coastal villages Cass had taken me to. The road kept going and going and going. It was a scenic drive, and the further I got, the farther my problems seemed to be. After some time, the dirt road became asphalt, and my surroundings became familiar. A few moments later, magic brushed over me, and I was back in the human realm, just outside of Silk City. I drove down the familiar streets of my neighborhood and parked in front of my chain link fence. It was odd stepping into my house and Gigi not being there either. I almost turned around and went back, but I decided to stop being a baby. I had to be ok with being on my own sometimes. The mere thought of being alone almost brought me to my knees. I was determined to get over it. I had to. I couldn't depend on anyone to make me feel whole.

Being around the men the past few days was changing me...for the better, I liked to think. Although kidnapping me was a messed up thing to do, I didn't harbor any ill feelings about it. And I found myself relying on them and enjoying their company. I missed them already and it had barely been an hour.

With a deep breath, I moved further into my home and immediately turned on the television. The news came on with a report about a Category 4 hurricane heading to the East Coast. I changed the channel to a silly talk show. Not even five minutes later, an important news bulletin flashed on the screen. An earthquake had rocked Asia killing thousands. I turned the darn thing off and went to the kitchen to fix something to eat.

There were a few rotted things in the refrigerator so I emptied it out and got back in Phin's car to do some grocery shopping. I was hungry and ended up purchasing more than I needed and realized I had to take all this stuff back to the kingdom or it would all go to waste.

I decided to cook up everything I just purchased and got out Gigi's recipe cards and went to work. Gigi was a southern woman and kept her recipes on little index cards that had been passed down for generations. I had already copied them all digitally so we'd have them forever, but I still liked pulling the cards out. I poured a glass of wine to sip on as I worked.

It would take a while to tackle the menu of mashed potatoes, fried chicken, collard greens, and mixed berry pies. When I finished, I planned to find my way to the healing village, drop off food and take some back to the lair. There were five grown men there, and as far as I could tell they weren't picky eaters.

Five men were a lot to handle, but so worth it. They were good men, all of them. They worked hard, had integrity and they all seemed to genuinely care for me. And having Thadd around made me happy. It was as though all the puzzle pieces had finally come together. Interestingly enough, the thought of being with them didn't make me want to run for the hills. Perhaps I was getting over my trust issues.

I'd never thought much about having multiple partners, even though it wasn't unusual for elementals. Unlike humans, female elementals were fertile, while males were not. Males could sire two children in their lifetime. Elemental women were fertile and could bear many children throughout their long lives. Thus female elementals took more than one partner. Cassian's mother had four husbands and six children. And she could have more children if she wanted to. No one could say why we were made this way. It was the will of the Goddess. She blessed us with our magic and that gift came with limits as to how many children we could have.

I never thought about having children until Calla asked me if I wanted her to leave contraception herbs. I had completely forgotten about turning twenty-eight and being vulnerable to becoming pregnant. Gratefully, I accepted. Linc had been spiking my coffee every morning.

All five men would make excellent fathers though. *Where had that thought come from?* Being around the children in the healing village and at the palace had tugged on my maternal heartstrings. I couldn't help but smile. *Am I seriously besotted with five men and contemplating having children?* Wonders never cease.

As I got through the daunting menu, the time passed quickly and I felt more grounded. Something about keeping your hands busy truly worked to relieve tensions, and it helped me to think through my problems.

It dawned on me that they weren't my problems, but problems of the kingdom. I had chosen to insert myself because I wanted to help. My poor father had been burdened with the weight of banishing his own daughter because his wife, her mother, had killed her in his dreams. That was royally fucked. Literally. And then, somehow, his youngest daughter got caught up in his wife's mess. I had hated him for years for what he did to me, but I found myself softening towards him. I would have hated to make the decision he had, only for it to fall apart. He lost his wife and a daughter. It would be cruel of me to make it worse for him.

The mines were an issue, and we were on a time crunch. We needed to figure that out, and the only thing I could do was offer to read through the crone's and Amina's nastiness. Gross. It had to be done though, and I was going to do it. Ugh. I sipped more whiskey and continued frying chicken.

As far as we could tell, the crone was indeed my biological mother. That was just weird. I wondered if she was more powerful than me. She was an earth elemental, and I knew without a doubt I had surpassed her power. Queen Anya could grow a garden like nobody's business, but I could create a quake and open sinkholes.

Elemental children were instilled with the knowledge that their magic was bestowed on their race to maintain balance in nature for the kingdom and other realms. The human realm was the most delicate because humans had no magic. They had the technology and there was a hint of truth to what Amina had said earlier; about humans mistreating the Earth. With eight billion people, the Earth could only take so much abuse. In time the universe would right itself and even things out, or so I believed. Unless the crone succeeded, which could not happen. I wouldn't allow it. If the elemental kingdom hoarded the magic to themselves, the human Earth would be left defenseless and deteriorate rapidly. There would be catastrophic storms humans would not be able to survive, not to mention food and fresh water shortages. From the brief glimpse I got of the news, it was already happening. The thought was depressing. I sipped more whiskey and then opened the oven to take the pies out and placed the mashed potatoes in to keep warm.

I settled the last of three pies on a trivet and a shadow caught my attention on my left. Without hesitation, I blasted out a force of air magic which punched out the window overlooking the back yard, and sent another shot of fire magic to my right.

"Zara! Stop!" Thadd's voice rang out knocking sense in me.

Phin summoned my flames from engulfing the living room wall, extinguishing my fire. Smoke alarms screeched. Beau did some magic to turn them off, while Storm sent a rush of air through the small house, blowing the smoke out of my now broken window.

"What the fuck guys?! You scared the shit out of me!!" I placed my hand on my chest, willing my thundering heartbeat to slow down.

Chuckling, Cassian wrapped me in his arms. "You disappeared, Z. We were worried."

"You could have called me."

"We did." The five men said at the same time.

I shrugged. I hadn't heard my phone ring and hadn't looked at it once since I arrived.

"We were worried, angel, and here you are playing happy homemaker." Phin pulled me away from Cass.

I kissed him and greeted the other guys with hugs and kisses.

Thadd leaned against the back of the sofa and held me tight for a long, sensual kiss.

"I'm glad you're safe and happy, baby, but I think something's burning in the kitchen." He laughed.

"Son of a bitch!" I ran into the kitchen and just barely saved the last few pieces of drumsticks.

Phin and Thaddeus called their contacts to fix the window and burnt drywall. I couldn't believe I damaged Gigi's house, but they assured me it was an easy and inexpensive fix. I trusted the men to sort it out, and Will, the big man who worked for Thadd, said he would stay in the house while the repairs were being done.

I had planned on packing up the food to take back to the lair, but the men couldn't wait. We sat around the small living room eating, and then we packed what was left to take to Gigi.

At the healing village, Gigi was happy to share the pie and the chicken with the villagers. I told her why I ended up going home and how much cooking her family recipes calmed me.

She teared up and gave me a bear hug.

"Oh Zara, I don't care about biology. You are my daughter through and through. I am so happy to see you cooking family recipes for me." She sobbed.

"Mama, don't cry. And I am so proud to be your daughter." I drew away from her. "Are you ok to be here? If not, I can get someone to stay at the house with you to keep you safe."

"I'm fine, Zar. Calla filled me in on your meeting with your sister. Stay. Fix things. You won't be happy until this is done. Besides, I like it here. The children are sweet and I feel good. Look how much weight I lost." She patted her belly.

She was right. She'd lost at least 5-7 pounds. I pulled her in for another hug.

"Hi, Gigi. You look good." Cassian said. I released my mother so that he could peck her cheek.

"Did Zara tell you about unleashing her magic at us? As children, we're taught not to use magic in the house, but Zara must've forgotten that lesson." Cassian continued.

I glowered at him over my mother's shoulder.

"My bad. I guess I wasn't supposed to say anything." He slipped away before I could swat him.

"Zara, what did you do at the house?" Gigi glared at me.

"Nothing that can't be fixed. It will be brand new. And no one got hurt, which is the main thing." I stammered.

Fucking Cassian Brooks. He stood several feet away near a water fountain, chuckling. I called up my water magic and splashed him in the face. *There, take that, big mouth!* I winked at him and he laughed harder.

We went back to the lair, and the men settled into the living area while I dropped off leftovers for Lulu and Linc. The gnome couple was thrilled to have food made for them. I truly hoped they enjoyed it and would be happy to share the recipe with Linc. I told him we'd be in the living area, and he promised to prepare a bar cart and bring it in for us.

I eyed the stacks of boxes; containing books and papers that were strewn about.

"Grab a box, babe." Thadd looked up and waved a hand at all the boxes. "We've got Evilness 101, How to do Sinister Shit for Dummies, or my favorite, Assholes Live Forever; learn how, I've been doing it for 1000 years, written in the crone's hand."

I laughed.

"Oh my, how can I pick just one?" I bent down to kiss his lips. "I'll take Sinister Shit for Dummies, please."

All the men had a stack of books and parchments beside them to study. Beau took on the crone's grimoire and sat in a recliner with a notebook and pen, scribbling away. Cassian was spread out on a large sofa with one leg draped over the back of the chair and a large tome propped on his chest. He looked comfortable and if I were a gambler, I'd bet good money he'd be fast asleep in no time.

Phin and Storm were seated on each end of an L-shaped sofa, and I sat between them, resting my head on Phin's lap and intertwining my legs with Storm's.

Thadd found a couple of cushions and plopped them on the floor next to me. He sat on the cushions, stretching his long legs in front of him while he leaned back on the sofa. We sat like this at his house often. I wasn't sure why he liked sitting on the floor like that, but I wasn't complaining. I found myself absently stroking his skin or running my hand through his hair. It was a familiar and comforting gesture.

For the most part, we all read in silence. Occasionally someone would have a question, but most of it was cringeworthy.

The stack Thadd handed to me was a book on basic spells all of which were designed to deceive, steal, maim, poison, or disfigure. The ingredients for each spell were mostly things I had never heard of. There were disturbing handwritten notes in the column. Some spells were starred which I deciphered to mean "favorite" or "worked better than expected". One particular note read, "Gave AL warts for six weeks" or "CW remains limp for three months!"

When I got to the part about physical torture, I couldn't handle it. I slammed the book shut and pinched the bridge of my nose.

"Had enough, angel?" Phin absently rubbed my belly.

"This is revolting," I muttered.

The darkness in these pages zapped my energy and made me feel icky. I would not recommend these books or give them a five-star review.

"Take a break, Z." Storm had earmarked pages with sticky notes for the magic wielders to review. He winked at me and began massaging my feet. I sighed gratefully.

Across the way, Cass was out while Beau concentrated on the pages in front of him, absently tapping his temple with the eraser end of a pencil.

Thadd sat in his same spot chewing on the tip of a pen. I rubbed his chest, and he put the pen down, picked up my hand, and pressed his lips to my knuckles.

Five sexy-as-sin men were lounging around me, and my libido was zilch. Stupid crone and her stupid evil magic.

I closed my eyes and drifted off to sleep.

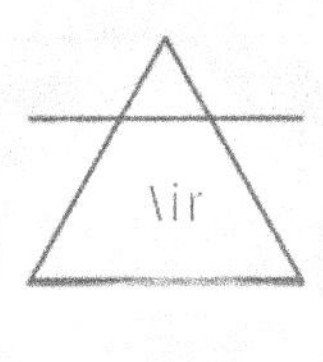

Chapter Fifty-Five

ZARA

Beau was lying on his stomach with his face smooshed in the pillow beside me. He was out and as much as I didn't want to disturb him, I needed to get out from under him. His arm draped over my torso weighed a ton, and his body heat made me sweaty.

With effort, I lifted his heavy limb, then gently lowered it back onto the mattress. He didn't flinch as I climbed off the bed.

The other guys weren't around. Sunlight barely shone through the room, and the morning air was crisp and cool. It was a new dawn, and I had gotten maybe seven hours of sleep. I vaguely remembered Cassian getting into bed shortly after me and wondered if the others had slept at all.

I rushed through my morning rituals and went to find them.

Thadd walked into the room as I was walking out.

He had dark circles under his eyes, and his hair was sticking up all over the place.

"Good morning." I embraced him "Have you gotten any sleep?"

My brain had short-circuited after the first book of evilness. I'd meant to take a short break, but Phin had brought me to bed while the other men continued their research.

"I did, babe." He kissed me, and his lips tasted like coffee.

"There's a lot we need to do. I'm..."

Beau grunted and turned over on the bed. Thadd frowned at the earth elemental then guided me to the balcony.

"This place is amazing." He whispered. "I can see why you like it here."

"Yeah, it is. Did Phin tell you it's sentient?"

Thaddeus nodded and smiled. "Did he tell you that he's been buying my mage tech?"

"No. What does that mean?" I asked.

"Here, see this?" He steered me over to the side of the copper door that separated the room from the balcony and pointed to a little box. "This is a sensor to open and close the door automatically, powered by solar and magic."

He picked up the box and opened it. There was a circuit board in it that had magical sparks moving through it. On the side of the box was a logo, for TS Limited.

"Thaddeus Sloane Limited?" I arched an eyebrow at him. I had seen the logo on things at his place.

"Indeed. He's one of my biggest customers." He grinned then put the box down.

"I had no idea," I said as he grabbed my hand and moved to sit on the day bed, bringing me down to perch on his lap.

The air was chilly, and he reached behind him to grab one of the blankets and draped it over my shoulders.

He kissed my neck, suckling on my skin. His kisses sent electrifying tingles through every inch of me. I wanted more, but we had other things to discuss.

"Thadd," I drew away from him. "Talk to me? What do we need to do?"

"We figured out a few things. Cassian found something before he went to bed. From what we can tell, they're ancient sigils that relate to the different elements combined with arcane symbols. Each line, each circle amplifies the other, and well, it's complicated. Our theory is to unravel each one. To do that, we need to make sure we're protected. I'm going to embed runes into everyone's skin, myself included, for an added layer of protection. It will drain my magic, so we need to get on it right away. I have someone in Silk ready to go. I'll go first and when I get back, I'll do everyone else. I'll need time to rest afterward, and then we'll be able to test our theory well before the full moon."

"Umm...I don't know if I like this. I don't want you or anyone of us to be compromised."

"It won't be forever, baby. Just a few hours."

"Thadd, there's six of us. Embedding each of us with your magic will be draining."

"Well, you'll just have to take care of me." He grinned.

"Don't be cheeky." I huffed and rested my chin on his shoulder. His plan would work, and I was confident in his skill. I just wished he wasn't taking on such an enormous burden.

"Thank you for doing this. Do you know how much I love you?" I asked.

"You don't need to thank me. There's nothing in this world I wouldn't do for you Zara. And yes, I've always known you were in love with me. I've just been patiently waiting for you to realize it yourself."

I pulled away to look into his eyes. "Seriously? You've always known? Impossible."

He tipped his head back and let out a hearty laugh.

"I've known since the day you threatened me and my date at the Convent. And just for the record, it was your idea for us to be open and see other people. I'm glad you insisted because that's when I realized you loved me and we were getting married someday." He shrugged as though he was stating commonly known facts.

"I've also known that you needed time to work your way through things. Considering everything you had been put through, I was determined to be patient and understanding." He added.

"How are you so ok with all of this?" I asked.

"Babe, the night I brought a date to the bar was five years ago. I've had plenty of time to prepare for this moment. Granted, I didn't factor in the crone and all the other nonsense, but it all comes with the whole package, and I wouldn't have it any other way."

"I love you, thank you for being patient with me," I whispered against his lips.

Thadd was right. I had been ready to kill the bitch at the bar. I just wasn't ready to admit how I felt back then. Perhaps I hadn't known myself.

"I love you too, Zara. Will you marry me? And the others, but I'm asking first. So they can suck on that."

I laughed so hard I nearly fell off his lap.

"I'm pretty sure proposals are supposed to be romantic and there's a ring involved," I said between giggles.

Thaddeus stood, bringing me with him, then deposited me back on the bed. He knelt between my legs and whispered a spell.

A tiny box appeared in his hands.

"Zara Angelique Cavendish, will you make me the happiest man alive by accepting my hand in marriage?"

My jaw dropped. Tears glistened in my eyes as Thadd opened the box, revealing a stunning enormous diamond ring.

"How? When did you?" I crushed my lips to his and nodded. "Yes. Yes, I will."

He placed the ring on my finger and kissed it. "Just hearing you say yes makes me happier than I could ever imagine. I know we have a lot to deal with, but there's no rush. My love for you doesn't have a time limit, Z. Nor do I have any misconceptions that you've chosen me and only me."

"Thaddeus Sloane, you are the most amazing man." I stared down at my ring, smiling, and thinking.

Why wasn't Thaddeus enough? I wanted him to be enough in my life. But my heart reached out in different directions, and I didn't have it in me to pull away.

"Hey." He tipped my chin to look into my eyes. "I can sense the hesitation roiling through you. And there is no need for that. Elemental women usually take more than one mate. Everyone knows that and I knew you'd need more than me. I've always been ok with it. You just needed to find the others. And just between you and I, the hesitation you're exhibiting is doing wonders for my ego. It is enough for me that you'd consider a life with me and only me. It wouldn't work though, Zara. It's not in your DNA. I will always want you to be a hundred percent happy all the time."

I crushed my lips to his again and told him how much I loved him over and over as I tore off my clothes and his.

Chapter Fifty-Six

STORM

Flying was as natural to me as breathing. I had been sailing through the sky before I turned five, yet my heavy heart threatened to drag me toward the ground like an anchor made of lead. After speaking with my half-brother, the burden of what needed to be done took a toll on me and then some. I only hoped the princess would agree with my plan; that thought alone made me eager to get home.

The lair had become home all because of the violet-eyed beauty that softened my heart. I loved my wife and children and still did. I missed them terribly and had never thought I could love again, until Zara. That mesmerizing woman had stolen my heart.

I banked left around Torch Mountain, towards Valley of the Goddess. The morning light bathed the valley in a golden glow.

Animals and critters were already going about their day, scurrying through the woods and gathering food for their young. I inhaled deeply letting the peacefulness of the kingdom wash away the taint clinging to me like a second skin from my morning visit to the dungeons.

Like a whisper in the wind, I heard her voice. My lips tugged upward, and then she cried out. Fear seized my breath, and I raced toward the sound of her cries, and nearly stumbled in the air.

The closer I got to her the more I realized she wasn't in danger, she was enraptured. Each moan and gasp from her lips was full of lust. My manhood stirred, and I flew closer.

Air elementals could see far distances with acute accuracy. It was necessary for fliers. From the distance I saw her on the balcony, a male between her legs. My vision was keen even from afar, but I wasn't close enough.

I landed on a solid branch of a Hyperion, its leaves shielding me from discovery.

It was an intimate moment, one I should have turned away from. But Zara was simply magnificent.

She writhed under Thadd as he deftly pleasured her. Her skin flushed, and her face exuded pure elation. She gripped him with her creamy thighs, her climax stealing her breath. He didn't stop. He pumped into her, and she encouraged him, pumping her hips in time with his. His muscles flexed as his body succumbed to his release, both of them panting.

He kissed her breasts and then her lips. I turned to leave, my own body aching to be with her as someone else approached the naked couple. Phin, no wait. Phin and Cassian.

I couldn't look away. My eyes were glued on the naked woman about to give herself to the other two men in her life.

Thadd gave her a salacious kiss then handed her to Phin and Cass. He wasn't the least bit jealous. He hesitated at the doorway leading to her room. He wanted to stay.

Zara greeted Phin and Cass with hungry kisses and tore off their clothes. She reached for their hard cocks, sliding her hands gently up and down them, making them moan and call out her name.

Damn, that could be me, I thought as she got on all fours. Phin lined himself up at her entrance while Zara opened her mouth and swallowed Cass whole. She was perfection, designed to please her men.

The men fucked her hard and fast. Judging by her moans and the wetness of her thighs, she loved every minute of it.

Phin gripped her ass, his muscles flexed. He tried to hold off, but her pussy must've squeezed him hard, milking his release.

He collapsed over her, both breathing hard. He kissed her back and shoulder, and then he moved away from her.

Cassian he flipped her on her back and slammed into her entrance. Her skin was red and used. He pumped into her with forceful thrusts, using her body until his climax tore out of him. "I love you," I heard him say. And she returned the sentiment, with kisses.

Cass pulled out of her, cum dripped down her thighs. She should have been exhausted, but she wasn't nearly sated. As soon as he released her, she reached down and rubbed her clit.

I groaned and realized my cock was in my hand and I was rubbing precum all over the tip. I could have gone to her, should have, wanted to, but I was about to explode in my fist.

Beau walked out on the balcony looking sleep-deprived. He tapped Cass on the shoulder who leaned over and gave Zara another kiss.

She moved on the bed, giving me the perfect angle to see her hot, well-used pussy. Her skin was flushed and wet. Beau and I both were savoring the vision of her. He ran his fingers down her slit, teasing her, and she bucked her hips.

He chuckled and knelt between her legs, bringing her pussy to his mouth. It was a dirty, messy affair, but she must've tasted like heaven. I licked my lips and pumped my cock furiously.

She moaned and bucked, and I shot my load, nearly falling off the branch where I was standing.

Oh fuck! I said under my breath. If she'll have me, I'll never leave her side.

I snuck back into the lair and cleaned up, then went to the kitchen. Linc was cooking something that smelled delicious. Bacon or ham, perhaps. I was ravenous.

"Good morning, Master Lockwood."

"Good morning, Linc. Have you seen the other guys?" I asked the gnome.

"Master Strait, Master Brooks, and Master Sloane have gone to Silk City. I believe Master Duray and Lady Zara are still asleep. Coffee?"

Still asleep. Sure. A smile tugged on the corner of my lips.

"Yes, please. And if possible, can you make a breakfast picnic for me and the lady. I want to take her somewhere this morning while Beau catches up on his sleep."

Beau was just going to bed when I left for the palace at 5 a.m. It was nearly eight and after what I saw earlier, I was sure he hadn't been sleeping the entire time.

"Right away!" Linc said and handed me a second cup of coffee, which had to be for Zara.

I went to her room with our coffee mugs in hand and found her in the closet.

"Knock, knock," I said before entering. She was pulling on yoga pants, and I turned my back to give her some privacy. After what I witnessed there was no need, but she didn't know that yet.

Her hand slid over my arm, and she cupped one of the mugs. "Good morning."

I released the mug into her delicate hand. She smiled and then rose on her toes to peck my chin. Compared to all the guys here, she seemed so little.

"Good morning, beautiful. You look like you're ready to begin the day."

"I was coming to find you. Beau hasn't had much sleep, and the other guys took off to Silk. So it's just you and me." She grinned.

"Perfect, I was hoping for some alone time. I asked Linc to prepare a breakfast basket. I'd like to take you somewhere if you're up for a little flying time." I grinned back.

"I'd love to." She encircled my elbow with her free hand, and we set off to the kitchen.

Linc had our picnic basket ready. He'd added a couple of thermoses to be filled with whatever was left in our mugs. We thanked him, and then we went to one of the many lair openings that allowed Phin and me to use as jump-off points for flying.

The first time I saw him jump and shift in mid-air made me envious. His beast was agile in the air and fast for being so massive. It was nice having a fellow flyer and now I had Zara as well.

The metal doorway opened, and Zara stepped back with a gasp.

"Are we supposed to jump?" She squealed.

"Sweet Zara, I would never put you in harm's way." I shifted the basket in my other hand and placed the other over her belly prepping myself for teaching mode. "For today, your magic is here, deep inside you." I patted her tummy. "With access to four, possibly five, you should be able to call on the one you require. For this lesson, you want to call on your affinity with air and imagine the air shifting and swirling itself around you and lifting you off the ground."

She closed her eyes and did as instructed. In moments her feet were off the ground, floating her over the valley. I followed closely behind her.

"Ok now what?" She whispered.

"Open your eyes."

She did and panicked, dropping a few feet.

I steadied her with one hand. "Calm down, Zara, you're ok."

"Whoa! I've never done this before. Usually, I take a running start." She gasped, her eyes wild with wonder.

"It's an instinct for flyers. You just haven't had to use all your magic yet. Come on, follow me," I said and drifted into the air over Valley of the Goddess, Zara staying close behind me.

We took our time as she marveled at seeing the valley from this perspective. Pure delight was written all over her face.

Flying was liberating. It was the best thing in the world. My heart soared seeing her so happy and to have found a partner that could enjoy flying with me.

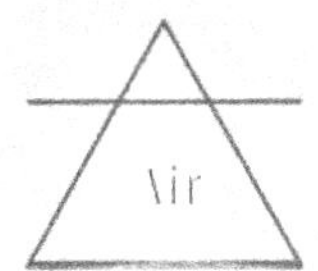
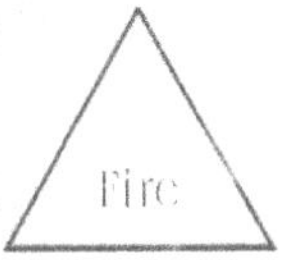

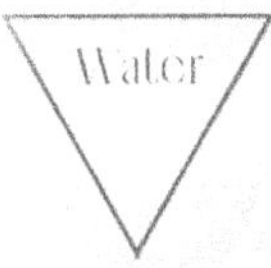
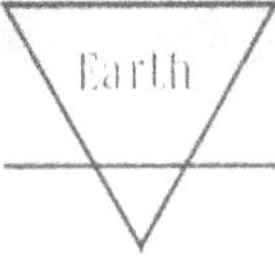

Chapter Fifty-Seven

ZARA

Valley of the Goddess, Glacial Mountain, and Torch Mountain looked different from the air. It felt like I was one with nature instead of being a spectator.

Storm took me high up Torch Mountain, eight hundred feet or so above my balcony. My balcony. Poor Phin. That room was no longer his.

We landed on a ledge near a cave carved out of the mountain. The wind was gusty, and the temperature had fallen at least another twenty degrees. When Storm insisted on me wearing a coat, I thought it was odd considering summer was in full swing, but at the moment I was grateful.

Storm lit a torch and moved further into the cavern lighting torches as he went. The cave wasn't very big, and it was mostly empty aside from the oversized nest that sat in the middle. The base of the nest was made up of twigs and leaves. The inside was overstuffed with cotton and covered with several pillows and blankets. I knelt next to it and pushed down on the cotton, surprised at how sturdy yet soft it was.

"Make yourself at home, Zara." Storm slid a wooden table beside the nest, and I flopped on it making myself comfortable.

"How'd you find this place?" I asked.

"Umm...well, this was Patrick's." He replied as he placed containers of food on the table.

I grimaced at the mention of his brother's name. I needed to get over it. The boy I had loved was no longer.

Storm handed me a breakfast sandwich, and I gratefully took it and dug in. After my morning with the four guys, I was ravenous. I reached for a thermos filled with water and filled cups for the both of us.

"Sorry. Are you ok to speak about him?" He asked.

I nodded as I chewed.

"Is that why you brought me here?" I asked after I swallowed, curious to know where the conversation was going.

"Yes, sort of. I went to see him this morning. Like I mentioned before, I needed closure myself," he said between bites. "Oh. Did you get the answers you were looking for?"

He shook his head. "No, he's not the same. Not that I spent much time with him before. We may have spent a total of four days together before my father was killed. Patrick, when we met back then, was guarded, a little on the shy side. Today he was just a shell of the man I'd met before. He's not well, Zara, and that is not your fault, of course. And I only bring it up because I fear it is time to let him go. He's not eating food or drinking blood. He's trying to kill himself. He knows that he's not right and he doesn't want to go on living."

"I didn't realize the extent of his condition," I admitted.

"When did he stop eating?"

"He never started. He's been in for three days now, and he hasn't had anything, not even water."

"What do you suggest?" I asked, trying to keep my emotions out of the conversation.

"We need to let him go. His obsession with you is not healthy and is dangerous. He realizes he's hurt you as it is, yet he doesn't have remorse, and he stated plainly that he will strike out again, though not at you because his original plan didn't work. He's looking forward to hunting your men. Me being number two on the list."

"You?" I gulped my water and he nodded. "Let me guess, Thadd is number one."

"Yeah, he is. How'd you guess?" Storm finished off his breakfast sandwich.

"I believe he knew Thadd and I were dating when he returned to

Silk City for me. And everything was fine between me, him, and the other guys for the first couple of days I was here until we stopped to speak with Thadd at his place in Silk. After that, he was mean to me." Nasty would have been a better way to describe the way he had treated me. I shook the thought away.

"Makes sense. His plan didn't work all those years ago and so he walked away for a time. My father found him and brought him here. He was busy trying to get to know his true lineage, but he never got over you." Storm got out another sandwich and offered it to me.

I shook my head and asked, "What do you mean about his plan not working?"

"Oh." He wiped his mouth with a napkin and finished chewing. "I thought you knew. He was turned. Asked to be. From what he said he asked his sire to turn him to keep you close. In exchange, he gave his sire six years, and then he was freed. I imagine he did all sorts of nasty things for his sire during that time. He didn't go into detail about that. And he only told me because I figured it out. I know vampires. They're fiercely loyal to their sires. They do whatever they're told."

I put the pieces together in my head. "So he asked to be turned into a vampire so that he could turn me, which would have made me his loyal whatever. Is that why he tried to bite me in the throne room?"

"Yes, that's why I thought you knew. He's figured out Thadd has provided you with protection against his kind and that's got him all in a tizzy. He can't be let out."

"Well, shit. I don't know what to say. How did he turn out to be so crazy? I mean he always had a jealous streak when we were kids. I just thought he'd outgrow it. Was I wrong?" I asked him not really expecting an answer.

"Zara, he loves you, but his love for you is not the healthy kind. He's jealous and obsessed which makes him dangerous because in his mind love means control. He wants to control your life, who you see, and what you do. This arrangement with the others would have never worked. And even now, if you ever decide to leave the rest of us and commit to only him, he will never let it go. Even twenty years from now, he'll remember and make you feel bad about your decisions."

"He admitted this to you?" I asked.

Storm nodded. "If he is freed, Zara, he will haunt us, me, and the others until we're dead. That is the only thing that keeps him alive. His revenge is his sustenance."

"Why are you telling me all this?" I exhaled. This was not the news I wanted to hear now or ever. I knew he was lost to me, and in some way, I had hoped he'd see reason. That in time he would return to his normal self.

"I'm not relaying this information to burden you, quite the opposite. He is suffering and as his brother, I want to relieve him of his misery. I'd rather chop his head off than have him starve to death and releasing him is not an option. I'm not asking for permission. I just don't want you to hate me once I've done what needs to be done." Storm stared into my eyes, searching for answers.

"Wow. I umm...I don't know what to say, Storm. I trust your judgment. And thank you for not making it my decision. I don't think I could. A part of me wants to believe he will change." I shook my head. "As I said though, he had a jealous streak when we were kids. He'd fuss and pick fights with guys if they looked at me too long, weird things like that. My father, Gigi's husband, didn't like him much because of it. He had a hot temper. We were so young though. I thought it was just a phase. I had a friend in college that had an abusive boyfriend, and she wholeheartedly believed his abusive behavior was an act of love. I never understood her."

"You've always known in your heart what it means to love and be loved. Your men love you. It's been interesting to witness and a privilege to be a part of it." He lay out in the nest beside me.

"Interesting how?" I picked up a scone and broke off a piece before putting it in my mouth.

"We are all so very different, yet we love you in different ways. Thaddeus, the druid, is obsessed with you in an endearing way. His magic is that of the universe and you are the center of it. He will spend the rest of his life giving you everything, like that ring." He ran his thumb over the rock and smiled.

"Phin is possessive. That's the dragon in him and it's not a bad thing because he doesn't want to control you. He wants you safe and happy. He would set the world on fire to keep you safe."

"Cassian is such a water elemental. He is fluid and adapts to whatever you're feeling. If you're happy, he's happy with you. If you're angry or sad he feels it too and wants to do whatever he can to change it. Haven't you noticed how he lightens the mood no matter what's going on?"

"He's always been that way since we were kids," I replied.

"Only around you, Z. Like the ocean, you never know the strength of the tide until it pulls you under. I've seen him annihilate opponents with force and cunning."

I stretched out next to him, and he turned on his side to face me, propping his head up with his elbow.

"And then there's Beau, the steadfast earth mage. He is the strong foundation for where you will always find your courage. Did you know that he hasn't used his healing gifts in like, ever? He never took a liking to it, but he does it now for you. He knew you'd feel more sure-footed here if he took care of your mother. Somehow, he figured out if she was healthy, you'd be willing to stay."

"I thought Calla was doing the healing for my mom." I turned on my side, mirroring his position.

He reached out for my hand. "From what I understand, Calla told him to do it himself. He came up with the remedies, and she's been doing the administering part of it all."

"Huh. I didn't realize any of that. I've always felt comfortable with all of them. It feels natural to be with all of them and you." I searched his gaze. "Where do you fit in?"

"I'm an air elemental, sweet Zara. My love for you is wherever you are. I am the breeze that caresses your skin, reminding you that you're worshiped and adored." He trailed his finger up and down my arms, and I closed my eyes, savoring his touch. "I'm the air in your lungs, reminding you with each breath that you are loved by me and never alone."

"Storm, that, that is the most beautiful thing anyone has ever said to me." Tears pricked my eyes, and I leaned in and kissed him, conveying I felt the same way.

He kissed me back and then pulled away. "Zara, I need to be honest with you about a few things."

I nodded and nervousness pooled in my belly.

"As you know, I was married. And I had two children." He began slowly then paused. He sat up a mixture of regret and sadness shadowed his silver eyes.

I sat up and grasped his hand, waiting patiently for him to continue.

"I want to be with you. I hope you'll have me, but...I won't be able to give you children." He couldn't meet my eyes.

I waited for a beat. He said nothing.

"Is that all?" I asked.

"Isn't that enough?" He glanced at me.

A wrought-filled gasp left me and my shoulders caved in. "I thought you were going to say something horrible. Like you remarried and your new wife was waiting for you or something."

I straddled his lap and cupped his face. "I am well aware of the constraints male elementals have regarding having children. The fact that you may not be able to have any more children doesn't bother me in the least. I want you just as you are."

I kissed him, tenderly then pulled away.

"Are you ok with me having children with the others?" I asked him.

"Of course. I would be honored to help father all of your children." Storm replied without an ounce of hesitation in his voice.

I gave him a big smile and a big kiss. "Thank you, Storm, that's the only thing that matters to me. Whose kid it is doesn't matter. I love all of you equally and will love our children all the same."

He captured my lips with his. His mouth hungry and wanting. We had restrained our passion for too long, and I did not want to wait any longer. I wanted him; he wanted me. We were in a frenzy filled with lust, desperate to satisfy our cravings.

I tugged his shirt over his head, while he unbuttoned my coat, throwing it on the ground behind me. My top followed behind it. I kissed a trail down his neck and over his broad shoulders. He unclasped my bra and palmed my breasts, and then he flipped us over, bringing his body down on top of mine. I kicked off my shoes. He suckled my breasts and then released me to pull off my jeans.

He knelt between my legs, staring at my core, and hesitated for a split second. I propped my body up on my elbows, and he crashed his lips to mine.

"Zara, one last thing." He kissed my neck. "It's not bad. But I have to be honest because I love you."

He stopped and I was about to panic.

"I umm...I saw you earlier and the other guys." He paused.

"Today, just now on the balcony."

My brain short-circuited. *Just now on the balcony? What was he going on about?*

Then it clicked.

"Oh." My face flamed hot. "You saw us having sex."

He nodded. "I'm not a perv. I just couldn't look away. You were so beautiful."

I bit the inside of my cheek to keep myself from laughing.

It seemed all my men had a thing for watching.

I spread my legs wider.

"Did you like what you saw?" I whispered against his lips.

"Yes. So much."

"Did you touch yourself?" I asked and began pushing his sweats down over his hips.

I grabbed his swollen cock and caressed it while using my feet to push his sweats further down his legs.

"Yes." He ripped my lacey panties and swiped a finger down my slit.

I moaned and guided him to my entrance.

"You're so beautiful." He sheathed himself in me with one deep plunge.

I gasped the pain exquisite. My hips undulated, meeting his thrusts. His mouth remained fastened to mine, stealing my breath and breathing into me at the same time. My nails raked down his back.

"I love you, Zara. I would never do anything to hurt you."

His voice deep and raspy. "Do you trust me?"

"Of course."

Storm's magic spilled out of him and caressed every inch of my skin. My affinity for air magic intensified and tangled with his. Wind swirled around us, our heated skin buffering us from the cold.

He held fast to my waist with a punishing grip. I arched into him, his cock burrowing deeper with every push. My hair streamed out behind me.

My eyelids flickered open. The blue sky framed a perfect background behind Storm's dark hair. I gasped and jerked upright.

"I've got you." Storm hooked my legs over his shoulders as we floated over Valley of the Goddess.

Holy shit! We were eight hundred feet in the air. Storm's magic held us up. He continued pumping into me, over and over again. I groaned his name, the thrill of being suspended in the air sparking my arousal, and my climax peaked. My pussy clamped him hard when I came, siphoning his release. His body drooped over mine, his hips bucking as we both came down from our orgasm. We panted, trying to catch our breath.

Storm peppered kisses all over my face, neck, and chest, and then stood upright, keeping himself firmly seated in my core, as we soared over the valley. I leaned back completely, my arms spread wide while looking at the world upside down, trusting him completely.

"Are you enjoying yourself?" He asked me.

I straightened my back and peered at him through my lashes. My air elemental looked like a god. Sweat covered his skin, making it glow almost translucent, his silver eyes reflecting the love I felt for him.

"Yes." I kissed him fervently, not ready to come down from the incredible high, literally and figuratively.

Elemental lovemaking was something otherworldly. It was magical. It was transcendent. It was everything.

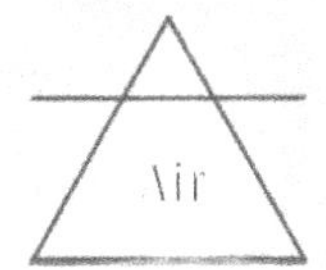

Chapter Fifty-Eight

THADDEUS

I couldn't wipe the grin off my face. Even with the tattoo gun penetrating my skin, I didn't feel a thing.

"What are you so happy about?" Will, the burly bearded man, asked me. We had been best friends since we were in college.

"What are you talking about?" I grinned harder.

"He's engaged to our girl," Cassian answered.

"Ah, so the princess accepted. All of you, I assume?" Will said, as he wrapped my skin.

I had told him about my feelings for Zara from the beginning.

"No, the shithead beat us to it," Phin replied.

"She said yes to me because she chooses all of us. You all just need to get your shit together and ask, when, and if, you're ready." I replied.

Zara loved me. I knew that, but I meant what I had said to her earlier. She needed all of us. Being an elemental was part of it. The other part was she loved it there and would want the kingdom to be her full-time home. And it should be. She thrived in the kingdom. Despite all the bullshit going on, she was the happiest I had ever seen her.

I wasn't about to tear her away from her happiness. I just wanted to be a part of it.

"Did she really say that or are you trying to make us feel better?" Cassian asked.

He was the youngest of all the men and Zara's childhood friend. He loved her and would follow her around for the rest of her life like a lovesick puppy.

"Guess you're gonna have to ask her yourself. After we deal with the mines. Come on, we have some shopping to do," I said and guided them through my place.

We were at my brownstone in Silk. It was the most unpretentious property I owned yet I found it to be the most comfortable. And it was close to Zara's house. I enjoyed all the nights she'd come over after work, or even better, when she came over after a date that didn't go so well. I loved that woman.

I led Cass and Phin down to the basement where I kept supplies, while Will went to check on the business. He was my muscle when it came to TS Limited. Not that I needed backup with my magic, but having him around just made it easier. One look at Will and people paid up as they were supposed to, and the staff I had, didn't ask questions or slack off when I wasn't around.

It surprised me that Z's father had done some digging into my business ventures. I wasn't expecting him to care that much. Not that it mattered. Most of what I did was perfectly legal. I was notorious for the magic tech gadgets I created. I've been messing with tech gadgets for a long time because it was easy for me, and it was lucrative.

In my basement I kept a surplus of supplies. Here we'd find things needed for the mines. The spells the crone and the mage had put up were complicated and volatile; it would take a lot of our power and we'd succeed as long as there were no nasty surprises. I had a feeling there would be nasty surprises and I wanted us to be as prepared as we possibly could and above all else, keep Zara safe.

"Grab one of the duffle's will ya'? Actually, grab two." I asked Cass and Phin and pointed out the duffle bags that were sitting on a shelf near the doorway.

"What is all this stuff? Is it legal?" Phin asked.

"Yes, mostly." The human government frowned on some magical tech gadgets, not all of them, but some. "I don't report everything, and I don't sell everything to everybody. I never create anything that will cause harm. But I have created things that make doing certain illegal things easier. Like this for example." I pulled out a simple baseball cap from a box and put it on my head.

"Whoa! That is so cool." Cassian gasped.

"A disguise. One of the best I've ever seen." Phin smiled. "Let me try."

The cap gave the user an illusion. It concealed their identity entirely, not forever, but long enough to do something law enforcement would certainly have issues with. I shrugged. Humans did nefarious shit all the time. Besides, I told myself this particular item had been sold to one person, for fifty million dollars. So worth it.

I showed them around the basement while adding supplies to the bag. There were also things Phin needed at the lair. The guy didn't even have Wi-Fi there. It was a cool place though. I owned several properties, but nothing compared to his lair.

Phin, Cass, and I joked around as we shopped in my basement. We were bonding which was kind of fun. Zara would be proud. After a few hours, I started to get antsy. I wanted to get back to Zara.

I packed up the last of the supplies, including the tattoo gun and accessories. We still needed to stop in to see Calla, Beau's mother. She was helping with the ink since I needed so much of it.

"Time to go guys," I called out and led them back upstairs to the office area where Will was doing something on the computer.

"Will, same as usual. I'll check in in the next couple of days. If there's an emergency you can't handle, you know how to reach me. But we all know there's nothing you can't handle. Oh, how're the repairs at Zara's going?"

"They put up the drywall this morning. Tomorrow I'll go over and add a coat of paint. I'll send pictures so you can share them with Zara." The big man replied.

"You're invaluable, my friend." I patted him on his shoulder and then put up a portal to the healing village.

We stepped out of the portal and strolled through the healing village. They could use magic tech here as well, but that was another task for another day.

We visited with Gigi first. I wrapped her in a great big hug. I had asked her a while ago for Zara's hand in marriage. She had told me to wait, saying it wasn't the right time. She had been right and I knew it. I had waited for years and was happy I did. Now that Zara had been allowed back into the kingdom, she was whole.

"I finally did it, G. I asked Zara to marry me," I said to her with a big smile.

"She told me. Congratulations! You just missed her. She was here with the earth and the air elemental. I'm happy for both of you. And I'm looking forward to having a wedding." She grinned at me.

"Well, in due time. The wedding may be a ways out, but we'll have an engagement party soon enough." I gave her a hug, and then me, Phin, and Cass went back to the lair.

At the lair we found Zara helping Linc in the kitchen. Storm and Beau sat at the kitchen counter.

"Hi, babe." I kissed her temple. "Are you cooking again?"

Zara smiled up at me. "Hi. Well, I'm trying to help, but Linc won't let me."

"Lady Zara! Get out of my kitchen." Linc shooed us away.

I tugged on her hand to give the gnome his domain back.

"Fine." Zara rolled her eyes and went to greet Cass and Phin with kisses.

"How was Silk?" She asked us.

"We raided Thadd's warehouse." Cassian grinned, holding up one of the overstuffed duffle bags.

"You got everything we need?" Beau asked me.

"Yep, we should get started, if you guys are ready," I stated.

The guys all grunted and nodded in response. I picked up one of the duffle bags and led Zara out to the living area.

Phin set up an extension cord and got the power going for my tattoo gun while Beau explained the process.

"Thadd is going to tattoo runes which will help shield us from the backlash of magic we expect when we dismantle the crone's sigils. This will take a lot of magic since there are five of us. So, we're doing this now," Beau said to everyone.

"After I'm done, we'll go over the exact steps we'll take when we get to the mines," I added, then patted the cushion near the tattoo gun. "You're first baby."

"Why me?" She brushed against my arm as she took a seat.

"Because you're my favorite." I leaned over and kissed her neck.

Storm cleared his throat. "Are you going to do your tattoo thing, or are you...you know?"

Zara chuckled and pushed me away. Beau handed me the stencil we had decided on the night before.

It was a Norse design known as the Aegishjalmur, commonly known as the Helm of Awe. It featured eight branches of magical staves, creating a circular design. Viking warriors decorated their helmets with the Helm of Awe to protect them when going into battle. It was a symbol of protection; however, the real protection would come from the ink we used plus the magic I would imbue in each tattoo.

"It's big." She peered at the stencil.

"That's what she said," Cassian muttered. I laughed. I really like that guy.

Zara rolled her eyes. "Where are you planning to put that?" She asked me.

"Well," I eyed her body. She wore a long blue tie-dye skirt that fit snugly around her hips and a matching T-shirt. I rolled up her skirt and ran my hands over her smooth, tanned legs. She closed her eyes and sighed.

"Hey!" Beau cuffed me upside the head. "Focus, we have work to do."

"I am!" I grinned. "I'm looking for a spot."

"Well, it's too large to be on her legs." Storm stood over my shoulder.

"It's got to go on her butt." Phin offered with a sly smile.

"Or her belly, right above her navel." Cass sidled up next to her and raised the hem of her shirt.

I placed the stencil in the spot Cass recommended and stepped back. The five men looked at it, tilting our heads.

"You all are ridiculous. This is my body. It's my decision," Zara said. "Is this going to fade under my skin, like this one?"

She pointed to the rune I had placed on her arm. It glowed when it had kept her safe from the vampire. Now the rune looked like a sexy golden brand.

"Yes, it will glow when the power is being used," I told her.

"Hmm...ok, I'd prefer for it to not be on my belly." "Why?" We all asked in unison.

"I have my reasons." She took the stencil off her tummy.

"Where are you all placing yours?"

I took off my shirt to show her the one Will had placed on my left pec earlier.

Zara knelt on the cushion to get a closer look. Her finger grazed around the sensitive skin. "I like it. It's sexy."

"If Zara likes it on his chest, I think that's where we should all get it." Storm chimed in.

"Great idea." Zara smiled at him and pecked his cheek.

"But you're not putting that on my boob."

She turned around, sat back her heels, and moved her hair.

"Back? And no, not a tramp stamp."

Her stunning purple eyes peeked under long lashes. She looked positively sexy.

Phin groaned and leaned over to kiss her shoulder.

I moaned and adjusted my dick. She was irresistible. The five men stared at her hungrily.

She tugged Phin's hair back and said, "Behave, Phin. We have work to do."

Phin's eyes turned red, and his dragon, who I had yet to meet, was shining through. He pecked her cheek and rolled away from her.

"Keep your pants on boys." Zara tugged off her top and then glanced back at us. "Shoulder blade?"

"Yep, shoulder. But I can't watch. I won't be able to keep my hands to myself." Cassian kissed her lips and walked out.

The rest of the guys muttered their agreement and followed him.

I gave my girl a sly smile and bent her over the chair.

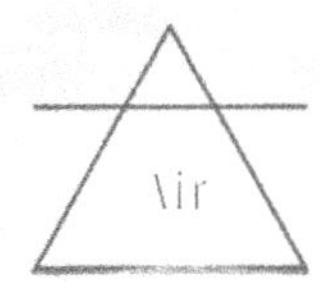

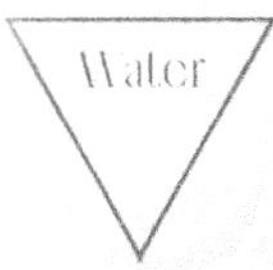

Chapter Fifty-Nine

ZARA

I buttoned up my jeans and winced. My lady garden was tender from all the activity yesterday. First Thadd had proposed on the balcony, and then the other guys professed their love. Then Storm and I had our first sexual encounter.

Later that day, Thadd and I had gone another round before he tattooed my shoulder. I wanted more, so I went after the other guys. I was lucky to be an elemental. If I were human, I'd have a UTI. Still, having elemental magic didn't save me from exhaustion, but the men were sweet and let me sleep in.

"Did you get enough rest?" I asked Thadd who was sitting at the kitchen counter sipping coffee. The magic he'd expended the night before was vast and had taken its toll.

He chuckled. "Yes, Z, I did. I love that you're worried about me." He kissed my nose. "Did you get enough rest?"

I nodded.

"You can have Beau heal you, you know. If your sex is feeling a bit tender."

My cheeks flushed. Before I could answer Beau came up behind me.

"I heard that," Beau said. "Are you feeling ok?"

He drew me away from Thadd and pressed his chest into my back. His hand slid into the waistband of my jeans.

"I'm fine, Beau. Honest." I leaned into him.

"Hey!" Phin snapped a dishtowel at Beau. "We don't have time for hanky panky. Come here, angel. I'll protect you from these sexual deviants."

Phin drew me into his arms. We all laughed. He was right. It was time to go.

We arrived at the Sanctuary ready to take on the spell the crone had left in the mines.

Once we got this done, my work here in the kingdom would come to an end. Butterflies swarmed my belly as we walked in the mines. I didn't want to leave the kingdom and hoped I could continue my relationship with the men that lived here.

"Alright everyone, as we practiced. We'll do this one segment at a time." Phin told us.

We all filed in line. Phin took the lead followed by Storm, then Thadd, me, Cass, and Beau at the rear. Each segment had five circles containing ancient sigils which signified the five elements of earth, air, fire, water, and spirit. Our plan was for each elemental to take on the sigils matching their magic. I'd break the connection sigil which in theory would unravel the entire thing. The rune Thadd had given us would protect us from entrapment and power drain. We were prepared as much as we could be.

When we came upon the first set of arcane symbols on the wall, Thadd and Beau wanted a minute to take a closer look before we got to work. They confirmed what we had prepared for, and we got to work. As instructed, the six of us called upon our magic and cast out.

The magic we were casting was powerful and heady. With the five men pulling on their magic beside me simultaneously, my magic responded. A vast well of power gaped open within me and swirled through my body. My hair stood on end and my skin buzzed.

The symbols glowed and pulsed. I felt the sigils start to give way, and then the dark magic pressed against us. The men pushed more of their power into breaking the sigils. The rune on my shoulder blade flared hot, I knew it was glowing without having to look at it.

My magic kept rising inside of me begging to be released. I couldn't hold it back much longer; it wanted out.

Beau had warned me against using too much because we didn't want the mountain to come down on us. I kept his words at the forefront of my mind, straining to keep a leash on my magic.

My body started to shake. I couldn't hold it back much longer.

I glanced at the men. Phin clenched his jaw, as lava rolled under his skin. Bolts of silver were etched all over Storm's face, and torrential lightning crackled on his fingertips. Cassian's arms flexed, his water magic assaulted the sigil, like a Tsunami crashing against the shore. A deep frown marred Beau's forehead as he concentrated on his sigil which vibrated, sending dust and pebbles to the floor. Thadd was the picture of peaceful meditation. He was used to using large quantities of magic and his sigils were spinning on the cave wall.

The guys were focused on their tasks, I didn't dare say a word and risk breaking their concentration. I had to do something before my magic went wild and escaped me. I analyzed the five sigils. The men were strong, their magic was winning, they just needed an extra boost.

I concentrated on our goal, *break the spell that blocked access to the Source.* As soon as the thought formed in my mind, my magic struck out. It flowed out from the vast well deep in my stomach through my arms and out of my fingertips. I placed my hands on the shoulders of Thadd and Cass beside me. My magic rocked their bodies and shot out toward the other men beside them until we were all connected by my magic. Our magics combined and bolstered their individual efforts.

A short, resounding pulse obliterated the symbols in front of us and our magic winked out.

The six of us stared at the wall for a minute, no one said a word.

"You did it, Z," Cassian finally said.

"Is it over?" I panted. I had used a lot of magic and my body felt it.

"This section is. Is everyone good?" Beau asked us.

Everyone nodded or murmured their responses. I looked at all the men and they all seemed to be fine.

"Let's keep going," Phin moved deeper into the cavern with the rest of us following him.

"Baby, you good to give us that power boost again?" Thadd asked.

"Yes, I'm good. I held back in the beginning, but next time I won't wait as long," I replied.

He reached behind his back in search of my hand. I intertwined our fingers and linked my other hand with Cass's.

The elementals had dug deeper into Source Mountain than I had thought. We had gone at least forty miles, and every five miles or so there were more segments of arcane symbols. We had gotten through seven of them and I began to see stars.

"Zara, are you good?" Cassian asked.

"I'm not sure how much more I can do, guys," I admitted.

Phin moved up the line to stand in front of me. He cupped my face in his large warm hands.

"It's ok, angel. Take a break. I'm going to run in and see how many more there are." He kissed my lips breathing into me.

"Don't go alone, please," I said, and he and Storm took off.

I moved back towards the opposite wall and slid down to the hard-packed dirt floor.

Beau sat beside me and handed me a bottle of water, while Cass sat on my other side and Thadd sat directly in front of me.

"It's working," Beau said. "It feels lighter in here."

I agreed, the oppressive darkness was still there, just less of it. In front of us was another story.

"Well, we could call it a day and return early tomorrow morning. We have about twenty-eight hours until the full moon. It might be good to go home and recharge." Thaddeus patted my leg.

"I agree. We've got at least three hours until sundown as is." Cass gulped a bottle of water in one go.

Phin and Storm appeared in a gust of smoke and wind. The rest of us stood.

"Well, there's good news and bad news," Phin said. "The good news is we're near the end. Just another five miles or so, which we can travel by magic to. The bad news is the symbols are huge."

We decided to give it a go. It was close and it was the last one. I would rally, somehow, someway I'd pull on all my reserves and get it over with.

Phin took Beau so he could open a portal to retrieve the rest of us. We were at the end of the mines, the last place the elementals had dug. There was a massive archway, which led into an even larger cavern.

He wasn't lying, the symbols were indeed huge. We had to spread out.

I rolled my neck and stretched, trying to rid the anxiety that gnawed at the back of my neck.

Storm approached me first. "You got this, Zara." He gave me a sweet peck on my lips.

Beau wrapped me in his arms, pulling me off my feet. I locked my ankles behind his back while Cassian pressed his chest against me. "We're right here, Z."

They both released me to Phin who slid his warm hand under my shirt, and his heat slid up my back. "One more, angel. And we can go home."

Thadd buried his face in my hair. "I love you, baby."

The love the five men had for me renewed my spirit, and I soaked it all in, determined to finish this and show them how much I loved them in return.

We started the process as we had done several times before. The size and strength of the symbols proved to be more difficult to dismantle.

Sweat ran down my back. I panted and steeled my spine. I couldn't spare a glance at my five men. The spell took all of my will, all of my strength. We poured our magic for what seemed like a lifetime. I struggled against the darkness. My magic and my entire body were ready to give way. I yanked on my magic with everything I had and blasted outwards. I cried out, my back bowed, the surge of power left me, and I crashed to the floor.

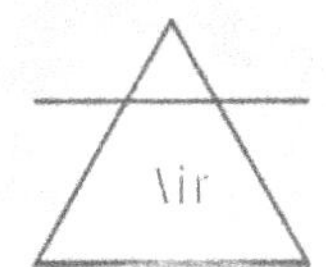

Chapter Sixty

ZARA

"Zara, baby, are you ok?" Thadd rocked me in his arms.

"I'm fine. Was I out long?" I looked around feeling disoriented.

"Not long, you just dropped." Thadd kissed my temple.

"Here, drink." Beau handed me water. "Do you need a protein bar?"

We had protein bars and water along the way, and I was tired of the cardboard healthy stuff, but I was also starving.

I nodded and gulped the water.

"We did it, Z. We're done." Beau stood a couple of feet away from me staring at the wall.

I stood with the help of Thadd, while Storm handed me a protein bar. The last remnants of the sigil faded to nothing, and I sighed in relief.

"Incoming," Phin announced, his muscular body taut with tension.

I followed his gaze into the darkness and couldn't see anything. The men stood in front of me protecting me from whatever was coming our way.

My eyes and ears hadn't detected a thing, but I trusted his dragon's senses.

A second later, a loud boom and a spark of light like a flash bomb ignited in the cavern. I shut my eyes from the blinding light and covered my ears with my hands. The bright light blinded me for a few precious moments, and there was a ringing in my ears.

The acrid stench of sulfur overwhelmed my sense of smell.

The minute my vision was restored I was on the ground again and my men were all encased in a bubble of magic.

"My, my, you are powerful, aren't you, dear?" A feminine voice echoed through the darkness.

"Let them go!" I demanded.

"What will you give me, princess?" The voice said from behind me, and I whipped toward the sound.

"What do you want? What is the meaning of this?" I shouted as I spun, tracking the movements of the voice.

"What is owed to me, of course." The crone stood in front of me in her elderly form.

"And what the hell do you think is owed to you?" I called on my magic.

"I wouldn't do that if I were you." She waved her hand and the men started to gasp for air. "I'll kill all of them so fast if you try anything stupid, princess."

I released my power into itself. "Let them go. Please."

"Sure, your life for theirs," She said.

"Fine, let them go. Now!" I demanded.

The crone cackled. She flicked her wrist, and the men began breathing normally. They were awake now. All of them called out to me, thrashing against their magical prisons, and began to float toward the way we had come.

"There, see. Their life for yours. You see it's always been you. I had it wrong the entire time. I thought it was the other sister, and she turned out to be useless. You, on the other hand, your power has grown. No matter, you're here now, and I have everything I need to make the transition."

"What are you going on about?! What have you done with my mother?"

She cackled again. And her body morphed from the old wrinkly crone into my beautiful mother. "I am your mother. Silly girl. After your exile, your mother gave herself to me in exchange for immortality. I couldn't begin my new life as the Goddess in my old body. Your mother offered me hers. Quite generous, don't you think?"

"You're doing all this to become a goddess?"

"Not a goddess, stupid girl. *The Goddess*. It should have been me, but that selfish sister of mine took what belonged to me. She stole all of the power and beauty and wasted it on creating a weak race of elementals and then promised to keep the other realms safe with her divine power. The humans don't deserve to roam the Earth. They have no appreciation for nature. They abuse what the land has given them. No more! My plans are already in place. Catastrophic storms have been released and billions will suffer. My time has come. I will take back all of it. I will no longer be the old crone, I will be the most beautiful, the most powerful Goddess and everyone will kneel at my feet."

The crone spun around with her arms open wide, cackling like she had lost her mind. She was a total whack job.

I gathered what was left of my magic, letting it build in my fingertips while the crone spun. The moment I got a clear shot I unleashed, hitting her square in the chest. The ground under me shook, knocking me off my feet.

The crone screamed in agony. She collapsed to the ground, bleeding and gasping for air. Fuck me. How was she still alive?

Dark magic hovered over her body. She punched the ground and the mountain rumbled, rocks and debris clattered all around me. I stumbled and then ran, dodging falling rocks. The opening we had come through was a few feet away. Rocks of every size rained down. The crone had started an avalanche, and soon that opening would be blocked off.

I picked up the pace, pumping my arms and legs as fast as I could. A rock clipped my shoulder and jolting pain ran down to my fingertips. I ignored it and pressed on. A large stone glanced off my skull and brought me to my knees. I half stumbled and half crawled my way to the opening. It was so close, just a few more feet. I pushed forward, climbing over the rocks that had piled up in front of it.

The crone let out another gut-wrenching scream that created another avalanche. Her scream cut off with a sickening crunch. Please let her be dead.

Liquid ran down my temples and into my eyes. I swiped the sticky wetness with the back of my hand, the coppery scent filling my nose. I clamored over the fallen boulders. Stones pelted me from all angles. Every step I took was painful and slow. The opening was nearly closed; rocks continued to rain down on me.

Almost there I convinced myself.

At the top of the rock pile, the opening had closed. I slumped over the rocks. My body was battered, and blood flowed down my face and into my mouth. My magic was nearly depleted, so I gave it one last tug. I pulled on my earth magic to wrench a boulder loose, and then I blacked out.

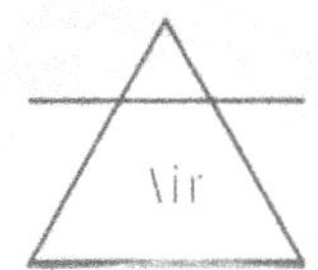

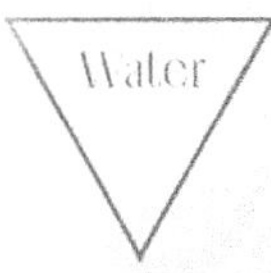

Chapter Sixty-One

PATRICK

I could barely lift my head and I stank. A hot shower would be nice. Since they'd dumped me in this dank cell, I'd refused water, food, and blood, but I wouldn't turn down a shower. My priorities were a bit skewed. And being locked up had nothing to do with my messed up thoughts and actions. It couldn't be helped though. A part of me knew I was misbehaving and yet I couldn't stop myself. Every bad decision I made was done out of love. *Why didn't Zara understand that?*

This cell was my punishment and I deserved it. No, not true. I deserved much worse. I had wronged her. Wronged was too gentle a word for what I had done. Betrayed. Destroyed. I nearly killed her. I wanted to change her, make her a vamp just like me. I would have done it, too. I would have drained her dry and then filled her with my blood. She would have been mine for the rest of our immortal lives. But she was protected by that fucking mage.

The very thought of him spiked my rage.

Zara was my obsession, the love of my life. It was an unhealthy type of love, but love, nonetheless. She consumed every part of me. Even now as I slowly wilted away, I longed to be near her. She was mine.

I shook my head. After all these years, I thought I had grown out of this insane obsession. Not even close.

The first time I'd left was on purpose. I wanted to change and had asked to be changed. I had done it for her. My adolescent brain was convinced that becoming a vampire would make me invincible. I'd have the power to change her, and we would both become powerful immortals. We'd rule the world together. I had thought she'd be pleased. She wasn't. She had moved on.

I was crushed, but my father had found me and while that relationship began to blossom, my sick obsession faded into the background of my mind. Never gone, just muted.

Darkness had returned with the death of my father. I was lost until Phineas, Cassian, and Beau befriended me. I found a brotherhood and for a couple of years, I functioned...normally.

Until her name came up and I became lost again.

We watched her for weeks, months even. The brotherhood all saw in her the things that I had seen. The things that I coveted for myself. I had told them I'd accept her choice whether she chose all of us, or none of us, or one of us. I tried to convince myself that I'd be willing to share or walk away. But that was a bold-faced lie. I fooled them and for a time I thought I could pull it off.

It all seemed to go as planned until she was right in front of me, and everything I had planned went out the window. The scent of her skin. The silkiness of her white hair. Those arresting lavender eyes. She was perfect in every way. She was mine. And I was certain she'd pick me. I loved her more than anyone else. *Why couldn't she see that?*

I scrubbed a dirty hand down my face, chasing those thoughts away. She wasn't mine. I needed to remind myself of that. I was stuck in this cell. I deserved to die for everything I had done.

Twice. I had left her twice. And both times I had said goodbye with a note. Coward. I was nothing but a coward. If I could only make it up to her somehow.

There was no way to help her now. Even if I could, I'd fuck up at the first opportunity I got.

The desire to kill those men who had stolen her from me was so strong. I dreamt about ripping their throats out and how I'd bathe in their blood afterward. The mage would be spared though.

I'd flay his skin and torture him as I feasted on his blood. I'd keep him as my private blood bank forever.

I jerked my head. Dark thoughts, too many of them, riddled my head. I was losing my mind. Or maybe I had lost it years ago.

Guards were coming down the hall. It was too early for a shift change. Something must've happened.

I slowed my breathing and listened.

"There's been a quake at Source Mountain. The princess and her men have been trapped inside." An unknown guard said.

"Stay alert, we're expecting trouble tonight. There will be two guards up top, everyone else is going to the mines. They're going to dig them out."

Zara! Worry blazed over my skin, like a feverish rash. I could handle being stuck in prison for life knowing she was alive. I couldn't handle the news of her being dead.

I banged on the door with my fists. The solid wood ripped the skin off my knuckles. Droplets of blood dotted the walls and floors. I kept hitting until the guards came to the door.

"I need water." I rasped. It was a lie, I just needed them to open the door and come closer to me. And I knew they'd open it. My half-brother ordered them to make sure I was fed and hydrated even though I refused.

"Back up," the guard said.

I did as I was told like a good little prisoner, doing my best impression of a docile lamb.

The guards shuffled around outside, and then I heard a key turn.

I kept my chin down, peering out through the strands of my grimy hair that covered my eyes. One guard came in with a cup of water while the other stayed by the door.

"Finally ready for something to drink, eh? Your brother will be pleased, not that you deserve his care." The guard threw the water in my face.

"You idiot, now I need to get more water." The other guard walked away.

I waited patiently while the water thrower sneered at me.

"You smell. Worse than the others. Must be the rank of your evil magic." He scrunched his nose up with disgust.

He was brazen, the fool. He thought I was a helpless prisoner. He was so wrong. With a sliver of stone that had fallen off the wall, I had etched away at the wards that neutralized my vampire strength and air magic. I wasn't at full power, but I had enough to take out these two. They wouldn't know what hit them until it was too late.

The guard returned and handed the water thrower the cup.

He held it out to me, and I waited.

Come on, just a little closer.

As soon as the water-throwing guard was in striking distance, I grabbed him by his hair and chomped his neck while incapacitating the other guard by using my magic to pull air from his lungs. I drained the first guard dry in seconds. His husk dropped to the floor. I released my air magic from the other guard before he suffocated to death, only to drink his blood.

With both guards dead, I dragged what was left of them into my cell. I took the keys from them and unlocked the shackles on my feet.

Blood dribbled down my chin, and I swiped it with my finger and wrote *Zara* on the wall, and left her a little present. I'd save her and then run far away, where she would be safe from me.

I had to leave something behind for her. It was the least I could do.

I dispatched the two guards at the dungeon's main entrance and took flight. My air magic set me free, and the blood I had consumed fueled me.

The elementals in the Sanctuary were in a frenzy. The mines looked to be sealed off. Zara and those damn men and their heroics. Earth elementals were removing the boulders one by one.

That would take hours. If the crone had her, Zara didn't have hours.

I stayed hidden and flew around to the north entrance. The crone and the royals had a secret entrance no one else knew about. They hadn't told me all their secrets, but I had skulked around and learned a few things.

Elementals wearing all black guarded the secret entrance. Crone flunkies. I dropped down to the ground and strode up to them.

The guards were sitting around having casual conversations oblivious to my presence until I was a few feet away.

They startled and jumped to their feet. They were too late.

"I remember you." A lanky guard pointed a bony finger at me.

"Aren't you supposed to be in the dungeons?" "The crone let me out. She in there?" I asked.

They all nodded.

"She said not to let anyone in," a young guard said.

These were the sheep amongst the elementals. Their magic was so weak they were practically human, making it easy for the crone to subdue them. And she had promised to give them a power boost. These guards, no doubt had come willingly. False promises, were easily believed by the weak-minded.

"Where's Issac? The Queen?" I asked, slowly moving towards them.

"She's... she's using him. Draining his power. He's in there with her," the young guard replied.

That wasn't surprising. I had cut a deal with the crone and her deals came with many caveats. All in her favor. It didn't matter to me. I had a way to lure Zara to a specific spot, and I'd save her from the evil crone, make her mine, and then we'd live happily ever after. That plan went to shit real fast.

I shrugged my shoulders. "Oh well. I best be on my way then. She's expecting me."

The guards blocked the entrance, and I released my monstrous self. My vampire side resurfaced in record time. These men did not have enough power to take me on and I ripped out their throats before they could defend themselves.

I took a torch off the wall and made my way into the cavern, following the only path in the place. The ceilings were too low for me to fly. I could barely stand up straight, and in some, I had to crawl.

Hours later, I still hadn't come across anything until I smelled it. Death. It wasn't Zara. She hadn't been here that long.

And she wasn't dead. I refused to believe otherwise.

The cavern opened to a small space illuminated by black candles. Issac sat in a chair, which was placed in the middle of an arcane symbol. I wasn't familiar with the symbols, but like the one in my cell, a small smudge would weaken or perhaps dismantle the spell all together. With the edge of my boot, I scuffed the chalk on the floor.

Issac bolted up, growling like an animal. His limbs hung awkwardly from his decomposing body, his movements uncoordinated and jerky.

He reached for me. I side-stepped and tore his head from his neck. It wasn't strength on my part. It was his rotting corpse. Disgust curled my lip. Somehow the crone had kept him alive for her diabolical purposes.

And I had betrayed my love to work with the evil bitch out of spite. Something was seriously wrong with me.

I kept moving through the cavern as quickly as I could. Perhaps I was lost and that would serve me right. But I had to keep going. I needed to find her.

Her family was total fuck wads. They didn't deserve her. They made me look like a saint in comparison, and I was an evil man. Even I was better than these assholes.

Her family was total fuck wads. They made me look like a saint in comparison, and I was a bad man. They didn't deserve her.

Even I was better than these assholes.

I searched the cavern for some time, but there was no other exit. Then I looked up, and there she was practically buried under stone and rubble that had fallen from the mountain. The avalanche had closed off the only other exit, and she had climbed over nearly twenty feet of rock to try and get out. Strands of her white hair glowed in the dark. I used my vamp speed to get to her and almost choked on my breath.

I dug through the rubble as quickly as my vampire strength and speed would let me. It would be nothing short of a miracle if she wasn't crushed. That couldn't have happened. She was strong. Her magic would protect her, I kept telling myself, until I gained access to her body and slid her away from the debris.

She was bloody. Numerous gashes were everywhere, from being pelted by rocks. Her pulse was weak, and her breathing shallow. Her long hair was matted with blood and plastered to the side of her face.

"Stay with me, Zara." Wet trickled down my cheeks.

I gathered her in my arms and spun around, looking for an exit. The one she had tried probably led towards the mine entrance and was now covered by boulders.

I went back the way I had come, running when I could which was not often. Most of the exit consisted of tunnels that were five feet high, and some were barely three feet. I crawled, dragging Zara through inch by inch.

After everything she had been through, the journey was causing more harm. Every bump and scrape over the rough path were surely cutting and bruising her body more than it already was. Still, she didn't flinch, not even a little. I checked her pulse often, making sure she was still with me. I prayed to the Goddess for the first time in my cursed life.

The journey took hours. But I kept going until the entrance was in sight. My body was drenched in blood, sweat, dust and prison grime. And I was running out of time. I could feel it. There was a time I would have saved myself first, but not now. Zara needed a healer.

I carried her out and used my vamp speed to where I left them. The shackles that chained me to my prison cell. I had fastened one end to a metal storm grate before approaching the guarded entrance just a few feet away.

Before I could change my mind I dropped Zara to the ground and cuffed the other end to my ankle. I wasn't going anywhere.

I shambled over to her limp body and gathered her in my arms.

"Please wake, Zara. Please. I'm so sorry." I cried.

I whistled a tune my father had taught me. It was an emergency signal we'd used while we were flying. He had to have taught Storm. I needed him. Zara needed him.

She groaned. Her body twitched in my arms.

"Zara, wake up." I prodded and whistled for my brother.

She groaned again and winced. Her head had to hurt.

"Help is on the way, Z. Hold on." The sun was shining through the leaves.

"Trick?" She raised her arm and touched her fingers gingerly to her temples. "What? What happened?"

"It's over now. The crone is dead," I told her.

"I couldn't get out." She sat up a little and looked around. "You saved me. You came in and saved me. Thank you. I don't know how you did it but thank you."

"I umm..yeah, the mine entrance is sealed off. I guess there was an avalanche, and I went in the other way. The guys are ok. They were working to clear the boulders. I couldn't go to them because, well..." I jiggled the chain adhered to my ankle.

Zara sat up and looked at it.

"You busted out of the dungeons." She smiled and then winced from the cuts on her beautiful face.

"I'm sorry, Zara." I hung my head. "I've been such an asshole. I hope when I'm gone you can forgive me."

She looked at me with a confused expression.

"I'm not right, Zara. I have a darkness that is dangerous to you and others."

"Not true, Trick, you saved me." She protested.

"Very true. You must accept this about me. Forget about me and live a life full of love and happiness. A life you deserve. I cannot give that to you. If left alive, I would be a constant threat to you and your men and your children. Those men, your men are on their way now, and a part of me is thinking about tasting their blood." My fangs dropped.

"He was right. Your mage, was right to protect you from me. I wanted to kill you, to turn you and make you mine and no one else's. You would have lived forever and hated me. And I would have painted the world in blood. I'm not right in the head, Zara. It's time for me to go."

"Stop, Trick, you're talking nonsense. I believe there's good in you. I believe there's love in you. We just need time to work on it. We all have issues stemming from childhood traumas or broken hearts. It's not the end of the world. It's just something we can work on together. I won't leave your side. I'll help you through it."

"No, Zara. This is the end. Know that I love you."

"Quit saying that. I won't let them put you back in a dungeon if that's what you're worried about."

Tears ran down her cheeks. She was a woman to love.

After everything I had put her through, she still cried for me.

"Dawn has come. I love you forever." My skin heated. I pressed my lips to her forehead.

"So, you have your ring. Right?" She shuffled off my lap.

"Where's your ring, Patrick?!"

She grasped my fingers, then patted me down, sobbing.

"Where is it Trick? I'll go get it."

Her chest heaved with each sob.

"It's gone, Zara. I left it somewhere far away. I love you."

"No! Trick, don't do this! I love you. Please. Don't. Not like this."
She pushed my body as hard as she could. Trying to keep me in the
shadows away from the rays of the sun.

"HELP!" She cried.

My skin burned.

"HELP ME!"

"Zara, it's ok. It's too late. Just hold me."

She draped her body over mine, trying to shield me from the sun.
"Trick, I love you, I don't want you to go. Please."

"I love you too, Zara. Forever."

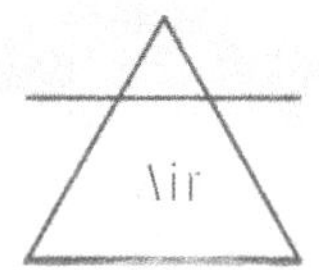

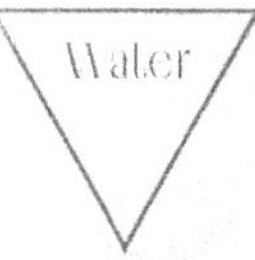

Chapter Sixty-Two

PHINEAS

"**S**hut it!" Storm yelled.

The crowd around us stilled. We were in front of the mines removing the boulders one at a time. The earth elementals did as much as they could, but it was painstakingly slow. We were being extra careful not to disturb Source Mountain any more than it had been. Another avalanche could bury our Zara.

A whistle carried with the wind, barely audible if not for my dragon's senses.

"Patrick. He must have her." Storm soared in the air and went north.

I shifted to my dragon form, knocking people out of the way. I didn't care. Zara was more important.

Halfway around the mountain, I heard her calling out for help. My dragon roared a battle cry. If Patrick hurt her in any way, there'd be hell to pay.

I sped around the mountain searching over treetops.

"Here!" Storm swooped down to the ground near a water pipe.

I followed him, shifting as I landed. And ran towards her.

She was sobbing, her body heaving.

Next to her was a male form with grimy black hair. She pushed the body as though she was trying to move it out of the sun.

Oh shit, Patrick. Storm and I looked at each other and ran toward her.

She draped her small body over Patrick trying to shield him. It was too late. His skin was burning.

"Trick, I love you, I don't want you to go. Please." She said.

"I love you too, Zara. Forever." Those were Patrick's last words.

Storm and I stood back a few feet, stunned and speechless.

Zara was a wreck.

The other men came up behind me, and I raised my hand telling them to slow down. We had to approach this delicately. Or so I thought. I honestly didn't know how to handle this. I was so happy to see her, yet she was experiencing pain I couldn't dare fathom.

Thadd held out a pair of sweats for me and I slipped it on while Storm went to her. He pressed his chest to her back and wrapped his arms around her body. They both cried.

"Patrick?" Cassian asked, eyeing the ashes that were flying everywhere.

I nodded.

"Fuck." Beau said.

Thaddeus didn't hesitate. He went straight to her, got on the ground, and nestled his head in her ash and blood-covered lap.

Royal guards were on their way, and I went to deal with them, leaving the others to help Zara.

I had no words. Aside from his crazy obsession with Zara, Patrick was a good man. And we all knew about the ring his father had given him. Where the hell was it? I had given the guards implicit instructions to leave the ring alone. If one of them took it, I'd have their ass.

"Sir?" One of the lieutenants approached me with a salute.

"There was an incident at the dungeons. You should come see it."

I nodded, took off the sweatpants, and gave them to him before changing forms and took to the sky.

When I arrived, four dried-out husks were found, two on the top and two in Patrick's cell. Incident was a mild term. I walked into the cell and analyzed the scene. On the wall by his cot was a note written in blood.

I'm sorry, Zara. Forgive me.

Beneath the blood-written note was his ring. He didn't want to live without her, but he couldn't live with her either.

I scrubbed a hand down my face.

"I heard it. I heard what happened." One of the prisoners chanted.

I grabbed the ring and closed the cell door. "Get the bodies out, they should be prepped for burial, and notify the families. No one goes in there without my permission." I told the guard and the lieutenant.

I strolled over to the vocal prisoner and peered in his cell.

He was one of the crones' sympathizers.

"What did you hear?" I growled.

"What will you give me?" He asked.

"Open the door," I said to the guard.

He opened the door, and the prisoner tried to get out. I pushed him back in so hard he hit the opposite wall and struck the ground.

"I will give you nothing. But you will tell me everything." My eyes flashed red.

The prisoner scampered to the far wall.

"He went nuts." He cowered in the corner.

Obviously. I gave him a flat stare.

"I'm not sure what happened. One minute the guards were talking and the next that guy started slamming the door. The guards went to check on him, and then they were dead."

Still not helpful. I had seen the specks of blood on the door.

"What were the guards talking about?" I asked.

"Something about an avalanche at Source Mountain."

As I suspected. He had heard Zara was in trouble and he got himself out. Fuck. It was hard to be pissed at the guy when everything he did was all for Zara.

I turned around and went up the stairs to the entrance. Beau and Cass strolled out of a portal.

"Thadd and Storm took Zara back to the lair. We need to update the king then head home," Cass said before I could ask.

"Is she ok?" I asked even though I knew the answer. She wasn't, but in time she would be.

Beau shook his head. "Should I take a look?"

I nodded. "You both should, then the others. I'm not sure if Zara should see it."

We waited for the king in his study. We were covered in sweat and dirt, not nearly presentable to have an audience with royalty. I didn't care. It had been the longest day of my life.

I sat there silent while the other two did most of the talking. We nearly lost Zara. The thought of losing her made me manic. I couldn't imagine what she was going through right now. Although Patrick's actions had been shit sometimes, he loved her. He just hadn't had a healthy way to express it.

"Phineas? You good?" The king asked me.

I shook my head. "It's been a long day, sir. I need to get back to Zara."

"Thank you for the update. And thank you all for everything. I'm glad we can put this crone business behind us. Pass my condolences to my daughter and please bring her back to the palace. I would like to honor all of you for saving the kingdom. Dismissed."

Beau put up a portal in the study, and we walked into my home on the other side.

Calla and Gigi's mother were walking out of Zara's room as we were walking in.

"Is she ok?" Anxiety laced my words.

"She will be. Mild concussion, minor blood loss, several cuts, and bruises. Physically she will be brand new tomorrow. But her heart is broken." Calla replied.

"Take care of my daughter. She needs to be surrounded by love right now," Gigi said.

"You're welcome to stay here," I offered.

"No, thank you. But maybe I can visit during lunch tomorrow. I'd like to speak with Linc about making her some comfort foods."

"Yes of course, anytime. You'll find him in the kitchen. And I'll make sure we get you a phone that will work within the kingdom."

I found Zara sleeping peacefully between Storm and Thadd. I reached over Thadd to stroke her cheek. He gave me a weak smile. The men were worn out. We all were.

Storm looked up at me.

"I'm sorry for your loss," I said to the airman.

"Thank you." He tucked his head into Zara's hair. "Yours as well."

He was right. Patrick was part of the brotherhood. The thought stabbed my heart.

"Take a shower, man," Thadd said. "She was asking for you."

I took a long shower and found the other four men in bed with Zara. It was a good thing my beast was huge, and I needed the big bed. I had never thought I'd be sharing it with four other dudes.

Thadd rolled over giving me space to lie next to Zara. I slid under the sheets and wrapped my arms around my angel.

"Phin?" she murmured.

"I'm here, angel. Sleep. You're home and safe."

"None of you can ever leave me. Promise me. No one leaves." She whimpered.

Her voice was soft, but the five men heard her loud and clear. And each of us vowed to do exactly as she asked.

Chapter Sixty-Three

ZARA

Four weeks later

We had a Celebration of Life ceremony for Patrick a week after his death. Despite all the shit he had put me through, I grieved long and hard for him. To watch someone I once loved die in my arms was no small thing. He had saved my life at the expense of his own. His passing left a mark on my heart. A scar that served as a reminder of a love that wasn't meant to be. In another life, perhaps, we could have made things right.

The five men and I got into a routine after the ceremony. I rearranged my schedule at the Convent. As a partial owner, I still had responsibilities. I worked on a few things remotely and went in during the day a couple of times a week. For the most part, all I did was change my hours which worked for Magz and me. And I no longer worked behind the bar. I went back once, and it hadn't worked out so well.

The last night I bartended, my five men came in and got a table in front of the bar. They wanted to keep an eye on me even though there was nothing to see. I was busy working but kept glancing at them and what I saw was not good. They were there for about one hour and that was all it took for me to lose my mind. Women of every magical species flirted with them. At first, it seemed innocent enough, sly glances, winks, flirtatious smiles. When the ladies upped their game by dropping napkins on their table with lipstick kisses and phone numbers, I began to lose my shit. One brazen bitch wrapped her panties around Phin's glass. I nearly killed her. I threw her ass out by her hair, finished my shift, and promised to never do that again.

Thaddeus' somewhat shady business dealings were revealed and perhaps not so above board according to human standards. His main line of work was combining human technology with a hint of magic. His inventions were in high demand, and he had developed quite a reputation from it along with wealth.

He adjusted his workload and coordinated his schedule with mine. We went to Silk together, worked, and then came home all via a portal. Sometimes Phin came with us when he had to visit his business as well.

Beau took on more responsibilities at the healing village. With his mage magic and connection to the earth, he was a gifted healer. Probably the best the kingdom had ever seen. Cassian, ever the diplomat, helped the refugees settle into more permanent living situations, some near the palace, some right where they were. Phin, my military commander, took on the responsibility of General of the Royal Guard. Storm, my ever-patient teacher, dedicated his time to training recruits, me included. He helped me go through the lessons I should have had had I not been banished.

For the most part, I didn't care what they did with their time, even if it meant they were working for the king. The most important, non-negotiable demand I had was that they'd always sleep at home. Losing Trick had made me needy.

Amina never regained her magic and her health had started to decline after the crone's death. She had linked her life source with her and her husband, Issac. Beau was working on it as well as the other healers, and they couldn't figure out what was ailing her. Only time would tell. I made a point to visit with her whenever I went to the palace. She ignored me for the most part. When she wasn't ignoring me, she spat vile words and told me how much she hated me.

Zander was healthier than ever. With the crone's death, the spell she had placed on him released its hold. He immediately had Issac and the crone's bodies cremated and the mines cleansed and sealed off. There were a few sympathizers to Issac's and Amina's cause, some of whom were council members, including Phin's mother and father. The king wouldn't tolerate their betrayal. All were stripped of their rank, had their magic neutralized, and had been imprisoned. He had much restructuring to do, and he offered my men seats on the high council and asked me to take up my role as his second, and we all declined. It was too much too soon for me to take on the responsibility. I wanted to hone my magic. I had power, but I lacked skill and knowledge.

We suspected the crone had manipulated my biological mother, Queen Anya. Somehow the crone had convinced her to share her power which in the end would allow Anya to become a powerful and immortal queen, while the crone became the Goddess herself.

We were still reading through journals and notes we had confiscated from the crone and Amina, and they all led to the crone wanting to harness the Source's power and become the Goddess. Some ancient text had led her to believe it was possible. It all seemed like wishful thinking and dark, sinister magic.

Despite the devastation of having to square off with the crone wearing my mother's face, I had Gigi, the mother of my heart to rely on. She was doing so well on the herbal remedies and magic that she was healthier than ever. She had also decided to spend her time in the healing village. The children loved her, and she loved feeling useful.

She and I decided to keep the house in Silk and rent it out since neither of us wanted to live there. I was reluctant to sell it. There were too many fond memories. Will Sharpe, Thadd's faithful right-hand man, had asked to rent it. He liked the coziness of the home, and he wanted a place close to Thadd's brownstone, where he worked most of the time. We rented it to him for a dollar.

Gigi was glad to have someone we knew making use of the place. After everything he had done for us, it was a fair trade.

I was busy painting my nails near the fireplace in my sitting room at our palace home. Zander wanted me and my men to take up residence in the palace, and I declined. There were too many bad memories in that place. The king had remodeled the throne room, and offered us an entire a wing of the palace. He even had palace staff, including the mages, do a thorough physical and magical cleaning. It wasn't enough. I still felt bad vibes there.

Our palace villa was erected in record time. My father brought in magic wielders from other realms to design a safe place for me and my men. It was reminiscent of an Italian villa off the

Amalfi Coast. I loved it. It was close to my father but not too close.

"Lady Zara?" Jacey, an earth elemental woman who had been assigned to me as an assistant of sorts, knocked on the door. "Come in." I wiggled my toes waiting for the polish to dry.

"Lady, we need to get you dressed. You'll be late." Jacey absently rubbed her belly. She had the radiant glow of pregnancy.

"How are you feeling, Jacey?" I smiled at her.

Jacey had almond-brown eyes and curly dirty blonde hair.

She resembled Nan, her grand-aunt and my former nursemaid.

Having her around always reminded me of my childhood.

"Perfectly well, my lady. Come now, time to get dressed."

I looked at the hourglass which said I had hours before the gala started. I shook my head. "It's too early."

"Oh no my lady, we don't have much time. Please."

I rolled my eyes and stayed put. I was being a brat, but it wouldn't take me that long. At the most, it would take me an hour.

Cassian and Storm both strolled into the sitting room. "Hey, what are you still doing here?" Cass asked me. "You should be getting ready."

"What's the fuss?" I shrugged.

"Zara, let the handmaidens help you." Storm helped me up and led me to the dressing room.

Zander had insisted on putting on a gala to celebrate our success in defeating the crone and restoring the Source. I told him no, it was overkill, but I had lost that round. He said it was important to let the kingdom know that I had been reinstated as the princess. I told him to send out an email. He grimaced and started planning things out anyway. Supposedly, as a princess I had to make an appearance.

"Have any of you heard from my mother?" I asked before the guys walked away. She was attending this gala as well, that much I knew, but she had requested to stay in the palace.

"Umm, well, the old mage, offered to escort her to the gala. She is already in the palace and is being pampered. She's perfectly fine, Z," Cass said.

"Maester Samuel? The palace manager?" I asked him.

Both he and Storm nodded. Hmm. That was interesting. He was old, like pushing five hundred at least, but he looked to be about Gigi's age.

"We'll get her on the phone for you in a little while. Go get dressed." Storm placed a kiss on my forehead, and he and Cass left me with Jacey.

I followed Jacey to my dressing room, which was also extra times a million, but whatever. The palace staff had outfitted the closet with an absurd amount of frilly and very expensive fabrics which I had been told were gowns fit for royalty. And I absently gave the men approval to choose my dress for this unnecessary gala.

Jacey prodded me until I got in the tub. Luckily, my polish had dried. She and another attendant were preparing themselves to get in the large tub with me, stating I needed to wash my hair and shave my legs. I gave them both a firm no, but Jacey perched on the edge of the tub, monitoring my bathing process as I told her how ridiculous this custom was.

"Lady Zara, you will be the queen someday, and when that happens your ladies will attend you. You must get used to this."

Fat chance in hell.

Once properly cleaned, an air elemental, helped me into a fluffy robe and then had me sit at the vanity. With her magic, she dried my hair and curled it while Jacey began painting my face. It was a painstakingly slow process, and I was beginning to fidget.

Phin came in with a phone in hand.

"Hi angel, your mom called." He kissed my lips, and I leaned into the kiss.

Jacey cleared her throat.

He pecked my cheek one more time and I called my mother.

"Mama, are you ok?" I asked when she answered the phone.

"Yes, of course. The staff here are very lovely, and my chambers are incredible." She replied.

"Good, I'm glad. You do have a room here with me and the guys." I told her while Jacey fluffed my hair.

"I know, Zar. I wanted to feel like royalty for once in my life. And besides, you and your men need your privacy."

"Ok Mama, I love you. See you in a little while." I hung up and decided to grill her on Maester Samuel later.

Jacey took the phone from me and started with the jewels. They placed crystals and gold plating on my skin around my face and chest, and then in my hair.

My tummy began to growl.

Beau and Thadd came in with wine and a small charcuterie board. Somehow, they had read my mind. Or maybe they heard my belly rumble. When the men tried kissing me on the mouth, Jacey swatted at them with a brush afraid they would ruin my warpaint.

Next, Jacey handed me my undies. The entire process was too weird. "I can pick out my own panties," I muttered.

"Your consorts picked these for you." She handed them to me.

My consorts. Ha! It was all about palace protocol and proper princess-like behavior. So, I kept my sassy comments to myself.

After my undies came the stockings with a garter belt. Ugh!

Then came the dress. It was a lovely silky fabric in a deep metallic purple and gold trim. The top was a bustier, which cinched my waist allowing the fabric to flow over my hips and down to the floor. It accentuated every curve and had an elegant train of purple satin that trailed four feet behind me. I slipped on five-inch gold stilettos with golden straps that laced over my ankle. Despite the cool winter weather, I had my fire to keep me warm and decided against wearing a coat or gloves. The gown was too pretty to cover up.

Just when I thought that was it, Jacey had me sit back down in front of the vanity mirror. She left the room and returned with a beautifully wrapped golden box.

"From the king, my lady." Jacey handed the box to me with a bow.

I read the card.

I had this custom-made for you. I hope you like it. Please wear it, at least this one time. Love, Your father

Oh boy. I looked at the box and hesitated. What was my father up to?

I unraveled the bow and lifted the lid. In it was a beautiful

golden crown. It was delicate but not childlike. It was perfect for someone of my age and birth right. I almost cried.

I fanned my eyes with my fingers not wanting to ruin my face paint while Jacey placed the crown on my head and made sure she didn't muss my hair in the process. It was exquisite.

Three hours later, I was ready. My men waited for me in the foyer of the villa. They were all so very handsome in black tuxedos with bowties matching my dress. Wow! I was a lucky girl.

The men greeted me with whistles, hugs, and light kisses on the cheek.

"Now, mistress?" Jacey asked me.

"Yes, please," I replied.

She nodded to someone behind a closed door and retrieved a black velvet box.

"I wanted to give all of you a little something," I told my men.

"As my consorts," I made air quotes with my fingers. "I wanted each of you to wear an emblem signifying my station in the kingdom and well, in my life. You are all important to me. It's just a little something."

Cass stepped up first, "Zara, I would be happy to wear your consort pin." I smiled at him grateful and affixed the pendant to his breast pocket.

I had the consort pins specifically designed with an infinity symbol and the ancient sigils and gems representing each elemental magic.

Thaddeus was last and unlike the others who were satisfied with chaste kisses on their cheeks, he kissed me full on the lips.

Jacey huffed at him and fixed my makeup when he was done.

Snow dusted the palace grounds in a powder of white. My skin prickled as we strode to the carriage, and Phin wrapped me in his fire magic before I could call on my own. I gave him a wink as we got into a horse-drawn carriage, which had been custom-made for the six of us. It was plenty comfortable and a bit over the top, considering the ride was less than a mile away. But supposedly, a princess isn't supposed to walk in the snow to her gala.

Ridiculousness all the way around.

We arrived precisely on time and were announced as we walked in. I took the lead with the five men behind me. I was suddenly nervous and turned around.

Phin was right behind me, blocking my path. "You got this, angel. We're right behind you."

"Right, ok."

The herald announced:

"Presenting Princess Zara Cavendish, Eldest daughter of King Zander Cavendish and sole heir to the throne of the Elemental Kingdom."

The crowd cheered.

I placed one step in front of the other, hyper aware of all the stares and murmurs. The herald continued and it took everything in me not to turn around and look at my men.

"And her consorts, Phineas Strait, Commander of the Royal Guard, Fire Element."

"Beau Duray, Master Healer, Earth Element."

"Cassian Brooks, Diplomat of the People, Water Element."

"Storm Lockwood, Master of Education, Air Element."

"Thaddeus Sloane, Master Druid, Spirit Element."

At the dais, I stood next to my father and the men fell in beside me. The crowd cheered and I smiled graciously. The weight of the crown sat heavily upon my head. I needed a drink.

The king made announcements, thanking me and my men for freeing the Source and welcoming me home.

Dinner was served as well as drinks and I nibbled. My stomach was twisted in knots. Lords and ladies of different clans approached us after dinner offering their gratitude and solicitations. I couldn't remember everyone; it was impossible. I smiled until my cheeks hurt.

I was beginning to feel overwhelmed when Gigi asked if I could accompany her to the ladies' room. Grateful for the distraction, she and I exited the dining hall with Phin and Beau trailing us. Princess protocol stated I had to be guarded at all times, and my men were taking their duties seriously.

My mother and I linked our arms together as we walked back to the dining hall.

"You look radiant, Zara," my mother said.

"You do too, Mama," I replied. "So, Maester Samuel seems nice."

She never looked healthier, and I hadn't seen her this happy in a while.

"Mmhmm. He's five hundred and two years old. He makes me feel like a spring chicken!" She replied with a wistful smile.

I laughed and we both took our seats at the royal table.

Music and dancing started after dinner, and I finally relaxed. My father and I had the first dance.

"I'm proud of you daughter. Thank you for everything. It feels right having you here and for the first time in many years, my heart feels lighter."

Tears pricked the back of my eyes. I didn't know what to say. For fourteen years, I had built up walls of resentment and distrust and had resigned myself to a life of solitude. Now I had the love of five men, a home, and my kingdom was whole.

"I feel lighter as well, Dad. I am happy to be home." I admitted to him.

He stopped on the dance floor to look at my face, his eyes watery. He pressed my hand to his cheek. "To our future, Zara."

"To our future."

Later that night after much dancing and mingling, my men took me home. They loved on me, like only they could for hours, and then we had some food brought to our room.

After we were completely sated, and comfortable in bed, Beau asked me, "What's next, Z? Is there anything that you'd like to do?"

We were young for elementals. Storm and Thaddeus were the eldest of us at thirty-three. We had a long life of at least five hundred years ahead of us. There was no rush to do anything, and I knew we'd never tire of each other.

"Well, we have a wedding to plan," Thadd said. He had proposed first, and over the last four weeks, the other guys did as well, one by one. It was sweet, and my engagement ring got bigger and bigger.

"Yes," I said, running my hand through Storm's hair. "A small wedding. Maybe fall?"

"That's almost a year away, angel." Phin massaged my calves. "Can't we have a spring wedding?"

I chuckled. "Umm... Well, I was kind of hoping..." I held back from finishing my thought.

All five men sat up to look at me. "Hoping for what?" Cass and Storm said, at once.

"Tell us, babe. We won't let you sleep until you tell us what's on your mind." Thadd added.

"There isn't anything in the world we wouldn't give you, angel." Phin chimed in.

Beau climbed over Storm to get closer to me. "Zara, what is it?"

I looked at each of my men and savored their adoring gazes.

"I want to have babies. I know we'll have hundreds of years together. But I don't want to wait," I said sheepishly.

I wasn't sure if it was being around all the children in the healing village, or Jacey with her swollen belly, or perhaps, it was all the love my men and I shared. One thing for certain, I couldn't wait to build our family together.

"So. Who's going to be the first to put a baby in me?" I teased, then squealed in delight as the five men scrambled over one another to get to me.

THE END

Author's Note

Thank you for choosing Zara's story! I hope you enjoyed it. Please leave a review as I'd greatly appreciate your feedback. As a new author I am whole heartedly interested in what my readers have to say. Your feedback helps me hone my craft and publish books you'll love. Visit my website to sign up for my free newsletter.

Website: genaviecastle.com

Acknowledgments

A quick shout out to all the wonderful women who help make this book possible. Self-publishing takes a village and I couldn't have done it without a team of beta readers, proof readers, my editor and my character artist. Thank you all for accompanying me along this journey.